Expulsion and Survival

Canadä

*The Publishers acknowledge the financial assistance of the
Government of Canada through the Book Publishing Industry Development
Program (BPIDP) for our publishing activities.*

National Library of Canada Cataloguing in Publication Data

Smallwood, Bill, 1932-
    Expulsion and Survival / Bill Smallwood.

(Abuse of power: Canadian historical adventure series ; 5)
ISBN 0-88887-328-X

1. Acadians--Prince Edward Island--History--Fiction.
2. British--Prince Edward Island--History--Fiction.   3. Acadians--
Expulsion, 1758--Fiction.   4. Prince Edward Island--History--Fiction.
I. Title.   II. Series: Smallwood, Bill, 1932-   Abuse of power: Canadian
historical adventure series ; 5.

PS8587.M354I84 2006   C813'.6   C2006-905966-7

Cover art by Eugene Kral.
Cover design by Bull's Eye Design, Ottawa
Printed and bound in Canada on acid free paper.

Ottawa August 2009

Expulsion and Survival

Bill Smallwood

Bill Smallwood

Borealis Press
Ottawa, Canada
2006

The book is dedicated to the memory of
W. Glenn Clever
Robert J. Endicott

ENJOY CANADIAN HISTORY
by reading other books written by Bill Smallwood

ISBN 0-88887-198-8   ***The Acadians*** (1749 – 1757)

You are witness to a truly great love story. There is action: Indian raids and massacres, a Royal Navy amphibious assault against a hostile shore, and sea battles. Don't miss it!

ISBN 0-88887217-8   ***The Colonials and the Acadians***
       (1757 – 1761)

You can sense the growth of a new nationalism along the Atlantic seaboard. The military campaigns against Louisbourg and Quebec are woven into the family stories with great attention to the actual events. The courage of the young woman to save her husband from execution and the dogged determination of the naval officer to remain loyal to his code of honour bespeak the difficulties facing all of the peoples who are trying to survive on the seaboard of the Atlantic Ocean.

ISBN 0-88887290-9   ***Crooked Paths*** (1755 – 1862)

A New England girl is captured by the Huron and taken to Canada. A boy is abducted at Halifax as an act of revenge against the father. Both children are lost to their parents but, on the long trek back – through priests and pirates, outlaws and judges, pestilence and war – they find each other. It is a story of bloody fights, sea battles, shipwrecks and courtroom dramas that are based on actual events.

ISBN 0-88887-281-X   ***The Planters*** (1761 – 1921)

The Elizabethan word for colonist was planter; they were the people who planted colonies.

William Brewster leads the Pilgrims of the Mayflower to North America (1620). Subsequent generations of Brewsters continue to seek their vision of religious freedom. In 1761, Samuel Brewster accepts the offer of free land recently vacated by the Acadians. The wars that are our history and the manoeuvrings of powerful men do not deter the Brewsters; they move to Baxter's Harbour where they live their faith as they follow the sea.

The Acadians IS NOW AVAILABLE ON CD AND MP3

*Special thanks to some classmates of mine
from the Royal Military College of Canada
for their interest and help in developing this book.*

3026 Walt Conrad

3108 Arthur Beemer

3164 Paul Ruck

Table of Contents

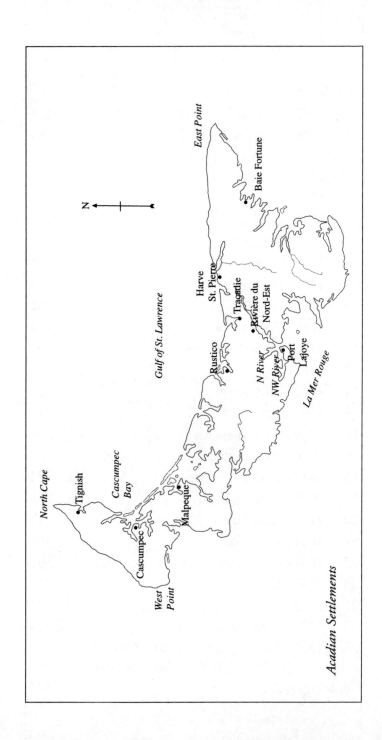

North Cape

West
Point

Tignish

*Cascumpec
Bay*

Cascumpec

Malpeque

Gulf of St. Lawrence

Rustico

N

East Point

Harve
St. Pierre

Tracadie

Rivière du
Nord-Est

Baie Fortune

N River

NW River

Port
Lajoye

La Mer Rouge

Acadian Settlements

Chapter One
Reine and Robert

August 1758
Port La Joye
Île Saint Jean

Drenched with spray from the turbulent waters of La Mer Rouge, Robert Cameron sailed his little craft into the shelter of the headlands of Port La Joye. He shaded his eyes against the afternoon sun as he picked out the landmarks. Then he pointed ahead, his whole arm shaking, as he was struck by another spell of shivering. "We should pass by the next p-p-point."[1]

"Pointe de la Croix?" his wife asked.

Robert tried to nod his head but his trembling was so intense he knew his wife would not recognize it as a response. "Y-y-yes. W-w-we should t-take the point and go up the North West River." Again the shivers struck him.

Reine Leblanc waited for the spasm to pass. During the past weeks she had watched as her husband had gotten progressively weaker: from his battle wounds, from their flight from Fortress Louisbourg, from the crossing of the Bras d'Or Lakes in a row boat, from his long exposure on the west coast of Cape Breton while Reine searched for a larger vessel, from the crossing in an open boat to The Island . . . She sighed. *We have come too far for it all to end in this wretched little boat,* she thought.

Patting his arm, she said, "Je tente de trouver un endroit où nous pouvons accoster . . . . I'll go forward and watch for a good place to land. If I remember, there's a beach beyond the point. Ce sera facile . . . It will be easy . . . to go ashore there. Maybe we can find some driftwood—build a fire—get you warmed up again."

As they rounded the point, she could see the beach, just as she remembered it. "Yes!" She pointed. "Steer to the left,

1

Robert. I see some driftwood." She blinked the salt spray from her eyes. *Was someone there, lurking in the bushes?*

Robert shoved the tiller to the right, the prow of the boat moving to the left so that he was no longer in the shade of the sail. He smiled as he felt the sun's warmth. "Il fait un beau soleil . . . . That sun feels good." He lapsed into English, repeating the advice of a Scottish friend, "Keep takin' the high road, Cameron." He answered himself, "Aye, laddie. I'll no be leavin' this life any time soon." Robert raised his voice so his wife could hear him. "I will rest on the beach. You can get some food from your cousin. What's his name?"

Reine was studying the shadows on the edge of the beach. Without taking her eyes off the bushes she replied, "Maurice. Maurice Gallant."

The boat was making its final run onto the shore. Robert gestured at the halyard. "Let the sail down, Reine. We don't want her to run aground too hard. She's got to take us home, yet."

Reine tore her eyes from the tree line and grasped the rope that would lower the sail. She freed it from its cleat and allowed the line to run through her fingers. With the sail out of the way, she could see soldiers emerging from the bushes, walking toward them. The boat crunched onto the beach.

"Home, safe and sound," Robert chuckled as he patted his chest. "Maybe not so sound, but safe, at least." He saw the approaching soldiers with their muskets at the port, bayonets glinting in the sunlight. "Sacre Bleu!" he said softly.

With a note of relief in her voice, Reine said, "It will be all right, Chéri; they are French soldiers from the La Joye garrison." She turned away from the soldiers as she secured the halyard to its cleat. "You were wounded in the throat," she whispered. "Do not speak. They would recognize you as English by your accent." *The soldiers must not learn that Robert is a deserter from an English regiment.* She quickly ran her hands up under her jerkin in a last-minute check that her breasts were still tightly bound. *And I must continue my masquerade as a boy soldier of the French Irregulars.*

The nearest soldier motioned with his bayonet "Haut les mains . . . Hands up!"

Reine smiled. "Je m'appelle Claude le Puant . . . I am called Stinky Claude. My friend and I escaped from Louisbourg . . ."

"Raise the hands!" The soldier turned his head somewhat, to shout over his shoulder, "Sergeant Pilon! I have some deserters from Louisbourg!"

A sergeant, standing at the edge of the bushes, spoke to someone and then turned to walk briskly to the water's edge. "Our officer has gone back to the barracks. Make them haul the boat above the waterline. Later, we will send someone for it."

Reine made a pleading motion with her hands. "My companion was wounded. He is too weak to . . ."

"You heard the sergeant," the nearest soldier said. "Move the boat."

"Fortress Louisbourg has fallen to the English! We only escaped because the Irregulars were allowed to leave; the English would have hanged us if we were captured."

"C'est idiot! Louisbourg can't be taken!"

"But . . ."

"Move the boat, now!" He jerked his musket back and forth near Reine's midsection. When he saw that Robert still hadn't moved, the soldier stepped to one side and raised the musket as if to shoot the figure slumped in the rear of the boat.

Weakly, Robert pulled himself erect. With apparent difficulty, he crossed over the thwarts and stepped ashore, where he collapsed in the sand. Reine rushed to his side. She indicated the bandages. "He was wounded." She cradled his head in her lap. "We must get him some help . . . some food . . . some dry clothes . . ." Her voice trailed away as the soldier placed his bayonet against the stricken man's throat.

Reine froze. She waited for the thrust.

With some delicacy, the soldier used the bayonet to move the collar out of the way, revealing scars.

"What are these?"

Her heart resumed its beating but she couldn't take her eyes off the point of the bayonet. "He was captured and the English hanged him trying to get information about the movements of Boishebert's Irregulars when we were fighting in '55."

The bayonet quavered and withdrew, slightly, but then pressed forward, punctuating each of the soldier's words. "So, he didn't die?" The soldier stepped back, steadied himself on the sand, and then kicked Robert in the leg. "So, he must have given up our positions to the English?" Robert moaned and the soldier kicked him again.

Indignantly Reine shouted, "No! They would hang him and bring him down and hang him . . . again and again until . . ."2

"Until he gave up our positions."

"He told them nothing."

The sergeant arrived and motioned for the soldier to step back. He looked at the two figures on the ground. "I can see you have had a sorry time." He thought, *they pose no threat, the older one in particular.* He turned his back on them and supervised his men as they pulled the boat up the beach above the waterline. When they were done, he detailed two of them to support Robert as they moved away from the beach toward the settlement. Sergeant Pilon walked alongside Reine. "You seem pretty young to be away from your mother's teats, son."

"Boishebert came recruiting last summer. He took me, my father, and our neighbour, Robert."

"Where's your father?"

"He fell during one of the raids at Louisbourg."

"Humph!" The sergeant watched for a reaction from the young boy. "Claude le Puant. Why they call you puant? You don't smell so bad to me." He rubbed the bristles on his chin. "In fact, you smell pretty good for a . . ."

Reine interrupted him. "The Acadian warrior Beau Soliel said I smelled bad—threw me in the North East River—but they still called me Stinky."

"Beau Soleil, you say? The Acadian raised by the Mi'kmaq? Who hasn't heard of him! If you were with Beau Soleil, you saw a lot of action."

"Yes, we did." She turned so she could look Sergeant Pilon in the eyes. "And Louisbourg has fallen to the English. You should get your men ready. The English might come here before winter."

"Merde!" Suddenly, the sergeant wanted to get back to town as quickly as possible. He turned to his men: "Wait here a minute!" He hurried off down a country lane and in a few minutes returned with a wheelbarrow. He gave Reine a friendly grin. "Au nom du Roi . . . In the name of the King, I commandeered this conveyance." With Robert in the barrow, they soon arrived at the settlement, the sergeant leading them directly to the army barracks.

The petulant voice of Ensign Richard Philippe Deschatelets preceded him through the doorway as the officer came out. "You are late for assembly!" Emerging from the split-log build-ing, squinting in the sunlight, the slim figure assumed a military pose—right hand to moustache, left hand to sword hilt. "Sergeant! What are you thinking of?" Ensign Deschatelets ceased grooming his moustache long enough to point at the captives. "Pinion the prisoner!" The hand, again grooming the moustache, screened the officer's smirk of satisfaction as he relished his alliteration. "Yes, pinion the prisoners, Pilon."

"Monsieur, I believe they are refugees from Louisbourg . . . ." "Really? You *believe* they are refugees from Louisbourg?" After a moment's hesitation, Ensign Deschatelets concluded, "Ah! They might be *English* fugitives fleeing from our finer French forces. Yes. Confine them to the gunroom—it has bars on the windows and a stout lock and door—until the commandant returns from the fort." He turned his back. "See to it, Pilon," he said as he re-entered the building, closing the door.

Sergeant Pilon pointed at the far end of the building. "Let's go!" Seeing a shadow in the window, he steadied his men and went to the trouble of binding the wrists of the pris-oners. Then he ordered, "Garde-à-vous! En avant, marche!"

Once inside the gunroom, Pilon released Reine and Robert from their bindings. Pilon shrugged his shoulders. "Not much here," he said. The room was bare except for the empty racks for the storage of the garrison's muskets, pikes, and sidearms. Pilon tapped his fingers on the powder tables where barrels of powder and shot would normally be stacked. "You can use these tables as bunks. Someone will bring blankets." He walked to the door. "Someone will bring food." He regarded Robert as he gripped the handle. "Someone will see to your wounds," he said as he left the chamber. He closed the door.

Later, while the corpsman was dressing Robert's wounds, they learned that four English warships had entered the harbour. English officers had come ashore under a flag of truce and were, at that very moment, discussing the surrender of Port La Joye with the French commandant.

"We are not going to fight?" Reine asked.

The corpsman pressed his lips together and put the finishing touches on Robert's dressings. He gathered his materials and stood up to leave.

"Well, are we going to fight the English or not?"[3]

The corpsman pointed at the empty gun-racks. "We do not have enough weapons." He hesitated but then continued, "You know the beach where you were found? We march there to practise our marksmanship and musket drills. We shoot three balls a week. Holding up his fingers and shaking them in Reine's face he repeated, "Three balls a week per man!"

Reine was about to continue making an argument for a spirited defence of the port but Robert stayed her with his hand on her arm; he knew from his military experience that the soldiers of this garrison would be unable to put up any sort of defence with so little training.

The corpsman left, promising to return with some food. Before they saw anyone else, they heard English voices ordering the French guards to ground their weapons.

Robert ran his fingers through his hair, trying to slick it down. He whispered urgently to his wife, "Fluff your hair. Unbind your breasts. Open your collar." He regarded her, "and a few buttons." Hurriedly he helped his wife. "I speak only English; you speak only . . ."

The key was inserted in the lock.

"Be a woman."

The key turned and the door was pushed open. Four redcoats entered with bayonets at the ready. As soon as they had fanned out, left and right, an English sergeant entered. He checked the room and its contents and barked, "All clear, sir!"

A tall thin-faced officer entered. He nodded at the NCO. "Thank you, Sergeant Brown."

Robert Cameron came to attention. "Corporal Herbert Miles, number 373M, Fortieth Regiment of Foot! Sir!

The officer tapped his stick against his leg. He stared at the rigid figure for a moment or so and then let his gaze rest on the woman. "I was told there were deserters from Louisbourg in custody, but this," he nodded in the direction of the woman, "is a surprise."

Robert's eyes were focused somewhere beyond the room as he responded, "Yes, sir!"

"Who is the woman, Corporal . . .?"

"Miles, sir! The woman helped me escape from the Micmac. I was a slave to the Micmac since '55, sir!"

The officer redirected his attention to the male prisoner. *He looks like a soldier . . . there can't be a Frenchman alive with freckles and red hair like that.* "Where were you taken?"

"Guard duty at Sackville, sir. Me mates was killed."

"How did you survive when your fellow soldiers didn't?"

"Beggin' your pardon, sir . . . they was fixen' to kill me too—had me hoisted by the neck—me feet swingin' clear—me world comin' to an end—hauled me up and let me down three, maybe four times—I . . ."

Showing his irritation, the officer commanded. "Get on with it, man!"

"If it would please you, sir," Robert bared his throat showing the scar ridges. "I was in sore trouble when a French priest ordered 'em to let me down. He saved me life."

"A priest, you say?"

"Yes, sir. Abbé LeLoutre was his name. The heathen Indians was in fear of him."

The officer tapped his stick against his leg. He seemed to have made up his mind about something. He pointed. "And this woman? She helped you to escape?"

"She helped me to escape, sir."

"Why would she take that risk?"

"I don't speak enough French to know, sir." When Robert saw that his answer wasn't going to satisfy the officer he hastily added, "She showed up at the Micmac lodge. Maybe she needed me strength to help her get away from Cape Breton, she bein' just a woman." He shrugged his shoulders, wincing from his wounds. "I dunno, sir. I was just glad that she was helpin' me to get out of there."

"So, she's nothing to you, Corporal?"

"Just grateful that she helped me enough to get me back to me old regiment. And here I am, safe with me own kind again, sir." Robert heaved a large sigh.

Sergeant Brown cleared his throat before speaking. "Beggin' your pardon, sir, she could be a Louisbourg fishwife just tryin' to get away from the kind attentions of our boys."

The officer tapped his stick against his leg. He stepped closer to the female prisoner. "You speak English?" he asked, keeping a watchful eye for any response. Seeing none, he backed away. "She could also be a spy. The French use women that way. I have a feeling that there is more here than meets the eye. Seize her!" he ordered.

The English soldier standing by Reine handed off his musket. Grabbing her by the arm, he twisted it behind her back until she was bent forward in pain. The officer watched the prisoner, Miles, for a reaction but there was none; Robert stared straight ahead as if he were not a party to the pain being inflicted on the woman.

The officer nodded his head.

The soldier applied more pressure to Reine's arm. She whimpered as she was forced forward and to her knees. She screamed as even more pressure was applied.

Robert maintained his rigid posture.

Again, the officer seemed to have made up his mind about something. "Release her. Take Corporal Miles to the mess tent . . . there should be one set up, somewhere, about now." He motioned for the redcoats near the door to get out of his way. He paused when Robert said, "Your pardon, sir." The officer slowly turned to face the corporal. "What *is* it?"

"Will I get me back pay? Sometime soon?"

"You will be returned to Halifax where the paymaster will check your records." For the first time the officer smiled. "I believe they will honour your time as a prisoner. It is the normal practice."

"And sir . . ."

The sergeant stepped forward. "Shut your face, man! Ye're botherin' my officer!"

"Thank you, Brown. Let's hear him out."

"Please may I have a chit to go to the surgeon? I got wounded makin' me escape. The frog corpsman tore the scab off."

"See to it, Brown." Again, he regarded the woman, staring at the white flesh exposed at the base of Reine's throat where the shirt had been opened. He swallowed. "Give her a meal, too. By all the appearances, she brought our corporal back to duty. We should at least feed her, the once." A trace of a smile and then he was gone.

When the sergeant was filling out the chit, Robert suggested it be made out for a "party of two." "That way you're shut of her, Sergeant. She'll be in me custody."

"Until she gets put on a ship." When he saw the questioning look on Miles's face, the sergeant explained. "They's all goin' on ships and then we burns this place to the ground."

"And good riddance," Corporal Miles affirmed. "I'm goin' to wash the French filth off me . . ."

The officer's voice boomed through the open doorway. "Sergeant Brown!"

"He's a mite irritated, my officer is. Gentlemen officers get that way late in the day." Brown hurriedly made out a chit for a "party of two" and then scurried out the door. "Right away, sir! Sorry for the delay, sir!"

"Even sergeants can have a sojourn in the stocks, my man."

"Yessir! I knows that, sir. I appreciates your for-bear-ants, sir.

"Take your patrol and herd the riff-raff out of the way."

Reine and Robert were listening as they stood in the shadow of the doorway. "Are you able to walk, Robert?" she whispered.

He nodded his head in the affirmative. "I'll keep on goin' but I need some food, right some quick." They peeked out the door—French inhabitants were milling aimlessly—Sergeant Brown had assembled his patrol in front of the military building—Ensign Richard Philippe Deschatelets was standing, somewhat apart from the gaggle of his soldiers, still fondling his moustache but missing his sword and scabbard. Two French priests were walking up the hill from the waterfront—and then Robert and Reine quickly ducked back in out of sight as Sergeant Brown turned to face his officer.

"Where does you want them put, sir?"

"Oh, out of the way, sergeant; out of the way of the supply train that must come up that hill to this building."

Reine and Robert believed that Sergeant Brown must have taken a look around because it was a few moments before he answered his officer. "Over by the Mass House will do then, sir?"

"That will do nicely, Sergeant."

"Just like Grand Prè," Reine whispered in her husband's ear. "They're going to lock them in the church and . . ."

Robert put his arm over Reine's shoulder and leaned on her. "Come on, Reine. We must go to the mess tent. Then we must find Maurice Gallant and get out of here. I can't have you taken from me and put on an English ship going God-knows-where." He smiled, grimly. "And sooner or later someone will remember the real Corporal Miles."

They slipped out the door as the redcoats advanced against the crowd, bayonets threatening anyone who didn't move toward the church. Robert lifted his head and sniffed the air, "I can smell shepherd's pie." They started walking down the hill. When they were accosted by another patrol, Robert held out his chit and they were allowed to proceed.

23 September 1758

Robert Cameron lifted his head from the mattress. Bleary-eyed, he looked around the small, dark shed. He was alone. He pushed himself up and swung his legs over the side of the cot. *Dizzy*, he thought. *Hungry.* He smacked his lips and then ran his tongue around the inside of his mouth. *Thirsty.* There was a jug by the side of the cot on the dirt floor. He grunted with discomfort as he bent over to get it. He slopped the water a little as he gulped down the contents. He was sitting there, holding the jug in his hands, when the door opened. Even with the glare from the outside sunshine putting the face in shadow, he knew it was Reine. He started to speak but all he could manage was a squawk. He tried again. "How long was I asleep this time?"

"Six or seven hours." She extended her arms to help him up. "There is food ready at the farmhouse. Maurice has news from the village. The English have about five hundred soldiers here now."

Robert stood at the side of the bed, steadying himself in his wife's embrace. "What is the news?" he said into the softness of her hair. He kissed her forehead and then pushed away. Tossing the empty jug on the bunk he walked, a trifle unsteadily, to the door.

"Father Cassiet and Father Biscaret met with Lord Rollo . . ."

Robert stopped at the door. "Who's Lord Rollo?"

"Colonel Lord Rollo was sent here by General Amherst to round up and deport the Islanders and to burn the settlements."

"Settlements? Not just here at Port la Joye where the fort is?"

"Tracadie, Malpeque, Port La Joye . . ."

"Rivière-du-Nord-Est?" Robert closed the door and, in the semi-darkness, felt for his wife's hand. He drew her to him and then they sat down, together, on the edge of the bunk. "You think they will burn our village, our home?"

"The priests spoke to Rollo, begging that the people of The Island be left in peace."

Robert closed his eyes. "The priests are right. These Islanders should be left alone. They are peaceable, hard-working . . ."4

"The mainland Acadians were peaceable and hard-working and yet look what the English did to us."

In the darkness, Robert could see the pout. He hesitated, but proceeded anyway. "The mainland Acadians took part in raids against . . ."

"It was expected of us. The priests"—she searched for a word and then fell back on the one that she had already used—"expected us to help defend our motherland And besides, the governor at Québec ordered us to resist the English. We could not disobey."

"Some of you . . ." Robert felt his wife tense. He started again. "Some of us, like Beau Soliel, were willing raiders against the English." He waited to see how upset she had become with this conversation—the first they had ever had about the root causes for the expulsion of Acadians on the mainland—before continuing. "You and I fought the English . . ."

"We were given no choice."

Robert nodded his head in agreement, "But none of these island people has ever lifted a hand against the English. They are no threat to the British Empire." Even in the half-light, he could see the gleam of anger in her eyes. He leaned forward and kissed her cheek and squeezed her hand. "For whatever reasons, enough mainland Acadians were willing to fight that the English recognized them as a threat." He patted her hand; she withdrew it, out of reach. He stood up. "These people— these Islanders—haven't hurt anyone. Hopefully, the English will leave them alone." In the darkness, he could see by the set of her square Leblanc jaw that even though this was the first time they had discussed the Acadians, it would not be the last. "We should go talk to Maurice." He held out his hand. She let him reclaim her hand and, together, they walked from the barn to the main house where Cousin Maurice and his wife, Angélique, were waiting.

Maurice met them at the door. He looked Robert up and down. "You are looking better," he said. "Good food, good sleep, and the attentions of a good wife are all a man needs for good health." He was enjoying his humour and didn't see the disapproving look cast at him by his wife. He flinched visibly when his wife spoke.

"Maurice!" Angélique's voice trembled with mortification. "The good Father has already warned you about that kind of talk." She lowered her head and spoke, sotto voce, "And Reine's husband is a stranger to us." She leaned forward and whispered, "And English."

Immediately chastened, Maurice made a placating gesture to Angélique as he invited the visitors to join him near the hearth; "The days are cooler now; come by the fire," he said, adding, "much has happened while you slept the days away."

There were only two chairs so, while Reine sat in the nearest chair, Robert settled down on the hearth stones near the fireplace. "Ah!" he said. "I appreciate the comfort of a good fire. It seems I have been cold ever since I was wounded at Louisbourg."

Angélique motioned for her husband to sit in the other chair. "I have some little chores to do. You talk to our guests."

Maurice directed his comments to the other man in the room. "The priests were given permission to take our petition to General Amherst at Louisbourg. This Rollo fellow was receptive enough to our plea but he said he would have to obey his orders."[5]

"To ship everyone out . . . to where?"

"To France, probably. But, on his own hook, Rollo agreed to wait while our priests went to Louisbourg to plead our case. They came back this morning."

Reine leaned forward in her chair so she could catch Robert's eye. "Do we know the result of their . . ."

Glancing at the woman, but returning his attention to Robert, he answered, "The priests were escorted ashore and taken directly to Colonel Rollo. From there they went to the French Governor's house."

"Nothing has been said?"

"Nothing."

For several moments the only sounds in the kitchen were the crackling of the fire and the slicing sounds of Angélique's knife. She was the first to speak. "I don't know anyone in France." She put her knife down. She came around the table, holding her arms out. "They wouldn't burn our homes, would they?" She wasn't asking her husband; she placed her hands on the shoulders of the only person she believed might really know. "Tell me, Robert Cameron, the English know we haven't done anything to harm them. We are no threat." Shaking her head from side to side she asked, in a pathetic little voice, "They wouldn't burn my house, would they?"

Gently, Robert tried to comfort her. He looked in the direction of the husband but Maurice seemed to be deep in thought, staring into the fire. Robert had his hopes for the future of the Island Acadians—he had discussed those hopes, earlier, with Reine—but he could not forget the English indifference to Acadian suffering at Grand Prè. In almost a whisper he pronounced his belief. "Expect little kindness from the English."

Angélique began to sob.

Reine reached out and patted her arm.

Just then, the village assembly bell rang.

No one made a move to answer the call. Maurice sat, watching the fire. Angélique continued gently crying into Robert's shoulder. Reine had stood, but she felt she had nowhere to go; there was nothing she would want to hear from the English.

The latch rattled and the door was roughly pushed aside as the three Gallant children stormed into the kitchen.

The mother separated herself from the Englishman and shook her finger at her offspring. "Mind your manners!" She quickly wiped the errant tears. "And you shouldn't track mud in here!

"Soldiers come to take us to the meeting!"

"Redcoats!"

"No! Red Lobsters!"

"No! No! Les Maquereaux!"

Angélique, using her "mother voice," admonished her eldest son. "Don't call them that. They might hear you."

In a soft voice, Maurice chided his wife, "Even if they heard, they wouldn't understand."[6]

The littlest boy, Simon, piped up. "I don't understand, Papa. I hear Uncle Jean-Baptiste call them Les Maquereaux all the time"

Through the door, they all watched the approach of a squad of the best-disciplined infantry in the world.

Simon persisted, "Well, Papa, why do we call them Les Maquereaux?"

"It's because they move all together and, when they move like that, we think they look like les maquereaux."

Angélique was the first out the door, followed by little Simon who was still chattering about the school of mackerel. She turned and shushed the child.

Walking slowly, they were caught up by a number of Islanders and they paraded as a closely knit group to the edge of the circle of bayonets. The English officer, known as Colonel Lord Rollo, standing tall behind the bayonets, cleared his throat, preparing to speak.

The Island Acadians of Port La Joye were about to hear what their conquerors were going to do with them.

27 September 1758
Port La Joye

Maurice rapped on the door of the shed. "Il y en a plus ce matin dans le havre. . . There are more of them in the harbour this morning."

Robert came out of the shed, tucking his shirt in and carrying his jerkin on his arm. "Let's go see what's going on."

"I don't think we should go into the village. The redcoats have penned the new arrivals from Tracadie near the church. They have shelter, food and water but they are not permitted to leave the small area by the church."

"Then we'll go to the knoll. We can see most of the harbour from there."

Maurice handed Robert a piece of crusty bread.

Robert nodded his thanks. "Still warm. Angélique makes good bread." He took a quick bite. "How many ships?"

"I counted five. Then there's the petit chasse-marée . . ."

Robert knew he was speaking of a fishing boat, which the English would have called a lugger.

" . . . that brought the people from Tracadie. It is supposed to leave tomorrow and go back up the Rivière-du-Nord-Est to gather in the people from Havre Saint Pierre."

"Is it far from the headwaters of the river to Saint Pierre?"

"Not far." He grunted. "And they won't be carrying much. The English make everyone leave most everything behind."

"Their possessions are being left behind?"

"And burned."

They had reached the top of the little hill. Maurice pointed. "The big ship is the *Duke William*. The smaller one to the left is the *Violet*. They were the first to arrive; that's why I know their names. The others I don't know."

They stood in silence as they watched the activity on the waterfront. Open boats were leaving each of the ships and approaching the shore.

"It looks like they are getting ready to move us onto the ships." Robert swallowed hard enough for Maurice to hear him. Maurice looked at his friend and reached over to squeeze Robert's arm.

Robert didn't take his eyes off the beach area as he said, "We have to leave here, right away."

"Yes, let's go back."

"No, I mean we have to leave La Joye. We can't stay here."

"Where would we go?"

"I don't know."

"They are going to burn everything. There won't be any food or shelter."

"Yes. I saw what they did at Grand Prè. If they are anything, the English are thorough. There won't be anything left." Then with a deep note of bitterness he added, "The English always plan their deportations for late in the season when there is little choice but to obey them."

"Well, I can't go off into the wilderness; I have a wife and three children."

They turned away from the view, walking in silence, each man with his own thoughts. The patrol of redcoats seemed to appear from out of nowhere.

"Hold there!"

Maurice and Robert stood still, facing the bayonets. Robert recognized several of the soldiers and Sergeant Brown.

The sergeant advanced. "Have you reported back to duty, Corporal Miles?"

Maurice, not understanding English, put on a blank look and shrugged his shoulders.

Robert answered, "I got up from my sickbed this morning, thank you, sergeant."

"Report to the quartermaster for your kit. Can't have you runnin' around lookin' like that, Corporal. Sets a bad example for the men, you know."

"Yes, Sergeant. First thing in the—"

"Meanwhile, we will take this Frenchie into custody . . ."

"Excuse me, Sergeant. I was billeted with him while I was making my recovery. He has a wife and family; they depend on him for . . ."

"Right!" *I'm not sure about this Miles fellow. Let's find something out . . .* "Lead us to your billet and we will take them all into custody."

"I can bring them in later . . ."

"Now, Corporal Miles!"

"Yes, Sergeant."

"Form squad!" Sergeant Brown bellowed. "Corporal Miles leading!"

Robert came to attention. "Right marker!" he called out.

A corporal stepped forward, marching to a spot three paces in front of Robert. He halted; smartly lowering his musket, he stood with the musket butt at the side of his right shoe, muzzle and bayonet supported at the side of his body with his right hand.

Robert turned to the right. Marching five paces he halted and executed a left turn. The soldiers of the squad now knew that, as soon as the order was given, they were to position themselves to the left of the right marker and face Robert.

"Squad, fall in!"

Maurice was pushed into the blank file in the middle; the rest of the column stood at attention in three lines, facing Robert.

"Carry on, Corporal Miles!"

"Yes, Sergeant! Shoulder arms! Right turn!" Awkwardly, Maurice belatedly turned in the same direction.

"By the left, quick march!" Robert had no choice but to give the orders.

Maurice was cursed at as he bumped against first one soldier and then another.

Sergeant Brown, marching alongside Corporal Miles, knew that an experienced corporal would immediately correct the unmilitary behaviour in the ranks.

"Quiet in the ranks! Take control of that prisoner."

Sergeant Brown beamed; Miles was, without a doubt, a good soldier.

The soldier next to Maurice reached over with his right hand and, grabbing Maurice in a very personal manner, led him to his proper position in the ranks. When the soldier was confident that Maurice was going to follow the movements of the patrol, he released his hold.

They marched down the hill until they were close to the little group of homes near the path leading to the fort.

"Halt your squad, Corporal!"

"Squad, halt!"

"Which house is it, Corporal?"

"The one with the bake oven in the front yard, Sergeant."

"You are relieved, Corporal Miles. Fall out!" Before Robert could obey, Islanders began coming out of the houses to see what was going on. Sergeant Brown acted immediately.

"Squad—section one to the left, section two to the right—surround the houses! On the double, double march!" The Islanders made no attempt to flee and they were soon herded into a tight little group.

"Does anyone here speak English?" Sergeant Brown rocked back and forth—heel to toe, toe to heel—as he waited for a response. After a decent interval, he gave instructions to his men, loud enough for the Islanders to hear: "Since I can't give them my instructions, march them away without any personal gear or effects." He turned his back on the Islanders, "Carry on, Corporal Farrow."[7]

"Yes, sergeant!"

"I speak English," a voice called out from the throng.

Sergeant Brown turned to see who had spoken.

Corporal Farrow took a deep breath: "Squad, take charge of your prisoners!" Bayonets were raised and the ring of soldiers advanced on the suddenly very frightened Islanders.

"I am here, Sergeant Brown," Reine said as she stepped clear of the small huddle of Gallants. "I speak English."

"As you were, Corporal Farrow!"

"Squad stand fast." The soldiers stood, muskets poised, eyes not leaving their quarry.

A large smile spread across the sergeant's face. He glanced over at Corporal Miles. *Ah ha!* He thought, *there's more to this fellow than meets the eye. He knows his squad drill so he's probably what he says he is . . . but . . . .* "Tell these people to go back into their homes and select those items they will need to travel—because they will be travelling." He again turned his back on the Islanders but continued pronouncing his instructions. "You may return to the houses, ten at a time. If any of you runs away . . ." he paused for effect, "the rest of you will be shot." He walked over to where Robert was standing. "And you, Corporal, you lied to my officer. You said that you didn't know why that woman was helping you. You said that you didn't speak to her."

Robert was standing at attention. "Permission to speak, Sergeant?"

"No. You can tell your story to my officer."

"I didn't know she could speak English."

Sergeant Brown was a fair man; he considered what the corporal had said and he came to a decision. "That may be so. I won't take you to my officer for lying, but you just disobeyed me. You didn't have permission to speak. You will appear on defaulters' in the morning."

"Yes, Sergeant."

"Get what you need from your billet. You won't be staying here any more."

"Yes, Sergeant." Robert marched into the Gallant house where he found Reine waiting for him. He picked up a shirt and wrapped some bread in it, adding a turnip and a couple of handfuls of dried peas.

"What are we going to do?" Reine asked.

Robert checked the edge of a knife and put it down, selected another one, and rolled everything up in the shirt. "Escape," he said. "You know where our boat is. Go there. Wait for me."

From outside, they heard the voice of Corporal Farrow: "Time's up for the first ten!"

"What if I can't escape?"

"You will escape, and I will be there."

"But, what if I can't escape?"

Robert shook his head. "I love you, dearest, and you will escape."

"Where is that translator woman?" They could hear from the testiness in Sergeant Brown's voice that he was losing his patience.

Reine whispered, "I will die if we are not together."

"Private Bagnal, shoot that first little man if she isn't here in . . ."

"I am here," Reine shouted, panic sounding in her voice. "I am here." She went outside.

"Tell them to get a move on. We can't wait all day."

Robert spied some flints and tinder. He scooped them up—to be included in his package—as he went out the door.

* * *

Boats were transporting Islanders to the largest of the ships in the harbour—*to Duke William*, Robert thought. *If Maurice had the names right, they are loading Duke William and then Violet.* From where he was standing—with the English soldiers who were being held in reserve in case any prisoners caused trouble—he could read the names from the boats as they picked up their human cargoes. There were boats from the *Nautilus, Parnassus, Hind, Duke William, Violet,* and the *Narcissus. There are more ships than he and Maurice had thought. Maurice! Where is . . . ah, there he is with his family. At least they are all together, huddled in the next group to be loaded in one of the boats.* Angélique gave him a small wave. He didn't dare acknowledge it. She looked hurt.

He kept his eye on the Gallants' boat. It went to the *Duke William;* all the boats were going to the largest ship. Two more boats were being readied for loading. Some clattering and military noises caused him to look away from the waterfront. He could see that the soldiers of the La Joye garrison were being marched down the hill toward the beach. When he looked back at the beach, two more boats were on their way to the *Duke William*. His heart lurched! Reine was no longer on the beach! Without thinking, he took several steps toward the water.

"Hold fast!"

Robert continued his search of the beach, taking a few steps first one way and then the other.

"Stop that man!"

Three redcoats of Brown's squad formed an escort around Robert and led him back to his proper position at the edge of the beach. "Christ, mate," one of them whispered, "you're already in deep shit with the sergeant. Breaking ranks like you did will get you the stockade. What the Micmac did to you will seem like a picnic."

Robert wasn't listening; he was hearing the officer's voice: "Where is that translator woman?"

"She went to the *Duke William* with the last load."

"I need someone to tell me what this frog officer wants. He's been making a fuss ever since he came down to the beach."

"Lieutenant Bradshaw speaks French, sir."

Another voice: "Your pardon sir, the lieutenant is not on the beach."

Sergeant Brown loomed large in front of Robert. Robert couldn't hear what was being said on the beach because the sergeant began giving orders.

"Corporal Farrow, march these men off to the mess tent. Have them fed early. Then take the defaulter to the QM and have him outfitted. I want him in proper dress when he is on defaulters' parade in the morning."

In a daze, Robert came to attention, right turned and marched off with his squad. *It couldn't get any worse*, he thought; *Reine a prisoner on the big ship and me a prisoner in the stockade.*

* * *

The Gallant children were excited; the ship was so-o-o big and there was so much going on—so many strangers—but they recognized Reine and ran right to her. She put her arms out and gathered them in. Holding the children close she looked over their little bodies at the black hole that other Islanders were being forced to enter. Occasionally family members were separated but the sailors would allow nothing to disrupt the flow of cargo into the bowels of the ship. There was crying and screaming but the flood of people into the dark space below decks continued, unabated. By the time it was the turn for the people around the Gallants to descend, the children had become infected with the terror and hurt that was going on around them. Angélique, ever the strong one, took charge of her distraught brood and they arrived at the lip of the ship's hold in good order—at least they were all together—and they still held their little packages of personal belongings tightly to their bodies.

Two sailors grabbed Reine by the arms and wrenched her out of the line.

Angélique caught a glimpse of what was happening to Reine but then a sailor put his big tarred hand on her head and pushed her down the ladder. For Angélique and her family, the world became a damp, dangerous place where fear-soaked bodies jammed up against partitions and each other in the half darkness of a few flickering candle lamps. It would be many, many days before she would wonder what had happened to Reine Leblanc Cameron.

* * *

Reine knew better than to protest or to ask questions. Although she tried to co-operate with the two sailors, she had been thoroughly handled by the time she had been lifted and dragged to the vessel's entry port. There a young junior army officer asked, quite timidly, if she were the translator woman.

She nodded her head.

"No, please. I have to be sure that you speak English and French. Please say that you do."

"I speak English and French."

Ensign Baker seemed to relax a trifle. "My major needs for you to find out what the French military want. You see, they are making a fuss and . . ."

A voice, heavy with authority, called down from the quarterdeck, "Make up your mind, Ensign. I mean to close the entry port and assume my station in the stream before the turn of the tide."

"Yes, sir. Thank you, sir. She is the prisoner my Colonel wants. I will take her into custody."

"Do you want manacles?"

Ensign Baker didn't give it a thought. "No thank you, sir. With your permission, we will proceed ashore." Baker saluted and took Reine by the arm. He was surprised at how muscular the young woman was. It should have warned him to be more alert with the prisoner but he was anxious to complete his immediate duty; he was going to deliver the translator woman to his major and the fuss with the French military would go away. Then Ensign Baker could go to the mess tent and spend the evening playing cards with his friends.

* * *

Corporal Farrow motioned for Robert to join him at the entrance to the mess tent. "Let's go, buddy. We havta do as we're told, don't we."

"Yes."

Farrow had stored his musket at the company armoury and considered himself off duty. He cast a sideways glance at this fellow corporal and asked, "Now that we are away from the men, what was that thing you wuz doin' on the beach?"

"Guess I went a little crazy. I thought there wuz Indians comin'. I had to do somethin' if the Indians wuz comin'. Couldn't just stand there. Had to do somethin'," Robert rambled. "Indians caught me last time. Hanged me mates. Tongues stuck out. Ol' Freddie bit his tongue right off. He bled to death, they hanged him so often."

"Christ!" Farrow looked at his mate with different eyes. "When it was goin' on, didja wanta die?"

"I wanted to die this afternoon on the beach. If the Injuns wuz comin', I wanted to go somewheres or die or somethin'."

The quartermaster stores were closed.

"He shouldn't be closed."

"I gotta have myself proper turned out for defaulters', I do."

"Ye're right about that! You can't go before the CO lookin' like this. You wait here. I'll go find the orderly sergeant. He'll get the place opened for us."

"Right. I'll just rest here." Robert hunkered down by the side of the tent. He watched as Corporal Farrow turned around to go in search of the orderly sergeant. Robert had a pang of guilt for this pleasant fellow who would soon be in a great deal of trouble. "You want me to come with you?"

"Naw. You rest."

"Ain't you worried about maintainin' custody of a prisoner?"

"You're not a prisoner until someone says you are." He grinned at Robert, "Tomorrow, after defaulters', you will be a prisoner."

Robert leaned over and selected a piece of straw to pick his teeth. "You got it right there, mate."

"I'll be back."

If Farrow had looked around, he would have seen Corporal Miles running and bounding like a deer over rocks and bushes as he sought cover in the woods.

* * *

Reine recognized the petulant voice before she could discern the face of Ensign Richard Philippe Deschatelets. She could see by the English officer's posture that he wasn't paying any attention to what the ensign was spouting. She wanted to slow her pace so she could pick up as much information as she could but Ensign Baker, with a firm grasp of her arm, urged her forward. Still, she heard enough to prepare herself.

"Vous avez mis un prêtre et son adjoint dans la cabine d'un bâteau le plus grand et le plus sécuritaire en route vers la France et . . .You have put a priest and his clerk in a cabin on the largest, safest ship going to France and assigned me, an officer of His Majesty's Army, to a closet on the miserable bastard of a ship, the *Violet*. It is unbecoming of my rank and the nobility of my family to be so treated." Deschatelets recognized the approaching person. "What's he doing here?"

Ensign Baker saluted the bored lieutenant. "I have the translator woman. She was on the *Duke William*."

"Mais oui!" Ensign Deschatelets interrupted, "*Duke William, Duke William!* I want to be assigned quarters on the *Duke William*. Remove the priests! God will look after them. I want a cabin on the biggest, safest ship."

When Deschatelets paused in his tirade, the English lieutenant dismissed Ensign Baker with a polite "Thank you, Baker."

Deschatelets stared at Reine. He became very agitated, screaming in rapid French, "You are the fugitive from Louisbourg!" His mouth opened and his jaw dropped in surprise. "An English spy! I should have you shot!"

When he realized that Reine had become a woman since the last time he had seen him—or her—he became truly excited. "He's a she!" he wailed.

The English lieutenant scratched his greying hair and then raised his hand to stop the torrent of French.

Deschatelets snapped his mouth shut as he attempted to discern what was going on.

The English lieutenant gestured at the French officer: "What does he say?"

"He says I am an English spy—as we say in French, espionne anglaise." She repeated "espionne anglaise," more loudly and slowly.

The French officer saw his opening and pounced: "Elle est une espionne anglaise. Es-pionne anglaise," he said a second time, more slowly so the older man, obviously promoted beyond his social station, might comprehend. He pointed at the woman. "Es- pi-onne ang-laise."

"He wants me shot."

The English officer smiled at the French woman. "What else does he want?"

"He says he is a member of the French nobility and he is entitled to a cabin on the largest and safest ship."

"Tell him there is no space left on *Duke William*."

"Oui, oui. *Duke William!*"

The English officer held up his hand again to silence the French officer.

"He says you gave cabin space to priests. Take them off and put them somewhere else. Give him a cabin."

The English officer rubbed his chin. "Nobility, you say?"

"*He* says." Reine smiled, "There's English nobility and French nobility. Both are the same except this one speaks French."

"Yes." The English officer wasn't a fool. He knew that noble families have a long reach. He made up his mind. "Tell him I will arrange for him to be given a cabin on the *Duke William*." When Reine stopped translating, the English officer asked, "What does he want done with his men?"

"He won't care about his men."

"Ask him, Madame, if you please."

Reine posed the question and then translated: "He has confidence that you will arrange suitable accommodation for his common soldiers."

"So be it." He nodded at the French officer. He turned away, leading Reine by the elbow. "Come, Madame. I will arrange for you to have at least one more good meal."

Reine smiled up at him. "A last meal? You are going to have me shot?"

"No, but tomorrow I will have our Intelligence Officer find out if you are one of them . . ."

"Or one of us," Reine interjected.

The officer laughed. "I am Lieutenant John Makin. And you are?"

"Reine . . ." She hesitated and then tried a bold move. "Cameron. French mother, Scottish father."

"My mother was a McGahern . . ." he began, but he suddenly excused himself saying, "I see my major has need of me," as he left.

Ensign Baker returned almost immediately. "The lieutenant was called away. The major is upset because one of our men, scheduled for defaulters' tomorrow, flew the coop."

"Flew the coop? My English is not that good."

"A corporal ran away rather than face punishment. It happens, but not often."

Reine's heart surged with hope; *perhaps Robert got away.*
"You look pleased about something."

"Ah, yes. Lieutenant Makin said he was going to arrange a hot meal for me and then somewhere to sleep."

"The first part's easy. Come along to the mess tent."

Just outside the mess tent, Reine landed a solid blow to the side of Ensign Baker's head and he fell to the ground. He recovered his senses in time to see the translator woman disappear into the forest.

17 October 1758

Reine stood as high as possible in the bow of their little boat and shielded her eyes as she scanned the next bay for signs of habitation. "Go in closer to the shore, Robert." She swivelled around to see if her husband had heard her. They were running with the wind, at a good clip, the boat's hull slapping the wavelets as it caught them up.

Robert signalled that he had heard. He adjusted the tiller to larboard and the bow of the boat moved toward the shore. "This one could be Malpeque Bay; it's big enough."

"I don't think so. There's supposed to be marine markers on some islands," she said as she scanned the bay, "and I don't see any islands."

"Too bad we don't have a map."

"Or some directions other than that Malpeque is in the west."

The boat shuddered. Reine grabbed for the jib to steady herself but missed a handhold. She squatted for better balance but, when the bow rose and the hull tilted to starboard, Reine was tossed into the water. The boat's forward momentum carried the boat over the sandbar and into deeper water leaving Reine in its wake, thrashing about.

There wasn't time for Robert to turn the boat before she touched bottom again, shuddering to a halt. The wind continued to fill the sails, forcing the lee-gunnel under the water; the boat began to fill with seawater. Robert had the good sense to release the sheets for the mainsail and jib, allowing the boat to right herself. Pushing aside the flapping canvas, he searched the surface of the bay for his wife. *Oh God! She doesn't swim! Help us, dear God!*

Reine surfaced about four boat-lengths back, sputtering and complaining about how cold the water was.

"You told me you couldn't swim, Reine."

"I am not swimming. I am standing here. Come get me, Robert."

"Reine, the boat has run aground."

"I tried walking after you but there is a deep channel between us."

Robert gazed toward the shore, about forty boat-lengths away. "There seems to be a series of channels and sandbars . . ."

"I must get out of this water, Robert. I am freezing."

Robert removed the sheets from the clew and tied them together, making one long piece of rope. He coiled the rope and threw it—just the way he had been taught as a Highland boy—upwind of his wife. She grabbed it. He hauled her in.

"Take your clothes off," Robert said as he slipped off the coat he had "borrowed" from an abandoned house at La Joye. With his dry shirt and coat, Robert tried his best to take the chill off her but their feet were in the cold water in the bottom of the boat, the sun was behind a cloud, and the wind was beginning to have a nasty feel to it. They were in serious trouble and they both knew it.

"We must get off the sandbar. We have no bailer . . ." He re-attached the sheets to their clew. "I will set the tiller. Once the boat is free of the mud, and the sails fill, she will want to go back to the first sandbar."

"How do we get her to move?" Reine asked before she realized what they had to do. "I don't know if I can go back into the water, Robert. I am so very cold."

"I will go. You stay here; try to get warm."

Reine stared at the green water. She shivered. "No, you will soon get cold." She began to get out of her clothes. "We have to do it right the first time."

Robert didn't point out the obvious; there was a second sandbar. They would have to do it right a second time, too.

Duke William
Canso

"Good morning, Father." Ensign Deschatelets gave a small— a very small—bow to the priest. "It is a lovely time of the day to take the air."

Abbé Girard and the ensign were on the quarterdeck. As cabin passengers, they were permitted to come out onto the quarterdeck for air or for exercise any time during the day, with curfew from twilight to sunrise. At the moment, aside from the ship's crew, they were the only persons on the upper deck. Below, on the main deck, they could hear the murmurs and the shuffling of many feet as a dozen Islanders tried to find space between the equipment, the crew, and the armed guards, to take advantage of their fifteen minutes in the sun. There was no doubt in anyone's mind. The passengers—even the exalted ones on the quarterdeck—were hostage to their good behaviour. One incident, one disturbance, and all prisoners would be confined.

"Yes, it is, quite."

"I have it directly from Captain Nicholls that our convoy will consist of seven ships." Deschatelets pointed toward the headland. "See! Another ship arrived last night." Importantly he added, "She's the *Nautilus*, Captain Dobson commanding."

"Oh. I see."

"We will remain here until the convoy is complete." With one hand he stroked his moustache and the other searched for the hilt of his sword; a futile gesture, of course, since his sword had been given up at the time of the surrender. "Oh, bother!" he grumbled, "I didn't expect they would actually keep my sword! It was an excellent blade, given me by . . ."

"Do you know how long it will be before our convoy is ready to leave? Did Captain Nicholls mention anything?"

"Yes, he most certainly did." Deschatelets furiously twirled the sparse hair of his moustache. "There is a plan . . ." he paused but was interrupted by the priest's impatience.

"Ensign Deschatelets! Would you please tell me when we can expect to leave Canso!"

"I don't know when *we* will leave because . . ."

"I thought you told me that you knew."

Obviously irritated by the priest's manner, the officer responded officiously, "My dear sir, over two thousand Islanders are being loaded on sixteen transports. It is expected they will leave for France during the first week of November."

"And?"

"Captain Nicholls's convoy will be obliged to wait for the last of the Island people to be gathered in and loaded."

"How long will that take?"

"The parish of Malpeque is far removed from Port La Joye. Lord Rollo has orders to collect *all* remaining inhabitants—even from as far away as Malpeque—and destroy their buildings, crops, and equipment. It will take some time . . ."

Ensign Deschatelets stopped talking when the priest turned away from the young officer and walked over to the taffrail. Deschatelets followed him to the rail.

The priest sighed. "If they delay departure until late in the season, it makes for a hazardous crossing."

The officer's demeanour changed. "Hazardous? You mean some danger to . . . to us?" He didn't wait for the reply; instead, he hastened on with some self-reassurances. "We have a large ship, a skilled captain and an experienced crew . . ."

"Yes, but . . ."

" . . . and they wouldn't give command of an entire convoy to Captain Nicholls if they didn't think . . ."

Exasperated, the priest laid his hand on the officer's arm and gave it a squeeze. "Listen, my son. The North Atlantic is not a nice place in December." The officer looked like he might interrupt so the priest squeezed harder on the arm. "Good ships with good captains have been lost in the winter storms on the Atlantic."

"Yes, but we have a good, big ship and a good, experienced captain . . ."

The priest shook his head and made one last attempt to explain his concerns about a December crossing of the Atlantic. "We are heavily laden. There are over seven hundred souls on these two ships." The priest saw a spark of insight in the other's eyes and he pursued it: "And when Lord Rollo collects the people from Malpeque, he might decide to stuff even more bodies into these two ships."

"That's terrible!"

"Yes, it is."

"I might be expected to share my cabin." Ensign Richard Philippe Deschatelets made up his mind. "I will not be put upon." He smacked his hand on the taffrail. "I will not share my cabin." When he saw the priest's look of incredulity, the officer hastened to add, "And I will insist that you be treated with equal dignity."

The priest bowed his head to hide his facial expression. "I appreciate your thoughtfulness," he muttered. With his head still lowered he raised his eyes. "With this delay, it will be months before we return to France. I plan to spend _my_ time giving religious instruction to members of my flock. How will _you_ pass the time?"

"Papers to write," Deschatelets sighed, "I am obliged, by my family's position, to report on the effectiveness of the officers I serve with."

"You continue to perform your duty to the King even in this trying circumstance. Admirable."

The ensign inclined his head to the priest, this time a little deeper. "I am mindful of my duty."

"Perhaps you may be able to do the Church a service?" Abbé Girard didn't wait for the objection he could see forming on the ensign's face to mature. "I require permission for boys to join me in my cabin so I may train them in their duties and obligations to the church."

"What could _I_ do . . .?"

"It would be much easier for an officer of some standing

to seek permission for three boys to join me for an hour each day. I would teach them their catechism and their duties at the altar."

"Every day?"

"Yes. And to ensure there would be no difficulty with the boys getting into mischief or becoming . . . involved . . . with . . . sailors, I would recommend that one of the adult passengers accompany them."

"And stay with them?"

"At all times."

"I will lay your case before Captain Nicholls."

"I would not forget that you used your influence on behalf of Mother Church."

"It is but a small service, Father, given with no thought of recompense or recognition," *although I might choose to remind you if I have a need of you in the future.*

22 October 1758

They had come to the northwestern end of The Island without finding Malpeque, or any other settlement for that matter. Having little choice, Robert turned the boat to a southeasterly heading, following the north shore of Île Saint Jean.

This course will take us back to the Islander settlements— and the English—and certain capture—and death for me. He looked over at his companion whose eyes were closed and whose head was lolling with the boat's motion—*and certain death for her if we don't find shelter and good food soon. The wind is cold and, coming from the north-east, it carries the smell of snow.*

Reine coughed. In her discomfort she might have fallen off the thwart into the water in the bottom of the boat if Robert hadn't reached over and steadied her. She opened her eyes. Seeing Robert, she gave him a half-smile as she collected the phlegm in her mouth. She spit. Some of it dribbled down her chin. She pulled Robert's coat closer to her throat and closed her eyes. Soon her head was lolling with the boat's motion.

Robert checked the set of the sails. He pulled his shirt closed at his throat. After a while, he opened his shirt again. With one hand on the tiller, he used the other hand to adjust the leaves and grasses he had stuffed under his shirt, next to his skin, trying to keep the cold out. When he had finished, he realized, with a start, that he was heading away from shore. Looking around, he could see that it wasn't really his fault; the coastline had bent away more toward the south. He was adjusting the tiller when he had that same old creepy feeling that had always warned him when the colour sergeant was looking at him—and only him—and that something dire was going to happen. In spite of the itching grasses and the penetrating cold, he grinned. *Well, at least the colour sergeant can't reach me out here. If there is one thing I can be grateful for, I'll never have to stand there and listen to* . . .

Out of the corner of his eye, he saw the large ship, bearing down on his little boat. Robert Cameron felt a strong sense of anger; if only he had remained in the shallow waters closer to the shore, this wouldn't have happened. "Damn! Damn! Damn it all to hell!" The other vessel was too large to sail the sheltered waters as he had been doing for days—except for today—and if he had only . . .

"What is the matter, Chéri?"

"We are being overtaken by an English ship." *At least, if they take us, the ship's surgeon will do something for Reine.* A flooding feeling of peace and resignation filled Robert. He turned his boat into the wind so the English ship could overtake them more easily. *At least my darling Reine will survive. Eventually I will be hanged as a deserter from an English regiment, but my dear Reine will survive.* He closed his eyes. *She will be deported to France. Perhaps in France she will find peace.* He opened his eyes and looked into the face of his beloved. *No, she would struggle to find her way back to Acadia.*

Reine opened her eyes. Her pasty-white face showed concern but her voice was listless when she said, "You must try to escape, Robert. Remember when they chased us at Rivière Habitant? We were ready to give up, but we didn't. Eventually, it was the English who gave up." Her chin lowered to her chest. "Don't give up, Robert." She sighed. "I can be of no help to you, now." She closed her eyes.

The voice carried across the water. "Qui êtes-vous? Who are you?"

Reine's eyes snapped open. She sat up. "Don't say anything, Robert! Remember our story!" Reine waved at the oncoming ship. "Nous sommes des Acadiens et... We are Acadians and we go to Malpeque."

* * *

In the ship's galley, Robert spooned pea soup into Reine's mouth as she soaked up the warmth from the cook's fire. Reine's head was tilted back but her eyes were locked on the movement of the spoon; she did not notice the suspicious looks from the burly seaman leaning against the bulkhead.

"Mon père veut savoir . . . My father wants to know why you were out in a small boat this time of year." When Robert didn't answer, the sailor pushed away from the bulkhead, taking several steps closer to the pair. "I want you to know, that I, Louis Arsenault, do what my father asks of me." He jammed his finger into Robert's chest. "You ignore me at your peril."

"Monsieur, I pray you leave him alone." Reine pushed the spoon away and sat up straighter. "Thanks to the kind attentions of the English, he is unable to speak." She swallowed, as if clearing her throat of the remnants of the soup. "Show him, Robert."

Robert unbuttoned his shirt. He pulled several handfuls of vegetation out to expose the scars on his throat. He jerked an imaginary rope up past his ear and stuck out his tongue as he teetered on the tips of his toes, giving a realistic imitation of a man being hanged.

"He wouldn't give information on the whereabouts of Beau Soliel and his Irregulars; the English hanged him."

Robert lowered his hand and steadied himself on both feet and then jerked the imaginary rope again, only this time even harder.

"They hanged him several times. They whipped him and then locked him up."

Louis regarded the delicate whiteness at the woman's throat. "You were not hanged, nor whipped . . . nor otherwise abused?"

"The English officer thought of himself as a gentleman. He did not molest me in any way." She smiled a grim little smile. "I suppose if he had known that Robert and I had fought side by side in Acadia and that we would go on to raid their positions at Louisbourg, he might not have been so noble."

"Why do you go to Malpeque?"

"The English came to Port La Joye. Before they could round up all the people, we left for Malpeque."

With a note of sadness, Louis said, "And they will come to Malpeque." He shrugged his shoulders. "My grandfather watched his home and farm burn at Beaubassin way back in 1741."

"That couldn't have been the English, not in '41."

"It was the French . . . but what is the difference who burns you out—French or English—you are left with nothing." He shrugged again, "He moved his family to Malpeque . . ."

"Who moved to Malpeque?"

Rather annoyed, Louis grunted, "My grandfather! My grandfather moved to Malpeque to get away from the French-English nonsense! He thought we Arsenaults would be left in peace at Malpeque." He turned to go. "I will tell the captain that you are escapees. Perhaps he will take you with us when we take the rest of our family to the Baie de Chaleur."[8]

"But the English will come there!"

Louis gave the woman a penetrating look. He sighed. Then he drew up his chest and squared his shoulders. "Not in my lifetime! With the French grand fleet and the guns of Fortress Québec keeping the English back, maybe never!" As he left, he repeated, "Not ever!"

Alone in the galley, Reine whispered to Robert, "Perhaps it is far enough that the English won't come?"

Robert cast his eyes down. He didn't respond.

"Robert, tell me what you think. You know these English. Is Baie de Chaleur far enough that they won't come?"

Glumly, Robert replied, "They will come to Malpeque." He watched the fighting spirit drain from Reine's eyes when he said, "And they will come to Chaleur."

* * *

Later in the day, as the *Marie-Fernande* passed between some islands, Robert stood next to the helmsman as the captain explained to his son, Louis, the particulars of the sea approach to Malpeque.

"Line up the first two markers and keep them lined up until the first marker is au bâbord—well to larboard—before you look for the next marker. Then line up the next markers and you will be through the channel." He waited as the ship turned to the right. "Then pass Bird Island on the right and look ahead to the western shore of the bay . . ."

Louis Arsenault gasped, "There's smoke!"

Captain Arsenault shaded his eyes against the setting sun. No one spoke as the captain made his assessment of the situation. "It looks like several buildings are burning." He turned to look at Robert. "The English burn houses?"

Robert nodded his head in the affirmative.

Irritated, the captain ordered, "Get me the woman! I want more information than this muet can give me!"

Louis was quick to respond, "You will have to put up with the dummy, Captain. She is no longer with us."

"She dead?" Then, obviously startled, Captain Arsenault shielded his eyes again. "There's a ship coming out the passage! Hand me the glass!"

Louis took the telescope from the *habitacle*, which housed the compass. "It might be an English ship." He handed the glass to his father. "Shall I break out . . .?"

"No weapons!" He raised the glass to his eye. "If she is English, we will make a run for blue water." Captain Arsenault adjusted the focus. "Bring us up into the wind," he ordered and then, softly, to his son he said, "The English may be here. If the English are already here, it will be too late to rescue our families."

Louis helped the crew to bring the bow of the *Marie-Fernande* around into the wind so there would be no more forward motion toward Malpeque. Meanwhile, the captain continued to examine the approaching ship. He muttered, "She looks . . . she might be a chaloupe . . ."

Although Robert couldn't see the details of the ship at this distance, the approaching ship reminded him of some French fishing boats he had seen with small mainmasts and the foremasts rigged for lug-sails. He strained his eyes but, of course, could not make out the type of ship without the magnification provided by the telescope.

The captain continued speaking. "DesRoches owns a chasse-marée." He rested his eye and looked over at Robert, explaining—as if it mattered—"He always sails her down by the head." He smiled at Robert and resumed his inspection of the oncoming ship through the telescope. "Yes, by the head— just as if he has stowed all his fish forward leaving lots of room at the stern for more catch—and she always seems ready to drop her bow into the next big wave and disappear into the bottom of the sea." He lowered the glass. Over the noise of the flapping sails, he ordered, "Resume course to Malpeque! She is not English! She is trimmed by the head!"

Captain Arsenault pulled a clay pipe from his jacket. He stuck the stem in his mouth. Through clenched teeth he said, "I am sorry about the woman."

Robert almost spoke but was saved from that mistake when Louis answered, "She isn't dead, captain. She fell asleep and we haven't been able to wake her, even to feed her."

"Unconscious?"

Robert nodded his head.

"She'll come around. Our women are tough." He nodded to his son. "Resume course and get the loud-hailer. I want to speak to Captain DesRoches."

The voice from across the water was strong and full of

authority. "Captain DesRoches of *La Tempête*. I bid you good afternoon."

Captain Arsenault accepted the metal hailer from his son and raised it to his lips. "Captain Arsenault of the *Marie-Fernande*. Where are you bound?"

"I take people to Miscou Island."

"What is burning at Malpeque? Are the English there?"

"Word is the English will come. These people burn their homes. They leave nothing for the English."

The ships were abreast of each other, now separating at the combined rate of seven or eight knots.

Captain Arsenault raised his voice a little as the two vessels separated. "Will you return?"

"No! Not ever!"

"I mean, sir, will you return for another load of people?"

"The families who remain await the *Marie-Fernande* and the schooner, *La Brise de Mer*. *La Brise de Mer* is out of Québec and might not arrive before the English. You may well be freighted beyond your load waterline."

Thinking of how the DesRoches ship always sailed with scant regard to proper loading, Arsenault hailed, "I note you are already sailing down by the head, sir."

"Je dois vous baiser, monsieur. Adieu."[9]

Captain Louis Arsenault chuckled. "I never did like DesRoches." He turned away and faced Malpeque. "Now, we must get in and get out, quickly . . . before the English come."

25 November 1758
Canso

"Papa, the ship is moving."

Maurice Gallant was getting his three sons ready for their journey "topside." Every day they dressed warmly and climbed the three decks to the priest's cabin where the boys learned their catechism and then practised the altar boy rituals. Maurice stopped what he was doing and studied the motion of the candle lantern against the beams of the deckhead.

"I think you are right, Simon." Maurice planted a kiss on his wife's forehead and herded the boys along in front of him. "Be careful of the ladder, boys; one of the rungs is loose."

"Yes, Papa."

On the upward climb, they were silent, saving their breath for the long ascent. When they reached the quarterdeck, they had a view of the other ships of the convoy. They had learned the names of the ships during their stay at Canso so Jacques, the oldest, was able to tell his father which of the ships had already moved out to sea.

"The *Hind* and the *Parnassus* are gone already, Papa." He pointed to the nearest vessel. "The *Nautilus* is still here . . ."

"So is the *Narcissus*," Simon piped up.

"Yes, but she is moving." Jacques resented Simon; Simon was always trying to steal their father's attention.

A deeper voice behind the three boys and their father added, "I am impressed with how good your memories are. What is the ship—the one way over to the left—that hasn't raised her anchors yet?"

"The *Violet*, Father." Of course, it was Simon who made the response.

"Good afternoon, Father," the other boys said in chorus.

The irrepressible Simon pursued the adults' attention. "Maybe she isn't coming with us!"

The long-suffering parent reminded the boy, "Say 'good afternoon' to Father, Simon."

Simon bobbed his head up and down a couple of times. "Good afternoon, Father. But maybe she isn't coming with us!"

"Who, my son?"

"The one that isn't moving."

Maurice picked up on the idea. "Perhaps she is waiting for the people from Malpeque."

Simon beamed with importance. "Yes! Maybe . . ."

"I was told by Ensign Deschatelets all the ships were leaving today." The priest shivered. "Hurry along to the cabin, my children. It is too cold out here."

"Yes, Father."

Simon hung back by the bulwark, watching the ships.

"Come, Simon. Don't keep Abbé Girard waiting."

"Yes, but I want to see the Violet hoist her anchors."

"Now, Simon."

"Yes, Papa."

Malpeque Settlement

A knot of people stood on the shore and watched the topsail schooner, *La Brise de Mer*, and a smaller schooner with two masts, *Le Volant*, move up on their anchors as they prepared to sail away from Malpeque. *Brise de Mer* was the first ship to be straight up and down on her anchor. When her uppers spread—they opened with a snap—the ship launched herself into the channel so quickly there was barely time for good-byes. The bystanders were better prepared when *Le Volant* sailed, the farewells trailing across the water and fading as the ship slipped out of earshot.

For a few minutes the group lingered as if trying to preserve the sense of community that was now forever lost to the village known as the Malpeque Settlement. There were scattered comments, a wave, and here and there an attempt at humour, as the individuals walked along their separate paths—past the charred ruins of a dozen buildings—to their homes.

Soon Robert Cameron was standing alone on the beach, watching the ships disappear into the sea mists. He glanced back up the hill to catch Joseph and Madeleine Arsenault waving. He waved back. When the Arsenaults had entered their little house, Robert took one last look out the channel toward Bird Island. *When they come*—he watched as *Le Volant* finally disappeared into the mists—*we might have as much as a half-hour before they can get soldiers into boats and come ashore.* He shook his head and sucked his teeth. *Only a half-hour to get our things together and disappear into the wilderness. What if Reine doesn't get better?* He sucked his teeth again. *Then we try to fool them once more.* He laughed out loud. *Who shall we have hang me this time?* He turned away from the beach and began a slow ascent to the house that had been left for them to use by the Bernard family. *Pierre Bernard was right to take his family on the Le Volant to Miquelon. Maybe we should have gone with them to Miquelon . . . or to Chaleur on the Brise de Mer . . .it wouldn't matter which . . .* Then he thought of how sick Reine was. *Every morning, sick as a dog. She doesn't get any better.*

Robert tapped lightly on the side door. He made a great deal of noise as he slowly scraped the mud from his boots. *She is so sensitive about the way she looks, always covering herself . . .*

"Come in, Robert."

He lifted the latch. He put a large smile on his face and pushed the door open. "Well, they've gone and now we have the place to ourselves."

"It is a lovely house. It is so sad that we will have to burn it when the English . . ."

"They won't come to Malpeque, my sweet."

"They will come. You said so."

"I can be wrong!" Robert tried to keep his voice hearty and his manner casual but it was difficult to hide his feelings when he considered the real picture. Most of the Malpeque houses had been burned to the ground, the families boarding ships for Miscou, Miquelon, or somewhere along the Saint Lawrence River. _They_ believed the English were coming.

The three families that had chosen not to sail away were resigned to the fact that they would be taken into custody and eventually shipped somewhere—possibly to France. France would be just as foreign to them as Miquelon or Chaleur so they had stayed, hoping for the best.

He and Reine, on the other hand, were given no choice; they were consigned to inactivity because Reine, usually the strong one, was sick and not getting better. He looked at her: *cheeks flushed, her hair glistening, and the fever giving a shine to her eyes that betrayed . . .*

He ambled over to give her a little hug. He touched her neck. The fever was gone. "Were you sick again this morning?"

"Yes, I was, Chéri." She sat up and ran her fingers through her hair. "I must look a sight!" She stood. "Would you like to have some hot soup? I am having some."

"Thank you, yes."

They sat at the Bernard family table and, for the first time in a long, long time, had a few moments of contentment.

Robert loosened his belt and leaned back, his head resting against the wall. He looked into the flickering fire. "Maybe . . ." he started.

Reine waited for him to continue and then smiled at her husband. "It isn't often you hesitate to say something to me, Robert."

"Well, your . . ." he searched for the word in French, "tes règles?"

She took his hand in hers. "Je me trouve . . ." here she searched for the English word but gave up, "enceinte."

Robert's jaw dropped.

She squeezed his hand, "Leblanc women often have . . . jumeaux, Robert."

"Two?"

"How do you say it in English?"

"Twins?"

"Yes, twins. Leblanc women often have twins."

Endnotes

1. I found different spellings used historically: Joye and Joie. The dictionary didn't contain Joye but it did have Joie so I was leaning to the latter until I saw the chart titled, "Carte de Port La Joye Dans L'Isle St. Jean (1734)." I decided to use Port La Joye in the story for the city we now know as Charlottetown. La Mer Rouge was the French name for the Northumberland Strait.

2. Those of us who have read the first book of the *Abuse of Power* series will know that a Mi'kmaq raiding party captured Private Robert Cameron of the 40th Regiment of Foot. In the first moments of his capture, he was raised and lowered by the neck a number of times until he became a docile prisoner.

3. The terms of the Louisbourg capitulation stated that the Island garrison was to be transported as soon as the English provided ships. French

officers from Louisbourg accompanied the occupying forces to forestall resistance but, at this stage, the local military would not know about the capitulation terms; they would expect terms of surrender to be offered and considered.

4. I had Robert Cameron present the view that the Island Acadians kept the peace and should not have been deported much in the manner suggested by Andrew Hill Clark in his book *Three Centuries and The Island.* "There were no reasons for the deportation associated with the conduct of the inhabitants. They were an inoffensive people. They had molested no one by themselves or in conjunction with the Indians and the Indians kept their hands free from blood."

5. Why would the English bother to depopulate Île Saint Jean? It was the supply colony for Fortress Louisbourg.

The English had captured Fortress Louisbourg once before (1745) but it was given back to the French during the peace negotiations of 1748. In 1758 we have the second capture and General Amherst, the Commander of the British forces, probably had the 1748 experience in mind when he ordered enough transport ships to carry the Louisbourg garrison away *and* the entire population of Île Saint Jean. General Amherst meant to destroy the fort and depopulate The Island that was the fort's source of supplies and manpower. If the English negotiators were to give the fortress back once again, the French would have to begin from scratch.

6. Maquereaux can refer to fish that are called mackerel in English. Maquereaux can also refer to pimps, procurers, and brothel-keepers.

7. I found the Joseph Farrow character in a 1792 edition of the *Royal Gazette of the Island of Saint John.* I gave him a military background and an association with the Camerons.

8. "Jean-Baptiste Arsenault was born in Malpeque in 1750 where his father had been living since he had left Beaubassin in 1741. To avoid being deported, Jean Baptiste and his parents moved to the Bay of Chaleur region. He married in Miscou in 1773 and later returned to his birthplace, Malpeque." From Georges Arsenault's book, *The Island Acadians 1720-1980.*

9. Je dois vous baiser is an old French phrase that I have been told is a formally polite way to tell someone to "kiss my ass."

Chapter Two
Death and Birth

February 1759
Duke William
La Manche

"Maintenant en penche vers la direction opposée! . . . Now we are tilted in the opposite direction!" Angélique waved her hands, theatrically, at her husband. "First we tilt to the left, and then to the right!" She pushed the hair back from her face leaving a dark smudge over her nose and forehead. "À droite, à gauche . . . left to right . . . no matter which side the water always drips down on us bringing foul-smelling filth from the floors above." She stamped her foot. "Now both ends of the bed are covered with slime."

Maurice Gallant didn't know what to say, so he kept his mouth shut.

Angélique shoved her finger under her husband's nose. "This time, you find out when we are going to get out of here." She turned and lifted Simon off the shelf of bare boards that served as their bed so she could have a place to sit down. She hoisted Simon onto her lap.

Simon squirmed out of her embrace. "I'm not a baby!" He moved as far away as he could—not more than two feet—so he might be able to sulk without touching anybody. He stepped on Jacques's foot and got a punch for his trouble. André, the middle boy, squawked that he was being hurt by Simon's elbows and pushed him back. They grappled and lost their footing, falling into the watery muck that was sloshing back and forth with the movement of the ship.

Maurice hit the nearest boy with the flat of his hand; it was Simon, who stopped fighting. Maurice then stepped between the other two. "We will go up early to the priest's cabin." He gave Angélique a sorry smile. "I will try to clean them off before we come down again."

Angélique's voice softened. "See what you can find out, husband." She made a tilting motion with her hands.

"Yes. I will see why we are going first one way and then the other . . ."

"And when we will get out of here."

"Yes, and when we can get out of here."

By the time they reached the main deck, even the older boys were breathing hard. Simon was crying that he couldn't go any further.

"I know, mes braves enfants. I know we haven't had any exercise for over two months and it is hard to climb . . . but we can do it! Only one more deck to go."

Maurice picked Simon up and hugged him tight. "Maybe the priest will have some sweets."

"The priest only had sweets the once," Jacques said in a complaining voice, "and Simon got more than I did." Jacques wiped some liquid from his face; it might have been spray from the ocean. "He probably won't have any."

"Well, we won't know unless we go up there to find out."

André leaned against the bulwark. "The ship is turning again. He grinned. "Mother will be angry."

Maurice thought he might be able to take advantage of the situation. "I think she might be, son. Let's go see if the priest has any goodies."

"Maybe we can take some to Mother," one of the boys suggested.

They started up the ladder to the next level.

Jacques pointed. "Look! Land!"

"And there's another ship!" André opened his mouth to add something else but Simon beat him to it.

"It's the *Violet!*"

A voice from behind them boomed, "What are you doing here?"

The Gallants faced the Second Mate of the *Duke William*.

Maurice turned back to watch as the *Violet* sailed along the line of white breakers. "Sont-ils en danger? Are they in danger?"

"I am an officer and you will obey me. Go below, right away!"

"Est-ce prudent d'être si près du rivage? . . . Is it safe for them to be so close to the shore?"

"I don't understand your frog-talk." The officer took two steps toward the boys, his eyes full of menace. "You must obey me or I will have you clapped in irons!" The officer pointed below. "Go below!"

"Ah!" Abbé Girard had come out of his cabin and was standing behind the officer. "But you will explain things to *me*, my son, won't you?"

If the officer was surprised that the priest spoke English, he didn't show it. He replied respectfully, "Yes, Father. We are trying to claw off the lee-shore."

Abbé Girard shrugged his shoulders. "And what does that mean?"

"We must beat to windward to avoid shipwreck." When the officer saw that the priest still didn't understand, he explained further. "We have been turning to windward all afternoon trying to get out of the trap."

"What is the trap?"

"The winds and the seas have driven us into Mounts Bay. The land you see is Cornwall, in England. There is not enough sea room . . . er, the wind is blowing us against the shore and the lee-tide . . . I mean, the tidewaters are also moving us toward the shore so we are not far enough from the shore to . . ."

"What can you do about it?"

"The commander has given orders to all of the ships of the convoy to lighten ship . . ."

"Like throwing heavy guns overboard?"

"We are cartel ships. We carry little armament but, yes, jettisoning heavy things would make it easier to—"[1]

"But our cargo is people . . ."

"Yes, too many people. The ships are heavily laden and there is little we can do about that."

"What *can* we do?"

"The captain gave orders for all ships to follow his manoeuvres."

"And the result?"

"Most of the convoy will be able to claw off."

"Most?"

The officer jerked his head in the direction of the *Violet*, "She's lost. It is a matter of time and she will run out of sea room."

"And be wrecked?"

"Yes."

Neither the priest nor the officer spoke for several moments. Maurice broke the silence, "What is going on, Father?"

"Eloignons-nous du vent . . . We should get out of the wind. Let's go to the cabin and have our lessons." He spread his arms out to guide the boys in the right direction. "Come along, now. I might have some sweets for you."

The boys made a dash for the cabin door but the ship began a sharp turn and the boys were thrown off balance, crashing into the door of the next cabin. It opened immediately.

Ensign Deschatelets towered over the boys. "You ruffians! Stay away from my cabin. I will not tolerate your noise and . . ."

The priest made an appeasing gesture with his hands and steered the boys into the cabin. As soon as Maurice was inside, he closed the door. "Now! I will see if I have some sweets."

They were halfway through the lessons when there was a quick knock on the cabin door and it was opened wide. Second Mate Armstrong beckoned the priest to the doorway. "Father, the other ships of the convoy have cleared Lizard Point and are on their way to France." He gestured toward the land and whispered, "The *Violet* is on the rocks." They both stepped outside where, with the last light of the day, they could see what was left of the *Violet* heaving and falling on the rocks below the steep chalk cliffs.

"Oh my! Those poor souls!" The priest began a prayer for

the dying: "Notre Père, qui êtes aux cieux, que votre nom soit sanctifié, que votre règne arrive . . ."

Armstrong placed his hand on the cleric's sleeve. "We don't have time to pray right now, Father."

Abbé Girard asked the question but he anticipated the answer as he pulled the door shut so that the boys would not see the destruction of the other vessel. "Why, what is going to happen?"

"Our ship will not get out of the trap, Father. She will beat upon the rocks and founder."

"How soon?"

"The captain is still holding true to his plan . . . he is counting on the turn of the tide in an hour and perhaps the wind will veer enough . . ."

"But you don't think so."

"He has enough sea room to claw to windward one more time and then . . ."

"Why did you come to warn me? You must have left your station to do that."

"I am a son of the true Church, Father."

The priest made up his mind. "So you have come to me and we must do what we can to save lives. We must warn the others . . ."

"There is no time, Father. Come with me. I need help to launch the cock-boat."

"Cock-boat?"

"It is a very small row boat." The sailor pulled on the priest's arm. "Come!" He repeated the command, this time with a tremor of urgency. "Come! We are wasting time!"

"You take the boys in the boat." Abbé Girard didn't wait for the officer's permission. He sprang forward and pushed open the door to the cabin. "Come, right away! Go with the officer!" When Simon went to the bed to gather up the sweets, the priest grabbed the boy by the arm. "You must do as you are told!"

Simon began to cry. "He hurt my arm!" he blubbered to his father.

Girard didn't let go of the boy's arm. Instead he pulled the boy toward the cabin door and pushed him into the arms of his father. "Take your boys! Follow Mate Armstrong. I must go below and save . . . "

The door to Ensign Deschatelets's cabin began to open. Armstrong lunged for the latch and slammed the door closed. He lifted a bar that was attached at one side of the cabin entrance and drew it across the latch to the other side. He hooked it tight.

It didn't occur to Abbé Girard right away that the door to the ensign's cabin was now locked from the outside. When it dawned on him, he asked, "What are you doing?"

"This is a cartel ship. There are restraining bars on all the cabins."

"But why?"

"He writes reports on everyone he meets. He told my captain I am Catholic."

They were all knocked off their feet. The ship had struck! She leaned further and further until it seemed as if she would tip over but then righted herself and sailed on. In the last rays of the setting sun, the land looked so very close and threatening. Armstrong pointed to the breakers not a stone's throw away. "She will strike again!" Armstrong took the priest by the arm. "Come quickly. We must go down to the main deck."

Maurice picked up Simon. "Shush, little man. We will go with Abbé Girard and everything will be all right."

The ship struck again as they were halfway to the main deck but they all held on and, when the ship righted herself again, they hurried along. Mate Armstrong drew a knife and slashed at the bindings holding a canvas cover over a very small boat. The priest took charge of the three boys while Maurice helped pull the canvas off and move it to one side. They tied a long line to the boat's painter and then the two men heaved the boat over the side. Even in the last light of the day, the men lost sight of the boat in the spume raised by the strong winds.

"Look after my boys, Father." Maurice looked deep into the priest's eyes. "I love them so very much, but I must save my wife. She is alone in the dark . . ." Maurice ran across the deck and lifted the hatch cover. He disappeared below.

"Jump now!" Mate Armstrong pushed the priest to the bulwark. "Hold on to the rope."

The priest lifted Simon but the little boy squirmed out of the priest's arms. He ran after his father.

The ship struck! This time she tilted to one side and then further. She did not right herself.

Armstrong grabbed Jacques and jumped.

Girard took André by the hand and they went over the side together.

The water was dark and cold. Girard was conscious of the boy's hand and, when it seemed that they might be separated, he held on with both hands. They settled deeper in the water. Something rough brushed across his face. Girard grabbed at it and pulled. *I've lost the boy!* He surfaced. *Where is the boy?* His eyes were full of salt water—it was dark—and he let go of the rope as he began flailing with his arms in search of the boy. He winced with the pain when he hit something solid with his arm. Hands pulled him out of the water.

From the bottom of the boat, Girard sensed there were three persons with him. "Thank you, Lord!" he said. A distress flare lit the sky for a moment and he could see who was in the boat with him: Mate Armstrong, Jacques, and another sailor. He pushed himself up on his elbows and looked over the side; there was nothing to see and, as the flare died, there was darkness.

Listlessly, he allowed Mate Armstrong to fasten a rope to his wrist. He could see that they were all tied to the boat. *What good would that do if . . .?*

The boat turned turtle. As Girard sank again in the water, his last thought was that somewhere, in the deepening darkness, he might find little André. He would look for him.

May 1759
Malpeque Settlement

Reine resisted coming out of the darkness. In the darkness there was quiet, solitude and—above all—no pain. Then the pain came and with it the calming voice of Madeleine Arsenault: "It will soon be over, Chérie." Reine felt her head being lifted, "Take a draught of this. I traded with the Indians to have it for myself when I was having children." Now Reine could see the woman's smile. "Nine children and, with God's grace, we will all live together here at Malpeque . . ."

Reine screamed. *The English are coming!* In her mind she had slipped away to Rivière Habitant and the English were going to take her Robert and . . . *hang him, and whip him, and hang him and* . . . she could feel the darkness overwhelming her fears. She welcomed the release.

* * *

Joseph Arsenault sipped his bière d'épinette. "My wife believes Madame Leblanc is built well enough to carry many babies. But my dear wife fails to understand the difficulty your young woman is now having." He glanced over to see if Robert were listening—it was difficult to speak to a muet—but he would keep trying to make the prospective father feel better. *Perhaps I will try another approach.* "It is not easy to go through this— sitting out here—waiting for the arrival. It is a difficult time for the husband." He checked the younger man's face again. *Nothing.* "This is the first time she is . . .?" *Well, at least this time, I got a nod of the head from him! So, it's the first time. Strange. They are old enough that they should have five or six children by now.*

Both men turned their heads at the same time when they heard Reine's voice: "Don't ever give up, Robert. Never give in to the bastards!" Then there were some muffled sounds and Madame Arsenault could be heard encouraging Reine . . . call- ing her pet names . . . telling her how well she was doing . . . muffled sounds . . . a scream . . . and then silence.

The firm voice of Madeleine Arsenault, filled with pride, called out to the two men, "The boy is fine! Monsieur Leblanc, you have a strong-looking son!"

Robert jumped up to go into the house but the other man restrained him. "How is she?" He shouted over Arsenault's shoulder, "Tell me! Is my wife all right?"

Taken aback, Arsenault let the new father charge past him. "C'est un miracle! It's a miracle! He has found his voice!"

Port La Joye

"Sergeant Brown!" Lieutenant Makin checked the company record book and then tossed it to one side. He put his elbows on the ammunition table and called out again, "Send Sergeant Brown in here!" He recognized the answering voice as belonging to Private Farrow: "He is at the Mass House, sir! With your permission, I will get him right away, sir!"

Makin casually picked up the company book and opened it. He ran his finger down the page. "Carry on, Private." *Yes. Corporal Joseph Farrow, broken in rank and twenty lashes for allowing a prisoner to escape, the prisoner being one Corporal Herbert Miles assigned to Brown's company about the date we shipped the Islanders out.* He could hear the clomping of several pairs of feet on the approach of Sergeant Brown. He checked another page. *Good man, Sergeant Brown.* Makin looked up in response to the firm tap on the doorframe. He waited for the non-commissioned officer to speak.

"You wanted to see me, sir?"

"Yes. I have been assigned to your company. As my sergeant, I will expect good things from you."

"Yes, of course, sir. What happened to my officer . . . er . . . my old officer?"

Well-connected officers do not do garrison duties, he was inclined to reply but, instead, Lieutenant Makin leaned forward and snarled, "Just so we understand each other, make that the last time you ever ask me a question about matters that should be of no concern to you."

"Yes, sir." Sergeant Brown snapped rigidly to attention, his eyes unfocused, staring straight ahead. "Of course, sir."

Makin leaned back in the chair. "Then stand easy, Sergeant." He steepled his hands in front of his lips. "I understand your men are working on the palisades for the new Fort Amherst."

"Yes, sir, they are and they sure have been grumbling about it."

Tough man, this sergeant—says his piece. "You will have to prepare our men for a little trip." Lieutenant Makin then outlined his plan for gathering in the last of the Islanders—what he called "the cleanup"—and shipping them out to France.

"I expect the cartel vessel will arrive here soon. We will embark our men and proceed to the western end of this island. We will exert the King's will on the remnants of the French population that Colonel Rollo couldn't gather up before the end of the last sailing season."

"We should do some re-kitting, sir. Give them a bit of boat drill; I'm a great believer that the men should . . ."

"Yes, Sergeant, yes. You can take them off construction work and get them ready for the cleanup." The officer grinned so the sergeant would understand that he wasn't putting one over on him.

"Thank you, sir. That will end the griping, sir." Brown snapped back to attention, "Is that all, sir?"

"Yes. Please carry on."

Six Days Later

"Sergeant Brown requesting to speak with his officer, sir."

Lieutenant Makin signalled with his hand that the sergeant could proceed.

"Sir, the ships to pick up the remaining inhabitants have arrived . . ."

"That's right, Sergeant."

" . . . but I also have your written order to re-assign the men to work on the construction of Fort Amherst."

Makin sighed. "Captain Johnson has intelligence that all the Islanders have escaped and gone off to Canada. There will be no cleanup."

"Very good, sir."

Endnotes

1. Special ships were hired to fulfill the terms of surrender such as, in this case, transporting an entire population away from a conquered area. The ships were known as cartel ships, were unarmed, and travelled freely from one side of the conflict to the other.

Chapter Three
The English Are Coming

Spring 1761
Malpeque Settlement

The baby, Robbie Leblanc, stuck his fingers into his mother's mouth. Usually this would bring forth a great deal of blubbering and pretend-chewing on the ends of his fingers but not this time. This time, his mother removed the fingers and abruptly sat the baby on the grass. To make matters worse, she then left him. The boy began to wail.

Robert came running around the house from where he had been stacking wood. "What's wrong with Robbie?" When he saw the baby unattended on the ground, he suffered a moment of real panic. "Reine! Reine, where are you?" He picked up the baby and tried to shush the child but the baby sensed his father's tension and screamed ever the louder. *Where is Reine?* Robert saw movement on the side of the hill; his wife was running along the hill to the Arsenault home. It was then he saw the ship. *My God! The English have finally come!* He cast another anxious glance toward the Arsenaults. Reine was now returning with Joseph Arsenault's eyeglass in her hands. *Good girl!* He jiggled the baby and made cooing noises as he studied the lines of the approaching vessel. There wasn't much to see: the ship was fore-and-aft rigged, black hull—bone-in-her-teeth as she caught the fresh onshore breeze . . . *I'll have to wait till I get the glass but one thing's for sure—she's too small to be an English sloop-of-war.* His mind a turmoil of conflicting thoughts—to risk waiting or to burn the house and run—Robert took the glass from his breathless wife.

"She's not English," he immediately said to relieve his wife's anxiety.

Reine took the child and cradled him, making shushing noises. "Who then?" she asked between shushes.

"I'll know in a minute as she makes the turn at the

channel." He continued to study the ship. "There's something familiar about her . . . *Le Volant!* She's the *Volant.*"

"That's nice, dear." Reine patted the baby's bum. "I must see to Robbie's bottom." She took the child inside.

Robert continued to watch as the ship came up onto the mooring. When she was secured, she dropped her stern anchor so she wouldn't swing with the tide. He watched as the boat's crew prepared their craft. When it was launched and steady alongside the *Le Volant*, the passengers began their descent.

The first passenger was Pierre Bernard.

Without taking his glass off the scene, Robert called out, "Reine! I think we have a problem."

Late Spring
Fort Amherst

"Sergeant!"

"What do you want now, Farrow?"

"There's a boat, over near the other shore. They been spyin' on us. I saw . . ."

"Farrow, I'm tired of your catchpenny tricks to get out of work. Ever since you were broke to private, you've been—"

"I mean it, Sarge. I saw the reflection off their spyglass!"

Brown was a careful soldier; he took the time to study the opposite shoreline and the waters of the bay before making a decision. Satisfied that the private was up to his usual tricks to get out of hard work he barked, "You take McIntyre's place at the bottom of the trench!" When he saw Farrow hesitate and open his mouth, Brown snarled, "Right now, if you know what's good for you!"

"Yes, Sergeant!" Farrow jumped down and took his position next to the other troublemaker, McIntyre.

McIntyre handed over the lever he had been using to position the bases of the stockade poles in the muddy bottom of the trench. "Nice try, buddy. Too bad it didn't work."

Farrow jammed the lever in the mud under the pole and

heaved. The pole slid over, giving room for McIntyre to climb out. "I saw what I said I saw. There's someone," he said, gesturing with his free hand, "over there—in a boat—watchin' us through a glass. I saw it."

"Sure you did, Joey."

* * *

In the boat, Reine exposed her breast for Robbie to suck. "I don't have much milk, Robert. I don't think the baby is getting enough."

Robert took some dried peas from the little sack. "Chew these. Put some on his tongue. We will have water tonight once we sneak past those redcoats."

Reine lifted her head. "What are they doing?"

"By the looks of it, building a redoubt."

"Like the English built at Louisbourg?"

"Yes. Just like they built at Gallows Hill."

"The English built that one in a day."

Robert stared at the opposite shore. He raised Joseph Arsenault's telescope and adjusted the focus. "These fellows seem to be lolling around."

"What does lolling mean?" They spoke both languages, now, switching from one to the other as it suited them because they meant for their little Robbie to grow up with a thorough understanding of both languages.

"I don't rightly know, Chérie. I guess what I am trying to say is, at Gallows Hill, the fortification was built by frontline troops." He inclined his head toward Fort Amherst. "Those fellows are lazy, garrison troops." He smiled. "I guess that's what I mean; they're being lazy."

"You think we will have any trouble slipping by them tonight?" Not waiting for her husband to answer she raised the subject that was really bothering her. "Maybe we should have stayed with the Bernards." She looked over to see if there was a reaction. *None*, she thought. "They were sincere when they suggested we stay with them another season and build our own home at Malpeque."

Robert chose to pursue the original question, avoiding his wife's eyes. "Yes, we'll slip by those . . ."—he searched for an English word that might distract his wife—"layabouts and go to our place at Rivière-du-Nord-Est. Perhaps the English didn't burn it. We should at least go have a look."

Reine was busy putting some well-chewed peas on her son's tongue. The boy smacked and smacked, making little mewing sounds. Both parents smiled.

"He's a real Acadian," Reine proudly claimed. "He likes his pea soup."

Robert patted his thigh. "Put him on my lap. Then sit next to me so you can lay your head against my shoulder and get some rest."

"You are every bit as tired as I am."

"I'll rest too." Robert collapsed the glass and carefully stowed it under the thwart. "I never thought I would have one of those." He pointed at the telescope.

"Yes, it was nice of Joseph to give it to us."

"Good friends, the Arsenaults."

There were a few quiet moments as Reine settled herself against her husband's shoulder. She smoothed his jacket. "Your jacket belonged to one of Joseph's boys."

"Uh-huh."

"We should have stayed at Malpeque where we have friends."

There was no more conversation until after it was dark and the two of them were unshipping the oars. It was Reine who spoke first.

"If there is nothing left at Rivière-du-Nord-Est, can we go back to Malpeque?"

"That's what you want to do? Go all the way back to Malpeque?" When there was no immediate response, he added, "You almost died the last time."

"I was pregnant then, and this time, we would know the way."

"Well, it was a hard trip," Robert said. He looked up when he heard a deep, deep sigh. "Yes. It was a hard trip."

One of the oars rattled in the rowlocks.

"Shhh!" Robert reached over to steady Reine's oars. "Those redcoats may be lazy but they're not deaf!"

"I'm sorry. I know sound carries across the water." She took Robert's hand in hers. "You are right about the trip back to Malpeque, Robert. We might not make it this time; we have little Robbie to look after." He heard another deep sigh. "And I am pregnant."

Robert raised one of his wife's hands to his lips. "Ma chérie," he whispered. He squeezed her hand and then released it. He unshipped his oars and slipped them into the water, waiting for Reine to get both her oars ready.

"Slowly, pull!" He chanted, "Back . . . pull . . .back . . . pull . . ."

After several hours of rowing, Robert allowed the thought to surface: *I pray our farm is still there at Rivière-du-Nord-Est.*

Chapter Four
Holland

July 1764
HMS Canceaux

HMS Canceaux, Lieutenant Mowatt commanding, had suffered a very difficult Atlantic crossing. In the calmer waters off Cape Breton, Mowatt had ordered the ship's company to render repairs at sea—a tricky task under normal circumstances, and made more difficult by a thick fog.

The *Canceaux*, a schooner-rigged sloop-of-war, was Mowatt's first command. Despite any difficulties repairs at sea might mean for his crew, he meant to have everything shipshape for landfall just as if Lord Coville, Commander of the British Naval Force in North America, were appraising him for a performance review board. *Our approach to Fort Amherst will be textbook perfect*, he thought. He cocked his head to one side. Above the noises made by the work parties, he heard something he couldn't readily identify. "Watch officer!"

A voice responded immediately out of the mists. "Aye, sir."

"Keep her full!"

"Full and by, sir."

Satisfied that his vessel was close-hauled and the helmsman was not steering too close to windward to cause the sails to make a shaking sound, Mowatt held his breath, the better to hear whatever noise was bothering him. *She's got her sails full and on a good reach to windward so the noise could not be fluttering sails, spilling out some wind. Then what is the sound . . .?* Mowatt just about jumped out of his skin when a voice spoke into his ear: "The fog is thick as pea soup."

He faced the person who would dare to intrude upon his space—the captain's space. *It's that jumped-up-civilian-appointed army captain who dares to accost me on my own quarterdeck!* "What, my dear sir, do you want?"

"We haven't had the opportunity to discuss our mission."

The mist was thick enough that the "jumped-up civilian," Captain Samuel Holland, Surveyor General of His Majesty's possessions north of the Potowmack River,[1] did not see the sneer on the naval officer's lips. Mowatt's voice dripped with charm. "Oh, I do hope you have finally acquired your sea legs. I am told that seasickness is a dreadful affliction. To your credit, I must say the seas were more than a little rougher than I have seen before on my many crossings."

"We should have some discussions before we arrive at . . ."

Mowatt's voice changed. "We arrive at Fort Amherst on the morrow. Ship's company will assist your men in transporting your survey equipment and supplies ashore and then the *Canceaux* will stand down awaiting further orders from Lord Coville." *The morning sun must be burning off the fog; I can actually see the stunned look on the miserable little bugger's face as he hoists in the fact that I am not going to be at his beck and call.*

"I beg your pardon? My orders state that you and your crew will aid me in my professional operations!" Lieutenant Mowatt was about to reply but he was silenced by the wave of the army officer's hand. "Your ship was fitted out by the government to assist me . . . to provide me with boats and men to survey the lands His Majesty acquired from the French by the 1763 Treaty of Fontainebleau. I was commissioned in March and . . ."

"I am aware of your date of seniority."

" . . . and ordered to begin by surveying The Island of Saint John."

Both men flinched when a musket was fired close at hand.

"What the hell!" Mowatt peered through the thinning fog at what appeared to be a fishing boat. A man was standing tall in the small boat, waving his arms. Suddenly Mowatt realized what the sounds were . . . the sounds he couldn't previously identify . . . the sounds that would have told him that his ship was perilously—perhaps fatally—close to land. The sounds were waves breaking on a rocky shore! *If only this miserable little man had let me do my job instead of . . .*

"Land ho!"

That's the goddam forward lookout!

The officer of the watch called, "Where away?"

"Ten points off the larboard bow."

That goddam fisherman was trying to warn us with his musket! Mowatt snapped out of his dithering, "Take her hard to starboard! Bring her about!"

The watch officer gave the order: "Ready to come about!"

The ship's captain beat the side of his leg with the palm of his hand. "Now, dammit!"

"Sir, some of the crew are working on the larboard side. We might lose them in the wash . . ."

Mowatt took two steps toward his officer and then changed his mind. He faced the helmsman: "Hard down, helmsman. The men will have to look out for themselves."

"Aye, sir." The sailor began his hand over hand turning of the wheel but Mowatt jumped to his aid and used his entire body weight to force the wheel to move faster.

"Coming about!" the watch officer shouted, with a crack in his voice as he caught sight of the black rocks of Cape Breton looming out of the mists. He raced to the wheel to help his captain. The three men were turning the wheel, turning and turning.

Captain Holland wore a bemused smile as the rocks came closer. He noted the seaweed on the rocks sticking out of the water not a score of yards distant. "Interesting," he said. *Reminds me of when Father identified the dark green vegetation covering rocks along the seashore as weir.* "It looks like weir, all right!" He thought to inform the captain that there must be a beach nearby when the ship heeled well to the left and, to maintain his balance, Holland stepped to the larboard bulwark where he steadied himself. "Well," he said. He knew enough about sailing ships that he recognized sloppy sail handling when he saw it—the crew were falling over themselves as they tried to bring the ship's sails around . . . Holland became mesmerized by one rock, which was much closer than any of the others—and getting closer to the bow of the ship.

"Take up a larboard tack."
That's Mowatt.
"What heading?"
That's the watch officer.
"East."
Mowatt.
The rock was passing them by, scant yards away.
"Steady as she goes." *Mowatt.*
"Aye sir!"

Holland chose to ignore naval goings-on. He also decided he would avoid the belligerent naval officer and returned to his cabin, taking his meals there just as he had during the months when he had been feeling poorly.[2]

Two days later, *HMS Canceaux* sailed smartly past Fort Amherst to her mooring in the inner harbour.

Captain Holland had not attempted another conversation with the naval officer. Instead, he allowed himself to be ferried to the fort where he was graciously received by Captain Hill, the commanding officer on The Island. As a consequence of the meeting and before the day was out, Lieutenant William Mowatt, his ship, and the entire ship's company were well and truly committed to Captain Samuel Holland's survey of The Island of Saint John.[3]

Oakwood Manor[4]
Handsworth, England

"They have already sent a stooge to Saint John's Island. Appointed him captain—not a brevet captain, but an honest-to-god captain of surveyors." Joseph Smallwood looked over at his daughter to see her reaction. *None. You never know what is going on behind those deep brown eyes.* He waited for her to speak. Just when he had decided that she wasn't going to say anything, Hélène Smallwood rose from her chair and walked to the window. With her back to the lord of the manor, she pronounced her opinion.

"I wouldn't worry about it, Father." She stood on tiptoe

trying to see beyond the hedge and over the lawns that reached all the way to the main gate on Church Lane. "Young Joseph is late getting back, Father." *She remembered how she used to wait for Cousin William by the hedge. Then they would go to chapel . . .*

"The Earl of Egmont presented a memorial to the King—"

Hélène never hesitated to interrupt her father. "Yes, but I am told that we could have heard the laughter all the way from London if we had but opened our windows."

"Then why did Egmont send his dogsbody to North America?"

"Because he could. Because he is First Lord of the Admiralty and it's easy for him to assign one of his ships—"

"But why? What is the point?"

Hélène turned to face her father. "His Majesty had just won a great war. He wants to count his winnings." She smiled her beautiful smile. "And our dear Earl told the King that he could send a ship—no trouble at all—and have the tally done for him, down to the inch, of just how much the King had won."

"At virtually no cost because he has a friend who . . ."

" . . . is a surveyor."

Hélène whirled around and almost pressed her nose against the glass. Her breath made a little patch of fog so she moved a bit to one side so that her view of the main gate was not obstructed. "I worry about Young Joseph."

"You fuss too much over . . ." Here the lord of the manor hesitated as he chose his words very carefully. " . . . the boy. He patrols for poachers and, I must remind you, he is not the first Smallwood to do so. I suggest to you that you must be careful not to mother him. Let my wife do that."

Oh yes! Cousin William used to patrol for poachers. I worried about him too, but in a different way; he wasn't my . . .

"You seem distracted today."

"Yes, I am distracted. It has been fourteen years since Cousin William left Oakwood to return to Maryland. This week, I wrote him three letters . . ."

There was note of impatience in Joseph's voice, "Hélène! Enough of wistful thinking! I must have your advice on these matters, today!"

" . . . but I tore them up, one after the other."

"Hélène! There is no one in the whole of England who understands the workings of the King's Party as well as you. I have need of your—"

In a musing tone of voice she interrupted her father, "Men talk in front of me, a mere woman, just as if I weren't there." Hélène cast a last glance out the window and, with a note of regret in her voice, got down to the serious work of running the family business. "You must use your influence with the Lord Commissioners of the Board of Trade and Plantations."

"To do what?"

Hélène stared at her father, wishing she had not been born a woman. *If I had been born a man, I wouldn't have to explain things all the time . . . to tell my father what to say . . . to show him how to use the Smallwood influence in the King's Party for the good of the family.* She shook her head. *If I were a man, I would do it first and tell my father about it afterwards.*

"Why are you shaking your head?"

She paused and then said, "I had hoped to spend some time with Young Joseph before we dressed for dinner." She walked across the room to where her father was sitting. She joined him on the sofa and took one of his hands in hers. "The Earl has ordered Captain Holland to measure Saint John's Island and bring the survey results back to England as soon as possible. In the meantime, Egmont estimates there are two million acres, which Egmont wants divided into fifty lots. With himself as Lord Paramount, there will be forty Capital Lords, four hundred Lords of Manors, and eight hundred Freeholders, all beholden to the Earl of Egmont. In its simplest terms, he wants to create a feudal state."

"The only thing I see wrong with that is . . . _my_ friends didn't get to suggest it first."

Exasperation showed in the young woman's face. She suppressed it and, squeezing her father's hand, continued with her instructions. "You must not say that."

Joseph Smallwood ran his fingers through his grey hair. "Then what must I say?"

"You and your friends must use your influence to delay every recommendation the Earl makes. You must be heard to agree with the Earl by saying that the nobles and other persons of rank and distinction should take the lead in the settlement of The Island. You, however, must go further by suggesting that officers of the fleet and army, whose bravery helped win the new lands, should also be rewarded and permitted to participate." She gave her father her best winning smile. "With that kind of mix, the feudal system won't be approved."

"Explain to me again, Hélène; why don't we want a feudal system?"

"We don't want any kind of system created by the Earl of Egmont; we want a system of our making." Hélène let go of her father's hand and dashed to the window. "I see Young Joseph!" She clapped her hands but then, quickly, pressed them together and held them in front, in a prayerful manner. "If you would excuse me, Father, I would go speak with him."

"I don't think it wise—for appearance's sake—that you spend so much time with the boy . . ." But she was gone.

Hannah, Joseph's second wife, came into the room. "I just passed my step-daughter in the hall. She seemed excited about something." Hannah kissed her husband on the forehead. "Do you know what it is all about?"

"Yes. She was helping me plan our next moves to acquire some holdings on Saint John's Island." He patted his wife's hand. "She is a very good schemer."

Hannah walked over to the window. "Where is . . . what's it called . . . this island?" She looked back at her husband's furrowed brow. "Oh, never mind. It doesn't matter. You and Hélène do whatever it is you do." Hannah turned her attention back to the window from where she watched Young Joseph spring down from his horse and toss the reins to the groom. She saw the boy give a casual wave to his sister and hurry along to the main house. Hélène stood still, gazing after the slim figure of the horseman. Hannah continued to watch as Hélène squared her shoulders and entered the chapel. Hannah turned away from the window. Her husband was dozing on the sofa. In a firm voice Hannah remarked, "She spends a great deal of time in chapel," but, if the sleeping form heard, it gave no indication.

* * *

Hélène Smallwood gently closed the door to the darkened chapel. *In earlier days*, she thought, *I would have run ahead to the second pew.* She hurried down the aisle and entered the second pew. *Cousin William, ever the cautious one, would check to ensure there were no supplicants before he joined me. I would lean over the front pew, like this,* she leaned over, enjoying the moistness that the memories always brought, *and William would throw my skirts up and over my head.* She hugged her breasts, tightly, as she remembered how William would fondle her as he pretended to have trouble with her underclothes. She pressed against the bench, moving against its hardness as she brought back sweet memories of her William. *If William would but return to me . . . we could visit, together, here, in the chapel.* She wiped the perspiration from her upper lip as her countenance glowed with the increasing pleasure . . .

After, she patted her face with the finely embroidered handkerchief taken from her sleeve. She sat, in the second pew, collecting her thoughts. *If William ever tired of soldiering in the colonies, he might return to Oakwood. This time, William and I might be allowed to acknowledge our relationship—there being no further family business to get in the way, and modern society being much more understanding of such things—and, yes, we would have a second son and this time we would announce him as our very own. This time . . .*

Yes, Hannah Barrett Smallwood was right when she observed that Hélène Smallwood did spend a great deal of time in the chapel.

Endnotes

1. "Potowmack River" is the spelling used in the Captain Holland's appointment documents.

2. The fog, the musket shot warning by a fishing boat, and the contrariness of Captain Mowatt are all as recorded in the *History of Prince Edward Island* (1875) by Duncan Campbell.

3. According to Duncan Campbell's book: "The ship barely escaped the rocks. Contrary winds were subsequently encountered, and Captain Holland resolved to proceed in a rowing boat to Quebec." Holland arrived on The Island in October and used his considerable influence to have instructions issued to Lieutenant Mowatt " . . . to render all the assistance in his power in forwarding the important service in which Captain Holland was engaged." I don't believe I left out anything important when I simplified the story.

4. Built in 1696 and known locally as "The Cottage," the Smallwood manor house and estate existed until after World War II. According to records, it was last occupied by a Smallwood in the 1930s.

Chapter Five
Plans

Out of the corner of his eye, Sergeant Brown watched McIntyre and Farrow as they wandered away from the survey team, their heads down, each with a long stick, poking at this and that, scuffing the dirt as if they were searching for something. Brown let them go until they were far enough away from the escort party guarding Captain Holland's surveyors that Brown could charge them with having left their assigned post. He had made up his mind that enough was enough when Captain Holland hailed him.

"Sergeant!"

"Yes, sir."

The officer pointed at McIntyre and Farrow, "Whatever those two men are searching for, have them stop. I want them to go out into the surrounding area and find me a Frenchie or two. I need information about the location of any trails."

"Yes, sir! Farrow, McIntyre! You heard the officer. Take your butts on a sortie and bring me back an Islander or two."

"Yes, Sergeant."

"And be quick about it!"

"Yes, Sergeant."

With their muskets at the trail, the two men moved quickly up the hill toward the woods. When they were out of sight, McIntyre stopped and leaned against a tree. "Pity we didn't find any peasants."

Farrow, half-turning to look back at his companion, continued walking into the forest. "The Sarge said…"

"Forget what the Sarge says; he can't see what we're doing in here. Let's talk about our gold." McIntyre settled down under the tree and leaned against its trunk. "Come on, buddy. We wouldn't find any Frenchies even if we did look; they

73

would hear us coming and hide." He waited for Farrow to return before he began talking about their search for the priests' gold.

"Do you think the priests would have buried their gold up on this hill?"

"It's the kinda place I'd bury me booty if I knowed the enemy wuz comin' and wuz goin' to burn everything . . ."

"But the priests wouldn't be so obvious, now would they? They would be crafty, for sure. They would try to outfox us. You remember, that Frenchie we found last week said that in '58, when the peasants up here heard the English were coming, they buried all their valuables so the English . . ."

"That's us . . ."

"For sure. So we couldn't find them."

"I know! They wouldn't put the good stuff in the houses 'cause they wuz warned we wuz goin' to burn everythin'."

"And they wouldn't put the stuff far away because they would want to find it again."

"Then we wuz goin' about it right when we was lookin' in the gardens and along the trails."

"No sense looking in the woods, then." McIntyre stood upright. "Joey, I think we just finished Sarge Brown's search for Frenchies."

"And we wuz quick about it, just like he said."

"Let's go back."

* * *

The next morning, when the valley was still filled with fog, the survey party ran a line down a path they had found. The escort party went ahead, marching the short distance to the head of the North-East River.

By midday, both groups of men had re-assembled on the banks of the river. It was there that Sergeant Brown asked permission to speak to Captain Holland.

"Beggin' your pardon, sir, but I must take myself off to Fort Amherst. I must catch ship to Halifax and thence home to my family what's waitin' for me at Birmingham. My enlistment is up, sir." When the officer didn't reply, Brown said, "It's, like, time I went home . . . to me family, sir."

"I'm sorry, Sergeant, but I can't spare you. Another month, perhaps, but not right now . . . not right here."

"The adjutant said I had to report to Halifax before my time was up if I was to qual-i-fy for trans-por-tation home. I can't travel back to the old country on the big ships of the Royal Navy if I am past me time. They won't take me on a Royal Navy ship if I am past me time. *You* knows that, sir. They made you a captain so's you could travel on the big ships. Besides, I can't disobey the regimental Adj."

"Maybe so, maybe not." The captain pushed his hat back and scratched his head, "Who would take charge of the escort party?"

The old soldier suffered a moment of panic—there was no corporal—and he knew he must stall while he thought of a way around the problem. There was always a way around any problem.

"Well, sir, you know that four of our men were sent back to Fort Amherst on the sick list. We could probably expect their return at any time and one of 'em might be an NCO since . . . He noticed that McIntyre and Farrow had wandered away from the main party . . . *of course! Farrow!* "But, in the meantime, we have good old, reliable Corporal Farrow. Yessir! Corporal Farrow could take my place! He has before, many's a time."

"I didn't know he was a corporal. He doesn't wear stripes."

"His stripes got took one time when he . . . "

"You mean he was broken in rank."

"Well, yes, he was demoted when he . . . when he . . . assumed authority over a situation . . . all proper and the right thing to do in the emergency that presented itself, sir. Believe me, sir, I was right some glad that he took the position he did . . . saved lives, he did . . ."

"But he lost his stripes."

"Well, sir, yes . . . he did, sir . . . he lost his stripes . . . because the young officer—don't take me wrong, sir, that officer was from a fine family, sir—didn't understand the emergency and wanted him punished." Sergeant Brown could see that he was making headway with his fanciful tale of a heroic Corporal Farrow so he continued, "I recommended the whip, sir, but the officer wanted more so Corporal Farrow was whipped and demoted."

"I see."

"Now that the young officer is no longer at Fort Amherst—his posting to a fine regiment finally arrived—Corporal Farrow will most likely be re-in-stat-ed, sir, yessir." He glanced over to where Farrow and McIntyre were slipping away again. Brown nodded in their direction. "You see, sir, there's Farrow, always doin' somethin' for the men—lookin' out for his boys—scoutin' to make sure there are no Frenchies . . . or Indians . . . sneakin' up on us."

Captain Holland looked around. "Well, I don't see how you would be able to go down river. We lost the use of our communications boat when we sent the sick back to the fort."

"That's not a problem, sir. This is the head of the river. A quick search around the shore and we will find someone's boat . . . a Frenchie's boat most likely, sir. We can use that."

"Very well." Holland turned away to join his survey party. "Carry on, then."

"Thank you, sir. Me family in Birmingham thanks you, sir."

"Ah, yes. Well, good luck, Sergeant."

Before Brown had finished his salute, he bellowed, "Farrow! Come here, on the double!"

* * *

Sergeant Brown sat down on the stern-sheets. He was grateful for the presence of the two members of the survey crew, one with a broken ankle and the other with crotch rot—neither malady preventing them from rowing Sergeant Brown into retirement. He stretched his legs and patted the side pocket of his tunic to make sure that his flask was tucked safely away. *As soon as I am out of sight of that friggin' officer, I intend to take a sip.* He had no intention of sharing with his boat's crew unless the one with the crotch rot started to scratch himself excessively and interfered with the boat's progress. Then he would pour some of his precious store over the man's sores.

Someone pushed the little boat away from the shore. Brown looked up to see who it was—Farrow. A sense of happiness and comradeship welled up in the old soldier's heart. "Take good care of my men, Corporal!"

"Yes, Sergeant." Farrow gave the boat a final push.

Brown was about to turn around and face the future, but he saw a man come running out of the woods. He watched as the man raced down the hill, past the guards of the escort party, past the surveyors sitting around the fire, past the startled officer, right to the edge of the river where the keel marks from the little boat were still filling with water from the boat's departure.

"Bring back my boat!" the man shouted through cupped hands.

The boat was almost at the turn to the river, moving swiftly with the current and the efforts of the two soldiers. Brown squinted as he tried to make out the stranger's features. He almost recognized the voice. *It was at Port La Joye the first few days; I was speakin' to a prisoner . . .*

The man stepped into the water, shaking his fist, "You are stealing my boat! Bring it back!"

Of course! The man's name was Milton . . . no, Miles. Corporal Miles who . . . Sergeant Brown stood up—causing the boat to rock—and he quickly sat down, grasping the gunnels, until the little craft steadied herself. By this time, the boat was at the turn in the river.

"Corporal Farrow!" Brown stood up, carefully. "Take that man into custody!" He shouted, even louder, "The man is a deserter!" But Farrow had answered, "Aye, Sergeant! What do you want?" at the first hail and had drowned out Brown's message. Brown would have to do it again.

An overhanging branch obscured Brown's view of the surveyor's camp. He had one last chance. It dawned on him that Farrow would recognize Miles. Farrow had been whipped and demoted because of that man's flight from discipline. *No, I don't have to worry about Miles getting what he deserves. Farrow will see to that.* He made another try, anyway. "Give him what he deserves, Farrow!"

* * *

Robert Cameron knew he was in serious trouble when he saw who was standing a few feet away holding a musket. *Merde! It's that corporal who was responsible for me when I escaped.* Robert moved his hands away from his body, palms up, to demonstrate that he had neither weapons nor an intention to make any quick moves. Robert kept a wary eye as Farrow approached, musket held at the port. Someone, standing off to one side behind Robert, spoke.

"What did Sergeant Brown say when he shouted from the river, Farrow?"

"Sergeant Brown knew this man, sir."

Robert tried not to show his sense of despair. *Not only do I have to contend with Farrow, but Brown is here too.* Robert's mind was racing, trying to devise a plan, hoping to get out of this trap. *Deserters can be shot! And they have an officer, right here, who would attest that I was shot while trying to escape, or properly executed for some other reason . . .*

"Brown said that this man should get what he deserves, sir."

With a note of impatience, the officer demanded, "And that is?"

"This man served with us at Port La Joye, sir."

"You mean Fort Amherst."

"Yes, sir. He served with us. Left us, saying he was going to take up land on this island—just like your friend, Lieutenant Burns."[1]

During the previous week, Captain Holland had been surprised to find an acquaintance, Lieutenant Burns of the 45th Regiment, living on what had been a Frenchie farm at Saint Peter's. Burns had built a substantial house and barn, *although they might have been built and used by the previous settlers*, Holland thought. *So, this fellow is of similar ilk . . .*

"This man is Corporal Miles, sir. He lives here some-wheres . . ."

Now, plainly irritated, Holland growled, "And what did your sergeant think this man should get? It didn't sound like Brown wanted him to have a nosegay of posies!"

"Sergeant Brown would want Miles to be given a chit for his boat. With a proper chit, signed by you, sir, Miles can go down to the fort and get his boat back after Sergeant Brown is finished with it." Farrow gave the officer a little smile. "That's all my sergeant wanted him to have, sir, a chit so his old com-rade, Corporal Miles, could get his boat back."

Holland was still upset about something. Farrow was not long in finding out what it was.

"Your men let him run through the whole camp, right to my very person. If he were intent on doing harm to this per-son, there was no one to stop him."

After the smallest of hesitations, Farrow replied, "My men probably recognized him, sir." Farrow looked around and seemed to randomly select one of his men. "Is that right, McIntyre? You recognized your old messmate?"

"Yes, I did, Corporal. Right some surprised I was to see him. Knew he had retired someplace but didn't know it was near here."

"That's enough!" The officer waved the problem away. "Find out what he knows about the area. See where he lives. Make a tally of animals, buildings, and persons for my report."

"Yes, sir."

* * *

Reine Leblanc picked up the baby and took Robbie by the hand when she saw Robert emerge from the forest in the com-pany of two redcoats. She relaxed when Robert gave her their secret hand signal that everything was all right. She waited for the group's approach.

"I brought two old friends, Reine," Robert said.

"Friends be damned," McIntyre snarled. "We want you to tell us where the priests buried their gold."

Reine crouched to put the baby in the crib-like basket. When she rose, she had a pistol in her hand. She pulled back on the hammer. "Take their muskets, Robert."

Robert pulled the musket out of McIntyre's hands. He took a couple of steps to Farrow and handed McIntyre's musket to the acting corporal. "You keep it. He's too bloody-minded to be carrying a loaded weapon around children." Without looking at McIntyre, Robert took the pistol from his wife and released the hammer. He put the pistol back under the crib.

"Where'd you get the pistol?" Farrow laughed. "It looks like an officer's weapon."

"It is. Borrowed from that lieutenant you were talking about. I dropped by one time when he wasn't home."

"You could be hanged for that."

"I could be hanged for a lot of things." Robert looked the corporal right in the eyes. "Why are you helping us? I left you in a lot of trouble when I escaped from custody."

"Yes, you did, but that officer shouldn'a had me whupped. He had me whupped and broke me one rank . . ."—he shook his head—"an' I don't hold with whuppin'." Farrow smiled at his friend McIntyre. "An' me and Donald here don't hold with officers no more. Me and Donald are on the lookout for me and Donald. An' there's no undoing what that officer had done to me and nothin' to be gained by turnin' you in. So you owe me." He grinned. "But I never thought I'd see you again to collect on the debt."

"Collect? We don't have much. What would you want?"

Joey Farrow leaned the muskets against the side of the little home that Robert and Reine had built in the forest. "Where can we sit?"

Robert pointed to a couple of logs that were placed next to a fire pit. "Over there is all we have."

As they sat down, Joey began. "They knowed the English wuz comin'."

"Who are you talking about?"

"The priests at Saint Peter's. They knowed the English wuz comin' and that we would ruin everything."

"So they buried anything of value."

Robert nodded his head. "I have heard the story."

"When we transported the Frenchies off The Island, we didn't let 'em carry much with 'em . . . all the good stuff is still there, somewheres."

"I can't help you with that." Robert shrugged. "I wasn't here; I was with you at Port La Joye."

"Yeah. That's right enuff. You wuz there." Joey thumbed at his back. "But not to watch me get me twenty lashes." He sucked his teeth and changed the subject. "How did you get away and where did you go?"

"We had a boat and we sailed to Malpeque."

"We were at Malpeque a couple of months ago."

Reine leaned forward and spoke for the first time since she had pointed the pistol at him. "How many families are at Malpeque? Are the Bernards still there? How are Joseph and Madeleine Arsenault? Did the English—"

"Three families and they are fine." McIntyre smiled. "I'm sorry, I interrupted you."

"Did the English come to transport them?"

"No. Lord Rollo couldn't arrange the transport that season and the next season when the ships arrived at Port La Joye, someone decided that everyone had left The Island."

"Aside from us, how many people are there on The Island?"[2]

"About thirty families."

"We used to live at Rivière du Nord-Est . . ."

"There's nothing there."

"Yes, we saw that. We came here, to the head of the river, and moved into the woods . . . far enough into the bush so we might be left alone.

Reine cautioned the redcoats, "We are the Leblancs."

Robert smiled. "Yes, I am known as a Frenchman who works on the English boats that sail out of Havre Saint Pierre."

"Saint Peter's?"

"Yes. There are English-owned boats there. I work for Englishmen; I get paid with supplies."[3]

The baby began to fuss and Reine jumped up to see to the

child. While she was tending the baby, Farrow asked, "Boy or girl?"

With pride, Reine answered, "Girl. She is Rosalie Cam . . . Leblanc.

Farrow held out his hands. "Let me hold her?"

"That would be nice . . . but don't spoil her. Most of the time we have to put her down while we do chores. Then Robbie keeps an eye on her for us." She patted Robbie's head as she walked by him. "And Robbie doesn't spoil his Rosalie, do you sweetheart?"

Farrow sat with the baby on his knee and told stories to the boy while McIntyre went scouting down the trail. When the boy tired and wandered off, Joey Farrow sang silly songs that he made up about a Rosalie

"who climbed a tree,
        to see the sea,
            but bumped her knee,
                on a honeybee,
                    who flew away,
                        but came back to say,
                            she'd tell the queen,
                                of what she'd seen,
                                    and that would cause a fuss.
The fuss would start,
        and the bees depart,
            to head for the tree,
                where they would see,
                    sweet Rosalie climb right down,
                        to run off homeward bound.
When I count to three,
        come down from the tree,
            sweet Rosalie, Rosalie.
                When I count three,
                    Come down from the tree.
                        One, two, three . . ."

and he would give her a little bounce and start over with another silly verse.

"What are you doing, Joey?" McIntyre sounded as if he was embarrassed by his comrade's behaviour.

Rather sheepishly, Joey answered, "Nuttin'. Did you find anything along the trail?"

"He has a lean-to shed, some hens . . . but nothing much else." McIntyre looked around. "It's soon going to be dark. We should head back."

Reine came out of the hut and took the baby from Farrow. Robert walked over and put his arm around his wife. He called his boy, "Robbie, come say goodbye."

"Just a minute. I'm doin' something."

"Viens ici tout de suite sinon tu y goûteras . . . Come here immediately, otherwise I give you a licking."

The boy came. The goodbyes were said and the redcoats took their leave.

On the way back, Farrow was quiet for a while and then told his friend, "My time is up in eighteen months. I'm gonna take my discharge right here; come live near the river. Find me a woman. Have some babies. It is good land . . ."

"And it's free!"

"Yes, and it's free."

The redcoats walked along for a while. When they were within sight of the surveyor's camp, Farrow asked, "Do you think the army will come after them?"

"Naw. The whole island is a prison. Keep 'em here. They can't go anywhere and they can't do any harm."

"That's not what I meant. I didn't mean the French woman and her kids. I meant, do you think they'll come after Miles?"

"Yeah. Probably. The sergeants can't stand insubordination. They won't let one of us get away with it—we might all try it."

As they entered the camp, McIntyre had one last thought on the subject. "Yeah, they'll get him."

September
Observation Cove Near Port La Joye

He signed the document "Captain Samuel Holland, Surveyor General." He gave it a moment's thought and then wrote, "dated at Observation Cove near Port La Joye, 19th September, 1765." He folded the pages and thumb-nailed the crease. He picked up a cloth and carefully wiped clean the nib of his pen. *Tomorrow I will have Mister Robinson transcribe the information onto proper parchment. Then, on the first available ship, I will have it delivered to the Lords Commissioners of Trade and Plantations.*

The Island of Saint John survey completed, he began his planning for the survey of the other islands: Cape Breton and the Magdalene Island. He spread the papers out on his little desk. He sat very still as he began thinking about possible problems that might beset him in this enterprise. After a while, he pulled on his lower lip with his thumb and forefinger. When he realized what he was doing, he dropped his hand immediately. "I might just as well be sucking my thumb!" He looked around to make sure that none of his staff were near enough to overhear him speaking to himself. *But what am I overlooking?* He began pulling on his lip, this time not stopping himself. *Of course! I must send a letter to my patron! He* half turned in his chair. "Mister Robinson!," he shouted as he gathered up the papers dealing with the other islands to put them away.

"Coming, sir!" He could hear Robinson walking through the front room—the floors squeaked badly. Robinson lifted the latch on the door between the two rooms, the door giving him serious resistance and grating on the rough, wooden surface of the floor as he forced it open.

Robinson entered the room and then turned to press his entire body against the door to force it closed.

"Let it be, Mister Robinson. Lieutenant Mowatt was ordered to build me a house but Lord Coville failed to specify the level of craftsmanship." He indicated for Robinson to take the chair on the other side of the little desk. "I call that door Mowatt's Revenge." He nodded at the pen and inkwell. "Take up your pen: I need to send special information to our friends." When Mister Robinson was ready, Holland began.

"Address the letter to the Earl of Hillsborough." Holland selected one of the pages of his folded report. "Take the information from this page; use it as the main text and fit in the comments that I will give you now."

"I am ready."

"Good. You may begin. There are thirty Acadian families who are regarded as prisoners and kept on the same footing as those at Halifax." He waited for Robinson to finish and then asked, "Do you think I need to mention that they are considered to be prisoners of war? That any livestock they might have is the property of the Crown and is being confiscated as the garrison requires it?"

Robinson shook his head. "It is perhaps better not to . . ."

"Good." He pointed to the folded page. "When you are using the information about surviving buildings . . . right here . . . where it reads that there are 11 mills, 2 churches . . . the cleared acres . . . and the number of houses that were overlooked in the burnings . . . add that there is a Lieutenant Burns and a Corporal Herbert Miles living near the North East River . . . no! Make that the Hillsborough River. Or better, the Earl of Hillsborough River."

"Your pardon, sir. I believe Hillsborough River would be sufficient."

"Yes. Perhaps you are right. Hillsborough River it is, then."

Mister Robinson gathered his papers.

"Clean the nib. I managed to get ink on my fingers and would prefer not to get more . . ."

"Of course, sir." Robinson sat down and picked up the cloth. "If I recall, sir, the plan for this island calls for a defensive system of proper forts. Shouldn't you say how badly The Island is defended at the present time?"

"Yes, of course! Good thinking!" Holland plucked at his lip and dictated, "Fort Amherst is a poor, stockaded redoubt with barracks scarcely sufficient to lodge the garrison."

"That should do it, sir. Anything else?"

"Ask Hillsborough to present my best compliments to my patron . . ."

"Earl of Egmont?"

"Yes, of course! Say that I am enamoured with the grant that I have numbered as 38 on the map." Holland placed his hand on his assistant's sleeve. "Lot number 38 encompasses the Head of the Hillsborough River which allows easy land access to Saint Peter's Harbour."[4]

"Admirable choice, sir." Robinson rose to go. "Is that all, sir?"

"Yes. You may carry on."

"Thank you, sir."

Captain Holland rubbed the blotch of ink on his index finger as he watched Robinson struggle with the door. He glanced at the table and saw the dirty pen. *He forgot to clean the nib!* He called out, "Robinson you forgot to clean the nib!" but Robinson continued out the side door to his tent—his master's summons and complaint drowned out by the squeaks of the wooden floor.[5]

July 1767
Oakwood Manor
Handsworth, England

"They lied!"

Hélène Smallwood sucked her teeth and took a deep breath. She turned and faced her father, forced a smile and then began the tedious job of getting her father into line. "It's not that they *lied*, Father. They told you—"

"They told me that I would get thousands of acres." He struck his fist into the palm of his hand. "They went through their tomfoolery of a lottery and I got nothing . . . my name wasn't even on the list . . . a bunch of admirals and the like got

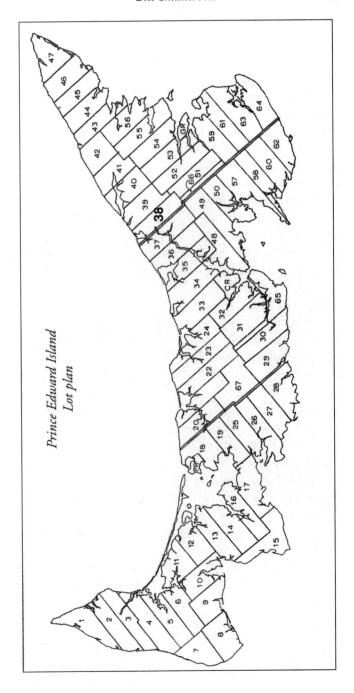

Prince Edward Island
Lot plan

land . . . petty nobility got land . . . friends of the Court got land . . ."

Hélène said nothing while her father took a breath.

" . . . I thought I was a friend of the Court . . ."

Hélène waited; it still wasn't time to begin her campaign to get her father to do what had to be done.

"Even that loser, the Earl of Egmont . . . even though his party was thrown out at the polls . . . even with the change of government, he had enough clout to be offered 100,000 acres—prime acres.

"He refused it, Father."

"More fool he." Joseph Smallwood began to pace back and forth in front of the hearth. He stopped and stared at the blank space over the mantel where the new family crest would be mounted as soon as it received royal approval. "And I suppose the Court will stall until . . . until . . . until I am dead and buried . . . six feet under . . ."

"You won't be put six feet under. You will be placed in the family crypt." *It's time to stop this foolishness.* "I will invite, with your prior approval, the new governor of The Island of Saint John to accept our hospitality for a week. During his visit, we can discuss with him how he will get our land for us."

"But Hillsborough should have already looked after us— like he promised—and we wouldn't have to bother with . . ." Startled, he looked more closely at his daughter. "Who is the new governor?"

"It hasn't been announced yet, but the governor will be Walter Patterson, a friend of the Earl of Hillsborough."

"A friend? Never heard of him."

"He is an Irish-born army officer. Hillsborough has used him before in land-grab schemes."[6]

"Land grab?" Joseph sat down; he stared at the blank space over the hearth. "Yes. Invite him here, by all means."

May 1768
Province House
Halifax, Nova Scotia

Michael Francklyn cleared his throat, bringing to silence the group of men that Joshua Mauger had left in control of Nova Scotia. Francklyn motioned toward the end of the room. "Close the door, Issac." When he saw the scowl on the face of his underling, Francklyn spoke in jest to the rest of the group, but there was an edge to his words that could not have been missed by the target. "I trust that when I appoint you to be officer-in-charge of the colonization of The Island of Saint John, you will be more amenable to my wishes, Issac Deschamps."

Deschamps was about to question his master but Francklyn waved him into silence.

"I have correspondence from our Mister Mauger but first I would cover the official situation with you." He consulted his notes.

"Last year, sixty-eight English proprietors were given title to all of the various parcels of land on Saint John's Island. By the terms of their titles, they were expected to pay quitrents to the Crown while arranging for tenants to be found and their labour used to improve the proprietors' holdings. One of the proprietors, a certain Walter Patterson, was later appointed governor . . ." He paused, expecting Issac Deschamps to question why, if there was already a governor, did Franklyn mention he was going to appoint Deschamps to be in charge of anything?

Instead, another voice questioned him. "You said Issac was going to be in charge."

Yes, of course, Richard Bulkeley would come to the point first—"It's quite simple, really."—*and that's why he has out-lasted any other government official in the history of the province.* "The new Governor Patterson won't be able to wind up his affairs in England for some time yet . . ."

"So what gives the Governor of Nova Scotia the right to appoint Issac Deschamps to a position on Saint John's Island?"

"The Board of Trade specified that all land titles be granted under the seal of Nova Scotia."

A snort of satisfaction and then, "We have control!" Bulkeley shifted in his chair. "Excuse me, sir; as Governor of Nova Scotia, _you_ have control."

His face flushed, Francklyn leaned over and squeezed his First Secretary's shoulder. "Yes, my dear Richard, I have control,"—he cast a quick look around at the rest of his cronies—"and I mean to share."

There was spontaneous applause from the eleven men present.

Now grinning, he waved an official despatch. "I have this despatch . . ." He waited while the men quietened. "I have this despatch, addressed to Lieutenant-Governor Michael Francklyn of Nova Scotia, from Secretary of State Hillsborough, detailing the afore-mentioned plans for settlement and requesting suggestions for the civil establishment on The Island."

As usual, Richard Bulkeley was the first to react. "That means patronage," he whispered, "and commercial contracts and money."

"Yes, bags of money." He paused, "I also have a message from our dear, dear Mister Mauger instructing me to proceed without delay."

"As I understand it, Governor, your administration was asked to send recommendations to Hillsborough, not lists of appointments."

Leave it to Richard Bulkeley to be first off the mark! "Not a chance! Mister Mauger believes we must strike while the opportunity exists!" He turned away from the group and gestured that they should follow him into the office. "I have appointments in mind . . . several contracts . . ."[7]

September 1768
The Cameron Farm
Near Saint Peter's Harbour

Reine noticed the figure leave the trail that led from the Hillsborough River to Saint Peter's Harbour. She slipped into the woods and watched to see if he would continue down the little path that led to their farm. He did.

Reine gathered up her skirts and ran. By the time she had reached what the family called Cameron's Brook, she was badly out of breath. She stopped long enough to splash water on her face and then climbed the embankment and struck out across the first field. Nearing the bushes at the end of the little open space, she ducked into the shade and stared at the trail on the other side of the brook. She waited. When it seemed that no one was coming, she hiked up her skirts again and hurried the rest of the way home. As soon as she saw her husband, she waved to get his attention and gave the signal for "strangers in the area."

Robert gathered up his tools, tossing them out of sight into the bushes. He picked up Rosalie who had been playing in the dirt by his side. Then he turned to face Reine and pointed in the direction of their orchard. Reine changed direction and went to fetch Robbie who must have been sent to do chores in the orchard. She found him in the grape arbour. The boy had been eating the unripe grapes and, expecting to be scolded, was relieved when his mother merely took him by the hand, telling him that he had to hurry back to the house. Robbie hurried.

At the house, Reine described what she had seen. "A man, dressed in a deerskin shirt, stopped at the beginning of our path. He checked the prime on his musket and came toward me."

"Had he seen you?"

"No." She continued, "He looked neither to the left nor to the right; he moved down the path as if he were going somewhere." Reine squinted her eyes as if she were trying to picture the man just the way she had seen him, "He wore a large pack and carried something else in the other hand but I couldn't see what it was."

"Alone?"

"As far as I could see. I waited at the first field to see if he would come . . ."

"But he didn't."

"He didn't."

Robert rubbed the stubble on his chin. "If he were English, he wouldn't be alone . . ."

"There would be redcoats if they were coming for you."

"No one knows I am here." He patted his wife's hand. "I think it's all right to wait and see. They wouldn't send one man to take me in."

* * *

An hour later, Joseph Farrow stumbled out of the woods into the sunlight. His clothing was in disarray and there were scratches on his face and hands. "Thank Christ!" he said. "I been lost! I thought I knew where you wuz but you wuzn't!" He smiled at the surprised couple. "Did you move or somethin'?" Still being faced with surprised stares, Joey spoke again. "I brought pea meal, flour, molasses, and . . ."

Reine threw her hands in the air and gleefully shouted, "Welcome, Joey!"

It was a pleasant time as they sat around the fire after their meal. With the children tucked away, Joey brought them news of the outside world.

"There's a new Island government now—in Halifax—and they mean to do wonderful things for this island."

Robert shook his head. "The further away the government is the better. Even Halifax isn't far enough for the likes of me."

"I might have fixed that fer you, mate. When I was in Halifax, I filled out some papers fer one Herbert Miles."

Both of the Camerons stopped breathing as they waited.

"I made an in-ce-dent report that a Corporal Miles had reported for duty at Port La Joye in 1759. Then I a-ttached the reco . . ."—Joey stumbled over the word—" . . . reco-menda-tion of one Sergeant Brown and company approval by one Lieutenant Makin that said Corporal Miles be given hon-ourable dis-charge from His Majesty's Service. A state-ment by the field surgeon that the corporal might not survive an Atlantic crossing due to the nature of his injuries sus-tain-ed at the hands of the Micmac led to the major's approval of an honourable discharge on The Island." It was Joey's turn to wait; he waited for some sort of reaction from the couple. When the Camerons continued to sit, dumbfounded, Joey prattled on: "It was McIntyre who did all the words." Joey smiled. "I did the sergeant's sig-nat-tour an' McIntyre did the officer's. Mac is right some good at that sort of thing."

Bemused, Robert could only say, "Yes, I suppose so." He sat there thinking of some of the possible consequences. Finally, he said, "But they will come after me when they find out it's fake!" Robert smacked his forehead with his open palm. "How could you do that to . . ."

"Don't you worry none, mate. Sergeant Brown is gone. Makin went off to a new regiment somewheres and the major died. I put the papers in the company files. They will be found someday. By then no one will give a tinker's damn." Joey shrugged his shoulders as he cast an apologetic look to Robert's wife. "Your pardon, Ma'am," he said.

Reine reached over and patted Joey's leather leggings. "A man who brings food and sweets for my babies . . ."

Robert punched Joey on the arm, playfully. "But don't do it again, she means to say." Robert deflected a return punch and then settled down to some serious talk. "What have you been doing since you were here on the survey?"

"I went back to Halifax where I was finally discharged." He dug in the pocket of his leather shirt and pulled out a fist-ful of shillings. "I got paid off . . ."

"Good Christ!" It was Robert's turn to cast an apologetic look at his wife. "I haven't seen coin since . . ."

Reine reached over and picked up a coin from the out-stretched palm. "So much money!"

"I didn't get it all from my mustering-out. I came back to The Island like I tol' you I wuz meanin' to do last time I saw you, and I meant to be here much earlier but they wuz hirin' men at Fort Amherst and payin' in coin . . . a lot of coin. I rowed Jonathan Binney around to inspect his new command."

"Who is . . .?"

"Binney was the senior naval officer for The Island of Saint John . . . an' it was good money . . . but when the easy rowin' wuz over, I thought I had better find you so's I could get settled in for the winter." He looked into the eyes of the couple, first the one and then the other: "You gonna give me shelter over the hard months at least until I can get me farm started?"

Reine put on a very serious face. "Well, we have the children to think of . . ." She smiled. "Jingle the shillings again, Joey, and I might have a change of heart."

Joey clinked the coins. There was laughter and some song. Later, Joey bedded down in the lean-to shed and immediately began dreaming his dream of a quiet life in the sheltered woods of The Island of Saint John.

Reine and Robert took one last look at their children before getting ready for the night.

"Do you think Joey's papers will fool the army?" Reine ran her fingers through her man's hair and kissed his forehead. She sat on the edge of the cot and then slipped in under the blanket; she turned on her side and held her arms out for Robert to join her.

Robert had finished washing his torso and dried himself with an old blanket. He blew out the lantern and snuggled in under the covers.

"Well, do you believe the papers will fool anybody?" When Robert still didn't answer, she repeated, "Well, do you?"

"If they can sit in the company files long enough, no one will give them a second thought . . ."

Reine punched him in the stomach. In return, Robert

pinched her buttock. They giggled. They lay in each other's arms, waiting for sleep to come.

Robert had almost drifted off when Reine whispered, "Are you still awake?"

"I am now."

"Do you think we are safe from the English?"

Robert gave a big sigh. "It might be safer for Bert Miles, but it will never be over for the army deserter Robert Cameron." He felt her tense so he added what he truly believed. "I think we are far enough into the woods that no one will come looking for us . . . and if they do, they won't find us."

June 1769
Oakwood Manor
Handsworth, England

Joshua Mauger clapped his hands to get the attention of the men who had gathered at the Smallwood estate. He waited for the bustle and conversation to die and then began to speak to the proprietors of The Island of Saint John.

"You are aware that the Board of Trade accepted our proposal. The deal was that they would recommend our island be removed from Nova Scotia's jurisdiction if we paid half of our quitrents up front and the rest to be deferred for twenty years. All but eight of the proprietors agreed and the Privy Council has approved a separate government for our little island. That's the deal, men! We get to run our own government and with one of our very own in charge . . ." He waved his hand in the direction of Captain Walter Patterson, who rose to a round of applause and then sat down again. "It should prove easy sailing to fat profits for all of us."

Admiral Rodney raised his hand seeking permission to speak.

Joshua Mauger nodded assent.

"Vice Admiral Sir George Rodney, proprietor of Lot number 43," he said by way of identification for the uninformed. "What will happen to the eight dissidents?"

Mauger laughed before he answered, "Our Governor Patterson will ensure they get what they deserve."

The admiral laughed too, and when the tittering had died out he asked, "What possessed the Board of Trade to change its mind at this stage and rule in our favour?" He hurried on. "After all, our proposal was not much different than that put forth by my friend the Earl of Egmont."

"British colonies are expensive to administer and defend; the cost to the motherland—and what I mean is, the cost to people like us—is horrendous. For example, the Board of Trade must take steps regarding our colonies in America . . ."

"Yes," the admiral interjected, "the American colonists resent being asked to pay for their own naval defence."

"And cost of government . . ." Mauger added.

"And a standing army," came from a voice in the back of the room. When the comment was followed by silence, the voice added, "Charles Lee, Esquire, proprietor of Lot 24."

"You are entirely correct, my dear Charles," Mauger said, agreeably. "The New England colonists were given too much say . . ."

"Their Lower Assemblies were given too much freedom, too much influence," the admiral said, irritably.

Mauger showed his own impatience as he closed off the discussion: "Suffice it to say that the American colonies are restive under the Board of Trade's attempts to reduce the costs of running the empire . . ." He paused and then hardened his voice. "And the commissioners are not going to make the same mistake with this colony as they made with the Americans." It looked like there might be further discussion so Mauger lifted his hands to quell discussion. "However, when the new costs for running the colony in the traditional manner were submitted by our friends in Nova Scotia . . ."

Mauger smiled slyly, as sounds of suppressed laughter filled the room. He waited for it to die down.

"The Commissioners told me they were horrified by the amount of money involved. If the Commissioners were going to reduce the costs of running the empire, they felt they were forced to try some other system on The Island of Saint John—other than the traditional system—and our offer was the only one still on the table." He paused and appeared to search the room for more comment but, with excellent timing, he closed off the meeting with, "Our gracious host, Joseph Smallwood, has clerks ready in the next room to process matters of great concern to our quest for adequate returns on our investments." He raised his voice over the clatter of shuffling feet and the grunts and groans of old men getting to their feet. "Please register your name with the lobby group we have formed so we may provide ongoing protection to our common interests."

Joshua Mauger walked away from the centre of the room seeking a glass of sherry from the manservant standing by the door. Through the rim of the glass, he watched as the "gracious host" worked his way through the throng. *No way to avoid the bugger! He's going to pester me again.* Mauger lowered his glass and extended his hand. "Mister Smallwood . . ." They shook hands, Mauger noting that the host's hands were damp and limp. "Thank you for your support over the years."

"Mister Mauger, it's not thanks I want . . ."

"My friends call me Joshua . . ." *That ought to soften the bugger up.* "So please do call me Joshua."

"Thank you . . . Joshua. I . . . I don't mean to be a nuisance . . ."

"I know, I know. It has been a long time that you have waited for what should have been yours from the very beginning . . . but politics, you know . . ."

"Yes, and I appreciate . . ."

"Just a moment . . . may I call you Joseph?"

Joseph Smallwood flushed with pleasure. "Certainly."

"Just a moment, Joseph." Mauger looked to the side of the room and then lifted his chin. Instantly, an aide appeared at his side. In a conspiratorial tone, Mauger spoke to the man. "Mathew, do you remember the lot number I designated for Joseph?"

Mathew, keeping his face impassive, leaned forward. "You gave me the information, sir, but I don't recall . . ."

"It was the same lot number that Captain . . . you know . . . that surveyor fellow . . ."

"Captain Holland, sir."

"The one Captain Holland wanted when it looked like Egmont was going to get control."

"Yes, sir, I remember now. It was Lot number 38."

"Lot number 38! That was it." Mauger took Smallwood by the arm, guiding him toward the other room where the administration for the new proprietor association was being handled. "Holland said he was enamoured with the location of Lot 38 and chose it above all others." Mauger stopped and turned Smallwood so he could look into the other man's eyes. "I can't get it for you right away, but I give you my solemn promise that you shall have it." He let go of the host's arm. "I must return to London." He beckoned to Mathew to step in closer. "Make a record of my promise that I make this day to Joseph Smallwood."

"Certainly, sir."

"We must leave, Mathew." Mauger nodded to Smallwood. "Thank you for all your efforts on our behalf."

Joseph Smallwood gave Joshua a courtly bow. "My pleasure, sir."

* * *

Mathew climbed into the carriage behind his master. They rode in silence for a while until, finally, Mauger spoke.

"Remember the story about the horse?"

Mathew's head nodded in agreement or with the motion of the carriage; it didn't matter to Mauger so long as it nodded.

"As the story goes, a horse-thief had been sentenced to death for horse-stealing. As he was being led away, he cried out that he had stolen the King's horse to give the King a gift. Stealing the King's horse for the King? Everyone laughed." Mauger struck his aide's knee with the flat of his hand. "Yessiree, everyone laughed!" He looked at his man to make sure he was properly attentive, and, satisfied, he continued.

"The thief said he had planned to teach the horse how to talk and then return the horse to the King. The King would own the only talking horse in the world." Mauger paused.

Mathew remained silent but cocked his head to one side to show continued interest.

"The King, after giving the matter consideration, granted the thief a year to accomplish this wonderful feat. If, at the end of the year, the horse could not talk, the thief would suffer a hundred terrible deaths."

As the guards led the thief and the horse away, the guard asked the thief why he had chosen a hundred terrible deaths in a year's time when he could leave this life easily, today, if he had just remained silent.

The thief replied, "During the year many things could happen: the horse could die, I could die, the King could die, or . . . the horse could talk."

Mathew laughed.

They rode in silence, Mathew wondering what the point of the story would be. He had no doubt that he would find out.

"After I read the Holland letters, I had decided I would acquire title to Lot 38. If Captain Holland chose that lot over all the others, it must be a good one." He looked over at the nodding head. "And, as long as Smallwood believes I can get him Lot 38 . . ."

Mathew smiled, bowing his head in acknowledgement of his master's shrewdness.

They rode in silence. After a while, Mauger chuckled. "Yes, for as long as our dear Joseph Smallwood Esquire believes that I can make the horse talk, he will be our loyal servant." Mauger laughed, "And, who knows? Maybe the horse will talk."

* * *

Hélène entered the main hall as soon as the last carriage rumbled down the driveway. She looked around for her father. The manservant took one step forward and said, in a soft voice, "He's in the anteroom, Mistress Hélène." She turned on her heel and entered the anteroom to find Young Joseph poring over a map.

When he saw his sister, Young Joseph asked, "Where is the damned island?"

"I thought Father was in here."

"No, sister, he's not here." He leaned over the map. "Do you know . . ."

"Not now." Hélène stormed back into the hall. "I thought you told me the master was in the anteroom!"

"Your pardon, Miss Hélène. You are usually looking for the young master . . ."

Tapping her foot, she growled, "I want to know where . . ."

The servant, cringing, pointed to the French doors leading to the side garden.

In the garden, Joseph Smallwood, Lord of Oakwood Manor, also recoiled when he saw his daughter's face. He stepped back and raised his hands as if to ward off a she-devil. "We will get Lot 38!"

"When?" Hélène stopped at the edge of the garden. "Is it on paper?"

"I don't know." Joseph sat down on an ornamental bench. He turned to face the warmth of the sun and closed his eyes. "I have his promise. We will get Lot 38 as soon as he can arrange it."

"Promise!" Hélène began her foot tapping again. "Promise? You've had promises before." When her father made no further comment, she sat down with him on the bench. She softened her voice. "I know, Father. You did the best you could with them." *I wish I were a man!* She patted his hand. "If they are men of honour, they will keep their word."

The father got up and hurried toward the house.

"What is the matter, Father?"

"I feel sick," was all he had to say as he disappeared into the manor.

Endnotes

1. In correspondence to the Earl of Hillsborough, Captain Holland reported that he had run across an old friend who was living at Saint Peter's: " . . . Lieutenant Burns, of the 45th Regiment, who had removed with his family to The Island . . . ."

2. Captain Holland reported, "There are about thirty Acadian families on the island, who are regarded as prisoners, and kept on the same footing as those at Halifax."

3. According to Georges Arsenault in his book *The Island Acadians (1720-1980)*, "At the time of the 1768 census the heads of the forty-one Acadian families on Île Saint Jean, enumerated in five different localities, all fished for Englishmen who owned most of the fishing vessels. The Acadians did, however, own two schooners, five shallops and one sloop."

4. Duncan Campbell quotes from correspondence from Egmont to Holland in which Egmont promises the surveyor land on the island. "For yourself, you may be assured of your Hundred, as formerly intended . . . ."

5. Holland is an historical character. I stayed as close as possible to what is known about him. Sergeant Brown is fiction. McIntyre is a character I found in a 1791 edition of the *Royal Gazette of the Island of Saint John*. I gave him his military background and associations with the Camerons and with Farrow.

6. From J.M. Bumsted's book *Land, Settlement and Politics on Eighteenth-Century PEI*: "Patterson was Irish-born, emerging out of obscurity to become a junior officer in the final war against New France, serving in the eighteenth-century equivalent of a commando regiment. He had come to Lord Hillsborough's attention in the course of a land grab in New York after the war, and, undoubtedly owed his appointment to Hillsborough's support."

7. Issac DesChamps was appointed chief justice. In all, eight senior appointments were made; salary costs were £1028 per annum. Charles Morris, chief surveyor of Nova Scotia, was ordered to make surveys of Island town sites. Over £3000 was quickly spent on supplies giving profitable contracts to many leading Halifax merchants. J.M. Bumsted's book *Land, Settlement and Politics on Eighteenth-Century PEI*.

Chapter Six
It's Happening All Over

1770
Le Volant

Captain Louis Arsenault studied the standing rigging of his father's ship. There was slack in the main shrouds, port side, which meant there was additional strain somewhere else. His eyes followed the line of the topsail yard on the foremast of his schooner-rigged ship; *there's trouble up there*, he thought. "Ease up!" The stiff west-south-west wind must have carried his order away because his nephew, who was training to be helmsman, made no move to obey. It gave Louis a moment to reconsider.

We have been sailing a constant heading during this whole passage south from the Magdalenes. He listened to the thrumming ropes and the whistle of the wind as it forced itself past *Le Volant*; he stared at the dark shape of Île Saint Jean now filling the horizon, hopeful of a good landfall.

A voice from forward called out, "Land's end to port!"

So much for one's hopes. That would be East Point to the left, placing their destination, Havre Saint Pierre, well to the right. He would have to sail west along the coast, a dangerous coast—the north shore of Île Saint Jean. *There is always the possibility that we could be driven against that shore. If I lose some canvas—and if the wind should change—I won't be able to beat to windward.* He heard a sharp crack in the rigging just over his head. His head snapped up, expecting to see falling spars and canvas . . . she's warning me! He cupped his hands around his mouth. "Antoine! Ease up!" He motioned to the crew. "Man the sheets! Joseph, make an easy port turn to due east!" He turned to face the crew. "Take your time, boys! Ease her off! Don't put any more strain on her."

Le Volant quickly settled on the easier, safer heading. The hum of thrumming ropes and the whistle of the wind disappeared. The decision to seek shelter behind East Point made,

Louis took a moment to look around; *it's actually a nice day*, he thought. He glanced at the north shore of The Island of Saint John and marvelled at how pretty it was—when it was no longer a threat. In his travels with his father, Louis hadn't come this far east and he was surprised by the intensity of the forest greens that came right down to the greyish sands along the shore. Pretty as the shoreline was, his ship would have been destroyed just the same as on any other lee shore.[1]

"C'est très joli . . . It's so pretty, Captain."

Louis took a couple of steps so he could place his hand on his nephew's shoulder. "Assez joli . . . Pretty enough, Antoine, but just as deadly as any other shore if you are driven onto it."

"Where are we going now, sir? I thought we were going to Saint Peter's Harbour."

"This old girl needs some repairs." Louis pointed ahead. "We must get behind East Point and take some of the pressure off her. The weather is unsettled and we mustn't be caught out here." He lifted his cap, rubbed the sparse hair, and slipped the cap back on.

Antoine took the opportunity to ask, "It's not far to St. Peter's Harbour. Why not . . .?"

"The north winds that come sweeping across the Gulf of Saint Lawrence don't need help to raise fierce seas; no, they do a good job all on their own." Louis inclined his head toward The Island. "But, when the wind drives the rough seas onto the north shore of that island, The Island's shallow waters give the north wind a helpin' hand; we get huge waves that are called 'ship killers'." Louis heard his nephew's quick intake of breath, so he hurried on. "Rogue waves we calls 'em and The Island hides the rogue waves here and there in the rough seas." Louis turned away to go below. "It's queer weather today." Glancing toward the shore, he saw hundreds of seabirds swooping along the tops of the waves, heading inland, making him feel better about his decision of doubling East Point instead of coasting to Havre Saint Pierre. *I'll snatch an hour or so of rest and then it'll be time to leave the gulf and sail into the quieter waters behind East Point. Yes, an hour or so of . . .* "There are several places along the eastern shore where we can seek shelter. There's Souris or perhaps Baie Fortune; I've a cousin at Baie Fortune. They'll probably have a carpenter." He patted Antoine on the shoulder as he turned away to go below. "Yes, we'd better find out what's ailing the old girl before we sail along that north shore again."

"Aye, sir."

"Let me know when East Point is well astern."

"Excuse me, Uncle, but why must East Point be well astern before we make the turn?"

"Mind your manners, son." But then Captain Arsenault gave a mental shrug. *So, he must learn. If I don't have a son, this boy will have* Le Volant *in his turn.*

He started without any preamble. "Just off East Point there are three reefs. The longest and most dangerous is called East Point Reef; it juts out about two miles. In the waters around that reef, there are tidal rips caused by the rocky submerged ledge and that just happens to be the very spot where the waves from the Gulf of Saint Lawrence break against the waves coming from the Northumberland Strait." He squeezed the boy's shoulder as he added, "Off that point, there is no shelter from the fickle winds and the heavy seas and—we must always remember—the reefs are there, waiting to take the unwary." He used his two hands to demonstrate the movement of the ship and the direction of the wind. "If the wind hauls around to the north east, and we are still beating up the north shore to double East Point, we would be in serious trouble."

A concerned Antoine Arsenault asked, "What would we do?"

"With a sturdy ship like *Le Volant*, we should be able to sail past the point and put the reefs well astern. Then we turn back and sail down the south side to our safe haven." Louis drew a "u" shape with his hand and said, "We double the point and spend a quiet day or two in Baie Fortune."

Antoine smiled. "Thank you, sir, for taking the time to . . ."

"But remember, sonny, the waves are treacherous and the tides are severe. Even in fair seas with a following wind like we have today, you could suffer a rogue wave off the reefs of East Point."

"If I see one, I'll be sure to call you, Captain."

The captain considered chastising the helmsman for his levity, but thought, *he's just like his father; he's always got to make the smart remark.* Louis put a stern note in his voice as he ordered, "See to your duties, helmsman," and descended below to his bunk.

* * *

Louis sensed the changes. He bolted from the cabin and out into the late afternoon sun.

"The mate was gonna call you, Captain!" Antoine pointed to starboard where a mackerel fishing boat was struggling against the waves. "They're having troubles!"

Louis glanced at the pinky—a small ship of about 45 tons, steered with a tiller in the pointed stern instead of a wheel and carrying a crew of ten or so. Yes, she was having trouble in the high seas kicked up by the strong north-east wind . . . but that was not Louis's concern. He looked beyond the pinky at the shoreline—a shoreline of wind-blasted spruce trees and steep cliffs with skirts of foam and spume. He gauged that the *Le Volant* still had enough sea room to double the point . . . but the pinky? The pinky probably didn't. She must claw her way out to sea, away from the coast, or she was lost. He scrambled across the deck to study the seas to port. A huge wave was approaching. He grabbed the nearest seaman. "Joe! Help Antoine on the wheel!" There wouldn't be time to handle the sails. "Hard away," he shouted. "Turn hard away!" The wave passed, drenching the decks with icy green water. As it left them and struck the pinky, he saw the sailor on the pinky's tiller disappear in the huge wave. With the firm hand gone, the pinky broached to and lost way. Louis couldn't spare the time to watch the pinky's recovery . . . she was behind them now. He raced to the wheel, giving help to the men trying to return *Le Volant* to her original heading.

Through gritted teeth, Joe explained, "We double-reefed but it all changed so fast."

"You should have called me."

Joe had a simple reply. "Yes."

"We'll be all right." He nodded to the two men. "Maintain course. I'm going to see what happened to the pinky." From the taffrail at the stern, Louis could see the pinky was hove to with a double-reefed foresail, bow into the wind, trying to hold her own against tide and tempest. He heard the shout of warning and gripped the railing as another wave passed over them. As he watched, the wave crashed into the pinky. When the wave had cleared, the pinky was gone. He wiped the salt water from his eyes but, in the closing darkness, there was nothing to be seen.

The next day, *Le Volant* entered the harbour of Baie Fortune. Louis was surprised to see an English ship moored in the stream. *This doesn't look good*, he thought. *What business do the English have here?*

Although Louis couldn't possibly know it, what was happening at Baie Fortune was happening all across The Island of Saint John.

It Happened at Malpeque

Earlier that year, the very same vessel that Louis discovered at Baie Fortune sailed past Bird Island and up the channel to the moorings in front of the little village known as the Malpeque Settlement. The ship took up her position. Joseph Arsenault and Pierre Bernard watched as the crew set riding lights and doubled up the mooring lines.

"Ils se préparent pour la nuit . . . They are getting ready for the night," Joseph said.

Puffs of smoke came from the ship's galley. Lights came on in the stern cabin. Somewhere on the vessel, a fiddle was being played and male voices could be heard taking up the melody, a refrain unfamiliar to the Islanders.

Madeleine Arsenault and Anne Marie Bernard came down the hill. Madeleine took her husband's hand in hers. "Que penses-tu qu'ils veulent . . . What do you think they want?"

The other families joined them at the shore until everyone was there, staring at the ship, wondering what it could mean to them.

Pierre Bernard summed it up. "Ils sont anglais . . . They are English. It can't be good." He took his wife by the arm and they walked slowly back to their cottage.

Eventually, only Joseph Arsenault stood on the beach, watching the ship, anticipating the worst. Toward the end of twilight, he saw a short man with heavy black whiskers come out of the main cabin and saunter across the deck. The man leaned on the bulwark and stared at the houses. Joseph waved. The man continued to stare at the shore.

In the early evening darkness, Joseph returned to his home on the hill. All the way back, he felt that the little man with the black whiskers was still standing where Joseph had last seen him, his eyes piercing the darkness—like an angel of death—seeking out the soft, vital parts of Joseph's soul.

At first light, the ship's bell was sounded—intermittently—for over fifteen minutes. At the end of that time, a longboat came around the bow from the far side of the ship where it must have been lowered, out of sight of the villagers. Seated in the stern was the little man, seemingly unmoved by the boat's motion or the waves on the choppy water. He stepped ashore, dry shod, and walked up the beach to the village well. He waited until the villagers had gathered closer and then he began to speak. He spoke in a conversational manner as if everyone could understand his English. The interpreter was hard pressed to keep up but did raise his voice enough to be heard even at the edges of the crowd.

"I am David Higgins, business agent for His Excellency, Captain Walter Patterson, Governor of The Island of Saint John. He sends his greetings and asks me to give you information that is vital to your survival."

"All lands on The Island of Saint John have been deeded to proprietors who will soon be coming from England to take possession of their property just as Governor Patterson has taken possession of Lot 19 on the eastern shores of the bay. When the new owner of Lot 13 . . ."—Higgins spread his arms to encompass everything that was in the area—" . . . which is this property, comes here, he might not want you to remain here. It might be in the depth of winter or the middle of the growing season, but you will be required to leave and go somewhere else."

The Islanders gasped. Joseph clenched his fists and moved as if to attack the little man but it was then the Islanders realized that the sailors were well armed and, apparently, quite ready to defend the governor's man.

David Higgins continued as if there were no disturbance. "Your governor offers his protection. He suggests that you move to lands under his direct supervision, and you will be free to carry on with your lives as before. As tenants of His Excellency, you will be given transportation to your new homes and a year of free rent to give you time to get settled in.

"I will be here for two days. During that time, my man"—Higgins pointed at the interpreter—"will take your names and acquire the details concerning your baggage. If there are any of you willing to risk waiting for the arrival of the new English proprietor for Lot 13—and gamble on the possible extent of his generosity—and he could demand rents from you for the past years of your occupation of these lands—then, by all means, make your wishes known and, when we sail away from here in two days' time, we will leave you on the beach."

Higgins squared his shoulders and walked past the hushed crowd to the beach where he stepped into the boat and returned to the ship.

Two days later, the English ship transported the residents to the eastern shore of Malpeque Bay.[2]

What Happened Near the Royalty of Princetown

Near the Royalty of Princetown, on Lot #18, the newly arrived tenants considered themselves lucky to be alive.

Hugh McKendrick was exhausted. As soon as he had gathered his friends and relatives about him further up the beach and in the shelter of the forest, he had hiked to where he believed there was a town only to find that the Royalty Town of Princetown existed mainly on paper. In truth, there were some surveyor's pegs and a few houses, but not much else. When he had told the only English-speaking person he could find that the freighter *Annabella* had been shipwrecked off Princetown, the resident had shrugged his shoulders and closed his door.

Hugh trudged back to where he had left his family to find that most of the eighty survivors of the shipwreck were gone. His eldest son, James, raced to him, "Father! Some Frenchies came and took the women and children away." He pointed in the direction of the foundering ship. "The men are scavenging along the beach, trying to recover anything that might drift ashore."

"Were the Frenchies hostile?"

"No, sir. They brought blankets and tended to the children right away. They were most Christian, Father."

"You sure your mother is all right?"

"Yes, sir. I went along. They are tucked in, warm and all cozy."

It was Hugh's turn to shrug. "Then we must see if there is anything we can rescue from the wreck." The McKendrick men went to the beach where James waded out, chest-deep, to pull in a package or two, but otherwise the supplies, personal belongings, seeds, and farm implements were lost. That evening, around fires on the beach, the Highlanders of Argyleshire considered their position.

Donald McDougald was the very first to complain about the proprietor, Captain John Stewart, who had convinced the McDougalds to leave Scotland for the fairyland that was to be

The Island of Saint John. "Milk and honey, he said. Told me that we could take the cleared land that used to belong to the French . . ."

"That was Nova Scotia where they got the cleared land." James McNutt was not from Argyleshire but he had earned the McDougalds' respect during the forty days at sea so there was no argument with his flat statement. "And the proprietor—if in fact he didn't lie to you—it was to his advantage to paint a pretty picture of this country."

The listeners waited; they were used to giving McNutt lots of time to develop his ideas.

"The proprietors got title to this land when they promised to bring new settlers at the rate of one person for every two hundred acres. They had to have 'em here before ten years were up, an' the settlers could only be Protestants from Europe and North America."

Hugh McKendrick got everyone's attention when he laughed. "Then I'm from Paris, I guess."

McNutt, a man with no sense of humour, countered, "There'd be no Protestants in Paris."

Not to be cowed, Hugh smiled and said, "There'd be no Europeans in Scotland."

McNutt persisted with his serious train of thought: "The proprietors got title when they promised to pay annual quitrents of say, thirty pounds, to the Royal Treasury."

A new voice from the far shadows of the bonfire spoke next: "Well, how do they profit from that?" The men craned their necks to see that it was young Andrew Grey speaking. "Thirty pounds is a lot of money."

McNutt spoke again. "They got title to a big piece of land. They got us to improve it and make it more valuable. They got us to pay them rents every year as we're improvin' their land makin' it more valuable."

There was silence around the fire.

Finally, Andrew Grey stood up. "I think I have had enough for today." He moved closer to the fire and scuffed a hollow in the sand for his hip. He took off his shortcoat and lay down on the sand, carefully fitting his hip into the hollow. Then he pulled his shortcoat over his torso and closed his eyes.

Soon all of the men were down, their eyes closed, but few of them were able to shut out their anger at the inept ship's pilot who had wrecked the *Annabella*—and their dreams—on the shores of Malpeque Bay.

The Acadians did what they could for the stranded Scots but it was a winter of starvation. Making matters worse, come spring, the men had no tools to clear the heavily wooded shores of Lot #18. Somehow, they learned of the abandoned French settlement where the land was already cleared and cultivation could be started right away. The Scots took matters into their own hands and moved to the abandoned farms of Lot #13—what had once been known as the Malpeque Settlement.[3]

It Happened at Other Places

The proprietors of Lot #24, Charles Lee and Francis MacLean, took title to their lands but made no effort to register the sixteen Acadian families who had settled near Rustico.[4] Nor did they arrange for Protestant European or North American settlers to come to Lot #24, or any other settlers for that matter. After 1787, title to the lands changed a number of times and the Acadians came to terms with each new proprietor but, eventually, some of the Acadians were not able to pay their rents. They were left with no choice but to migrate. Acadians in default of their rent went to Cape Breton.[5]

Hundreds of other unfortunate souls—returning Acadians, Catholic and Protestant Scots—suffered at the hands of unyielding proprietors as tenants and indentured servants.

Meanwhile, While It Was Happening at Baie Fortune

Meanwhile, at Baie Fortune, Louis Arsenault saw to the careful mooring of his vessel before he ordered the boat's crew to lower the longboat. When all was ready, Louis sat on the stern-sheets and looked over the heads of his men at the crowd of people gathered on the shore. He could see that a little man with black whiskers was at the centre of the crowd, while a half-dozen armed sailors provided a protective ring around him. The Acadians of Baie Fortune were restive and, as the longboat's keel grated on the beach, he could hear the anger as they shouted at the little man. Louis felt pity for the centre of such hostility—until he found out what was going on.

A big, rough-looking man, Luke Chiasson, was shaking his fist at the impassive face of the Englishman, making absolutely no impact there. The spittle that flew from Luke's lips as he harangued the stupid little Englishman made no apparent impression either.

"After the Grand Dérangement, the English told us to take the oath of allegiance and we took the oath of allegiance," Luke shouted.

Mister Higgins held up his hand to still the irate Acadian while the interpreter slowly worked his way down the sentence. When he was finished, Higgins lowered his hand and Luke continued with his angry arguments.

"We were told that we could live here, and we came."

The imperious hand went up and the interpreter completed the sentence. Luke didn't wait for the hand signal before he charged on.

"We were told the land was ours and each of us was given a deed by the English officers who were here at the time . . ." Luke ignored the hand but did stop when Higgins began to speak in a very quiet voice and the interpreter translated as he continued.

"I am aware that you were permitted to move here. Permission from the Board of Trade was given to you in 1764 and you gave your oath in the presence of the British naval commander who signed papers that said the land was yours—conditional upon your remaining loyal subjects of the British Crown—but those papers were worthless. The naval officer had no jurisdiction here. However, the permission to live here, granted to you by the Board of Trade, is still in effect . . . "

Mister Higgins stepped back within the ring of sailors as the anger of the Acadians rose but he continued with his speech.

"I am the business agent of Vice Admiral Sir George Rodney, proprietor of Lot 43—the lands hereabout at Baie Fortune constitute Lot 43—and he invites you to continue to live here in quiet enjoyment of your possessions." The Acadians had become less vocal so Higgins stepped forward again to the edge of the armed sailors. "The acreage that you use will be tallied by my men and you will be provided with a reckoning of the annual rents that you will pay"—the uproar was more threatening than before, and Higgins raised his voice—"and the arrears for"—he stepped back into the middle of his escort—"the past years that you have been occupying the Admiral's land." The sailors formed a wedge around the little man and they marched to the beach where Higgins boarded the craft. The sailors were on the alert for trouble as they took turns stepping into the craft. Most of the boat's crew remained on guard, holding their muskets at the ready, while two of their number plied the oars. When the boat was deemed to be far enough from the shore, the muskets were stowed and the craft speedily returned to the ship, where Higgins disappeared into the main cabin.

Louis walked past a weeping woman who was holding an infant to her breast. She glared at him, probably thinking he was English. Louis was very prompt with his "Bonjour, Madame," accompanied by his hand to the forepeak of his hat as a polite salute. "Does this village have a carpenter?" he asked.

With her free hand, the woman wiped the tears from her cheek and pointed to an older man with rounded shoulders. "He makes caskets," she said and, weeping again, ran into the arms of a young man who consoled her with small mewing sounds. As Louis passed them by, he heard the woman ask, "What shall we do? Where shall we go?" The baby began bawling and Louis did not hear the reply.[6]

The casket maker was in the middle of a heated conversation, so Louis stepped to one side and waited. He thought, *I wonder what these people will do?* He shook his head. *It has nothing to do with me; I live at Miscou. These people should move away, just like we did.* He saw that the casket maker was finished with his argument.

"Good day, sir. I need to replace some spars on my ship. Can you do it for me?"

"If you bring me one, I can shape some wood for you. How many pieces?"

"At least two, but I will probably need some spares. She's a fine old ship but every new day brings its own problems." Louis touched the peak of his cap. "I will see you tomorrow."

Endnotes

1. There aren't many places on The Island that had grey sand, but this was one of them.

2. Acadians who fled the Malpeque Settlement for the largely uninhabited area of Tignish and Cascumpec (Lots 1, 2 and 5) were confronted by their proprietor (John Hill) in 1814 who demanded his rents for the "improved" lands. Some Acadians attempted to come to terms with this owner and subsequent legal owners, while others were forced to move on to somewhere else where they would have been confronted again.

3. According to J.M. Bumsted in his *Land, Settlement, and Politics on Eighteenth-Century Prince Edward Island*, Captain Stewart did not pursue these settlers. Another group of seventy Scots arrived at Lot #18 in 1771. Their first winter was also one of starvation.

4. When parcels of Lot #24 became available (probably during the distraint proceedings of 1776 and the land sales of 1781), several well-to-do Acadians bought their properties but the majority remained as tenants. *The Island Acadians 1720-1980* by Georges Arsenault.

5. *The Island Acadians 1720-1980*

6. According to Georges Arsenault in his book *The Island Acadians 1720-1980*, the residents became tenants but were not provided with leases. When Higgins died in 1783, the tenants were unsure of their position relative to the absentee proprietor. In 1786 and 1787, a number of families emigrated to Cape Breton; a dozen settled in Cheticamp. In 1788 another group sought escape from the proprietor system in the Margaree area of Cape Breton. Baie Fortune residents who believed they had valid title to their land sought relief in the courts but the system was unfairly tilted against them; when they lost, more residents moved to Cape Breton. In 1801 and 1802, others bought small farms on Lot 44 and became the first settlers at Rollo Bay.

Chapter Seven
Beginnings

July 1773
The Farm
Near Saint Peter's Harbour

They both looked up when they heard their son's whistle. It was the "a stranger comes" call. Reine and Robert knew that the boy would lead the stranger around the end of the brook and approach the cottage across the open field; in that way, Robert could get a good look at the stranger and assess the situation. Meanwhile, it gave the parents the opportunity to hide their precious possessions.

Reine took the iron pot from the crane in the hearth and placed it—contents and all—in the hole in the ground that was made for it. Robert hid the musket but shoved the pistol in the slot by the door where it could be readily available; if it had been the danger signal, both weapons would have been left out. Reine was wrapping their knives in a leather pouch when she realized that her daughter had not yet left for Joseph's place, which was further into the woods. Reine continued wrapping the knives but the tone of her voice betrayed her irritation: "Rosalie! You know what your duties are! Now, go!"

When the girl didn't move, Reine stuffed the knives in the hollow log at the end of the woodpile and turned on her daughter like an old she-cat. She was advancing on the girl when Joseph Farrow came running up the back.

"I heard the whistle but Rosalie didn't come." He looked at the two women—he realized at that moment that he no longer thought of Rosalie as a child—who were acting like a pair of fighters getting set for a match. Knowing Reine's fascination with English words, Joseph asked, "Which one of you is the grimalkin?"

If Joseph thought he might defuse the situation by using

117

an old-world word for a spiteful woman, he was mistaken. Both women turned on him, Rosalie being the first to react.

"I don't appreciate it when you talk down to me."

"And I don't like it when you use words that you know I don't understand."

"I didn't mean no harm." He stepped back a pace or two. "I just thought—"

"Well, you thought wrong," Rosalie said but, seeing the concerned look on her dear, sweet Joseph's face, she relented somewhat. "What does grimal— whatever mean?"

As an old soldier, Joseph saw a chance to seek cover, which he did. "My Ma used to . . ."

Reine had lost all patience with her daughter. She pointed at the door. "You go, now! Take her with you, Joseph."

Rosalie smiled at Joseph. "It's Robbie and his whistle. He whistles all the time. There probably isn't a stranger within forty miles and, if there is, he's no more a threat to me"—she faced her mother—"than he is to you, Mother."

Mother grasped her daughter by the arm and turned her toward the door. "You go, now! Go with her, Joseph."

The girl pulled away. "I don't have to—"

"This is not the time to discuss it. Your father made the rules—gave us our duties—and yours is to go to Joseph's house." Reine flicked her hand in a form of dismissal. "Take her, Joseph. I must go to the front and back up Robert." Reine left.

Joseph shrugged his shoulders and offered his arm to the twelve-year-old.

Rosalie stamped her foot and was on the verge of refusing when they heard voices from the front. Rosalie smiled and took Joseph's arm. "Take me, my dear Joseph Farrow, but take me out the front."

By this time there was some laughter, so Joseph again did what he was told. He led the young girl out the front where Robbie was saying to his father, "Antoine Arsenault has dropped by for a visit." Robbie saw a hint of amusement in his parents' eyes at the thought that a young man, from Miscou, sailing into Havre Saint Pierre, would leave his ship and stroll through the woods to the Leblanc farm—just for a visit. "Should I fetch Rosalie back from Joseph's farm?"

Rosalie walked through the door. "I'm right here, brother dear." She smiled her prettiest smile at the young sailor with the large biceps. "Hello again, Antoine. How nice of you to come by."

So it begins, Reine thought with a sense of pride in her beautiful daughter.

So it begins, Joseph Farrow thought with a distinct sense of loss as Rosalie let go of his arm.

September 1773
Oakwood Manor
Handsworth, England

The elder Joseph beckoned his twenty-three-year-old son to join him at the desk, his hands shaking with excitement as he moved the documents around on the desktop so that Young Joseph would be able to read them.

"This deed gives us title to land on The Island of Saint John. We have an estate in the new world larger than Oakwood!"

Young Joseph picked up the deed. He saw the Smallwood name and the description of the property.

His father shuffled the papers and withdrew from the file a sheet with a large red seal. "This is our undertaking to pay a yearly rent to the Crown."

"Why do we have to pay rent if we own the land?"

Joseph was always disappointed in his son's limited grasp of family business. He cast an exasperated look, as though expecting to find the extra hole in the boy's head where all practical sense had fallen out to the floor! *Good God! I paid for this boy to be given lessons in everything but if it didn't pass from the lips of his tutors or appear on his Eton slate, it doesn't exist! The insufferable whelp!*

The elder Joseph forced a weak smile to his lips. "When I was a boy, I asked questions around the estate. I wanted to know how things were done and I grew to understand that the Crown was the source of our wealth and power." He stopped, hesitated, and then cast his eyes down so his son would not see his indecision. *Nobody had to teach me that! Damn! To think that someday* . . . Joseph felt the lump in his groin . . . *perhaps someday soon . . . this boy will be Master of Oakwood.* He decided to try another approach.

"Son, you must pay more attention to the workings of the family business." Joseph indicated the smaller chair on the other side of the desk. "Sit down, opposite me." He waited for the boy to get settled before he went on to explain that the fortunes of the Smallwood family were inextricably attached to the fortunes of the English Crown.

"Smallwoods contributed mightily to the victory of English arms over the heathen Indians and French in North America. Your great-great-uncle James and cousin William were in the fore of the battles during the French and Indian wars and, while we didn't have a Smallwood at Louisbourg or Quebec, our money was there . . . permitting our King to field the finest army money could buy to win North America for the Crown in 1763."

The father studied the face of his son to see if there was any understanding. Dissatisfied with what he apparently saw, he asked, "Did your tutors instruct you about the wars in America?"

"No, Father. I was taught about the European wars, the subjugation of the Scots and, of course, India." Young Joseph said with some pride, "I can list the treaty maharajahs—" The boy was visibly disappointed when the father interrupted.

"The decisive battle was the capture of Fortress Quebec. From that moment on, the success of English arms in North America was assured and, for families in royal favour like us Smallwoods, it was an unprecedented opportunity to increase our wealth and influence. With the French vanquished, new lands were open for colonization and that colonization would be accomplished in an orderly, English manner."

It was the boy's turn to interrupt. "I understand the principle of 'to the victor go the spoils,' Father. I do understand that . . . but I don't understand why, if we have royal title to lands, we must pay rent for those lands."

"Son, I will explain about the rents." Joseph seemed annoyed as he waved away the boy's question and continued, "But first, I must say that this wonderful day has been a long, long time coming. Why, as far back as 1764, I had been told that I would get an estate on The Island. Of course, I didn't know which of the lots we would get." He noted the quizzical look on his son's face, so he continued, "Saint John's Island was divided into 3 counties and 67 lots. Let's see." He picked up the first document and read it for a moment. "We just acquired ownership of most of Lot number 38. That's our land now."

Young Joseph forgot about the rent because another thought struck him. "Does this mean we will leave Oakwood?"

The father paused for a moment and again studied the face of his only male offspring. *He's a good-looking enough lad but is he really this dense? Somehow, the role the Smallwoods play in the grand march of the British Empire across the face of the world is lost on this youth.*

"No. Smallwoods will never leave Oakwood!" He riffled through the file and extracted a document, holding it up for the boy to see. "This gives us title to the North American land." He selected another impressive-looking parchment, and handing this one to the boy to hold, said, "And this one ensures we understand our obligations to the Crown."

The boy attempted to read the document but the legal prose defeated him. "What does it mean, Father?"

The boy's respectful tone reminded Joseph of the role he had to play in the development of his son. His irritability faded. "Pull that chair around here so we can both look at the documents while we discuss the terms of the land grant."

When the boy was settled and the documents spread out before them, the father gave meaning to all the dry words on the various documents. He concluded by saying, "It is our responsibility to ensure that Saint John's Island is developed properly which, by the way, we can do ourselves by emigrating to The Island or by renting the land to peasants and remaining at Oakwood. In either case, as landlord, we are obliged to pay annual quitrents to the Crown to finance the cost of governing and colonizing." Joseph put the papers down. "As I said, son, English development of this new land will not be done haphazardly."

The elder Joseph opened a drawer in the desk and pulled out a decanter and two glasses. "We will engage a competent overseer and money will pour into the Oakwood estate coffers," he said as he poured a generous portion of port into one glass and a token amount into the other. He handed the second glass to his son. "The combination of healthy peasants, competent overseers, and English law backed by the invincible power of the Royal Navy, will ensure our prosperity."

Joseph raised his glass. "Our title became effective last week. In approximately six months, we will receive our first rents from our tenants. Here's to our prosperity!" Joseph drank his port. He poured another.

Young Joseph seemed puzzled. "How did we get people to move to The Island so quickly?"

Joseph sipped from his glass, pleased with the wine and the intelligent question. "As I understand it, there were some French settlers who have been living there since 1715." He sipped his port and reached for a cigar. "And some Acadians who came when the Governor of Nova Scotia warned them off."

Young Joseph tried the port. He put it down. "The governor warned them off for what reason?"

"If they didn't swear allegiance to the English Crown they were obliged to leave Nova Scotia. The ones who didn't leave of their own free will were expelled in 1755."

"There have been people living on The Island for up to fifty years?"

"No matter, Île Saint-Jean is English now. The Acadians and the French and," here, Joseph waved his arms wide, "anybody else who wants to, can live on Lot number 38 as our tenants."

Joseph offered to top up his son's glass.

Young Joseph shook his head "no." "The payment of rents; tenants to Oakwood and Oakwood to Crown, do we make money on the rents?"

"Not really."

Young Joseph was confused. "We don't make money on the rents?"

"By the time we pay an agent to manage our business there won't be much left but—I don't mean to mislead you—there'll be some profit. The big thing is the land. It's the land that's important, my son."

Joseph had helped himself to another glass of port. He made another broad, sweeping gesture with his free hand. "Behind the mighty shield of the Royal Navy and the British Army, English Law provides a system of ownership and land title. British Peace gives stability. Where there is stability and a system that provides for the orderly transfer of wealth, land values steadily increase. Tenants come and go, governments change, but the land is always there. It's always the land, my son."

A servant's voice could be heard in the hall. "Both gentlemen are in the master's office, Miss Hélène."

Young Joseph jumped to his feet. "Would you excuse me, sir?"

"What's wrong, son?"

They could hear the footsteps coming down the hall.

"Sir, she's always trying to mother me—giving me advice, telling me what to do—and she's just my sister!" Young Joseph anxiously glanced at the door. "Please, sir, may I be excused?" He saw the continued hesitation on his father's face, so he made his most telling argument. "You don't like it when she tells you what to do!"

The father pointed at a little door set into the woodwork. "Use my private door to the biffy."

Young Joseph disappeared into the concealed door just as his sister entered the office.

Hélène Smallwood scanned the room. "That dumb servant said that Young Joseph was here." She sucked her teeth. "He must be getting old. You should think of replacing him—move him out to the barns—get a younger servant."

Joseph waved the thought away. "I have the deed to our land in the New World! It arrived today."

"Why didn't you call me?"

"I thought the men of the family should go over the documents first." When he saw the scowl on his daughter's face, he added, "You want Young Joseph to know his place . . . that he will be master of Oakwood Manor . . ."

It was Hélène's turn to wave a thought away. "Tell me the details."

"Captain Patterson had acquired several lots for his own use." He could see his daughter getting ready to pepper him with questions so he hurried on, "One of the lots—Lot number 38—he has granted to us."

"*Granted* to us?" Hélène was suspicious of Irishmen, particularly this Irishman; she didn't like the man. When her father didn't answer right away, she prompted, "How much did you give him?"

"Eight hundred pounds."

"My God!" Hélène paced back and forth. "And the folderol about finding Protestant tenants . . . he has done some of that?"

"Some of it."

"How much of it?"

"I don't know. I will hire a business agent. He will find out for us and report back."

And so it begins, Hélène thought, *I will have two estates to manage.* She gave her father one of "those looks."

Her father flinched. *What is she going to tell me to do now?*

"How are you going to find an honest manager?"

Joseph beamed. "I already have someone in mind." *Yes, Captain Patterson gave me his name.*

October 1773
Charlotte Town Waterfront[1]

"We were lucky!" Joseph Farrow clapped young Robbie on the back. "This is probably the last ship for Halifax this season."

"Yes." Robbie fingered the leather sack of coins in his pocket, feeling uncomfortable that he had accepted it. "Yes, we are very lucky," he repeated as his mind wandered. He fingered the little sack again. *I wonder what the old guy had to do to get all this money.*

Joseph seemed to sense what was going on in Robbie's mind. "Don't you worry none about the money. It's like . . ." —he searched for the word—"like found money." He shrugged his shoulders. "I didn't have to do much to get it." He gave the young man a sly wink. "It was mostly McIntyre's doin'. Besides, there's nothin' to spend it on at the farm. And you . . . you wouldn't be gettin' to Montreal unless you had some money."

"It's the chance of a lifetime! A new fur company that's hiring . . ."

"You follow your heart, Robbie. Your father and I did." Joseph put his arm around the young man's shoulders and led him toward the entry port of the Halifax-bound ship. "You know better than I do why your father couldn't come down to see you off." Joseph leaned close so that he could whisper, "I thought we had it all fixed up for your Pa when we signed off on Corporal Miles at Halifax." He patted Robbie's arm. "But I am honoured that you shared the family secret with ol' Joseph Farrow."

Robbie hoisted his duffel bag onto his shoulder. "I plan to leave Halifax as soon as the ice is out of the Saint Lawrence. McTavish, the chairman of the North West Company, is looking for Scots to go out into the wilderness and trade with the Indians. In the spring, I'm going to be his man."

"I know you will be successful." Joseph Farrow stepped back as the sailors closed the entry port. There was a lot of activity on the deck. Robbie said something but Joseph couldn't hear it. He pointed to his ear and shook his head. Robbie nodded that he understood.

The ship moved very slowly away from the pier but, before very long, Joseph Farrow was a small figure in the distance, soon to be lost to sight as the ship left the harbour and sailed into the Northumberland Strait.

Robbie gave one last wave, just in case the family friend could see him. He pulled his collar closer to his neck as he felt the chill of the waters in the strait. *That's that*, he thought. *The deed is done. For better or worse, it is a new beginning for Robbie Cameron.*[2]

December 1773
Alexander Richardson's Tavern[3]
Charlotte Town

"Gentlemen, we are going to have to make some serious changes." He looked from face to face of the government officials he had called to a meeting. "We must have a new beginning and what I am talking about is our salaries; actually, the fact that we have not been receiving any salaries."

Most of the faces remained non-committal, but Governor Patterson was not concerned. He would appeal to their greed. *Gets them every time*, he thought.

Patterson cast a glance at his Irish compatriot, Attorney General Phillips Callbeck. *No, Callbeck is probably the one person in this room who has no need for his salary; he receives graft, not only as attorney general, but also as surrogate-general and as judge of probate.*

A tiny frown of worry crossed Patterson's brow as he considered David Higgins next. *And David has plenty of opportunity as a business agent to skim off sizeable amounts with no one the wiser. And to think I made him responsible for licensing all departures from The Island. It was a fine idea at the time— to prevent indentured servants from escaping from The Island— but I certainly handed it over to the wrong man if I thought it would produce any revenue.*[4]

Thomas Wright? Our Surveyor? Well, maybe I can count on him.
Patterson shook his head, and maybe not. *Wright's development plan for Charlotte Town originally called for building lots
eighty-four feet wide. When he was finished with it, the sneaky
little bookworm had provided for some prime lots—one hundred
feet wide—that fronted on the river. One-hundred-foot lots that
fronted on the river! How thoughtful! How clever! How profitable
for the little bugger!*

Governor Patterson glanced at the rest of his entourage:
Burns, Duport, Lawson, Allanby, Fergus—*yes, even my old
friend, Fergus*—they all have their scams. He smirked. *As I have
mine.* The smirk left his face as he recalled that he had been
forced to dip into his wife's money to keep things going. *When
Hester finds out how much I have spent, there will be the devil to
pay!* He forced that tender thought from his mind. In a very
cheerful manner he signalled the barkeep.

"Master Innkeeper! A round for the gentlemen, if you
please! We will begin our business with a toast to the King!"

By the time the rum had been served and the toast given
and answered, Patterson felt his confidence returning, as he
watched the familiar rum flush creep up the faces of the governing body of Saint John's Island. *We'll do a much better job
of running this island than those Halifax scallywags . . . a much
better job of lining our pockets, too.* Governor Patterson
cleared his throat. "The Earl of Hillsborough is gone but
the principle that our salaries would be paid out of the
quitrents is not." He picked up his rum glass and savoured
the contents. He smacked his lips as he put down the empty
glass.

"We now have to deal with Lord Dartmouth. Perhaps
Dartmouth is not aware that our personal well-being—our
salaries—are not dependent upon some of the proprietors
paying the quitrent to the Crown; they are dependent upon all
of the proprietors paying what they owe."

Patterson signalled the innkeeper to top up the glasses.
Soon the pungent smell of dark rum filled the room.

Fergus raised his glass and downed it in one gulp, then

looked around to see that he was the only official to have done so. He belched. "It's not sippin' rum, it isn't."

Patterson smiled, weakly. "In '71 we passed a bill that would allow us to distraint lots upon which the quitrents were in arrears. That would have given us the right to sell the seized lots at public auction. The proceeds would have paid off the overdue quitrents, the arrearages in our salaries would have been made up . . ."

"And we would be as happy as pigs in shit," Fergus quipped.

"Er, yes."

Patterson could see that Chief Justice John Duport had not touched his drink since the toast to the King. That was a bad sign; the lawyer in Duport might be troublesome to Patterson's plan. It wasn't long in coming to the fore.

"Your legislation was disallowed because there is no legal recourse for us to recover the salary arrears. Salaries were to be paid out of quitrents. If there were a shortfall in quitrents, our salaries would be reduced, proportionally." He leaned forward as he made his point. "We all knew that when we accepted our appointments here." John Duport shifted in his seat so he could have eye contact with the governor. "Unless you have something hidden up your sleeve, Walter?"

"I plan to seek the support of the influential group formed by proprietors—resident in England—to bring pressure to bear on . . . "

"For what purpose?" It was Patrick Fergus again. "They're not so special! We are the same as they are,"—he tapped his glass on the table—"except one of us is an Irishman with an empty glass." He swivelled his head around. "A lot of us are Irish but I'm the only one with the empty glass."

When Patterson didn't signal the barkeep to look after Fergus's drink, John Duport said, "Put it on my tab." He smiled at Fergus, "The point is well made, Patrick. What can this . . . lobby group . . . in England accomplish that we haven't tried to get done ourselves?"

Suddenly very serious, Patterson explained in depth. "The

proprietors maintain a close relationship with the parties in power. Aside from this intimate social contact with the nobility and senior officials, they are the people who have given good and faithful service to the Crown and, consequently, their requests always bear special consideration. The proprietors also cultivate friendships with secondary government officials so that they are kept well informed; under-secretaries have been known to promote the proprietors' views with no inducement other than wishing to please a particular proprietor."

John Duport nodded his head to show that he understood.

Patterson continued, "I plan to ask the proprietors to present a memorial to the Secretary of State for the Colonies for an annual parliamentary grant to support our salaries. That way we get away from the quitrent problem."

"Yes, the proprietors would be pleased to have the matter fade away too; they are the ones who are delinquent in the payment of their quitrents." John Duport rubbed his chin. "The Secretary of State will want something in return. What have you got to give?"

"I'll promise to give the money back." Patterson spoke loudly over the flood of questions, suppressing them while he explained. "When our proprietor friends tell us that there will be positive results from their efforts, we will pass legislation that will frighten the pants off anyone who hasn't paid their quitrent; it will say that the arrears of the quitrents should be enforced by legal proceedings. It will further state that the money so obtained from the sale of properties will be used as a refund to Crown coffers."

"But—"

"I know, I know. We will have to give certain assurances to our proprietor supporters that any legal actions taken under this legislation will be quite selective . . . or perhaps none will be taken. We will see how much delinquent quitrent is forthcoming before we decide what we choose to do." The governor looked around the room. "If I have your acquiescence . . . ?"

Most of the members responded in the affirmative. Patrick Fergus was asleep.

As Patterson shook hands all around he explained, "I will have to go to England in the near future to make sure that all goes well." He was shaking hands with Phillips Callbeck when he said, "You won't mind acting as governor in my absence, Phillips?"

"Not at all, Walter."

As Phillips stepped back to allow other supplicants their moment in the limelight, he was quick to sense the changes in the room. Certainly there continued to be a feeding circle around the governor, but a growing number of the Governor's cronies were attaching themselves to the group around the newly anointed acting governor. Phillips Callbeck could hardly contain himself as he realized what was happening.

Walter gets a law passed in England that guarantees our salaries—my salary—and promises to threaten delinquent proprietors so they will pay what they owe to the Crown. But not all the proprietors will have to take the threats seriously. No, not all of us; just the ones the current administration believes to be disloyal. And who will head that administration? Who will have a say—a large say—as to which proprietor is a genuine troublemaker or even merely a bothersome bane to our . . . my existence? His grin grew so wide that members of his coterie thought he was in pain and brought him a chair. He refused the chair as he assured his toadying friends that he was in excellent humour. *Phillips Callbeck, that's who! Me!* He suffered a true moment of weakness as he realized what this would mean to his wife. *Anne loves power. After I tell her, she won't be able to keep her hands off me!* He excused himself to his circle of friends and hurried out of the meeting, trying not to run.

Endnotes

1. Please note that, at this time, Charlottetown was spelled as two words.

2. In another book of the *Abuse of Power* series, *Crooked Paths*, Robbie Cameron joins the North West Company seeking riches and adventure as a fur trader in the far west.

3. According to J.M. Bumsted in his book *Land, Settlement, and Politics on Eighteenth-Century Prince Edward Island*, government meetings were held in Richardson's house/tavern because there were no public buildings.

4. For story purposes, I show David Higgins still on The Island in 1773. According to J.M. Bumsted, Higgins disappeared from The Island late in 1772. He didn't apply for a departure licence.

Chapter Eight
Visitors

June 1775
The Farm

Reine and Robert watched as Antoine Arsenault turned at the edge of the forest to wave farewell.

The couple raised their arms, Robert saying, "Rosalie! Step out of the house and give him a big wave." When his daughter didn't come out from behind them, Robert looked around; Rosalie was not there. Robert had kept on waving but their visitor was gone. He lowered his arm. "Where did she go?" Without waiting for an answer, he complained, "That girl has a fine young man who travels hundreds of miles to see her but she isn't even here to say goodbye."

"She was here. She said her goodbyes. She went off to Joseph's," Reine said, rather matter-of-factly. Reine looked at the surprised expression on Robert's face. "What do you expect?" Reine picked up the bucket of water she had been bringing from the brook when Antoine had announced his departure. "For years now, every time something is going on, we send her to Joseph's—a stranger comes, we send her to Joseph's." Reine grinned. "You want to make love . . ."

"I know, I know, we send her to Joseph's, but it doesn't mean that she should discourage a suitor . . ."

"A suitor? You think of Antoine as a suitor for your daughter's hand?"

"What else could he be looking for here?"

"I do truly believe he likes to listen to your stories about the British Army,"—Reine turned to place the water bucket on the table, averting her face so her husband wouldn't see her grin—"and he keeps coming back for more."

Robert caught his wife up in his arms. "Robert wants to make love," he whispered in her ear.

"Send Rosalie to Joseph's," Reine replied with the throaty

giggle that she knew he liked so much. She withdrew from her husband's grasp and backed up toward the ladder to the sleeping loft.

Robert pretended to stalk his wife but he stopped. "That sounded like a horse," he said, surprised.

"Hello, the house!" Someone was in their front yard!

Robert made sure that the pistol was in the slot before stepping into the doorway. He could hear Reine in the back, getting the musket, checking the prime, laying out powder and ball on the ledge where it would be accessible. He knew she would remain out of sight with her finger on the trigger.

The rider dismounted. "I wouldn't have known that you were in here if I hadn't seen the young man coming out onto the trail. I'm Liam Phelan, business agent for Joseph Smallwood Esquire, proprietor of Lot 38."

Robert nodded his head in acknowledgement of the introduction but otherwise said nothing.

"I came through last year, collecting rents from tenants, but I guess I missed you." Phelan craned his neck, looking beyond the cottage to see if there were any more houses. "You the only ones in here?"

Robert, secure that Reine was behind him with the musket, took a couple of steps forward. "You all alone?"

Suddenly very alert, the agent tied off his horse and stepped back, closer to his saddlebags. "My men are out on the road but we won't need them, now will we."

He's lying. He's alone. Wonder why he's all by himself? I heard that these bustards always come with an armed guard . . . "I don't know anything about a proprietor."

"He owns all the land around here." Phelan was breathing easier. *If I can get 'em talkin', I got 'em sewn up.* "Like I said, I came through last year collectin' the rents. If they couldn't pay, I warned 'em off; told 'em they had to be gone in a month. If they weren't gone when I came back, I would get the sheriff to move 'em off."

"You don't say."

Phelan pulled out his folder and ran his finger down a list.

"Most of 'em paid. The one's who didn't: John Sassong, Lewi Longapee, and Joe Arsnoe . . ."

"Did they leave?"

"Of course; it's always the Frenchies that move along. People who speak English understand tenancy and have a proper sense of accountability to their betters; I don't have to move 'em along."

"I don't intend to move along."

"Good!" He stepped off to one side. "Is that another house I see down the glen?"

"No."

"I see. Yes, well . . . well, I will have to calculate your annual rent." He consulted his folder again. Most of the farmers on Lot 38 take up fifty acres." His stylus poised over his little slate, Phelan politely asked, "And your name is?"

"This is my land. I am not paying rent. I am not moving on."

The agent's eyes shifted from Robert's face to the muzzle of a musket that protruded through the darkened doorway.

"Y-y-you are m-m-making a mistake." Without taking his eyes off the musket, Phelan stuffed his folder and slate in the saddlebag. He very slowly moved to untie his horse. After he was mounted and had gathered up the reins, he snarled at the unseen person in the doorway, "You took unfair advantage of me, sir!"

The musket was raised as the shadowy figure sighted along the barrel, the musket pointed true to the chest of the horseman.

Liam Phelan galloped off. Lying in the dust where it had fallen was the little slate with the stylus in the holder. Robert picked it up. He was going to toss it into the fire pit where they burned the trash but Reine told him not to.

"We can't afford to throw anything away, sweetheart."

"Maybe we just threw our lives away," Robert said with real concern in his voice.

"Yes. Maybe we did." Reine held her hand out for Robert to take. She led him toward the house. "We had better put the shutters down; he might have men waiting for him on the road." She grunted as she lifted the heavy wooden shutters off their pegs and lowered them. "When you wanted to build these things, I never thought we'd ever need them." She ran her hand around the edge of the gun port in the middle of the shutter. "Spider webs," she said. She shook her head. *This is no time to think about housecleaning.* "I'll finish up here. Go get Rosalie. Bring them both here," she said to her husband's back since he was already running down the path to Joseph's.

When she was finished with the shutters, Reine sat down and began to line up more powder and shot. *It was on the Bras d'Or Lakes that we promised ourselves that the English wouldn't ever push us off our land again.* She could see in her mind's eye the Highlanders coming down the hill, their bayonets thirsting for Acadian blood. She shivered.

She heard a commotion outside. She grabbed her musket and, crouching, sneaked a look out the gun port. She breathed a sigh of relief and stood up, waiting for the rest of the family to arrive. *Yes, Joseph Farrow is family,* she thought, when she saw Rosalie clutching his arm.

There were four of them so they could each take a window, standing watch on constant alert for hours. The family maintained a cautious vigil for many days, but after several weeks they returned to their old routines.

By the end of the summer, they had begun to believe that they would not see the agent again.

July 1775
Oakwood Manor
Handsworth, England

Young Joseph took his mother's arm as they walked down the path to the carriage. He could feel her hesitate at her favourite flowerbed but Joseph maintained a firm but discreet pressure on the arm so that she wouldn't linger.

Hannah Barrett Smallwood was a strong-willed woman and she wasn't being led by anyone, even if he was now the

Master of Oakwood. She stopped. "Your father loved his roses, didn't he?"

"Yes, he did."

"You will place some on his crypt, from time to time, won't you?"

"Yes, of course, Mother." Joseph took a step away but the woman did not follow his lead.

"Joseph, I want you to listen to your sister's advice. Your father listened—paid close heed—and the family prospered."

"Yes, Mother." Joseph stood still, waiting. He recognized the signs; *I am going to get a lecture.* Inwardly he was smiling: *this will be the last lecture I will ever have to endure. Father is dead. Mother is gone. And I will soon put that overbearing sister of mine in her proper place; yes, she may tend her flowers but I will tend to the Smallwood family interests. What is she saying?*

". . . still have our family concerns. This war in the Colonies; we have an estate there. I knew your Uncle James; he would not have wanted politics to come between the branches of the Smallwood family."

Joseph wore a pained look, but he did not interrupt his stepmother.

"Even with the war, you should be able to get letters through to Cousin William. Tell him of your father's death. Oh yes, don't forget to inform him about the coat of arms." She began walking toward the carriage. "Be tactful when you explain that the arms were only granted to the male descendants of Joseph's line. Your father asked for a boon from the heraldry people—that James's line be qualified—but your father was too weak near the end to follow through and make it happen."[1]

"I understand, Mother."

Joseph waved the carriage footman aside, saying, "I will help my mother in her ascent into the carriage."

The man bowed.

Hannah got in and sat down. She leaned forward to hold the little door so Joseph could not close it. "I hope you don't mind that I take your man with me?"

"No. Not at all, Mother." Joseph closed the door. "He used to work in the house but sister Hélène had him moved outside. You should find him doubly useful as an inside and an outside servant."

"Then it is goodbye, Joseph. Serve your King and your family, wisely."

"It is not goodbye, Mother. Au revoir would be more apt. I will let you know when I can visit at Barrett House."

"Yes, of course you will."

Joseph tapped the side of the carriage and the old Mistress of Oakwood was gone.

He returned to the house, where he found the new Mistress waiting.

"You didn't come out to say your goodbyes, Hélène."

Hélène ignored the comment. "You had letters and a dispatch this morning. Father would let me peruse them . . ."

"I am not Father."

"What was in the dispatch?"

"We are at war with the American Colonies."

"Any word from Cousin William?"

"He has raised a regiment . . ."

"A Royal American Regiment! How brave! Cousin William always yearned to be a soldier."

Joseph strode away from his sister, hoping to leave her female yapping behind. She followed him so he decided to be brutally frank about Cousin William's "yearnings to be a soldier."

"I did not bother to tell Mother, but William is a traitor!"

Hélène's mouth dropped and it was several seconds before she could bring herself to speak. "No! Never!"

"He has raised a regiment—using Smallwood money—in support of the rebels."

Hélène sat down. "I can't believe it!"

"He uses the family name. He is Colonel of Smallwood's Maryland Rifles. When he is caught, he will be hanged." Joseph leaned forward with what he believed would be the most telling thrust. "He will never, never be allowed to come back here." He watched for a reaction but there was none. "Your pipe dream with your lover—oh yes, I have heard the servants talking—is over." He smiled. "He will be hanged. He will die a traitor. You will never see him again."[2]

"I am disappointed in you, Joseph. You are petty." Hélène rose and smoothed her dress. "Have we heard from our business agent on The Island?"

"No. Our father had confirmation from Governor Patterson that Mister Phelan had undertaken his duties, but there has been nothing subsequent to that."

"I have been told that Governor Patterson will be coming to England. He has been granted a leave of absence to sponsor—"

"Would you stop your prattle, woman!" Joseph turned on his sister. "You have no idea what you are talking about!"

Prattle! Hélène was tempted to lay it all out—what should be done in the best interests of the family—but she knew Joseph would probably . . . Suddenly, Hélène decided how she was going to handle him. She began.

"When Patterson arrives in England, host a meeting here like Father did."

"Then what?"

"At that meeting you can support the governor's plan for The Island because what is good for the governor is probably most appropriate for his supporters." As if she had had a moment of revelation she added, "You can ask about our business agent and find out why we haven't heard from him."

With the gleam of satisfaction in his eyes, Joseph crowed, "So much for the all-seeing, all-knowing Mistress of Oakwood Manor!" He was going to continue in that vein but hesitated. *My bitch-sister—always hounding me—always telling me what to do. Sticking her nose in my business. Well, I am master here and soon she will be . . .*

Hélène saw the hesitation. *He was on the verge of telling me something. I would wager it was about Isabelle.* She pushed. "Well, the little man has something right! I am Mistress of Oakwood."

Joseph turned his back on the argument and reached for a decanter of port. He poured himself a glass but the gentleman in him would not let him ignore his sister. "Would you care for some port?"

"No, thank you. I prefer to have my wits about me when I am talking business with you." *A bit of flattery and* . . .

"It has nothing to do with our disagreement, Hélène, but you will not be Mistress of Oakwood much longer."

"Because you have . . .?"

"Because I have spoken for the hand of a suitable lady— a lady of substance—to become Mistress of Oakwood." He placed the top on the decanter. He raised the glass to his lips. "To Isabelle Ankatel-Jones." He sipped his port and then put the glass down. "Her father has blessed the union although I have yet to tender my proposal to Isabelle."

Tender his proposal . . . *my God!* "I am pleased for you both."

"As to the other business at hand, I apologize for my rudeness earlier, Hélène, but you couldn't possibly understand that this Patterson fellow is out to feather his own nest. His proposal, which the proprietors have been asked to sponsor, would place our family's interests at risk."

"How so?"

"He would have us obtain approval for a parliamentary grant to pay the salaries of Island officials—putting money into his own pocket, by the way. In return, he would have the Island government pass laws forcing proprietors to pay their quitrent arrears; that way the Crown would get its money back."

He is leaning the right way, I think. A little push . . . "You seem to have a fine understanding of the situation. However, you and Father left us in the position of being in arrears of our quitrents."

"Yes, but the governor has promised not to apply the law against his supporters."

"The promise was also made that we would be on the list of the original grantees. Instead, Father had to pay eight hundred pounds before he could become a proprietor."

"But he did eventually become a proprietor . . . just like they said he would."

One more push, Hélène thought. "It still cost us eight hundred pounds."

"It still was good value."

"Yes, but it was another broken promise."

Seeing his sister was going to argue further, he raised his hand. "Enough! I will not have that snake Mauger or that Patterson fellow in this house. I will not be seen to support his proposal"—he smiled slyly—"and I will not be seen opposing it, either."

Great! Hélène bowed her head. "You are the Master of Oakwood, Joseph."

Somewhat mollified, Joseph offered an olive branch. "In normal times, I would agree with you that we should take the first opportunity to check on our agent . . ."

"Phelan is Patterson's man . . ." *so by all means, we should check on him. I don't trust any of Patterson's minions,* she thought.

" . . . but these are not normal times." He picked up a dispatch case and held it out as though it was a bad fish. "I have been informed that American privateers are interrupting our commerce in the Gulf of Saint Lawrence. The King's Navy does not normally patrol that far off the trade routes and the brigands are having a high time." He dropped the case on the table. "Most likely our agent's correspondence is being intercepted." Joseph suppressed a yawn. "I will not become agitated about the situation until we are operating under more normal conditions."

"You are not going to ask the governor about Phelan?" She recognized the petulant are-you-going-to-lecture-me-again look. *Oh dear. This isn't going the way I planned. But he could be right; there might be nothing wrong with our agent. It might just be American pirates interfering with the empire's lines of communications. It won't take long for the King's Navy to correct the situation.* "Yes, of course, you are right, Joseph. We can wait for things to return to normal." She gave the young man her best-practised smile. "Thank you for being so patient with me and answering my questions." Hélène kept her eyes demurely downcast so she would not reveal her satisfaction that the Smallwoods were disassociating from the likes of Mauger and Patterson. *I did pretty well,* she gloated as she went down the hall. She turned the corner and feasted her eyes on the new manservant. *Found him in the stables.* She licked her lips. *Clean 'em up and they all look good.*

November 1775
Charlotte Town

Donald McIntyre leaned against the side of the house, carefully licking the last of the brown sugar from his fingers. When he was finished, he wiped his hands on his leggings and then stepped away from the house and strolled down the trail leading to the waterfront. He stopped and stared with surprise at the ship that was making the bend of the channel leading to the mouths of the rivers, easily following the buoys that had not yet been removed for the winter season when the channel would be frozen. There was something odd about the ship. He studied her as she came up right in front of the town and dropped anchor where she had a commanding position relative to the rivers and the settlement.

No flags! They aren't flying any colours at all!

He watched as the sailors backed the sails until the ship was broadside to the town and then the crew dropped the stern anchor to hold her in that position. Gun port covers were raised and cannon run out; McIntyre could see the flickering matches held by gunners ready to serve their weapons. For a few moments there was concentrated activity as the sails were furled; then the ship sat there, silent and sinister, as the sun continued its descent to the horizon.

Not long afterwards, during the early twilight, a second ship sailed boldly to the fore and performed the same backing of the sails but, this time, the broadside of the ship was pointed at the harbour entrance. Gun ports were raised and the guns run out. It was then that the first ship broke out her colours.

McIntyre wished he had one of the telescopes from his trade goods. In the gathering darkness he strained his eyes but he was unable to determine the nationality of the flag. He knew the ships were not Royal Navy. If not British, then whose?[3]

Donald had come to Charlotte Town on the last scheduled freighter of the season. He had acquired some pots and pans, a few mirrors, knives, six telescopes . . . in all worth about £11. He figured he could turn that small investment over through barter, and hopefully some cash sales, at a 200 per cent profit—more, if he considered that the telescopes had been stolen from naval stores and would give him a fatter mark-up—if he could just get his goods out to the settlements where they were sorely needed. Now, here was the hazard of any independent businessmen—competition from an unexpected source. Those ships were probably American privateers—he had learned in Halifax that the Americans were at war with the British—sent out by bad old George Washington to prey on the weak and defenceless outports of good old King George.

Couldn't find a more weak or defenceless outport than Charlotte Town, he thought. It dawned on him suddenly— *Christ! My flaming' telescopes! My sugar!* He began to run to the shed where he had stored his wares. A scream of surprise, followed by the report from a pistol, told him that the American invasion of The Island of Saint John had begun.

He ran faster.

Three Weeks Later
The Farm

Robert cupped his hands on either side of his mouth. "Reine!" He took several steps in the direction of the garden where Reine had been digging around trying to find any sort of vegetables they might have missed. "Reine!" He had her attention. "The bastard's back. Fetch Joseph! We have to fort up!"

So far, I see two horses. No Highlanders in sight! Oh dear God! Don't let there be Highlanders.

A man on a horse hailed the farm. "Hello, Robert!"

I didn't tell him my name. Robert went to the doorway. The stranger was down off his mount and was leading both animals toward the house. *McIntyre! McIntyre in leather leggings and green pea-jacket! McIntyre, of all people!*

He turned to cancel the alarm but Joseph Farrow had already come into the front yard and had recognized his old friend from army days. Rosalie came next and smiled at the visitor. It was a little while before Reine, breathing heavily, came into sight. When she saw the family standing around, she realized that the emergency, or whatever it was that had set Robert off, must have taken care of itself. She sat on a stump, wiping the cold sweat from her face. Everyone walked toward her. When she saw Donald McIntyre, she gave a husky laugh and a shaky "Welcome . . . Mis-ter . . . McIntyre." It was all she could manage but it brought smiles of relief from the family; they were not accustomed to any sign of weakness in Reine Leblanc.

Hard physical labour and very little food is taking its toll on all of us, Robert thought as he took a moment to pat Reine's shoulder. He glanced at the load on the second horse. *It looks like Donald McIntyre is a trader.* Robert didn't hesitate. "Do you have any food, Mac?"

"Some brown sugar, a half-pound of dried peas . . . but that's all. When he saw the crestfallen look on all the faces around him he quipped, "I have telescopes."

"I have a telescope," Robert replied. "And you are welcome to it for some of those peas."

With a quick look around the circle of gaunt faces, McIntyre went to his horse and pulled out two small packages. He tossed them to Robert. "I hope you plan to invite me to supper."

Robert opened the first package. It was the sugar. He peeled back the leather bag and held it out to McIntyre. "You want first lick?"

Mac shook his head.

Robert went to his wife and got down on his knees. He bit off a small chunk and put it on her tongue. He tossed the bag to Joseph. Then he put his arm around his darling and rocked her. When he felt some strength in her again, he asked McIntyre, "What is going on? Is the world coming to an end?"

* * *

They all felt better after some hot pea soup with fox meat in it. They began to talk about how hard life was this year, 1775.

Robert talked about conditions on the north shore. "There is no food at Saint Peter's Harbour. My English bosses haven't been able to pay me in supplies. They have let me keep some fish but the season is past and the fish they gave me is gone."

"The supply ships didn't get through?" McIntyre hastened to explain that he understood the difficulties, that there was a war on. British supplies were probably being diverted to where they were needed for the war. "But didn't any ships get through?"

"The supply ship for Malpeque Bay ran aground on the sandbars, dumping a load of settlers on the beach with no food or shelter."

"The cargo?"

"Lost, mostly. Provincetown sent a small boat to Saint Peter's looking for help but we didn't have much to give."

"What's been going on at Saint Peter's?"

"The American privateers have been raiding all along the north shore. The Arsenaults and their boat have disappeared, probably taken by the Americans. One ship escaped and told us of others that were taken." Robert stopped talking and there was silence around the table.

McIntyre cleared his throat . . . but then Robert continued. "There are no small animals left in the area." He pointed at the empty soup pot. "That was probably the last fox for five miles. We have tenants to the north of us—the Curry family—and another tenant family to the east—the Andersons—and all of us go hunting, every day." He shrugged his shoulders. "But, no matter. Soon the snow will be too deep to hunt. No matter what the personal risks, we had decided that we will have to go to Charlotte Town before the snow comes."

"Well, I have news but, before I give you news of the south shore, explain to me what you mean when you say that you have personal risks in Charlotte Town." McIntyre stared into Robert's eyes. "So what's the secret?"

Reine pressed her lips together and looked away.

Rosalie took her father's hand in hers. "I'm sorry, Pa. It isn't really a secret any more. Robbie was using our name when he left for Halifax." She leaned her head against Joseph. "Joseph asked me what it was all about."

"You told him?"

"Robbie had already . . ."

Reine stood up. "We are Camerons. Robert Cameron was a British soldier who couldn't stand the cruelty of English officers."

"I deserted. I ran away. I left my post and I don't feel the least bit guilty about it. I married an Acadian—lived and fought as an Acadian—and I'm more Acadian than most Acadians. "

"If they find you, they will hang you . . ."

"Amongst other things." Robert reached for Reine's hand and kissed it. "We both fought against them and if they knew that, they would treat us as renegades and kill us both." He let go of his wife's hand so he could use his hands while he talked. He grinned. "Je parle moi aussi comme les Acadiens . . . and I talk like an Acadian, too." That brought a laugh. Robert hurried on. "There is no food here, and not much hope of finding any. We have to go to Charlotte Town." He looked at McIntyre, expectantly. "You said you had news?"

"When I left, the Americans had captured the town and have most probably looted everything of any use by now. I travelled along the shore to Lot 57—Orwell River—where some Lowland Scots were brought last year on the *Lively Nelly*. They had been provisioned by their proprietor but field mice took their first crops and another form of vermin—American privateers—took their supply ship—and the proprietor won't resupply them. If they can arrange a ship next year, they're going to Pictou." He looked around the group. "Imagine! Things are so bad for them that they would voluntarily go to Nova Scotia!"

Robert summed up the situation: "Things are bad here . . . but not so bad that we would go to Nova Scarcity!"

Endnotes

1. The citation for the coat of arms reads: "The Arms of The Smallwood Family of Birmingham as registered in the College of Arms, and legally borne by all of the existing descendants in the male line of Joseph Smallwood of Handsworth and Birmingham (died 1774) and Hannah Barrett his wife."

2. The saga of Colonel William Smallwood's Maryland Rifles will be told in a later book of the *Abuse of Power* series.

3. " . . .two American armed vessels which had been sent to cruise in the Gulf of Saint Lawrence, in order to intercept English ordnance store-ships, supposed to be on the way to Quebec, entered the harbour, and a landing was effected without any opposition . . ." Duncan Campbell's *History of PEI.*

Chapter Nine
The Raid

January 1776
The Cameron Farm

"Would you like to know how I met Annie?" Donald McIntyre searched the faces around him: the beautiful features of Rosalie Cameron showed him the encouragement to "please begin" as it did any time there was a mention of storytelling, his long-time comrade wore that "here we go again" look of resignation which Donald had come to expect of Joseph—cooped up as they were in the little cabin by the deep snows—and Robert? Well, Robert was always respectful of the far-fetched creatures Donald invited from the ether-world to join them at the small fire. It was the last face that Donald found to be troubling. For just the smallest moment, there was the shadow on that face soldiers come to recognize; Donald could see that Reine was dying. He cast a quick look at Robert. *No, the husband has not yet seen the shades of death in his wife's face.* Donald McIntyre sighed. *No matter; Reine is dying. It is now Annie's time.*

"Who is Annie?"

Trust Joseph to ask the sensible question. Donald nodded at his friend in acknowledgement but instead of answering, opened up his arms to include everyone in their span. He began. "One night, the Americans came to Charlotte Town."

Always irrepressible, Rosalie taunted the storyteller, "Shouldn't you begin, once upon a time?"

Donald gave her a severe look and then ignored her. "They came in two warships—bold as brass—right to the front of the town."

"I don't want to hear about the Americans," Rosalie pouted. "You said the story was about someone called Annie."

Joseph patted Rosalie's hand. "You know by now that Donald's stories are a long time coming. Be patient, my dear." His face flushing a deep red, Joseph cast a quick look at the father to see if there was any reaction to his use of an endearment with the daughter. There was none. Everyone was smiling in anticipation of Donald's tall tale—everyone except Reine, who had her eyes closed and was leaning her head against Robert's shoulder.

"As soon as I saw the armed sailors leaving their ships, I ran to the undertaker's." Donald settled down on the floor of the shanty and tried to make himself more comfortable a bit closer to the fire. He took a deep breath to begin his story. "I could see that the privateers were converging on the public house and the governor's."

Joseph couldn't stop himself. "Why were you going to the undertaker's?"

"It was at the undertaker's where I stored my boodle." Donald smiled a wide, toothy smile. "He always had a couple of caskets made up for walk-ins . . . well, maybe they wouldn't be walk-ins"—Donald waited for the snickers to end—"but he kept a couple of boxes, ready-made, for unexpected customers." He shrugged. "I couldn't think of a safer place; nobody looks inside a casket." He waved away the thought. "But, that night, when I saw the raiders heading for the governor's house, I decided to pass by the governor's stable. You see, with all the commotion and goings-on, I thought I might be able to borrow a horse or two."

"You'd steal a horse?" Rosalie asked.

"Sure he would," Joseph affirmed as he playfully put a finger under Rosalie's chin to close her gaping mouth. Looking deep into the young woman's eyes, he explained, "You think of him as a sort of Uncle Donald. I know him as a true comrade who has served by my side for many years." Joseph glanced over at Robert for some support in his attempt to save Donald's reputation with Rosalie. "Donald was probably going to use the horse to ride through the countryside and raise the settlers to repel the invaders . . ."

Robert didn't rise to the occasion.

Donald wasn't having any part of it either. He butted in.

"Er, not quite, old buddy. There were too many of them

. . . and they had rows of cannon pointed right down our throats." Suddenly Donald rubbed his shin—the one that was closest to the fire—and squirmed away from the heat. "No, I wasn't thinking of much other than finding a way to carry my trade goods out of town—away from the clutches of the pirates." He extended one of his hands as if he were parting a curtain. "I peered through the bushes at the stable. No one was there although there was a bit of screaming coming from the house." He smiled. "The woman who was doing the screaming was more angry than hurt, I could tell. I thought about going to her aid but, just then, she bolted out the side door hollering and spitting that she was Anne Callbeck, the governor's wife, and she would have them skinned alive if any one of them laid a hand on her." Donald grinned. "One of the Americans hoisted her over his shoulder and carried her back inside and all the while she was shouting that Governor Callbeck would hang them from the highest tree." Donald shifted around to present the other leg to the fire. He sucked his teeth. "Not likely."

"What do you mean, not likely?" Robert asked.

"I sidled over to the house and peeked in the window. I could see that Governor Callbeck wouldn't be doing much harm to anyone since he was trussed up like a highwayman going to the gallows. In fact, I watched as they took him and a couple of his cronies to the ship."

"As prisoners?" Robert didn't wait for the answer. "Besides, they had the wrong man; Patterson is governor."

"Patterson's gone to England to get permission to swing some sort of land deal. Callbeck was sworn in as acting governor. Anyhow, I could still hear the woman—"

"Missus Callbeck?"

"Yeah. I could still hear her screaming that she was Anne Callbeck, the governor's wife, when I was in the governor's barn looking for horses. There was only the one. When I took her, I named her Annie."

Rosalie rocked back and forth with amusement. "You named the governor's horse after the governor's wife. Where did you get the other horse? You have two."

"The undertaker's."

Rosalie had a shocked look on her face. "You stole your friend's horse?"

Donald acted as if he were crestfallen at this lack of confidence in his honesty. He hung his head and twiddled with a bootlace. "He is more of a business associate—not a friend—and he told me to take his horse to keep her out of the hands of the Americans." He stuck out his lower lip as he solemnly declared, "I wouldn't use anything of his without permission." Donald could see there was still a lingering doubt on Rosalie's face so he hurried on. "He said I should bring her back, if I could." Giving up his attempt to salvage his good name he carried on. "Anyhow, the Americans ransacked the town and stole everything that wasn't nailed down. They even carted the governor and some of his officials off to the American colonies." He sucked his teeth. "In one fell swoop, The Island lost its government . . ."

"No harm done." Joseph chortled at his own humour.

Donald continued. "The undertaker probably lost his caskets and I would have lost my boodle if it hadn't been for Annie."

Joseph broke the silence that followed the end of the story. "That's a nice story, Don."

"Yes, thank you for the nice story." Rosalie wore an impish smile when she added, "Uncle Donald."

Robert stood up. "But, now that you have brought it up, we have to do something about the horses."

"Yes, I know. There's no feed left."

"At least there isn't enough feed for two horses."

"That's why I told the story." Donald gave the little family a sheepish smile. "I am supposed to take the undertaker's horse back, if I can. Of course, I can never take Annie back. Missus Callbeck would have me skinned alive."

"Yes. Especially if she found out that you named the horse after her." Rosalie giggled, not realizing the nature of the decision that was about to be made. "Wouldn't it be fun if we could find some way to tell her."

Businesslike, Donald McIntyre brought his story to its sad conclusion. "Annie saved my boodle from the Americans. She brought me here where I was able to share what I had with friends."

Reine spoke for the first time. "With family, Donald. To share with your family."

Donald's eyes glistened as he patted Reine on the arm. "But Annie is out of food. Starving is not a pleasant way to go. I can save her from that." He kept his eyes away from Reine as he added, "And Annie's goodness might keep us alive."

Spring

It had taken the sacrifice of both horses for the little family to survive until the snows had receded enough for Robert and Donald to trek to Saint Peter's Harbour in search of food. Fortunately, they found one of the returning English ships moored in the harbour. The owner advanced Robert some supplies against his labour in the upcoming season.

Late summer
Handsworth, England

Joseph Smallwood hated to admit it but he was worried about his sister. Sitting across the table from him, Hélène Smallwood appeared pale and listless; the veins on her forehead were blue and very pronounced. She seemed even more stooped and fragile than the old seamstress who had spent her days in the little room on the far side of the kitchens and was found dead there one cold morning. He smiled at the thought—*the old woman looked better that morning than she had for years*—but his smile faded as he contemplated the current problem that was his sister.

It had been quite some while since Hélène had shown any interest in politics or the estate or the family's lands on Saint John's Island. More recently, she had ignored the planning for Joseph's wedding, the preparations for the round of parties and receptions, and, as far as Joseph had been able to find out, she had not availed herself of the services of the estate's staff, choosing neither to go riding nor to be ridden. Yes, he was worried about his sister.

Joseph signalled one of the dining room staff to pull his chair away from the table. Joseph rose and excused himself and, as he passed by on the way to the main hall, he patted her shoulder. If Hélène Smallwood was conscious of his touch, she made no outward display. He slowed his pace, uttering a long, deep sigh. *A trifle overdone,* he thought, *but it usually gets a rise out of her—an expression of motherly concern.* He glanced back. *Nothing. Not even a raised eyebrow.* This time, Joseph's deep sigh was real. *It's almost like she isn't there any more.*

Once in the hall, Joseph picked up a leather bag. He hefted the mailbag as he walked back to the dining room. *Perhaps there might be something in the mail to interest her.* As he re-entered the dining room, he noted that, during the few moments of his absence, the serving staff had removed the remains of dinner. Hélène was sitting, her heavily veined hands worrying the edge of the napkin she still held in her lap. He paused—ostensibly to force the wax seal as he opened the mail pouch—studying his sister's profile, the line of her chin, and the wrinkles on her throat. *How old could she be? I never thought to ask Father. There must be some papers . . . somewhere.* He tossed the pouch to the nearest servant and returned to his place at the table. He spread the mail out in front of himself and sighed heavily as he settled more comfortably into his chair.

Joseph dropped his eyes and scanned the pile of letters. *Perhaps there might be news about the rebellion. Information about the American traitor might spark her interest.*

"Is there a letter from Cousin William?"

My God, she can read my mind! "No. Sorry. Nothing." *Should I tell her what I heard? Maybe not.*

"Have you heard anything? I wrote last year but he doesn't answer."

I didn't know she was still trying to get a rise out of the man. He suppressed a grin at his unintentional humour. "Yes I heard something but I wasn't aware of your interest." For a fleeting moment he saw the old furies flare in her eyes but then, just as quickly, die. He hastened on. "I was told that Smallwood's Maryland Rifles had marched north to join George Washington's army. I was assured that William was at the fore of his men."

"Oh!" With a quaver in her voice she whispered, "I asked him to come back to England."

"When was that?"

"Before . . ."

"Before he joined the rebellion."

"Yes. It seems like a long time ago."

Joseph fanned the stack of mail. "There is one letter from the colonies . . ."

"From him?"

Joseph opened the letter and silently read the first few lines. He was going to tell her that the letter was from Saint John's Island—in fact, he had opened his mouth to speak—but he quickly thought better of it. He continued to read. He had read the entire contents of the letter several times, delaying his response, hoping to force her to show some interest. He heard some movement; when he looked up, the servant was holding Hélène's chair.

"If I may be excused, brother, I shall retire early."

"Yes, of course. Of course, if you didn't want to know about the letter."

"It's not from him." She rose and, pulling her skirts closer as she moved past his chair and lowered her chin so that her eyes were shadowed. "I am particularly fatigued."

"The letter is about the land."

"I supposed as much." She continued her way to the door. "If not from Maryland, then it would be about your land on Saint John's Island." She turned at the door. She gave him a small curtsey.

"My land?" Joseph stood up so quickly that the surprised servant barely caught the chair as it fell backwards. "My land?" he repeated.

"Yes, brother. You have made it plain . . . ever since Father's death . . .." Hélène lifted her chin. "Ever since Father's death, you have made it very clear that you have no need for my . . ."

"That may have been true . . . ." He started again. "I might have resented your mothering at one time . . . I . . . I . . ." he stammered. "Come. Rejoin me at the family table. I have need of your advice." He gave her what he hoped was a sincere-looking smile. "I was a dolt." He held out his hand for her to take. "I am older now."

Hélène Smallwood glared at the boy who had become Master of Oakwood—who had become Master, not because he was smarter, or older, or more deserving—who was master because he stood up to pee. She thought to tell him. *I have tried it. I can stand and pee, little boy. I just can't pee as far as you can.*

"Before she left, Mother Barrett told me that I should seek your advice."

If Cousin William had not gone to Maryland, I would still be Mistress of Oakwood and not that fop of a wife you imported. She speaks such twaddle . . . but then you haven't noticed . . . you don't listen to her, either.

Joseph inclined his head at the servant who eased the chair forward. Hélène sat.

Obviously relieved, Joseph made a grand to-do about spreading the letter from the colonies flat. He traced a line with his forefinger as he read its contents. "A certain Benjamin Coffin claims that he is a tenant on our land . . ."

"Have you heard from our agent—what's his name?"

"Liam Phelan and no, we haven't had a word from him."

"More importantly, have we received any rents?"

"There has been no accounting from Mister Phelan. I don't even have a list of tenants." He picked up the letter and shook it. "This is the first indication . . ."

"What does it say?"

Heartened by Hélène's quick interest, Joseph replied, giving as much detail as he could. "Mister Coffin claims that, when he paid his rent again this year, he asked that there be a footbridge constructed over the neck of the river. He explains that, at the present time, he must backtrack through the woods and rely upon the good graces of a Mister Leblanc who allows him trespass to reach the Saint Peter's Harbour trail."

"In a way, that's good news. At least now we have some indication that Mister Phelan is on the job." Hélène frowned. "If Mister Coffin can get a letter through to England . . ."

Joseph raised his hand to interrupt the thought. "I'll read directly from the letter." He leaned forward and squinted as he traced again the words with his finger. "Mister Phelan claimed that he had proper instructions from Joseph Smallwood Esquire that said Joseph Smallwood had already made his improvement allocations for the foreseeable future." He placed the letter flat on the table. "According to Mister Coffin—who has loyally paid his rents to the aforesaid Phelan—I am quoted as having said that I have made provisions for certain improvements that, apparently, do not include Mister Coffin's coveted bridge." Joseph picked up the letter and, holding it pinched between thumb and forefinger, offered the limp paper to his sister. "It provides other information that can only lead me to believe that—"

"We have a fox in the poultry yard." Hélène looked longingly at the door to the main hall. She seemed to be hesitating about becoming involved. Joseph hurried on.

"Yes. Patterson's man."

Hélène gave an evil smile. "Didn't I warn you about trusting Patterson?"

In a very contrite voice and manner, Joseph quietly responded, "Yes, you did and I am truly sorry that I didn't take your well-intentioned advice." Joseph waited. He continued to hold the letter out, dangling like bait. He lowered his arm so that the letter was now closer to his sister and within her easy reach. He sighed when she finally took the paper. "Yes, you did. Patterson is now in England claiming that his policies will bring recalcitrant proprietors into line."

Hélène raised her eyebrows. "Which means?"

"He has sold off some of the lands belonging to proprietors who are not up to date on their quitrent payments to the Crown."

"Which includes us."

Joseph swallowed hard before answering. "Yes, it does include us. We have paid no quitrents."

Disgustedly, Hélène waved her hands. "Yes, you and Father decided that you could . . ."

"That's old history now, Hélène," said the Master of Oakwood, who instantly regretted his rashness. "That was our mistake . . ." He waited, not knowing what to expect. It wasn't long in coming.

"And now, we have made an enemy of Patterson."

"Uh, yes. I suppose you could say that."

"A Patterson dogsbody is running our estate,"—when her brother didn't answer she continued—"and we know that certain lands have been sold,"—again she paused but continued before the hapless Master could form a reply—"and we don't know if any of our property has been sold . . .."

Joseph Smallwood nodded his head.

" . . . and we have not had any communications with the Patterson viper who is collecting rents on our behalf?" She stared at the young man's bowed head as if she were looking for fleas in his thick, black hair. "Men!"

Silence fell in the dining room of Oakwood Manor as Hélène Smallwood read and re-read the Coffin letter. Without looking up she said, half to herself, "This letter made swift passage." Her brother flinched when she raised her eyes to meet his. "The American insurrection isn't stopping the royal mails." She tossed the paper across the table where it almost slid onto the floor, being stopped only at the last minute by a sweaty palm. "The only thing I can think of is skulduggery on the part of Phelan . . . or Patterson . . . or both."

"Patterson is here in England. We could ask him . . ."

"Ha!"

"What, then?"

Hélène smiled her evil little smile. "Someone will have to go to the colonies . . ."

"Who, then?"

"Only the Master of Oakwood would have the authority to act in the best interests of the Smallwood family."

"But . . . who would look after Oakwood? It won't run itself, you know."

"That's right." This time, the lady's smile was one of pure delight. "That's right. The estate won't run itself."

Chapter Ten
The Will

Spring 1781
The Waterfront
Charlotte Town

The well-dressed man seemed completely relaxed as he sat on his campaign chair in the shade provided by the wide umbrella. All around him the busy, dusty bustle of sweaty people serving the needs of the newly arrived vessel ebbed and flowed, but he sat untouched by it all. He spoke to the two black men standing behind him, who by their size, were providing some of the man's shield from the human traffic. The taller of the two men separated himself from the little island. His progress toward the ship could be followed through the throng only because he was head and shoulders above most of the crowd. The slave's progress was stopped momentarily at the gangplank while the sailors secured its footings but he ascended, quickly, to the main deck. After a few words with the deck officer, the black man was lost from sight.

Some time passed. The white man lit a cigar but butted it before long, showing some distaste as he did so. He stood. He glanced at the ship and then up and down the pier. Gesturing at the chair, he watched as the black man folded it and then collapsed the umbrella, tucking both under his muscular arm. "Samuel," he said, pointing at the chair and umbrella, "take them to the carriage. Be sure to place them directly into the hands of the driver. Then fetch me a flask."

"Yessir, Mister Tierney." The slave did not move.

"Well?"

"Water or spirits, sir?"

"Rum, Samuel. I am not thirsty." He gave the slave a friendly, open smile. "It is always an experience when one meets his new master, don't you find it so, Samuel?"

Samuel knew better than to participate in the moment. He nodded and left.

Although the crowd on the pier had thinned considerably, Francis Tierney suffered some jostling as he made his way along to the foot of the gangplank that was now being replaced with a sturdy walkway. When the ship's crew had secured the walkway, Tierney grasped the railing.

"Francis Tierney, I presume?"

Tierney looked up to see Joseph Smallwood for the first time.

"You would be Francis Tierney, steward of my lands at Lot 38?"

Tierney stepped back and gave the arriving passenger room to step ashore while making a deep bow. "Your humble servant, sir."

"You have accommodations for me?"

"Yes sir, such as they are. This isn't the old country."

"You're not English, are you?" Smallwood pointed at the three travel cases that had been brought to the ship's entry port. "Have them looked after, if you please."

Samuel had returned. The handsome black man wiped the pewter flask with a linen he had taken from his side pocket and then, with two fingers, held the flask out to Mister Tierney.

"Not now, thank you, Samuel. You and Cecil take Mister Smallwood's luggage to Richardson's where he has chambers. Unpack the cases. When you are finished, go to the kitchens. Make certain that you eat well; we will be busy tomorrow. Await my return."

The two blacks moved up the walkway against the flow of persons who stepped out of their way without comment or gesture.

"No sir, I am not English. My family was . . ."

"Irish?" Joseph frowned. "You're not one of Patterson's men, are you?"

"You mean Governor Patterson? I have had neither the pleasure nor the opportunity." Tierney looked past Smallwood's shoulder. Samuel had hoisted one of the cases to his shoulder. Tierney grimaced. *Now both of his shirts are dirty.*

Smallwood recognized a look of distaste when he saw it. "Anything amiss?"

"No, not at all, sir." He then made a sweeping motion with his hand. "Come along to the public house while the blacks look after things."

Smallwood raised a quizzical eyebrow. "They think on their own? Unsupervised?"

"They are from fine Maryland stock. I always buy the ones with blue eyes. Then I pay for two years of social schoolin'—dress 'em up—give 'em manners—give 'em clear orders—and they can pass well in society. " He was still smiling but his eyes took on a steely glint as he said, "And they know better than to disappoint me." He took stride, but quickly matched his pace to Smallwood's unsteady land-legs. "I'm third generation out of Maryland," he said, by way of continuing the conversation.

Joseph Smallwood had lost interest in Tierney's antecedents. "I want to know about my land. Where is the scoundrel Liam Phelan?"

"Whereabouts unknown. He collected this year's rents and had left The Island by the time I took up my duties on your behalf. I just returned from upriver." He gave his master a beautiful, reassuring smile. "You have title to probably the most promising lands on The Island and some of the tenants are doing well for you but . . .." Tierney held the door open for Smallwood to enter the dark interior of the public house.

Smallwood hesitated. "Isn't there somewhere better than this?"

"There's naught to choose from. Richardson's Tavern is the best public house on The Island because it's the only public house on The Island." They sat down at the one empty table in the large, crowded room. Tierney waved to a beefy, red-faced man, who brought two mugs. Tierney tossed several coins to the publican. "This is Mister Richardson. When we

had news of your ship standing up the harbour, I asked . . .
well, Richardson was kind enough to save us a table."

Richardson nodded to the customers, made a swipe at the
table with a wet rag, and returned to his taps.

Smallwood could smell the pungent rum. He didn't touch
the mug. "What have you learned?"

"You have eleven tenants who claim that they are up to
date in the payments of their rents."

"And, of course . . ."

"We have no way of proving or disproving . . ."

"They have receipts?"

"Phelan had a ledger which he signed and they counter-
signed." Tierney shrugged his shoulders. "All seems to be in
order at the courthouse. The eleven families are listed as residents of The Island of Saint John and attested to by one Liam
Phelan."

"Who passed himself off as my agent."

Tierney made no comment.

"Other problems?"

"Three men bought land on Lot 38 when it was made
available by the Island government: two are regimental—soldiers who took their discharges here—and one is a Frenchie."

"The devil!" Joseph Smallwood sucked in his breath and
held it until his face turned red. He exhaled, slowly. When he
was breathing normally again, he lifted the mug and drank the
contents in one draught. He placed the mug on the table
before he spoke. "Get them off my land."

"It might be difficult to get rid of the two soldiers. They
would have the ears of the officers of their old regiment."

"So?"

"It will take some planning . . ."

"Start with the French, then."

"They will be gone by next spring, sir."

"Good."

Summer 1781
The Cameron Farm

Robbie Cameron was filled with regret that he had left good old Montreal and come back to the farm.[1] He leaned the hoe against a tree and wiped his upper lip with his sleeve. *Life had been good in Montreal. Lots to eat and drink . . . swordplay had been stimulating . . . until she got fat and pregnant.* He took his hat off. "Christ! It's hot!" He cast a quick look around to see if he might have been overheard by his strait-laced parents— so Acadian in their thinking—who would have surely started a rumpus if they had heard him use the Lord's name in vain. Reassured that he had not been heard, he pulled out the end of his shirt and tried to dry off the sweatband of the limp hat. *Summers in Montreal; winters in the wilderness.* He fanned his face with the brim of the hat. *My marriage to the squaw meant nothing . . . a passport to another female crotch.* He placed the hat lightly on his head, *but then, the marriage to Marie Celeste had no meaning either. At least, it had no meaning until my son came along.* "I should have stayed in Montreal!" He grabbed the hoe and viciously struck at the clay. *If only she hadn't let herself go. Stupid, fat bitch! I could've stayed on in Montreal as a trapper.* He had a flashback to the irate face of his supervisor when he was being fired. *No, maybe not. I had to leave.* He worked the row until he could feel the perspiration pop out all over his face. He stopped and pulled off his hat, starting the whole mopping-up process over again. *She could have cleaned herself up. It's not my fault she let herself go until she was as fat as a pig. I could still be in Montreal and not here.* He looked around . . . *not here!* Certain that he was alone; he gratified himself by venting some of his pent-up frustrations. "Christ! Christ! Je–sus–Christ–All–Mighty!" he hollered.

"Are you all right?" It was a voice from the far side of the trees that served as a windbreak between the two first fields. "Is anything wrong with Little Robbie?"

He could hear the rush of movement through the brush as his mother came running to find her grandson. *Damn!*

Where is the little bugger? Robbie thought. "Cuddy," he called, softly. Robbie raised his voice. "It's all right, mother. Cuddy is playing at hide 'n seek. I just missed him for the moment but he's right here . . ." he lowered his voice, " . . . somewhere."

Reine Leblanc, ashen-faced, burst through the bushes. "Is Little Robbie all right?" She looked left and right. "Where is he, Robbie?"

Robbie Cameron, erstwhile Northwest Company fur trader, didn't know—hopefully just for the moment—where his son was. "Well . . . he was playing right there, next to the tree stump . . ." *Damn! I don't have to answer to her!* He drew himself up and, setting his jaw, he countered, "Mother! I wish you would stop calling him Little Robbie. Father is Robert. I am Robbie and, just because my wife"—Robbie crossed himself—"may she rest in peace, named him after me, there is no reason why the boy should be saddled with a worn-out name."

"I don't like what you call him." Reine turned away from her son. "Where is he? He was supposed to be with you this afternoon."

Robbie Cameron was not to be turned aside by reason. "His name is Cuddy Cameron, Mother. As the boy's father, I ask that you stop being silly about what to call a three-year-old boy."

Reine recognized her son's delaying tactics. "Where is he, Robbie?"

On the verge of admitting that he didn't know, Robbie made a great show of cocking his head and listening to some noises in the distance.

From across the fields came the voice of Robert Cameron. "Rob-bie! Robbie! Cuddy is over here. Isn't he supposed to be with you?"

Reine made a sound of exasperation and pushed her way through the bushes in the direction of her husband's voice. "I'll come, Robert."

"Well, goddamn!" Robbie whispered.

His mother spoke from the other side of the bushes. "I have asked you not to swear."

"Yes, Mother."

"Finish what you were doing and come along. Rosalie will have our evening meal ready by now."

Reine crossed the field and pushed through the next windbreak. She smiled when she saw her husband, on all fours, romping with their grandson who was squealing with joy. She frowned when she heard Robert sing out, "Got you! Got you, Cuddy!" *So much for the grand plan of teaching French to the boy.* She cupped her hands so that she might be heard over the happy sounds. "Today is supposed to be a French day, Robert!"

Now Robert was tussling with the little fellow. After a short while—when he was lying, pinned to the ground by the giggling wrestling champion of the New World—Robert shouted back, "What did you say, Grandma?" He sat up, pulling the child to him in a great bear hug. "Here comes Grandma!" He put the boy down. "Run to Rosalie, Cuddy. Tell her Grandpa says you are a good little boy and deserve a treat." As the boy took off as fast as his chubby legs would move him, Robert cautioned, "Be sure to clean off your feet at the door." Robert shielded his eyes against the late afternoon sun. "You wanted something, Reine?" He looked past his wife, expecting to see the boy's father close behind. "The boy got away from Robbie?"

"Yes, he did." *I'm going to spoil this nice time by . . . no! I'm not going to bring up the French thing again.* "It's hard to work and watch the boy at the same time."

"You know, as well as I do, that our son is lazy. No wonder he came back from Montreal with little more than the clothes on his back."

"He brought Little Robbie."

Robert took his wife's hand and they walked down the rows toward the house. "Thank God the boy is thriving. He was a sad-looking little tyke when he first came home."

"Tyke?" Reine was like a sponge, always picking up new English words. "I haven't heard that word before."

"Perhaps I shouldn't have—"

"You tell me, Row-bear," she said, smirking as she adopted the thick French accent she had years ago when she first attempted to speak English. "Beeg English-mahn tell lee-ttle French wo-mahn whot is . . ."

Robert used his free hand to turn his wife's lips to where he could plant a soft kiss. He was about to give her a second kiss but she pushed him away. "Tell me!"

"Tyke is a sad little . . . thing."

"Thing?"

"Like a stray dog. Everyone thinks it is worthless so they don't give it much food . . . or . . . love. It's a tyke."

"You thought Little Robbie was a dog?"

"It could also mean an unfortunate person." He stopped and pulled her around so that he could look directly into her eyes. "Remember how the boy looked when he first came home?"

Reine knew what would come next; her husband would say something unkind about her son. "Robbie did the best he could."

"Maybe so, but he shouldn't have taken the baby away from Montreal."

"There was no job . . ."

"He was fired."

"Marie Celeste died . . .

"There would be more help for the child in Montreal than on a shoddy coastal freighter."

"Marie Celeste's entire family died of the 'pox. There was no one."

"The Church . . ."

"Robbie was lucky to come back from the wilderness to find the boy still alive." Reine pulled her hand away and tried to run ahead. Robert restrained her by grasping her elbow. "We shouldn't argue," he said, in a pleading voice. "Robbie is . . ."

Reine relented, a little. "Well, then . . ."

"I know, Reine. I know." Robert knew he was making a mistake, but he couldn't let the pretence lie between them, unacknowledged. "It doesn't change the fact that . . ."

"You don't know what it was like in Montreal! Or you wouldn't keep bringing it up."

Robert Cameron clamped his mouth shut. "Yes, my dear."

Again Reine pulled her hand away and continued walking toward the house. "Robbie had no money. He had a baby to look after." Reine looked back to see if Robert were following her. He was. "Robbie was lucky to find a ship that allowed him to work his passage."

"I know, dear . . ."

Reine interrupted. "Look, I think Donald is back."

The couple moved quickly through the end of the rows to the house where Cuddy was running around holding a coloured ball in his hands. "Lookit! Lookit," the boy screamed with delight, "Unc'e Donnal give me somethin'."

Robert made catching motions with his hands; Cuddy threw the ball in the general direction of his grandpa. Robert went to retrieve the ball but his son, who had been coming down the rows, picked it up and tossed it back. "Nice-looking toy," Robbie said.

Donald McIntyre pulled another one from his saddlebag. "I have a new job at the Customs House." He lobbed the second ball to the little boy, who went scrambling along the grass trying to catch up to it. "I didn't think they'd miss a few . . ." He recognized the distaste that was registering on the Reine's face. "There were hundreds of them . . ." He could see that there was no acceptance of what he was saying so he finished up, "Besides, even the Customs Agent took a few home for his boys."

Laughing, Robert asked, "How many did you take, Donald?"

"Just a couple for my little family." He cast a quick look at Reine's retreating figure as she went into one of the outbuildings. "And a couple for every family on my route."

The three men guffawed at the humour. Reine came to the shed door for a moment to see what was so entertaining. Donald gave her a big smile and she retreated back into the shadows. Still keeping an eye on the door, he added, "The Customs House is a perfect job for me—"

Robbie interrupted. "Why did they give *you* the job?"

"They need someone to take inventory, tally the accounts, and write up a monthly report for the Customs Agent." Donald grinned. "Some bigwig told them that I was their man."

Robert slipped the saddlebags to the ground. He grunted as he hefted them. "Heavy," he said. "What happens to your tinker's route?"

"No real change. On my way to Charlotte Town, I take the orders from my customers. On my way back, I drop off their supplies." He lifted the bags and slung them over his shoulder. "If I can't find what I need at Charlotte Town, I order it in from Halifax." He winked at the two Camerons as he started to carry the bags to the shed. "Might even be cheaper orderin' in like that, given that there's a new, open-minded customs clerk doing the accounts." Suddenly alert, Donald eased the bags back down to the ground. He pointed up the track. "Strangers coming." He squinted a little as he gave them the once-over and then turned away, disinterested. "Whoever they are, they're Acadians."

Robert recognized the men coming down the track: André Bernard—from two farms over—and Abraham Bernard, his brother, both dressed in dark suit coats, black breeches, ankle boots and, set well back from their foreheads, identical wide-brimmed black hats. *Yes, Donald's right. Even from a distance, I would know they're Acadians by the way they dress. It's never dawned on me before that . . .* "Bernard, from two farms up," Robert informed Donald. "Haven't seen them for a while." . . . *that we . . . that they . . . are so different from English settlers.*

Robert waved. "Messieurs Bernard! Comment ça va?"

The Acadians waved back.

Donald made a perfunctory wave. "They brought their women. Must be something going on."

Robert cast back in his memory. *Catherine and Marie-Josèphe?* He raised his voice. "Reine! We have visitors." *She will remember their names.*

It was when Reine came to the door that the full impact of the Camerons' differences from the Acadians became apparent to Robert. Where all of the women wore their shoulder-length hair tied back and covered by a simple bonnet, Reine's hair had no covering whatsoever. The Bernard women's garments, tightly enclosed at the throat and wrists, allowed an occasional glimpse of tidy black shoes. Reine, on the other hand, wore a calf-length skirt; her grey blouse—open at the throat—short and loose at the sleeves—tucked in at the waist—was practical for field work but, obviously, not in the Acadian style.

Reine gave a small wave to the visitors and ducked back into the house to take off her field boots. She returned, barefoot, standing behind her husband as he welcomed the visitors.

Donald shouldered the bags again, making motions to leave. When he saw Joseph Farrow coming around the corner of the Cameron house, he excused himself and joined his friend.

"What's goin' on?" Joseph asked.

"Can't tell. I get lost as soon as they start nattering in French . . ."

"Did you bring somethin' for me?"

"You mean, did I bring something for you to give to Rosalie?"

"Well, did you?"

They were bent over the sack as Donald searched for Joseph's gift for Rosalie when Robert called out, "Donald! Would you please join us?"

Donald patted his friend's shoulder. "It's a purple stone. Nova Scotia amethyst they call it." He patted Joseph again. "I'll find it for you as soon as Robert is through with me."

Joseph's disappointment showed in his face.

"Don't worry. I'll be right back and Rosalie will love it." He grinned. "It's worth the wait, you'll see."

"Donald!" This time it was Reine calling. Donald McIntyre hurried.

Robert began explaining as Donald joined the group.

"I told the Bernards that you had just come back from Charlotte Town and you would know about any laws passed recently."

"There's a problem?"

"A new proprietor's agent visited them and told them their land purchase was unlawful. The agent said the King has rescinded the law that allowed the Bernards to buy their land. The agent said—"

Donald raised his hand to interrupt the story. "Tell him the King has been asked to rescind the Charlotte Town law that permitted some delinquent proprietors to have their lands sold out from under them. The proprietors have great influence . . ."

"But the law hasn't been rescinded yet?"

"Right. But, even if the law is rescinded, Governor Patterson bought some land too . . . under the same Charlotte Town law. I don't think anything will happen. Governor Patterson won't let it happen."

Robert didn't translate for the Bernards. He explained further to Donald. "They are frightened. The agent came a second time, the morning after something killed their livestock."

"Something killed their . . ."

"It looked like a bear got into the pens." Robert paused and then said, slowly, "There aren't bears around here."

"No, there are no bears."

"The agent said it was a shame the livestock was gone. Tierney—that's the man's name—Tierney said he would have been willing to give a fair price for the livestock if the Bernards had agreed to leave the day before. Tierney hoped there wouldn't be a wildfire; a wildfire would destroy all the improvements and make the land useless for years to come."

Donald sucked his teeth before answering. "Tell the Acadians to take what they can get and move on."

Robert couldn't hide his surprise at his friend's quick—and negative—response. "Why would you say that?"

Donald watched the eyes of the nearest Bernard to see if there was any understanding as he spoke. "This Tierney fellow has served notice that he would burn them out. We don't need wildfires in here because there's no real way of stopping them;

we would all be burned out." He turned away from the Acadians and said, in a very low voice, "Get rid of the threat. Get rid of the Acadians." Donald turned back to again face the visitors. He gave them a broad smile and bobbed his head up and down a couple of times. "Goodbye, mister and missus. Good day." He strode back to where Joseph Farrow was still digging in the bag. "Lay off, Joe. I'll find it for you."

* * *

After the evening meal, Joseph Farrow chose not to sit in his usual place near the window. He moved, purposefully, to the other side of the room. He hesitated, but then sat on the floor near the end of the bench usually occupied by the young woman. He patted the stone in his side pocket, watching the women as they cleared away the meal's remains, praying that Rosalie would be the first to turn away and join the men near the hearth.

Rosalie did turn away first. She noted the anxious look on the older man's face. "Anything wrong, Joseph?" She sat on the end of the bench, her eyes searching for evidence of something that might be bothering him.

"No, I . . ."

Robert gained the attention of everyone in the room when he announced, "They were good neighbours. I hate to seem them go."

Donald McIntyre cackled, "Heh, heh. You took my advice? You warned them off?"

Robert, his face flushing, shook his head "no." "I didn't have to. They had made up their minds to go before they came for the visit. They said they would rather have the proprietor's few pence than—"

"Than be burned out." McIntyre stoked his pipe. "Lucky for us." He reached for a switch and poked it into the base of the fire, seeking a light for his pipe. "We'd get burned out along with them."

There was quiet for a few moments as Donald lighted his pipe.

The family waited for Robert's response while Robert fought his sense of guilt that he would even consider warning off his neighbours.

Donald took a good draught and sighed. "It's a pity that we don't grow tobacco here. I wager there would be a good market in Charlotte Town and Halifax. Instead I have to pay—"

Robert finally conquered his embarrassment with the situation. "Something really bothers me, though," Robert interrupted. "We haven't seen hide nor hair of any proprietor's man since that first time."

Reine had been drying her hands as she joined the group around the hearth. Finally satisfied that her hands were dry enough, she slipped off her apron and hung it over a peg on the wall. "We scared him enough that he didn't want to come back."

"Maybe so." Robert didn't want to appear to contradict his wife so he chose his words carefully. "Facing the wrong end of a musket would unsettle any man," he said, smiling, "and you sure had the drop on him. But we don't own the land like the Bernards and they are being forced off; we don't pay rent like the Currys who, according to the Bernards, have already had a visit from this Tierney fellow demanding rent payments. I can't understand why we are being left alone."

Robert and Reine missed the quick guilty look between Joseph and Donald but the younger Camerons, Rosalie and Robbie, caught it. Rosalie opened her mouth to question the two family friends but Robert continued speaking.

"There's something really fishy going on. We are Acadians and we are living on English land and we are beholden to no man? Not likely."

Reine cleared her throat. Everyone waited for her to speak. "While you men were talking, Marie-Josèphe Bernard commented that we do not look like Acadians and we do not speak like Acadians. She asked if we didn't care that we were losing our heritage, that our grandson, Little Robbie, would never know—"

Robert, his face flushed, interrupted his wife, his voice showing some irritation. "What more do you want, Reine? We speak French. We—"

"The sense of belonging. To be a part of a community is what it means to be Acadian." Reine spread her arms wide. "There is no community here. Our children and grandchildren will never know the songs, the stories of our people—"

"We will speak of this at a later time, Reine."

Reine Leblanc Cameron stood and faced her husband, her hands on her hips, her teeth clenched, her jaw thrust forward. "And an Acadian husband would never speak to his wife like that, Robert."

In the moments of silence that filled the little house, Donald McIntyre was the first to move. As he stood up he said, "I believe I hear the horses . . . restless . . . perhaps something bothering them."

Joseph Farrow was quick to join his friend. "I'll help you, Donald."

"Me too!" Robbie took his sister by the hand and led her out the door. Once outside, they ran to catch up with the two men. "Wait up," Robbie said, *sotto voce*, so as not to be heard inside the cottage. "We have some questions we need to ask you."

Joseph and Donald slowed their pace but did not stop. They had reached the barn before the Camerons caught them up. Joseph turned to face the young siblings as Donald picked up the candle lantern. "I didn't bring a flint," he muttered. "I won't be able to see what's disturbing the horses."

"You know there's nothing wrong with the horses."

If Robbie could have seen Donald's face in the semi-darkness, he would have seen the *dour* smile of a man who knew he was being corralled. Donald shrugged his shoulders. "I know there's nothing wrong with the horses. I just wanted to give them some space."

"Never mind about my ma and pa. They will be fine."

Rosalie took something from the folds of her skirt. She handed it to Donald as she said, "Ma and Pa always work things out." She gestured at Donald's hand. "Use the flint. Light the lantern. I want to see your face so I will know when you try to lie to me."

Donald opened the front of the lantern and manipulated the flint against some tinder. "I wouldn't lie to—"

"Yes you would. You have done it before . . ."

"Not for a long time. Not since you were a little girl."

A firm-jawed Rosalie Cameron remained silent as Donald serviced the lantern. "There!" he said. He placed the lantern back on its hook and turned to face the young woman. "What is bothering you, little one?"

Rosalie ignored Donald. She stepped forward and jabbed her finger into Joseph's chest. "I want to know, Joseph, what you two are hiding." She pressed so hard that Joseph winced and took a step back. "Pa thinks you are his friend. What are you hiding about the farm that we don't know?"

Joseph Farrow didn't hesitate. "I bought title to a hundred acres from the governor's agent." He smiled and shrugged his shoulders. "I own the land around my house."

What followed was a silence so still and prolonged that the stealthy movements of a mouse in the rafters could be sensed by the humans below.

Joseph was the first to speak. He held out his hands in a pleading gesture as he blurted out, "We didn't mean no harm!"

Rosalie looked at him, sharply. "What do you mean, 'we'?"

"Donald bought title to this land . . . to your Pa's land."

"Aw, shit, Joey!" Donald moved quickly to repair the apparent damage, placing a tender hand on the girl's arm, patting it, hopefully reassuringly.

Rosalie stepped away at the first touch.

Undeterred, Donald took her hand in his. "They were selling the land . . ."

"Where were they selling the land?" Robbie had found his tongue.

"At Charlotte Town. I heard it while I was picking up my goods from the Customs House."

Joseph had found himself again and piped up, "At the time, we didn't think this land would be for sale . . ."

"But when we found out it was, we bought two hundred acres." Donald nodded his head at his old friend. "Joey took the one piece and I took the other."

"You took my Pa's land."

"I always meant to sign it over." Donald kissed the tips of the captured fingers. "I did it to protect my family." When he saw the disbelief still lurking in the woman's eyes he said, "I would make out my will, right now, and sign it over . . . if you wanted me to."

Rosalie had heard too many McIntyre promises and stories; she pounced. "Do it."

Donald McIntyre looked around the barn, a half-smile on his face as he said in a bemused tone of voice, "There's nothing to write on."

Rosalie strode across the barn and pulled a stylus and a dusty slate from behind a beam. "Use this," she growled as she thrust the writing implements into the soldier's hands. "You write contracts and letters all the time, so do a good job."

"Now? In the darkness?"

"Now." Rosalie pointed at a storage bin. "Sit there. I will watch." She took the lantern from the peg and stood over Donald as he wrote. In a conversational tone, she asked, "Where did you and Joseph get that much money?"

Donald seemed to relax as he settled into his favourite role: the family storyteller.

"When you were just a baby, Joseph and I came through here with a survey team. Sergeant Brown was in charge of the military escort party." Donald looked beyond the circle of light into the remembered past. "We were camped across the way—just on the other side of Cameron's Brook—when Sergeant Brown asked permission to return to Charlotte Town so that he could take ship for Halifax. At Halifax he would be given his mustering-out papers. The regimental adjutant had promised him transport on a warship so that he would have a swift Atlantic passage and be home for Christmas."

Joseph cleared his throat.

Donald paused, giving his friend time to speak.

"Sergeant Brown left."

"And that winter, we both believed that Sergeant Brown was back in England with his family."

"The next year, when it was our time to muster out, we went to Halifax . . ."

" . . . and found our Sergeant Brown was NCO in charge of the regimental orderly room." Donald looked up and smiled at his listeners. "Our Sergeant Brown was a bitter man."

"Yessiree. The adjutant had loaded an officer and his family onto the manifest . . ."

" . . . leaving no space for our sergeant."

"Yes. He had missed his ship and was stuck in Halifax over the winter."

"We saw an opportunity to get official papers for our friend, Corporal Miles . . ."

" . . . and some money."

Donald grimaced at what Rosalie must have been thinking but he faced up to it. "Yes . . . and some money."

"We planned to give your father his share . . ."

Both Robbie and Rosalie grunted in disbelief.

It was Joseph's turn to put on a sour face. "No, no! It's true! We planned to give your Pa his share . . ."

"Until?" Rosalie looked at the two soldiers through slitted eyes. "You planned to share the money with Pa up to the point where . . ."

"Up to the point where Sergeant Brown suggested that we could muster-out all of the missing, absent . . ."

" . . . or all the dead soldiers that we had ever heard of."

"Which we did and everything was coming along just fine until . . . "

" . . . Lieutenant Makin found out what we were doing..."

" . . . and he wanted his cut . . ."

" . . . so then Sergeant Brown created a pay list for detachments of soldiers that he made up out of thin air . . ."

" . . . that the lieutenant issued orders for them to proceed to . . ."

" . . . some god-forsaken places like Chebogue Bay, Tangier and Cornwallis . . ."

" . . . and we took their pay, too."

Donald McIntyre laughed. He bent his head down and went back to writing his last will and testament; but not before he added, "At that time we took our mustering-out for real before the major found out and wanted his slice of the pie." He shook his head. "Yes, we left before anyone else got involved."

Without realizing it, Rosalie had allowed the lantern to lower as she had followed the story. Donald tapped the slate with the stylus. "Raise the lantern, Rosalie. I can't see to finish this thing."

With eyes as big as saucers, Rosalie did as she was told.

Robbie swallowed. "How . . . how much money was involved?"

Donald continued with his writing; it was Joseph who answered. "Enough to buy the two hundred acres . . ."

" . . . and set me up with a small inventory as a tinker . . ."

" . . . and to send a young Robbie Cameron off to Montreal."

Donald slid the stylus into its holder. He held the slate out for Rosalie to take but she shook her head. "I can't read it, Uncle Donald." She gave him a sweet smile in an effort to make up for the evil thoughts she had had about her Uncle Donald. He smiled back in understanding. He handed the slate to Joseph. "You read it, old buddy; then sign it as witness. I left you some space at the bottom."

Joseph took a moment or so and then signed. He handed it along to Robert.

"What does it say?" Rosalie asked.

Robert took his finger to trace along where he was reading.

"Don't do that!" Donald snatched the slate back. He took the stylus and corrected the smudge. He handed it back to Robbie. "Be careful not to rub the writing," he said.

While Robbie read the slate, Joseph asked, "Is a letter on a slate legal?"

"It's just fine. Sometime, when we can, we should go to a man of the law and have it transcribed to paper and have a fancy seal put on it."

"But, in the meantime, it's good?"

"It's good," Donald affirmed.

"And it says that Robert Cameron inherits all that is owned by Donald McIntyre in the event of McIntyre's death or disappearance."

Rosalie held her hand out for the slate. She placed it in a leather bag and hid it in the crevice behind the beam. "It can stay there until we get a chance to get it . . ."—she hesitated— "to get it . . ."

"Transcribed."

She gave a nod of appreciation to her Uncle Donald. "Yes. In the meantime, what do we tell Ma and Pa?"

"Nothing." Donald gave his storyteller's smile to his audience. "I don't mean to die any time soon." And then, with his usual dramatic flare he added, "Or disappear."

Everyone looked toward the house as they heard the quiet whistle.

Joseph was the first out the barn door. "That's Robert giving us the all-clear. Let's go have us some tea."

Endnote

[1] In book three of the Abuse of Power series, *Crooked Paths*, Robbie Cameron joins the North West Company as a fur trader. He marries Marie Celeste (Kendrick) Tsawenholi at the Company's headquarters in Montreal. They have a son, Robert (Cuddy) Cameron.

Chapter Eleven
Gallant Ghost

Spring 1785
Oakwood Manor
Handsworth

Hélène Smallwood looked up from her accounts, slightly annoyed at the hesitant knock on the door to the master's office. She pushed the ledger away. *There's only one reason any-one would disturb me at this time of day, so it must be . . . She* didn't have time to complete the thought before the house-keeper entered.

"The village church bell rang twice, Mistress. I have already alerted the house staff." It was the signal that Joseph Smallwood had been seen riding up Church Street toward the estate.

Hélène gathered her skirts and moved sedately through the door to the main hall. Over her shoulder she said, "Open the window." *The last time he came back from a trip I had left a telltale trace of lavender.* She smiled. *I'm not fooling him in the least but this way, it is not a point of discussion between us, first thing upon his return.* "Tidy up the desk. Put the ledgers I was using in the seamstress's room."

"Yes, Mistress."

The Mistress of Oakwood turned and fixed her deep brown eyes on the housekeeper. "Madame Smallwood is still . . . in the town?"

"She has not returned, Mistress."

Hélène strode across the main hall to the front door where she expected to find the outdoor staff assembled. "Get the boys. Have them stand by my side." She didn't wait for the housekeeper's response as she stepped outside into the fresh-ness of a beautiful morning. Members of the outdoor staff were assembling, lining up by seniority of position. She cast a practised eye over the outside staff—mostly men—and noted an absence. "Where's Digger?"

"He's gone workin' in the pens this morning, Mistress, and then swillin' the pigs."

Unconsciously wrinkling her nose at the thought of an excrement-spattered field servant, Hélène ordered, "Have him not come to assembly."

"Yes, Mistress. Digger won't be here."

Through the trees, she could see movement on Church Street. Without looking around she asked, "Where are the boys?"

"Coming up to your left side, Mistress."

She put her hand down. The older boy, Joseph, thrust his hand into hers and positioned himself close to his Aunt. The smaller boy ran around and grasped her other hand. Everyone had done this before; they were very much aware of the role they were to play in *The Master's Homecoming*.

The rider passed through the gates where he urged his horse to a canter. He was smiling as he dismounted.

"Good news, brother?"

Before he could answer, the smaller boy, John, took two running leaps and threw himself into his father's arms.

"Oh, it's always you, first. Always wanting the attention." Giving the boy a playful spank he handed the child off and held his hands out to the older boy. He saw the hesitation. "Not getting shy at the ripe old age of six, are you, Joseph?"

"No, Father, but Aunt Hélène advised me it would be more seemly for us to shake hands."

Very sternly, and formally, father and son shook hands. The boy stepped back into the care of his tutor.

"Where is Madame Smallwood?"

Without hesitation, Hélène answered, "She had appointments in the town. I expect her back before dark." *I'll make sure of it*—she suppressed a grin—*I'll send Digger to fetch her in the enclosed carriage, where the essence de manure will linger even if she makes Digger get off and walk home.*

The Master of Oakwood waved a dismissal to the staff as he entered the main hall. The only movement was the butler at the entrance taking his master's outer gear.

Hélène nodded her head and the staff dispersed to their duties. From inside came the call, "Hélène! Where are you? We have things to discuss."

"Coming, brother."

When she entered the office, she sniffed. *Nothing, no lavender.* She held her hand out to take the glass of sherry from her brother. She waited for him to become comfortable behind his desk before taking one of the little chairs.

"I don't know how you always manage that grand ceremony upon each of my returns."

Hélène countered, "And how was London?"

"Fine, thank you. I have news from America."

Hélène raised an eyebrow. "Our dear Mister Tierney has removed those two bounders from Smallwood lands?"

Joseph scowled. In an attempt to disguise his displeasure, he turned quickly away to stare out the window. "Tierney is doing a fine job—"

"But he hasn't been able to rid us of those two . . ."

"It is difficult to harass Englishmen—particularly two Englishmen who have served their monarch—without garnering a great deal of official attention." He harrumphed. "You know . . . a man's home is his castle . . ."—his voice dwindled away as he lamely finished, "and all that sort of thing." He shrugged his shoulders and, in a smaller voice he added, "Tierney assures me that the very laws that protect the rights of Englishmen will be used to get rid of our two interlopers." He gave an encouraging smile to his sister. "It will take some time but English law will be used to—"

Hélène interrupted, "So that was the message from America?"

Joseph turned to face his sister; he wanted to see her face when he broke the news. "Our Cousin William is now the Governor of Maryland." He searched her face, looking for a reaction. *None.*

"At least Mister Tierney has been making regular deposits,"—she indicated the ledgers—"all correct and in good order." She smiled at the Master of Oakwood. "You made an excellent choice when you hired Tierney."

"Did you not hear me, Hélène? I said Cousin William is the Governor of—"

"I heard you." She opened the ledger and ran her finger down a column. "I seem to remember you saying he was a traitor."

"Major General William Smallwood is now the head of a large province of an independent nation. I believe it would improve the family position if we invited General Smallwood to—"

"You said we should never allow him to set foot here again."

Joseph turned his back on his sister in exasperation. He stood clenching and unclenching his hands. Finally, he ordered, "Send him an invitation. It will be good for the family business and, besides, I thought you might be happy to renew an old—how should I say—contact." He turned around and attempted to stare her down. After searching her expressionless face, he made a cutting motion with his hands. "See to it. I want him invited." When there was still no discernible response, he hardened his voice. "Just see to it." Joseph Smallwood, Master of Oakwood, stormed out of the office.

Hélène sighed. She closed the ledger and reached across for some writing paper. She smiled as she heard her brother finding fault with every servant he met in his journey across the main hall and up the grand staircase. In the upper hall he must have startled one of the maids because there was a crash, closely followed by a sharp oath and female weeping. Finally, the door to the master bedroom slammed. She listened, but an uneasy quiet had descended over the manor. Hélène dipped the nib into the ink, hesitating as she considered the salutation.

She put the pen down. *No! I have written him several times. I will not write again. He is a traitor. He betrayed me. We can well do without the presence of Major General William Smallwood on our social calendar.*

Hélène Smallwood sat for the longest while before she took the blank sheet of foolscap and replaced it in the drawer.

* * *

Late that same night, with the rest of the household hushed in sleep, Hélène returned to the office. She settled herself into the big chair behind the master's desk and, opening the drawer, she chose a fresh sheet of foolscap and selected a good pen. Dipping the nib she began: Dearest William.

Midsummer 1785
The Cameron Farm

"Aren't you afraid you'll get caught?"

Donald McIntyre smiled. "Not likely, chum. I do the inventory. I make the reports. Besides, even if they catch me, there's no real punishment for a government official." He lifted a bale from the horse and tossed it to his friend. "Even if they were real pissed at me . . ."

Both of them looked around to see if either woman was within earshot. Satisfied they were alone, Donald continued but with a lowered voice. "Even if they were . . . tremendously unhappy with me, the most that would happen is a couple of hours in the stocks followed by a stint of free room and board in the jail."

Robert hefted the bale. "Seems soft. What is it?"

"Diapers. Can't get enough of them for my clients." Donald looked past Robert toward the trail. "Someone's coming." Donald squinted. "My eyes aren't as good as they once were. Can't make out who he is but he's Acadian. Young chap." Donald took the bale from Robert's arms and carried it into the barn. "You go talk to him," he said over his shoulder.

Robert raised his arm in greeting and walked out to meet the stranger.

Through the open door, Reine could see the two men talking. Suddenly, Robert put his arms around the stranger and hugged him close. "Reine!" he shouted. "Come see who this is." Robert took the stranger's hands and danced around and around. "It's Jacques!"

Reine untied her apron and placed it carefully on the table. "I don't know any Jacques," she muttered as she went out into the sunlight. "Certainly not anybody named Jacques that I would expect my husband to dance with." Yet she felt there was something familiar about the way the stranger stood there, now with his hands on his hips, waiting for Reine to say something . . . or do something. *Strange, he makes me think of Maurice, but it couldn't be. This man is thirty . . . perhaps thirty-five. Maurice would be much older. Besides, they were sent to France.* As she got closer, she knew the smile; it was a Gallant smile. *My God! He's one of Maurice's boys.* She ran forward and drew the young man into her embrace.

During the next hours, through a good meal and into the evening, the cousins reminisced. There were tears at the loss of Maurice, Angélique, André and Simon—old wounds for Jacques but a fresh and sudden loss for Reine. Robert, Joseph, and Donald maintained a respectful silence while Rosalie wept as the tale was recounted how there were only four survivors from the over seven hundred passengers on the two vessels that foundered off England: two sailors, Jacques and a priest.[1]

"I lived with English priests for years. An English priest at Charlotte Town, Reverend DesBrisay, reported back to my priests that some Gallants at Rivière-du-Nord-Est would give me a home. Et voilà! Here I am."

Reine leaned forward, excited. "We lived at Rivière-du-Nord-Est before the English came." In a halting voice she asked, "Are there . . . does anyone still remember us?"

"Yes. Old Francis Gaudet remembers you. He was the one who told me you were here, living with an Englishman." He glanced at Robert and fell silent.

Rosalie asked about each of her cousins so that she might know of them.

Manfully, Jacques attempted to paint a word picture of his family until, beset by his grief, he shook his head and covered his eyes, the tears flowing through his fingers. Hoping to ease his heartache, Reine hummed a song—from the old days—and before long, Jacques joined in, the two of them singing, seeming to invite the flickering shadows to resurrect the essence of the Maurice Gallant family. The songs had lilt, the words had meaning, and the verses were repeated to encourage the listeners to join in. Everyone clapped their hands to the rhythm but only Rosalie sang the songs and shared in the love that enfolded the three of them around that Acadian fire.

Joseph was the first to leave, soon followed by Donald.

At the end of one of the songs, Rosalie said, "Robbie would just love this."

Jacques raised his head. "Who is Robbie?"

"Our son; he went to Havre Saint Pierre for some supplies." Robert gave Jacques a knowing look accompanied by a furtive encircled forefinger signal for sexual encounter. "Sometimes, if there's reason enough, he stays over."

Jacques shrugged. "I can't imagine what would keep a young man away from chez soi." Jacques misunderstood Robert's look of incredulity as one of enquiry. "It's like you English and your evensong," he went on to explain, "although we Acadians don't pray very much." He reached over to pat Robert's knee. "But we sing a lot." He withdrew his hand but maintained a friendly smile. "You should sing with us. It is the Acadian way." He motioned with his hand. "Singing eases life's burdens." He motioned again. "Come closer, Robert Cameron. We would want you to be part of this chez soi."

Bashfully, Robert demurred. "I don't sing very well."

"Yes, you do!" Rosalie explained that her father had taught her all the verses of *The Hundred Pipers*. She moved quickly to sit at her father's feet, where she encouraged him to join her as she sang the verses. Finally, as Rosalie began the final chorus, Robert Cameron raised his voice in pride of his race.

"Dumbfounded the English, they saw they saw.
Dumbfounded, they heard the blaw, the blaw.
Dumbfounded, they ran awa, awa,
'fray the hundred pipers and aw' and aw'."

"Pa said that the English were afraid of us and they ran away." She stood. She took her father's hand and pulled him over to sit by the fire. "And you have heard him; my Pa has a fine voice."

Later, after Robert had excused himself from the chez soi and gone to check the animals, Jacques brought up the obvious. "Living on this farm, you are far removed from any community. You should move back to Rivière-du-Nord-Est where your family awaits you."

Reine could see the shock and alarm on her daughter's face. She squeezed Rosalie's hand to prevent an outburst of anger. "Rosalie, he means no harm. It is his place—nôtre patriarche—to give advice where he thinks it is needed."

Rosalie was not to be stilled—not by hand nor by reason. "He's no older than I . . ."

Reine interrupted. "He *is* older and he is family to us."

Rosalie shook her head. "My father is the head of this family."

Jacques nodded his head in agreement. "Your father has done a wonderful job; you survived when many didn't, but there are things that he cannot do for you."

"Like what?"

"Did your husband die?"

"I haven't taken a man."

"You will soon be too old for a man to take you."

"Oh!" Rosalie jumped up. Red-faced with anger, she stomped her foot once, twice. "I don't have to put up with this!"

Reine tried to stop her daughter from going out into the night but she was shrugged off. Reine came back to the fire and sat down. "She will be all right. She'll go to Joseph and have a good cry."

"You leave her alone with . . .?" Jacques suspended that line of reasoning when he was confronted by the mother's anger.

"Joseph is as much family as anyone else!" and, as an after thought, "so is Donald. They are like uncles to the girl."

Jacques Gallant persisted. "There are elders in Rivière-du-

Nord-Est who would be uncles who could teach her Acadian ways and values. You should do the right thing and bring her home."

The fire crackled and a log fell. Jacques pushed the burning piece back with the toe of his boot.

"You will ruin your boot that way."

"Maybe so. There have been no men for Rosalie?"

"There was a nice boy but the American pirates took him."

"No one since?"

Reine thought for a moment before answering, "No. There has been no other."

Robert clumped his feet against the boot scraper before re-entering the house. He shut the door softly and looked around. "Where is Rosalie?"

"She went to visit with Joseph."

He turned around. "I will go get her. There are so many more tenant farmers around these days, I don't like the thoughts of her being out alone after dark."

With the door closed, Jacques took Reine's hand in his. "I don't mean to cause you heartache but I feel I must ask. Is your grandson being brought up Acadian? Does he speak French? What kind of name is 'Cuddy'?"

Reine patted Jacques's hand to release his hold. "Robbie was a fur trader with the North West Company in Montreal. His wife died after giving birth to my grandson. She named the boy Robert Cameron."

"And the name Cuddy came from . . ."

"My son had no money but he wanted to come home to The Island. He was fortunate to find a ship's captain who was willing to take them both if Robbie worked his passage."

"What did he do with the baby?"

"The cook had the warmest place on the ship. The boy stayed there. The cabin was called the ship's cuddy."

Jacques smiled. "They called the boy Cuddy."

Reine grimaced. "Yes, they named my grandson Cuddy." She looked up as Robert and Rosalie rattled the door. "Yes, they call my grandson Cuddy Cameron," she repeated in a softer voice.

Rosalie entered with her arms outstretched to Jacques. "I am so sorry, cousin. I understand your well-meant intentions and concerns." She reached back to take her father's hand and bring him closer to the group. "Father says we should be more aware of Acadian customs."

"Yes, we should," Reine said. "Yes, of course we should."

Endnotes

[1] Originally it was believed that the *Duke William* and the *Violet* sank in the English Channel with tremendous loss of life. There was supposed to have been only four survivors: two crewmen of the *Duke William* and two Acadian passengers. The priest was one of the survivors. Research has led some historians to believe that the leaky old *Duke William* just settled into the water and more passengers were able to save themselves. I was brought up on the original story and have used it in this book.

Chapter Twelve
I Shall Be Master

Spring 1790
Oakwood Manor
Handsworth

Joseph watched his sister cross the West Lawn on her way back from the gardens. Impatient to speak with her, he grunted with annoyance when she turned and waited for the gardener to catch up with her. They had a conversation, the senior gardener showing her something and Hélène bending slightly to examine whatever it was. *That's a pretty picture,* he thought as he watched the two of them—their grey heads almost touching—standing as they were in the middle of the sun-dappled lawn. The gardener, cap in hand, sun-browned wherever his blue work clothes allowed, stood with his feet planted squarely on the lawn—reminding Joseph of the oak trees for which the manor was named. On the other hand, the mistress, clad in gold and white, seemed to have as much contact with her surroundings as an alabaster figurine left on the green playing area of a billiard table. Joseph shook his head. *Damn! I wish they would drop whatever little root or stem they are talking about so I can get on with it. I have business to discuss with that woman!* He turned away from the window. *I must set the stage.* He looked around his office. *Yes, of course. I know what to do . . .*

A few minutes later, Hélène entered the office. "You wanted to see me, Joseph?"

"Yes, my dear." He gestured: "Why don't you take the chair behind the desk. It will be more comfortable; I know you have been having a bad time with your old rheumatiz lately." He sat in the smaller chair that had been placed squarely in front of the desk.

"Uh-huh! He wants something."

Sensing his sister's hesitation, Joseph smiled his very best. "You shouldn't feel awkward about sitting behind the desk;

191

you do it every time I go away."

Hélène shrugged. "Yes, that's right." She sat down and pulled the chair forward so that she was comfortable. "These old bones need all the support they can get." She sat back, waiting. "I am reminded of the day that Father explained we were going to have more land in North America." Joseph stood and walked over the cabinet. "I remember Father pulled out the documents dealing with the land and explained in detail what it meant to be a Smallwood in the most successful empire in history." Joseph caressed the satiny wood, allowing his fingers to sense the generations of family-living. He paused, enjoying the moment.

"You must have had a letter from Tierney."

"No, I mean, yes . . . I will come to that later." He started again. "I can well remember Father's very words." Joseph made a broad sweep with his hands. "Behind the mighty shield of the Royal Navy and the British Army, English Law provides a system of ownership and land title. British Peace gives stability. Where there is stability and a system that provides for the orderly transfer of wealth, land values steadily increase. Tenants will come and go, governments will change, but the land is always there. It's always the land, he told me. It's always the land, my son."

"Are they gone?"

"Er, what do you mean?"

"The two soldiers. Did Tierney get rid of them? In every report Tierney says they are soon gone from our lands but . . ."

Joseph interrupted her. "Our Mister Tierney will get rid of the soldiers. He has done everything else he promised so I do believe he will get rid of them." Exasperated at the woman's interruptions, Joseph seized the port decanter. "Would you join me?"

"Yes, thank you."

"And, would you please allow me to say what I am meaning to say?"

Hélène accepted the glass of port with a nod of her head.

"Good." Joseph took a sip from his glass and then began

to pace. "I am of the opinion that the American Revolution spawned many ideas of individual liberties and personal worth that have raised the expectations of loyal Englishmen throughout the empire. And not just the Americans; see what happened with the Canadians—they were granted special language and religion rights—"

"That was an inexpensive gesture to buy their loyalty. Besides, in a sea of English, they will soon enough be integrated into the empire."

"Yes, of course . . . but it is seen as an increase in their personal liberty, nonetheless." He could see that his sister was about to argue further so he waved her quiet with both hands. "Hear me out!" he ordered, hurrying on, "I believe that with the independence acquired by the Americans and the special treatment awarded to the Canadians, loyal Englishmen—no matter where they live in the empire—will expect the same liberties and benefits that they would have if they were living in England."

Impatiently, Hélène said, "Yes, yes." *Get on with it! What are you after?*

"Saint John's Island is the only place in North America where there is no land available for the rabble to hold in freehold."

"I know that! All the land belongs either to the Crown or to the proprietors. What's wrong with that?"

"As I said, the spawning of this sentiment . . ."

"What sentiment?"

". . . that every Englishman should have the same rights and privileges no matter where he lives in the empire. An Englishmen would expect that, if he works hard and betters himself, he should be able to acquire title to the land he works."

"Humbug! Most of our tenants are non-English." She looked up sharply and voiced her sudden thought: "The Frenchmen would never be able to hold title . . . would they?" When her brother didn't immediately answer, she pressed on with her query. "They are Papists. They can't vote or hold public office; why would they expect to have title to the land?"

"Some of the moneyed Acadians on Saint John's Island bought title to land after 1780."

In a smaller voice Hélène said, "I didn't know that." She experienced a sudden insight. "You acquired this new theory from Tierney, didn't you?"

Joseph settled into the little chair, lifted his chin, and said, somewhat defiantly, "So what if I did? Tierney believes the tenants will form interest groups and, eventually, seek political office and pass laws that will put absentee landlords . . ."

"Like the Smallwoods . . ."

" . . . at a disadvantage. Initially, we won't like the laws and—sooner or later—we will be hurt by them; perhaps even to the extent that the laws force us to relinquish title." Joseph pulled a file from the cabinet. "I went over our accounts and can now give you a reckoning."

Hélène leaned forward, very interested. In all her time of working from the master's desk, she had been unable to find the account book for Lot 38. Her lips parted slightly, in anticipation of what might be revealed. *I had no idea where he kept that ledger*, she thought.

Almost in answer to her unasked question, Joseph volunteered, "I gave it to Reverend Matheson in the village for safe-keeping. By the way, he told me about the church warning bell."

"Ah yes."

"No matter. I think we can both agree; it is always the land, just like Father said." He riffled through the pages of the ledger, finally settling on a particular page. "But Father couldn't have foreseen the problems." Joseph tapped the bottom of the page. "There has been a litany of problems: some years we haven't been able to collect all of the rents causing a shortfall when you take into account our payments to the Crown, there have been support costs for some of the tenants who would have starved to death if we hadn't helped them, and Mister Tierney doesn't come cheaply. Altogether, the accounts for Lot 38 show an accumulative loss of £1,118 12/2." He pressed his lips into a thin line. "And I intend to get rid of the red ink."

"I am listening."

Joseph gave her an appreciative look. "I believe Tierney when he says that the tenants will begin to put pressure on the local government to force sale of the land to residents by distraint proceedings. They might not succeed at first, but time is on their side. I believe that the residents will eventually have their way, winning title to the land they live on."

"What does Tierney propose?"

"He proposes nothing. It is my plan to have a Smallwood resident on Lot 38. That way we will have someone on the winning side." Joseph offered to refill Hélène's glass but she declined. He filled his glass to the brim and studied the colour before taking a mouthful. "As we develop the skills, we can eventually do without the services of Francis Tierney, thus reducing our costs significantly."

"I don't know who you would send. I probably wouldn't survive the crossing."

"I agree. At your age, you would find the trip very difficult."

"Then who? Cousin William is the only other family we have and he won't be much interested in—"

"If you will take over the stewardship of Oakwood, I will accompany John to Lot 38."

Hélène almost purred as she answered, "Of course, brother dear. I will do anything I can to help, you know that." *This time, when the little bugger goes away, it will be no sham; I shall be Mistress of Oakwood.* "I will help any way I can," she repeated.

"As soon as Mister Tierney unburdens our property of one of the soldiers, I have instructed him to build a modest house and barn at that location." Joseph was startled into silence by the piercing look his sister gave him. He waited for her to speak.

I won't live long enough, she thought. *My nitwit son still believes we will be rid of those . . .*

"What bothers you, sister? That I await the departure of one of the soldiers before I have our man build a place to stay? The soldiers chose well . . . probably the best location on Lot 38. It is secluded, yet close to the river and near enough to Saint Peter's Harbour that we can easily . . ."

Hélène wanted to say, "Oh Joseph! You are such an ass! Build your house somewhere else; you have plenty of land. Don't waste another year. Take control of the situation . . ." but she restrained herself. *I never get my own way when I make him angry.* She pursed her lips as if considering a reply.

". . . get supplies except at the coldest times of the year." He reached over, taking her hand in his. "What troubles you? Is it something else?"

"You must remember that I am in my declining years." She saw he was going to interrupt so she squeezed his hand to forestall comment. "I can't always be here for you, Joseph." She had his full attention now. "If it is your considered judgement that we wait years"—she allowed her voice to weaken and trail away as she looked up to give him her sweetest smile—"then you can always appoint a stranger to help Isabelle manage Oakwood while you are tending family business in the New World." She believed she had gone too far when Joseph dropped her hand, stood abruptly, and began waving his arms in wide sweeping motions.

"You believe Isabelle could manage all of this?" He snorted a half-laugh. "She can't even . . . He searched for words. "She's not . . . she's not a Smallwood."

"But Joseph! If we are forced to wait until—"

"I will give Tierney his orders . . ."

"In your most forceful manner?"

"In my most forceful manner. Those soldiers are as good as gone."

Hélène couldn't stop herself; victory was in sight and she pursued it. "And building the Island house? Tierney will be told to begin this year?"

Joseph regarded Hélène as if he were seeing her for the first time. Now it was Joseph Smallwood who pursed his lips as he considered his reply.

"We don't want to lose a year. We have plenty of sites to choose from and . . ."

"I have chosen the site, Hélène. When the soldiers are gone, the Island house will be built."

Chapter Thirteen
Gaol

23 February 1791
Jailhouse
Charlotte Town

Sheriff William Winter rattled the keys in the lock of the main door to the jailhouse. Through the bars he gave some advice to the visitor. "You can only have a few minutes; they'll be comin' for him in a short while and I got to get him ready for court. You his lawyer?" He motioned the visitor in, allowing barely enough time for Joseph Farrow to enter the building before the door was slammed shut. "I have three of them for today. Yours is in the last cell on the right. They wanted him kept solitary-like. He's the one they want manacled, for sure."

"Why is that?"

"Manacles or solitary-like?"

"Why is Mister McIntyre to be manacled? What's he charged with?"

"Don't they tell you lawyers nothin'?" Sheriff Winter shook his head in wonderment. "How do they expect you to put up a proper defence unless you know all the facts . . ."— he winked—"unless the fix is in?"

Angrily, Joseph turned on the sheriff. "What are you sayin'?"

The sheriff backed away, raising his hands in a disclaiming motion. "I didn't mean harm, counsel; just thinkin' out loud." He motioned for Joseph to follow him down the long, narrow hall.

The voice from the far cell was strong and confident. "Then take your inappropriate thoughts back to your office, Sheriff, and leave us be."

With keys rattling and his tread echoing in the hall, Sheriff Winter pushed past Farrow and started back to the front of the building. "You should tell your client that I can make his time here a lot easier if he's polite." Still smarting he hissed, "Special things happen to those that deserve them."

Joseph opened his mouth to challenge the court official on his threat, but snapped his mouth shut and turned to speak to his friend instead. "I should have . . ."

"No. You made the wise move, buddy." Donald extended both arms through the bars to grasp his comrade's hands in his. "I should have kept my trap shut too; he can make it very uncomfortable for me."

"He thinks I'm your lawyer. Don't you have a lawyer?"

"Naw. Don't need one."

"What's the charge?"

"Petty larceny. Since I don't have a lawyer, they gave me the specifications of the charge." Donald tilted the paper to one side so he could better catch the light from the window. "It says here that previous to the detection of Donald McIntyre in the alleged thefts of the property of his master, James Douglas, Esq., Comptroller of His Majesty's Customs and other sundry small articles from different persons, he had generally been considered and received as an honest man . . . ."

"We need a lawyer, Donald. That sounds like you've already been found guilty. If you had a lawyer . . ."

"I don't need a lawyer." Donald silenced any further protests by holding up the flat of his hand. "Listen to me!" Satisfied that Joseph was going to pay attention, Donald explained. "They got me dead to rights. Remember the new lining that Rosalie sewed into my jacket? Well, she used the diaper cloth that I had brought home that very first time. She used the oznabrigs . . ."

"What? What the hell are oz-na-brigs?"[1]

"It's a cloth that is one hundred per cent linen. Well, she used the oznabrigs to reline the pockets."

"That was a long time ago. Surely they can't charge you at this late date?"

Donald ran his finger down the page. "I'm charged with stealing ten yards of diaper cloth, ten gallons of rum, fifteen gallons of molasses, one hundred pounds of beef and . . . let me see . . . ten pounds of nails."

"My God! How could you carry all that stuff?"

"Simple. I didn't carry it because I didn't steal it." Donald looked around as if he thought someone might overhear them. "They found me with two bottles of rum . . ."

"Was that all you took?"

"Yes. Well, it was all I took this time. I take two bottles a trip."

"And what else did they find?"

"They found a hat . . . but that was none of my doing. A friend of mine gave it to me. It was too big for him but it fit me just fine." With a rueful smile Donald added, "Besides, I needed a hat. February is a cold month on The Island and the guy who gave me the hat—his name is John Allen—probably found it somewhere. He wouldn't have known that the owner's name was under the hatband."

"If you had a lawyer, he would call this Allen fellow as a witness."

"Maybe so, but I don't mean to get John in trouble."

You're the one in trouble, Joseph thought. "Is there anythin' else?"

"No . . . well, yes. I was supposed to have stolen a water pitcher from the priest Theophilus DesBrisay."

"And did you?"

"Me? Steal from a priest? Not on your life!"

"Then how did you get the blame?"

"The sheriff found the pitcher in my trunk." Donald shrugged. "Not that it matters much, but I can explain that one. A friend of John Allen—John MacDonald—gave me the pitcher. I had seen it in his chest and thought it was just the thing for you to give young Rosalie, all japanned like it was. He also had an axe—barely been used—he said he was willing to give me. It would have been a nice gift for Robbie but the sheriff came before I could pick it up."

They heard the footsteps coming down the hall and the jangling of the keys.

Joseph, who could see down the hall, said, "Three men: the sheriff, a short guy carrying manacles, and a big man carrying a gun."

Sheriff Winter pointed at Joseph. "You, step back! Go out the door at the end of the hall, turn left and it's just a block to the courthouse." When he saw that Joseph was trying to whisper to the prisoner, the sheriff hurried forward and thrust his arm between the visitor and the cell. "Go now, lawyer!"

"Yes, sir," Joseph quickly answered. "Mister McIntyre needs more competent help than I can give him." Joseph spoke over the sheriff's shoulder "I will try to find someone to act as counsel for you, Mister McIntyre."

* * *

Joseph Farrow chased through the slush and cold trying to find some legal aid for his friend but no one was willing to talk to him. By the time he returned to the courthouse, the prosecutor was summing up the case against Donald McIntyre.

"You have seen from the samples of the diaper cloth and the oznabrigs provided by the Customs House and that they corresponded in colour, consistency, and make to the materials used in the linings and pockets of the prisoner's clothes." His voice dripping with sarcasm, the prosecutor leaned toward the jury as if telling them a secret. "And Mister McIntyre claims he brought the diaper cloth and oznabrigs from Scotland." He stepped back to the evidence table and raised one of the bottles of rum for all to see. "At first, the prisoner said he bought the bottles from a Negro man of the name of Davy. You will remember, when I suggested it would not prove difficult to find such a person in our little community—if indeed such a person existed—our prisoner changed his story, saying that he had purchased the rum in the dusk of the evening from a black man that was unknown to him."

The prosecutor took his time replacing the rum bottles on the evidence table. He seemed to hesitate before picking up the japanned pitcher. He examined it, turning it this way and that, seeming to admire the finish. Abruptly he put it down.

"Stealing from an Anglican priest! Despicable!" He selected the hat and put it down almost immediately. "The prisoner didn't even bother to remove the true owner's name from the hatband. Oh, Mister McIntyre is guilty, all right."

The prosecutor took a deep, deep breath. Speaking slowly and emphasizing each word he said, "I ask you to view the evidence and to remember the prisoner's attempts at prevarication. I know that in the breast of every man of the jury there can be no doubt remaining as to the prisoner's guilt." The prosecutor bowed his head in the direction of the Chief Justice and sat down.

Then, solemnly, the Chief Justice charged the jury to return an impartial verdict agreeable to their conscience and the spirit of justice.

* * *

Joseph Farrow was not surprised when the jury returned shortly with the verdict—guilty—but he was astonished when his friend was sentenced to receive corporal punishment.

As Donald McIntyre was led away, Joseph continued to sit in his place as he considered the consequences of the trial. *Donald had expected to spend time in the stocks and a month or two in the jail if he were found guilty. Where did the judge get the authority to impose a whipping on a prisoner found guilty of petty larceny? Not in the history of The Island had anyone been whipped!* Joseph cringed; *my time under the lash was bad enough but it could have been worse if they used a cat o' nine tails. Oh, please dear Lord, don't let it be the cat. Donald hasn't been whipped before. Don't let it be the cat on his first time.* He was shaken from his trance by the words of the Court Clerk: "The King against John Allen." *John Allen. Isn't that Donald's friend— the one who gave Donald the water pitcher?*

Joseph listened as the charges were read and the evidence presented that John Allen had been identified as the person who had stolen a bedtick and japanned water pitcher from Reverend Theophilus DesBrisay—the very same Theophilus DesBrisay who later recanted his identification of John Allen as the intruder and thief. The verdict was predictable; the prisoner had a plausible reason for borrowing the bedtick and Donald McIntyre had already been convicted for the water pitcher. Bemused, Joseph heard the "Not Guilty" as if in a dream. He was not surprised when he heard the clerk announce, "The King against John Macdonald." The charge was theft of an axe from Mrs. John Boyer of Stanhope. *An axe? Someone offered Donald an axe* . . . but before Joseph could follow that thought much further, MacDonald was acquitted, following convincing and irreproachable testimony from respected members of the community.

This is a set-up. Someone went to a great deal of trouble . . . but to what end? I must speak to the Court Clerk.

Joseph waited until the room had cleared and made his way to the prisoner's dock. He cleared his throat to get the attention of the clerk, who was tidying up his papers.

The clerk looked up and sighed. "Now, how can I help you?" he asked in a barely polite, bored voice.

"I didn't know petty thieves could be sentenced to a whuppin'."

"Since two months." Warming to the subject, the clerk explained, "In fact, our new criminal law statute encourages the use of the whip. Judges now follow the dictates of the 1530 Whipping Act of King Henry the Eighth which specifies that the offender be tied to the end of a cart and whipped until the body becomes bloody."

"Oh!"

"Yes, indeed. The customary punishment is one hundred and eight stripes . . ."

"No one can live after one hundred and eight stripes."

"Ah! Yes, they can." He riffled through papers on his desk apparently to find the name of the prisoner. "Now, take this McIntyre fellow; he'll get one hundred and eight stripes. He'll be tied by his arms to the end of a cart. They will probably begin the whipping parade opposite Richardson's Coffee House. I expect the town bell will be rung to announce the beginning of the parade. I have no idea where they will take him from there because McIntyre is the very first prisoner to be whipped under the new law."

"One hundred and eight stripes?"

"Not all at once. Day after tomorrow"—he checked his papers again—"one Donald McIntyre will receive thirty-six stripes." He glanced at his little calendar. "And on March 9 he will get thirty-six more and—la-de-da—eight days after that there will be one more parade so he gets his full one hundred and eight stripes." Unconsciously the clerk licked his lips. "Oh, his body will become all bloody, for sure." He looked up in time to see Joseph running out of the courtroom. The clerk shouted after him, "Listen for the bell . . . you won't want to miss the parade!"

Joseph ran all the way to the jailhouse. *I must warn Donald. I must tell him what they are doin' to him.* He rattled the main door but, this time, no one answered. He went to the side door but he couldn't see in. Joseph returned to the front entrance in time to see the door being held wide open for a well-dressed gentleman to enter. The door was slammed in Joseph's face. He grasped the bars and rattled the big door. "I must see my client! He must be told what is going on." Joseph put all his weight against the door and attempted to force his way in. Of course, he failed; the door had been built in anticipation of much stronger forces than a middle-aged Joseph Farrow could muster.

Joseph heard the key being turned in the lock. He stepped back and waited to see who was there as the door slowly swung wide; it was the well-dressed gentleman.

Francis Tierney adjusted the collar of his coat; the sun was going down and the breeze off the water was penetratingly cold and damp. *It's hard to imagine this little man as a soldier of the empire,* he thought. He sniffed his disdain. "I wish to assure you, Mister Farrow, that your friend will have it all explained to him how he fell afoul the law and his options to avoid the whip . . ."

"What kind of options?"

"None of them beyond his capacity, believe me. As I said, I can assure you that Donald McIntyre can avoid the whip."

Francis Tierney smiled a sad little smile. "In this world we all have roles to play. You and McIntyre served your monarch well and were amply . . . nay, may I suggest that you both were more than generously rewarded . . . along with Sergeant Brown, weren't you? Now, your friend McIntyre has a role to play here in Charlotte Town and it doesn't have to be a tragedy. Trust me. He can come out of this drama unmarked. On the other hand, your role is to return to the farm and take care of your ladies, Rosalie and Reine, as best you can during the time left to you. Hold the youngster Cuddy close to hand, Mister Farrow . . . ."

Joseph blinked at the implied threats and the extent of the man's knowledge about his past. He swallowed hard but continued his quest to help his friend. "I must speak with McIntyre."

Tierney showed some anger but quickly replaced it with his warm smile. "That won't happen, Mister Farrow. If you are still in Charlotte Town on February 25th, I can foresee you playing a role of your own in the Supreme Court of The Island of Saint John." Tierney stepped back and an unseen person swung the door shut. Tierney spoke through the bars. "Leave town. I have the temerity to suggest you make plans to leave The Island. Take your pseudo-family with you."

"Why? Why are you doin' this?"

"It should be enough that you can see that I am able to do it; the why is not important. I go now to speak with your friend. If he is smart, he will take my advice and he will come out of this tragedy unmarked. In fact, McIntyre could be free to join you wherever you want to go. But if I were you, I wouldn't linger in Halifax. The Halifax authorities might want to have a word about your clever little schemes."

Joseph stared into the darkness behind the bars. He sensed there was no longer anyone there.

25 February 1791
Richardson's Coffee House

At the first toll of the town bell, Francis Tierney stepped out into the weak sun of a crisp February morning. He had expected to see a crowd but not one as large as had gathered to witness The Island's first whipping. Across the street from Richardson's, a cariole with runners was being positioned so that the tailgate of the little carriage was facing the coffee house. Sheriff Winter was reading the charges, twelve soldiers of the Queen's County Regiment were standing with their rifles at the ready, while a large man, all dressed in black, was off to one side, caressing the end of a mean-looking whip.

Tierney viewed the scene and then took a little sip from the steaming cup in his hand. "Too much sweet," he complained and handed the cup off to one of the blacks who always seemed to anticipate their master's wishes. "Did he make any kind of signal, Cecil?"

"No suh. I deen't see no signal."

"It is more correct to say, I didn't see a signal."

"Yes, suh. I didn't see a signal." Cecil studied the prisoner for a moment before adding, "He has a big case of the shivers, Mister Tierney, but I don't see a signal from the prisoner."

Tierney smiled at the slave. "That was just fine, Cecil. You'll soon be speaking the King's English as well as Samuel."

Cecil stepped back several paces into the shadow of the building.

The crowd noises stilled as the prisoner was stripped to the waist, revealing leather thongs tied to his wrists.

Samuel appeared and approached his master.

"Yes, Samuel?"

"That other man you were interested in . . ."

"Yes."

"He didn't leave town. He stayed the night. Is it all right for me to point, sir?"

"That would be most appropriate, Samuel."

"He is standing in the shadows of the old grey building."

"That's too bad." Tierney turned to look in the direction that his slave was pointing. There was movement in the small group of spectators in front of the grey building as someone hastily left the gathering.

Anticipating that his master's short-sightedness would provoke another question, Samuel said, "He saw me point. He is running away."

"Have Cecil follow him to ascertain which direction he takes out of town. If he remains in town, I want to know where he is." When Samuel didn't move, Tierney pursed his lips in annoyance. "Ah, yes. The word ascertain means to learn, Samuel. Tell Cecil to go learn which direction he takes out of town."

"Thank you, sir."

He redirected his attention to the spectacle. The prisoner's thongs were securely tied to the carriage tailgate. *That must be an uncomfortable position—stretched out like that—neither standing nor kneeling.* That thought made him uncomfortable; he didn't like being the author of unnecessary pain and suffering—there was so much of it in the world already. His eyes drifted to the officer dressed in a coat of scarlet with green facings who was positioning himself to give commands to the military guard. *That's Lieutenant Albert DesBrisay. I must say that family does well: a DesBrisay as lieutenant governor, another is colonel of the Queen's County Militia, and this young whelp gets company lieutenant.*

The lieutenant barked his commands and the guard moved smartly to the right—white cross-belts, regimental gold lace, elegant epaulets, fixed bayonets, and glinting metal-tipped scabbards dancing across an otherwise sombre scene.

While the soldiers were marching off to one side, the man with the whip was laying out the distance to give his whip full play across the exposed flesh. Once the soldiers were turned into line, the whip was manipulated a few more times and then the man with the whip assumed a firm stance and nodded to the sheriff that he was ready.

Sheriff Winter offered the prisoner a piece of leather to bite down upon but McIntyre showed no inclination to accept the object. The sheriff folded the leather once, twice, and then pushed the wad into the prisoner's mouth, where it stayed. Sheriff Winter stepped back and nodded to the man with the whip.

The noise of the whip moving through the air must have frightened the horse, causing it to bolt. Carriage and prisoner were dragged far enough for most of the stripe to fall across the prisoner's lower back and buttocks.

McIntyre yelped with pain as he was hauled on his knees across the frozen slush.

The sheriff growled with anger. "Didn't you put the brake on?"

"I did, sir," the frightened handler cried. "Honest to God, Sheriff, and I had her firm by the harness, I did."

"Then hobble the beast or I will have you both flogged." He pointed at the man with the whip. "Begin again."

Shaking his head, Francis Tierney turned away and re-entered the coffee house. He chose a table near the door but quickly changed his mind and moved to the far end of the hall, near the fireplace. Even there he could hear the noises from the crowd with each crack of the whip. Eventually, when there was quiet, a number of customers entered the coffee house, stamping the cold from their feet. The whipping parade had finally moved on.[2]

6 March 1791
Jailhouse

Francis Tierney watched his two boys minister to the sorely injured back. It was obvious that the whip had been applied professionally; the pattern was so plain to see. "Tsk, tsk," Tierney said with what he hoped would sound like a sympathetic voice. "Your back is almost ruined and there are only three more days before they will do it again."

Donald McIntyre was lying on the cot, face down, so his voice was somewhat muffled. "Don't jerk me around, you bastard! I gave you the signal that I was willing to talk." With a groan he lifted his head so that he could see his tormentor. "You said you could stop it if I gave the signal. I gave the goddamn signal and you let them whip me."

Today was the first time Tierney had seen the prisoner since the whipping parade and he was startled to observe how deep and black were the circles under the eyes, how gaunt the face and how tremulous the voice—even in the middle of its owner's display of anger.

"I saw no signal. I confirmed with Samuel that you gave no signal before my sensibility forced me to depart that dreadful scene."

"It's goddamn hard to give a signal when both arms are tied . . . . And who the hell is Samuel?"

"Samuel is my boy who is dabbing the balm into your wounds. Cecil is working on your wrists."

"You and your goddamn Samuels and Cecils caused all this. I didn't do anything this last month that I haven't been doing for years; suddenly you haul me up and get me whipped!"

"It was not sudden, Mister McIntyre." Tierney nodded to the slave and Samuel moved out of the way while Cecil placed a chair where Tierney could sit and look right into the prisoner's eyes. "I considered having you called to account for your Halifax fiddle but there would have been difficulties getting you to leave The Island and"—he sighed—"one can never trust strangers to handle one's business; my friends are here at Charlotte Town. No, it was not sudden. Patience and planning was what it took . . ."—he spread his arms—"and here we are."

"All because you want my land?"

"Your land means nothing to me. I am just a soldier—like you—who has a duty to perform. Orders are given and it is a soldier's duty to obey." Tierney leaned forward and lowered his voice. "If you will sign over your land to Joseph Smallwood, I will arrange for the remaining punishment to be remitted."

Again the prisoner lifted his head. "I told you I can't do that!"

"Or I can request that the second flogging be laid on much harder."

McIntyre lowered his head as his tortured frame was shaken by his sobbing. "I signed the land over to Robert Cameron."

Startled, Tierney leaned forward and blurted, "That's not true! There has been no change of title registered."

"It is true. He just hasn't registered it yet."

"Then write another to supersede Cameron's title."

"I wrote it as a final, irrevocable assignment of title. It was signed and witnessed." A note of despair coloured McIntyre's voice. "You see, I can't help you." He began to sob. "Please don't let them beat me again. Please."

Tierney rose from his chair. "Our business is done." He watched as Cecil lifted the chair and placed it against the wall. With a flick of the wrist, he ordered his slaves to leave the cell. "I hope you survive, McIntyre."

"No-o-o-o-o! Don't leave me here. Please don't leave me here."

"Good day and good luck."

"I can tell you where the slate is!"

"Slate? What do you mean by slate?"

"I wrote it on a slate. Cameron didn't know about it. He probably still doesn't know about the slate."

"Where is it?"

"Rosalie hid it behind one of the beams in the barn. It's probably still there."

"I will think on it." Tierney walked to the cell door and rattled the bars. "I may return tomorrow with some papers for you to sign."

Donald McIntyre pushed himself up and swung his legs over the side of the cot. He tried to stand but fell back. He sat there, breathing hard. "I will sign. Please don't let them . . ."

"Good day, Mister McIntyre."

" . . . beat me again." He raised his voice to carry down the hall. "Please, sir. Don't let them beat me again."[3]

8 March 1791
Jailhouse

Francis Tierney watched as McIntyre feverishly signed the several copies of the legal document. "Yours was an interesting assignment," Tierney said. He took the first copy from the bed and examined the signature. "You have a nice hand, Mister McIntyre." He blew on the signature and then accepted the second copy from the prisoner. "In the beginning of the assignment, I had considerable influence with the judge and the local political chiefs. I used up a lot of that influence to get them interested in resurrecting that old law from King Henry the Eighth's time." He blew on the second signature. "I expended more goodwill when I asked that you be the very first thief to be tried under the new law." He folded the foolscap and placed the sheets in his leather case. "Finding you guilty cost me nothing; you accomplished that yourself."

Donald McIntyre pushed himself erect. "I signed your papers. When do I get out of here?"

Tierney stepped into the hall. He motioned for the guard to close the door. Not until the key was turned did he answer the question. "Any time after tomorrow." He placed his hand on the guard's arm. "When we go to the sheriff's office, I need you to witness the prisoner's signature. It's just a formality." He turned to go.

"Wait! Wait, please."

"Yes?"

"Why do I have to wait until the day after tomorrow? Isn't my punishment remitted?"

"Yes, your punishment has been remitted . . . at least to the extent I was able to arrange."

"But why must I wait until the day after tomorrow? Tomorrow is the second whipping parade."

"Yes. That is correct and I am truly sorry that I was not able to do better for you."

17 April 1791
The Cameron Farm

Reine placed a bowl of pea soup in front of the desperately hungry man. "Did you see Donald again . . . after the whipping?"

"No, I didn't." Joseph shovelled a couple of spoonfuls into his mouth and swallowed, choking a little. He tried to speak but had to clear his throat a couple of times before managing to say anything. "I was warned to leave town but . . ." he coughed again.

Robert put his hand on his friend's arm. "Just eat your meal. We can wait."

"Yes, don't choke yourself to death," Robbie said. He beckoned to his son to join them around the table. "You're old enough to learn about the world, Cuddy."

Reine shushed her son. "It's late, Robbie." She faced the boy. "It's time you went off to bed, Cuddy."

The fourteen-year-old looked to his grandfather for a response. When there was none, he cast an enquiring glance at his father before starting to move slowly toward the loft. Goaded by the boy's sullenness, both men spoke at the same time.

"Grandma's right, of course, but it wouldn't hurt for the boy to . . ."

Robbie was more direct. "Mother! You have to let the boy grow up. He should learn about . . ."

Reine stared, open-mouthed, at her two men. She took a deep breath and, with nostrils flaring, allowed the poison caused by years of hardship and oppression to spill out.

"You men! The English don't care if we understand them! They don't care if we are agreeable to what they are doing! We have something they want; they can take it because only the English have a say under the laws. Acadians have no vote, no schools, no priests . . ." She stopped and pointed at the men. "And you three English are no better off." Reine put her fingers to her lips when she saw the look of dismay cross her beloved husband's face. "I'm sorry, sweetheart; I didn't mean to hurt you."

Robert, his eyes averted, nodded his head. "Yes. We are English. Even though we are English, we have no say."

"Am I English, Grandma?"

"Yes, my dear."

"Then why do I have no say if it's only the English who have a say on this island?"

It was Robert Cameron, ex-soldier of the King, who answered the young man. "Catholics are not allowed to hold public office or vote in elections. And we Camerons are Catholics."

A look of wonderment flitted across Cuddy's face. "I didn't know I was Catholic. I thought Catholics have a priest."

Joseph pushed the empty bowl aside and leaned on his elbows. "There's a priest in Charlotte Town. I saw him in the courtroom. His name is Reverend DesBrisay; he is English Church but serves Acadians as well."

"And English Catholics like me?" Cuddy didn't wait for the answer. "I should go to Charlotte Town. I would like to have a priest."

In a stern voice, Reine declared, "You should go to Rivière-du-Nord-Est. You would be safer among the Acadians." In a more subdued voice, Reine asked Robert, "And you want Cuddy to learn to be a part of this system?" She didn't wait for an answer. "Cuddy should go to Rivière-du-Nord-Est and stay with my relatives . . . like Rosalie is doing." Reine held her hands out to her grandson; he came quickly into her arms. She stroked his unruly dark hair. "My baby should go where he can be appreciated for what he is."

Robbie shook his head, this time in disagreement. "The same English laws are in place over there. Nothing changes by leaving the farm."

"You are blind, my son. At Rivière-du-Nord-Est, if the English come, the family will stand together. They will support one another."

"I don't mean to be rude, Mother, but those seven hundred Acadians were probably standing together when that ship sank off England."

Reine almost snarled at her son. "At least at Rivière-du-Nord-Est, the families have standing in the English courts as tenants. Here, at the farm, we have nothing: no recognized tenancy, no title to the land, no—"

For the first time, Joseph Farrow interrupted. "You do have title. Donald bought the title to the farm. He gave his title to Robert."

Reine regarded Joseph in disbelief. "Why would he do that?"

"Because Rosalie asked him to."

"Show me the document."

"It's in the shed, behind the main beam. Donald signed it. I witnessed it. It was ear-re-vokabell—forever—Donald said and Donald knew about those things."

Reine thought about it for a moment or two. Then she asked, "So, where is Donald McIntyre now? He has his place with us; why didn't he come back?"

"Perhaps he couldn't come back. I know I-I-I w-w-was warned not to come back." Joseph swallowed the last of the soup and stuttered, "If–if–if . . . I c-c-came back, I was to t-t-take my family and l-l-leave here." He pointed at the members of the little group, each in his or her turn. "He said I should l-l-leave here with my family and look after Cuddy in p-p-particular in the small amount of time that I have left."

"He threatened you? Just like that?'

"Yes. I believe he meant it."

Robert broke the small period of silence that followed that. "He's English. He can say things like that and get away with it."

Joseph wore a small smile as he said, "He spoke with an Irish accent but I know what you mean."

This time, the silence was prolonged. Finally, Cuddy asked, "What happened to Uncle Donald?"

"He was paraded through the town, twice. He was supposed to go a third time, but there wasn't a third parade. No explanation; it just didn't happen."

"So, where did Donald go?"

Cuddy pulled himself loose from his grandmother's embrace. He pointed at the crack under the door where there was a yellow, flickering brightness. "Look!"

Robert could guess what it was the moment he saw it. "Fire!" He thrust open the door and ran outside. "The barn's on fire! Get buckets! Water from the brook!"

"I'll get some pots," Reine shouted as she ran back into the house.

Joseph saw something none of the others noticed—a dark figure running away into the bushes. *That bastard Irishman sent his slaves to burn us out!* He had another thought: *the slate is in the barn!* "The slate is in the barn," he shouted.

Robert was the only one who heard him. "Donald's slate? Where is it?"

"Behind the centre beam." When Joseph realized that Robert was going to enter the flaming building, he shouted, "Don't go in there, Robert! It's too late."

Robert disappeared into the smoke and flame. He was still in the building when it collapsed.

28 April 1791
Richardson's Coffee House

Mister Richardson wended his way through the tables to where Francis Tierney was sitting by the fireplace. Richardson stood, respectfully quiet, until Tierney looked up from the newspaper he was reading.

"That was a fine account of the trial and the whipping parade. Did you get a chance to read it, Mister Richardson?"

"No, sir, not yet. I usually avail myself of a copy a patron might leave behind."

"I'll leave this one for you, my friend."

"Thank you, sir. It would be much appreciated."

Richardson gave a little bow as he said, "I came over to tell you that your other slave is at the back door. Do you want to do it here or out back?"

"Let him in here. When I give the signal, have your boys join me."

"Of course, sir," the hotelier said as he bowed himself away from the table.

Tierney put his paper down as he watched his slave approach. Tierney gestured toward the chair opposite. "Sit down, boy."

Cecil's face remained impassive but he was surprised; he had never been asked to sit with his master before. He hesitated.

"I told you to sit, boy!"

"Yassuh, Mister Tierney."

"What did you accomplish?"

"I couldn't find a little slate, like you said. I burned the building."

Tierney scowled but said nothing.

Now Cecil's anxiety began to show in his face and in his speech; he was really worried because his master was annoyed about something and that boded no good. "They didn't see da fire 'til too late."

"You think the slate was destroyed?"

"Yassuh, and the man you wuz worried 'bout too. He went in but deedn't come out. Frum da woman's screamin' and hollerin' ah could tell—"

"You think that Robert Cameron died in the fire?"

"Yassuh and the house burned too. Da way da wint wuz blowin' da fire went to da wattah . . ."

"Not much else burned?'

Yassuh, I mean nosuh. Just a little bit... Like I said, it burnt to da wattah."

"That's a good job, Cecil. We don't have to worry about the slate any more because you killed the man." Tierney waved to the barkeep. "I'll buy you a drink for a job well done."

Cecil looked around. He now knew that something was terribly amiss.

The three men came from behind and slipped the manacles and leg irons on the unresisting and shivering black man.
"Wat'd ah do, mastah?"

"I checked the passenger manifest for the ferry to Pictou It
showed that Mister McIntyre left The Island accompanied by
his slave Samuel . . . all properly documented . . . bill of sale
attested to by the Reverend DesBrisay . . . everything fake, of
course. By now they should be in Halifax . . . probably on their
way to Boston. You, Cecil, will be sold here." He picked up his
newspaper. "At least I recoup part of my investment." He nodded his head to the white men. "Sheriff Winter says we can store
him in the jailhouse until I find a buyer. Don't mark him."

Francis Tierney raised the newspaper and began reading.
Cecil left quietly. He knew better than to beg.

July 1791
Oakwood Manor
Handsworth

This time, I've got the old bat! Joseph Smallwood drummed his
fingers on the desk as he waited for his sister to respond to his
summons. *She is always so high and mighty about Tierney's
progress. This time . . .* His thoughts were interrupted by the
movement of the door handle. *That would be her,* he thought,
but it wasn't; it was the new houseboy—the one that used to
work in the gardens. *What was his name?*

Beggin' yer pardon, Master Smallwood, it's Digger here to
tell you that the mistress . . .

"You will knock and gain permission to enter before you
. . ."

"Yes, sir. The mistress sent me t'tell you . . ."

"Well?"

"Yes, sir. Mistress Hélène wants you to . . ."

"I meant, well, go back out and knock and then gain permission to enter."

"Why do that, sir? I'm already in and the mistress wants
me t'tell you that she is in the gardens and will come up . . .

shortly, she said. She knows how you hates to be kept waitin'
so she sent me ahead to . . ."

The door opened wider as Hélène entered behind the servant. "That will be fine, William."

Digger flushed with pleasure. "That's me proper name. I
shurley likes it when you calls me Willum, Mistress Hélène."
He made an almost courtly bow and held it as he left the
room, drawing the door closed behind him.

"Insufferable!"

"Perhaps, but he is a rare commodity in this world."

"Oh?"

"Yes. He is humble and straightforward. He does what he
is told when he is told to do it." The silence hung between
them, Joseph waiting for the conclusion that Hélène never
failed to draw, and Hélène . . . well, Hélène liked being dramatic when she was baiting the Master of Oakwood. It was
not long in coming.

"Yes, my man Digger certainly accomplishes more than
your dear Mister Tierney."

Joseph beamed. At long last he would be able to twist the
knife. "I have correspondence from my dear Mister Tierney"
—he waved the letter in her face—"yes, indeed I do."

Hélène didn't like the sound of that but she was committed. She took a slightly less aggressive position about the
manager of Lot 38 than she had for years. "More promises
perhaps? Or has he accomplished something?"

"Well, he *has* made another promise."

"Ah," she said with some satisfaction creeping into her voice.

"He hopes that he will have the second soldier removed
from our land by next year."

"What happened to the first one?"

"Gone." *Oh wonderful!* "Title has been transferred—all
nice and legal—to one Joseph Smallwood Esquire, of
Handsworth, England. Since it is one of the best locations in
the whole area, I have ordered Tierney to begin construction
of a modest house and outbuildings." He pointed at his sister
while saying, "Oh, ye of little faith."

"I'll have to admit that I am pleased as you obviously are."
Hélène had a thought. *He said that Tierney <u>hopes</u> to remove the
second soldier. Is there a problem?* "Does Tierney anticipate any
sort of difficulty?"

"The Island is a proper English Colony now and everything must be done by the book."

"You told me the first removal was done legally. What's
the problem with doing it a second time?"

"Tierney had the element of surprise in the first goings-
off. He anticipates they will take some protective measures,
making it more difficult this time, but he seeks permission to
proceed."

"And you said yes."

"He has had some unexpected expenses . . . he lost a treas-
ured possession to one of the culprits and asks that he be
compensated."

"Pay him and have him proceed." When she saw the look
of hesitation in Joseph's face she pronounced, "We are English
landowners seeking redress in an English court from the despicable actions of a now discredited government."

"We will be seen as taking action against an honourable
servant of the Crown—a veteran."

"Then discredit the soldier."

"You are shameless," Joseph whispered, all the while grinning broadly at his sister, "and I love you for it." He stood up.
For the first time in many, many years he showed a moment
of real affection, planting a kiss in the middle of her forehead.
He was humming as he left the office.

Endnotes

1. One hundred per cent unbleached linen. This fabric is often called
"oznabrig" after the German city that produced considerable amounts of it
in the eighteenth century. In the nineteenth century, as with many fabrics,
oznabrig was made of cotton. Oznabrig is a cheap unbleached fabric often
used for poor-to-middling men's shirts, hunting frocks, trousers, and over-
alls, and women's shifts and pockets.

2. The details of the laws, the trial, and the whippings are taken from the *Royal Gazette of the Island of Saint John* (1791)

3. The entry in the *Royal Gazette* reads: "March 9.This day Donald McIntyre was again whipped through the town pursuant to the sentence of the Crown." I could find no record of a third whipping.

Chapter Fourteen
Grim Reaper

January 1792
Near the Farrow Farm

Looking across the open space where the Cameron house and barn used to be, Robbie could see the yellow light from the Farrow house in the next glen. Robbie was breathing so hard from the effort of snowshoeing through the deep snow that clouds of white vapour hung in the still night air around him as he stopped to orient himself.

I don't want to fall into the brook, he thought. I know it's 'specially cold right now but we've only had one night of deep freeze. That brook probably isn't . . . He felt the give from the rubbery ice underfoot and jumped back, his snowshoes catching in the snow, tripping him. Robbie landed flat on his backside and could immediately feel the cold, cold water entering his clothing, numbing his privates. He felt his heart racing as the water crept higher—now to his waist—and entirely covering his outstretched legs.

Mother warned me not to travel in January . . . *to wait 'til spring.*

He gasped as he rolled over to kick off his snowshoes. Robbie paddled and crawled his way in the direction of the yellow light. He shouted. "Joe! Joe! Come help me!" Robbie sucked in a deep breath but the cold air caught in his throat, making him cough. He lay there until the coughing stopped.

* * *

"Did you hear something? Cuddy looked out the window. "It sounded like someone . . ."

Joe laughed. "You're hearing things, young feller. Nobody would be out there on a night like this. It's so cold you can hear the hearts of the trees snappin' and bangin'."

"I don't know, old-timer. It did sound like a human voice."

"Then *you* go outside and look. I'm stayin' here by the fire."

Cuddy went to the door and opened it. He cocked his head—first to one side and then to the other—like an animal confronted with something new or strange. "I don't hear anything now."

"If you don't close that damn door, you'll hear some complainin' from me!"

"Well, I guess it was nothing." Cuddy closed the door.

* * *

It doesn't seem so cold now. I'm tough, I guess. Robbie shook his head, clearing his thoughts. *That's stupid! I have to get out of the water.* He pushed himself upright and then to a standing position. In a couple of steps he found the edge of the brook by tripping over it and falling backwards into the water.

If Rosalie were here, she'd have laughed at that. Robbie started to laugh but that made him cough too. He waited for the coughing to end. It took longer this time. He moved his arms and legs.

Where is the yellow window light? Robbie was out of the water, he knew that much, but it was impossible to push himself up . . . to stand up . . . he couldn't feel his legs . . . no, it was his hands he couldn't feel. He was moving through the snow, his chin pushing the snow aside like the prow of a boat. He giggled at the thought—*mustn't laugh. Laugh starts cough.*

"Maybe if I rest a while . . . then I can stand up." He realized that he had spoken out loud; he seemed to have forgotten that he could speak so he bellowed, "Joe! Joe! Joe Farrow! Joe Farrow!" He put his head down, his left cheek resting on the warm snow. Robbie Cameron closed his eyes.

It was nice visiting at Rivière-du-Nord-Est. They are nice enough people and I should have stayed with Mother and Rosalie, at least until the break-up of the river ice . . . but I don't belong

*there . . . too French for me. Anyway, I'm almost home. It will be
. . ..*

Robbie opened one eye. *Must have been asleep. Rosalie looked
nice dressed like the other Acadian women. She looked like she
was born to it. Mother looked . . . uncomfortable in the Acadian
get-up. I think Mother lived too long with an Englishman. She
likes being English . . .*

*. . . Was I asleep? I shouldn't rest too long. Have to get up . . . go
home . . . but we don't have a home here . . ..*

This time, Robbie didn't try to open his eyes. *I must have been
asleep again. Mother and Rosalie won't be at The Farm any more
now that Pa is gone. No, they won't be coming back to The Farm.
We don't have it any more.*

I was sleepin' agin. I gonna miss Mother and Rosalie.

I'm sorry about . . . endin' like this.

* * *

On about bedtime, they played their game, the loser to fetch
one of the twisted, knotted logs that would hold the fire until
morning. Cuddy, pulling on his boots, thought he would have
one more try at sweet-talking old Joseph Farrow into a
rematch. "Best two out of three," he suggested as he laced up
his boots.

"Don't forget to pull your cap down over your ears. It
won't take a minute for frostbite to get you on a night like
this."

"I know. I know, but we should have the best two out of
three."

"Whistle when you're ready to come back in," he chortled, just loud enough so Cuddy could hear, "and I can open
the door for you."

"It's not fair! You always win."

"Old age and cunning will overcome youth and ability every time."

Cuddy yanked the door open and stepped outside into the frigid night air. He grunted as he tried to pull the door closed against the frost lip.

Joe heard the grunting. "Close the damn thing, will you? It's cold in here."

Cuddy slammed the door shut. "I always lose when it's time to get the night log," he grumbled. He eyed the woodpile of the regular split logs stacked close to the house where they would be sheltered from the weather by the overhang. Pulling his jacket close to his neck as he walked along to the other side of the barn, he continued to gripe. "I'll have to watch him closer the next time we play." He stepped over a mound of rubble and examined the piece of knotted wood at the top of the pile. It was a tree root. *Ol' Joe must have had to struggle to get this miserable piece of root out of the ground . . . but it will keep the fire goin' tonight. Looks froze-in but I might be able to shake it loose.* He tried pulling the root, first this way and then that. "They're all frozen together," he complained. He lifted his foot to kick it loose but he changed his mind: *it's too far up on the stack.*

Cuddy grabbed hold of the twisted root and pulled with all his might; it wouldn't budge. *I could go over to the barn and get the hammer . . . knock it loose . . .* He looked at it again. *Naw, one good kick should jar it loose.* He lifted his foot and lost his balance. *I hope there's nothing sharp,* he thought as he fell backwards into the pile of farm rubble. He should have landed hard, but the landing was soft. He rolled over and searched through the snow—a face! Cuddy dragged the body to its knees. *At least he's not frozen solid, he thought; maybe we can do something for him.* He hoisted the body over his shoulder and staggered through the snow to the house, where he banged against the bottom of the door with his foot.

The door opened a crack. "I thought I told you to whistle. No sense kicking the hell out of . . ." Joe finally looked up. He pushed the door open so hard it crashed against the wall, knocking traps and snowshoes off the pegs. "Put him down by the fire. Is he breathin'?"

"I don't know," Cuddy said as he let the body slip to the floor where—in the light—he saw who it was. "Oh God, no!" Cuddy then fell to his knees, hands brushing snow away from the white face. "What the hell was Robbie doin'? He knows better'n this!"

"It was dark and . . . I didn't know who it was and . . . I didn't think I could lift him and . . . I brought him in as quick as I could—honest to God—I moved as quick as I could and . . .." " Cuddy fell silent as he watched Joe loosen Robbie's clothes and, leaning down, search for signs of life.

"He knows better'n bein' out on a night like this!"

"Is he breathin'?"

"Yes, he's breathin'!" Joe gestured toward the fireplace. "Get off your ass and help me get him nearer the fire. We gotta see what we can do."

"He's breathin'; do you think he'll be all right?"

"Breathin' is a good sign." Joe tried to slip Robbie's leggings off. *Must have been in the brook. Froze solid.* He was able to work the jacket and shirt better, slipping his hand in to feel how warm Robbie was under his armpits. *Cold, too cold.* "Have to get his clothes off."

"Will he be all right?"

As Cuddy helped remove the clothes from his father's body, he didn't ask the question again.

* * *

In the spring, Reine and Rosalie Cameron returned home to bear witness to Robbie's life and to tidy up affairs. They were accompanied by several cousins from Rivière-du-Nord-Est, one of whom, André Gallant, proceeded to make all the burial arrangements as if he were the head of the family.

When Cuddy learned that André planned to bury Robbie in the Acadian cemetery at Saint Peter's Harbour, Cuddy suggested that Robbie Cameron had never thought of himself as being a part of the Acadian community and should be buried on the farm next to his father. Cuddy knew his suggestion was doomed when Reine compressed her lips and pronounced that Robbie was born of an Acadian mother and, if he hadn't had the opportunity to join the Acadian community in life, he would do so in death.

* * *

Interment at Saint Peter's Harbour was dignified and simple. André Gallant led the group through the rituals. Reine meant to say a few words of goodbye to her son who was her last contact with the man who had been her lover, husband, and comrade, but she broke down and André continued speaking on her behalf.

"Ce que cousine Reine allait vous dire monsieur . . .What Cousin Reine was going to tell you, Monsieur Cuddy, be content to know that your mother will be safe in the bosom of her family at Rivière-du-Nord-Est. She will share a house—very close to the ruins of your first home—with the widow Arsenault, related to us by marriage. Your sister, Rosalie, is betrothed to Jean-Pierre Gallant—a fine young man—who will, hopefully, give Rosalie some children to carry on the Cameron seed, if not your name." André paused and lifted an eyebrow in Cuddy's direction.

Cuddy shook his head in the negative and turned away.

André Gallant led the group in a simple prayer and then they filed out of the little cemetery leaving the remains of Robbie Cameron to the services of the gravedigger.

No one noticed that Joseph Farrow had turned away and left the cemetery at the first mention of Rosalie's betrothal.

15 June 1792
Charlotte Town

Cuddy gave a quick rap on the door of the little shanty that he and Joseph Farrow called their Charlotte Town home when they were visiting the capital. He didn't wait for an answer but barged right in, slamming the door behind him. He could see his roommate hunched over the kitchen table. "Joe! Guess what!"

Hurriedly, Joe adjusted himself and his clothing and turned around, revealing a young girl straddling the end of the table. She lowered her legs and slid down, allowing her dress to cover her more modestly.

"What the devil!" Cuddy's face got even redder as the young girl smiled at him and said, "Good evening, Mister Cameron," as she walked toward the door. She flashed another more professional smile at Joseph. "You were finished, weren't you hon?"

Neither man said anything until the door was closed and the footsteps had died away.

"I'm sorry, Cuddy. I shouldn't have brought her here. I won't next time."

"Next time? I'm surprised as hell that you were doin' her this time."

"Never did it before because . . . because I was savin' myself for Rosalie. Even when Robbie wanted me to go . . . Oh!"

Cuddy finished the thought for him. "Any time my father went to Saint Peter's Harbour for some entertainment, he asked you to go, right?"

Joseph nodded his head. "I didn't ever go because I thought that I might have Rosalie . . . someday. But, there's no point now. I just satisfy myself as I have the need. If I need a drink . . . if I need to sleep . . . if I need a woman . . . I just do it." A tear formed as the older man whispered, "I was saving myself for Rosalie." He shrugged. "Now that she's gone, there's no reason for anything—any more."

"Go find yourself another Rosalie. You have money. You have land. You can have your pick of almost any . . ."

"I would 'preciate not speaking of this any more." He rubbed his hands as if to rid himself of something dirty. "What did you want?"

"What? What did I want?" Cuddy scratched his head. "Oh yes! I wanted to tell you about that slave owner—the one with the fancy clothes—he lost a slave." Cuddy was almost beside himself with excitement. "And guess what!"

"He's here? Tierney is still here?"

"Yes, and he lost his slave to—guess who, of all people— Donald McIntyre! Uncle Donald stole the slave from under his nose." And as an afterthought he said, "The other one was sold off right here in town."

In an apparent daze, Joseph sat down. He put his elbows on the table and cradled his head in his hands. "He's still here," he mumbled. He suddenly jumped up. "Get your things together! Forget about joining the County Regiment! Let's go back to the farm!"

"Slow down, old-timer, I have already passed my name in to the recruiter, volunteering to serve." He winked at the older man. "With a handsome uniform, I won't have to settle for the likes of . . ." He stopped as he realized what he was saying. "Like I said before, you don't have to settle for her either. I'll have the uniform and you'll have the money. We should be able to have our pick of the nice girls."

"You're a dumb, stupid kid!" He stopped when he saw the shocked, hurt look. He began again. "Tierney told me that I had better protect my family in the short time that I have left. Reine and Rosalie are away; we should leave too!"

"Short time? He threatened you?"

"Yes. He made that threat while he was taking Donald's land. I believe he wants my land now." Morosely he added, "Nothing can stop him from getting what he wants. I've seen him at work." He shook his head. "Nothing will stop him."

Cuddy watched as the dejected-looking old soldier slumped down in the chair. "Just give me a couple of weeks," he said. He squeezed Joseph's shoulder. "You came down to help me get my enlistment in the regiment. We can't just . . . give up, now."

Joseph shook his head. "I don't want anything more to do with that man."

It's not fair! Things are looking up for me but he still sees a bogeyman behind every bush. The young man stared at the bowed head, willing the older man to see things the right way. "I tell you what; if I am not accepted by the end of the month we'll go straight back to the farm."

He's too young to be afraid . . . like I was when I first joined the army. Joseph Farrow sighed. Just like I was when I joined up. But it really doesn't matter much any more. He swallowed once, twice, and then said, "We'll go straight back to the farm?"

"Let's make that six weeks." When he saw the hesitation, Cuddy offered five weeks.

"A month. Tierney will get me if we stay longer."

* * *

On July 20, at the Charlotte Town Court House, the Grand Jury was called and sworn. After a short but pertinent charge from the Chief Justice, the jury retired for about a quarter of an hour; when they returned, a bill of indictment was found against Joseph Farrow for the rape of a twelve-year-old girl. The prisoner was arraigned—pleading "not guilty"—and the jury empanelled. The evidence was presented by the Attorney General with propriety and delicateness so as not to cause more distress for the wretchedly unhappy mother of the unfortunate girl. Defence Counsel was equally circumspect, being very cautious that, during his attempts to vindicate the accused, he did not trespass on the good name and reputation of the girl or her family. It was a long day for Joseph Farrow.

28 July 1792
Charlotte Town

Late in the afternoon of a soggy day, Reverend Theophilus DesBrisay picked his way carefully around the deeper puddles, clutching his cassock at the knees so as to keep it free of the mud and water. Suddenly, the wind took his hat and he watched as it collected a fair amount of mud along the brim, bouncing up the footpath until it came to rest against the jail-house step. With a sense of detachment, DesBrisay watched as it teetered back and forth, back and forth, until it settled flat into the mud, completing its ruination.

The Reverend lowered his head and closed his eyes. *Dear Lord, what did I ever do to deserve that?*

"I'm afraid your hat is spoiled, sir."

Without looking up, DesBrisay answered, "Yes, I believe so." He continued to pick his way, carefully, along the pathway to the bottom step. When he finally glanced up, he saw a nice-looking young man holding out the errant piece of clothing for him to take. "Thank you," he said with a smile.

"Sir, my name is Cuddy Cameron."

"I don't believe I know your family, son."

"No sir, you wouldn't." Cuddy grimaced. "We are Catholic, Father."

"I attend Catholic families as well as Anglican."

"Then, sir, would you please help me get into the jail to see my uncle?"

"They won't let you in?"

"No sir, they won't. They say there are no visitors allowed."

Reverend DesBrisay considered the situation for a moment before answering. "Your uncle must be Joseph Farrow."

Cuddy nodded his head.

"All right. If your proper name is Robert Cameron . . .."

"It is, sir."

" . . .then I happen to know that Mister Farrow wants to see you."

The priest rapped on the door. Eventually the door was opened and the priest entered the inner darkness. When it was Cuddy's turn to enter, a big hand was raised flat against his chest.

"You, go no further, sonny."

Cuddy's eyes quickly adjusted to the semi-darkness and he recognized Sheriff Winter.

"The young man is with me, Sheriff."

"There are no visitors, Padre."

"Not even me and my acolyte?"

Sheriff Winter scratched his head. "You know that you can always come, Padre. The prisoner has been asking for you but I don't know about . . . what did you call him?"

"He is young and inexperienced. We are all a novice at one time or the other."

Suddenly, Sheriff Winter smiled. He shrugged and pointed over his shoulder with his thumb at a shadowy figure: "I got one of them, too, except mine is real green—my daughter-in-law's son."

"We all have them, Sheriff."

Sheriff Winter grasped Cuddy's shoulder and pulled him into the hallway so he could close and bolt the door. Winter pointed. "Go down the hall. Turn left at the corner. Farrow is in the very last cell." Winter accompanied the visitors to the corner. "You go left," he said with a smile. "The cell isn't locked. There's a chair for you, Padre, but your rookie will have to stand because the prisoner is shackled to the bed."

"Thank you, Sheriff." Stamping his feet to knock off some of the mud and water, DesBrisay motioned for Cuddy to follow as he marched down the hall. Halfway to the blank wall at the end of the hall, the priest held up his hand—signalling that he wanted Cuddy to stop. They stood there, Cuddy holding his breath, DesBrisay cocking his head to one side, listening to the melody wafting down the hall.

> "My soul He doth restore again;
> and me to walk doth make
> within the paths of righteousness,
> e'en for His own name's sake."

Cuddy whispered, "That's Joe doin' the singing!"

"Sh-h-h!"

After a moment's pause, the voice began again. "Yea, though I walk in death's dark vale . . ." The pleasant baritone voice faltered—closely followed by a sob.

DesBrisay immediately took up the refrain, waving his arms at Cuddy as if he were conducting a choir. "Yet will I fear none ill;"—he beckoned to Cuddy, trying to encourage the boy to sing—"for Thou art with me; and Thy rod . . ."

Cuddy shook his head. "I don't know the words."

" . . . and staff me comfort still."

The two voices continued—the one leading, confident and triumphant, while the other, initially tentative and searching, grew stronger as the priest paced down the hall ever closer to the cell door.

"Goodness and mercy all my life
Shall surely follow me . . ."

Reverend DesBrisay entered the cell, his voice swelling with the final lines of the psalm: "And in God's house for evermore my dwelling place shall be." He went directly to the side of the bed, kneeling with outstretched arms to enclose the fettered and manacled body lying on the bed. "In the name of God, why have they done this to you?"

Even though Farrow's voice was muffled beneath the folds of the ecclesiastical robes, Cuddy could sense the strength of the man as he said, "I almost got away last night. After you left, I got the cell door open and was on my way down the hall when they caught me."

DesBrisay leaned back. With Cuddy's assistance he rose and reached for the chair. He pulled it closer to the side of the bed and sat. "There was a petition being circulated in the town on your behalf asking for a lesser punishment." He sighed. He gestured at the shackles. "I suppose this incident will silence it."[1]

Joe's face fell but almost immediately brightened as he tried to hold out his hand to Cuddy. "It's good to see you, Cuddy."

Cuddy grasped the hand and squeezed it. "Where did you learn to sing like that?"

Joe smiled a sad little smile. "Father has been teaching me as I wait for the day."

"The day?"

"Yes, the day I go home to God." Joe saw the stricken look on Cuddy's face and he hastened to reassure the boy. "I was found guilty and sentenced to be hanged by a jury of my peers but I am innocent in the eyes of God."

Cuddy swallowed, hard. "The innkeeper said you wouldn't defend yourself . . . didn't make any sort of defence."

"They had a witness who said he saw the whole thing and I can't deny it. I was there . . . and . . . I was deep in my lust and carnal pleasure with . . . well, you know who."

Cuddy nodded his head, acknowledging that he knew the woman Joe was speaking of. "Then we'll find her! She would tell them what is true!"

Joe tried to shake his head but the fetters held him firmly. "If she is still on The Island, she is dead." He closed his eyes. "Tierney was here."

"Here?"

"Yes. He didn't mention the land. He didn't have to. I know what he wants." Joe Farrow smiled. "Yesterday, the sheriff gave me some paper so I could write a letter to my loved ones." His smile got broader. "With the good Father's help I also wrote a legal document giving you my land." Joe tried to lift his head but gave up. "Under my pillow, Reverend."

DesBrisay reached under Joe's pillow and pulled out two pieces of paper. He examined them and then handed one to Cuddy. "I advise you to take this to the County Clerk as soon as you leave here and register title in your name." The priest's face clouded as he added, "The way the world is today, you should leave here long before dark."

"But I want to stay here with—"

Joe interrupted the boy. "I have a few things I want to say, Cuddy." He looked over at the priest. "Would you excuse us for a few minutes, Father?"

"Of course." Reverend DesBrisay rose, making complaints about his creaking joints. "I will go down to the sheriff's office and see if I can stop this barbaric treatment of a human being." He mumbled as he went down the hall, "It's not right to treat a man like a dog. Unchristian, I call it, to tie a man to his bed. The world is not . . ."

Cuddy sat in the chair.

"I want you to remember us: Uncle Donald and me. We were soldiers of the King defending the empire—raising England's flag wherever we were ordered. We always did as we were told. Right or wrong, our officers were always right and we followed them right to the death if needs be."

"I won't forget, Joe. Grandpa told me the stories of how . . ."

Joe held up his hand to silence the boy. "Your father was different. I know he was a good soldier but he was a better human bein'. He tried to help English settlers durin' a massacre and got flogged by his officer for his troubles."

Cuddy's face brightened. "He told me how he saved the life of a naval officer at Halifax and, later on at Louisbourg, the same officer returned the favour, helping him and Grandma escape the English."

"He didn't have much use for Injuns . . . . Did'ja ever see his neck? The Injuns hanged him by the neck a couple of times or maybe more." When they both realized what they were talking about—hanging—they fell silent for a spell.

"I liked the story where he escaped from Grand Pré." When Joe didn't say anything Cuddy went on. "I liked that story a lot."

Joe had a faraway look as he said, "But when he found a people worthy of his love . . . well, he threw his lot in with them . . . all the way. He was a good soldier . . . even in a losin' cause . . . ." Joseph lowered his voice as if he were telling a big secret; "the Acadians were a losing cause, y'know." He raised his voice again. "But he fought for them at Beausejour and Annapolis and . . ."

"Louisbourg ."

"Yeah, Louisbourg and probably some that we don't know much about."

The priest reappeared at the door. "The turnkey will remove your fetters, Joe, but the shackles will remain."

"Every little bit is a help, Padre."

"And you, Robert . . . Cuddy . . . should leave. It is late in the day. Run along to the clerk and get your business done."

Cuddy grasped his friend's hand. Joe held it firmly as he said, "I want you to remember your Granddad. I want you to remember him as a good soldier, a good soldier who followed his heart and never went back on his friends." Joe released the boy's hand.

"I will come back tomorrow, Joe." He moved to the door. "See you then."

"Yeah, see you then."

It was not to be; even the priest was denied access the next-to-last day of Joseph Farrow's life, probably as a consequence of Cuddy's business with the County Clerk.

Monday, 30 July

Reverend DesBrisay finished his exhortation and prayers. He patted Joseph Farrow's shoulder. Making the sign of the cross, he stepped back and to one side.

Now Joseph Farrow stood alone, facing the quiet crowd who had come to witness his launch into eternity. Joe opened his mouth as if to speak.

"Have you any last words?" It was Sheriff Winter, intent on fulfilling his every obligation to the Crown. He leaned in close to the prisoner and whispered, "You don't have to speak, you know. Why don't you just get it over?"

When Joseph cleared his throat, obviously preparing to say something, the sheriff also stepped to one side and took up a position next to the priest.

"Notwithstanding . . .." Joseph cleared his throat and started again. "Notwithstanding that I have been condemned to die for rape; I declare to the world that I am not guilty of this crime." He lowered his chin to gaze into the upturned faces of the crowd. "But I am not innocent." Joe must have meant to step closer to the edge of the gallows to better reach his audience but his feet had been tightly bound and he fell over. Joe would have fallen into the arms of the nearest person—the hangman—but that official stepped back so that there would be no physical contact. It was the priest who broke the fall and struggled to set the prisoner back on his feet. No one else moved.

"Thank you, Padre," Joe said, slightly out of breath. When he had regained his balance, he began again.

"I am not guilty of the crime of rape. I am guilty of living a sinful life. If it has pleased God to awaken in me a sense of my unworthiness by this heavy stroke, then I can only praise His Holy Name for His loving kindness. It is better that I die now, with an interest in the blessed Jesus, than to have a longer life in unknowing sin." Joe lowered his head as if in prayer. Without lifting his head he said, "Jesus is the Rock of My Salvation. I go to him now."[2]

No one on the scaffold moved. All eyes of the spectators were on the silent figure.

Sheriff Winter pointed at the hangman. "You may carry on, sir."

The hangman produced a black bag from somewhere and with a fluid, almost graceful movement, slipped it over the unmoving head. Ensuring that the bag was neatly tucked under the chin with the one hand, he reached behind him with the other and pulled the rope free from the hook on the side of the gallows. He dropped the noose over the victim's head, now using both hands to snug the knot tight just behind the left ear. He gave it a little tug, allowing the slack to trail over the left shoulder. He stepped back a pace. If he had not been wearing a black mask, the spectators might have been able to see the look of professional satisfaction as he examined his handiwork.

Again, no one moved.

Someone in the crowd called out, "Well, what are you waiting for? Get it over!"

Reverend DesBrisay whispered to the sheriff, "What are you waiting for?"

"He had his speak, which was his right, and now he is to be executed at twelve all right and proper."

"How would you know when it's twelve?"

"The town bell will sound at noon."

The bell sounded. The hangman moved swiftly and pulled the lever, hard.

Joseph Farrow fell with a swishing sound. He stopped, abruptly, just below the floorboards of the scaffold. When the jerking stopped, something fell from his grasp; it was a Nova Scotia amethyst.

October 1792
Oakwood Manor
Handsworth

Digger, standing near his mistress Hélène, watched as the Master of Oakwood approached from across the lawns. *This can't be good news,* he thought. *The master never comes into the gardens during the day . . . and seldom at night.*

"Sister!"

Hélène looked up from what she was doing with her favourite roses. She compressed her lips enough so that only Digger would be able to hear her. "Either he wants something or it is bad, bad news." She saw the despatches in his hands. "Bad news," she said.

"I have news."

"Well, get on with it." She straightened up from her crouch, placing her hand in the small of her back to relieve the arthritic pain somewhat.

"The parliamentary assistant to the Secretary of State knew of our interest—possibly because of the name—and passed a copy of this news item for our information."

"Joseph! If you don't get to the point I'll—"

"Yes, of course. I'll read it." He searched first one pocket and then another to find his spectacles, Hélène becoming more impatient as the moments passed. "Ah!" He unfolded the sheet and then, examining it, turned it right side up. "Now, let's see which item it was . . ."

"Oh for pity's sake, Joseph! I'm not going to wait for you to get to read some nonsense or other that I have no interest in."

"Here it is. Major General William Smallwood, three times Governor of Maryland, died July 4, 1792. According to the general's instructions, he was buried in an unmarked grave with little ceremony."

"Oh!" Hélène staggered against her servant, who held the distraught woman in his arms until the master ordered, "Carry her to the house!" Joseph took a second look at the grey-haired servant and asked, "Are you capable of that or do we need help?"

"I will carry her, m'lord."

"I am not a lord."

If Digger heard his master, he gave no sign. He strode so swiftly toward the manor that Joseph was not able to keep up. "Ye'll be all right, my dear, dear Helen," he whispered in her ear. "By the time we get to the house, ye'll think of some reason other than your Cousin William's death for your weakness. The master believes in women's weakness. Tell him so. You won't want to have him hold Cousin William over you at this late stage. Tell him . . ."

"All right, Digger put me down."

"For appearances' sake, mistress, I suggest that I not put you down until we are in the manor and out of sight of the master." He felt her tense as if to resist, but then she relaxed. "I'm sorry he's gone, Digger."

"So am I. William Smallwood was a nice man, although a bit difficult to get along with—but still, a nice man."

"Put me down now, Digger."

"Yes, mistress."

"You may return to the gardens, Digger. Tell the master that I am in the family office."

"Yes, mistress."

Still feeling unsteady on her feet, Hélène walked close to the wall, tapping her knuckles against the panelling like a child might do. She recalled that her tutor of many years past had called her a knuckle-knocker nitwit. *I do believe that I would fall over if I don't stay in contact with something firm and solid.* She kept moving along, tapping the wall with her knuckles. *Imagine! William has been dead for weeks and I didn't know a thing about it. I thought that lovers had some sort of sense about the other's condition . . . and he's dead! But I truly loved him.* She pushed open the door to the office and hurried to the big chair behind the desk. When she was safely settled, she steepled her fingers as she examined her feelings about the loss of her William.

He didn't marry. Perhaps he had children? Illegitimate, of course, and since he didn't marry they would be of no consequence. Gradually, she began to feel better as she pursued that line of reasoning. *Not like my son. My son is Master of Oakwood and proprietor of many lands in the New World. Our line—the Joseph Smallwood line of Handsworth—is unsullied by any hint of illegitimacy since official recognition was given years ago to my son as rightful heir to the estate. The James Smallwood line of Maryland—the more senior branch of the family tree—would now probably die out with the death of one Major General William Smallwood.* She snorted. "Pity," she said.

"What's a pity, my dear sister?"

Hélène had failed to notice Joseph standing in the doorway, watching her, and was startled by his question. She was very quick to recover her composure. "I was thinking that we probably won't be able to garner title to any of the Smallwood lands in Maryland."

"Ah, you are feeling more like your old self. I am relieved."

Recalling what Digger had suggested, she jokingly passed off her moment of shock as a moment of female weakness. "Would that I had been born a male," she complained but then quickly changed the subject. "You're relieved? Is there something I should be aware of?"

"Yes. I have other correspondence." He handed her the document. As she read the details, Joseph explained the thrust of the letter.

"Tierney has rid us of the two soldiers. He has accomplished that much, at least. However, before the second soldier departed the scene, title to the land was passed to Robert Cameron."

Hélène sensed there was more to the story so she asked, "Departed the scene? Does that have some hidden meaning?"

"Not really. Tierney says both soldiers are gone. The nature of their departure matters naught."

"And he suggests?"

"He suggests that we take no further action to recover the second farm lot."

Hélène read from the letter. "He says here that the opportunity to recover lands sold as a consequence of Governor Patterson's cavalier treatment of proprietors' rights has passed." She looked up. "I suppose he is the best judge of that." She let the paper fall to the desk, dismissing it. "That's all very interesting." Hélène produced a handkerchief and dabbed her forehead. "I am fatigued, brother." *Yes, I must take time to mourn the passing of my William.* She rose from the chair. "If you will excuse me . . ."

"I plan to take the boys with me to The Island."

Hélène Smallwood sat down with a thump. "When?" she asked.

"Next season."

I shall be Mistress of Oakwood after all. "Both boys are going with you?"

"Yes. They are too young to be schooled in the management of Oakwood and their experiences in the new world will have . . ."

" . . . a beneficial effect. Yes, I do believe so." She rubbed her hands together. "We can't get started too soon. Let's get down to work."

"Right now?" Joseph hesitated, but then strode to the cabinet, where he selected several file jackets. He opened one of them. "You're right; there is a great deal to be done." He opened the second file. He ran his finger down the page. "You will need access to my personal accounts as well, so that you will have a complete picture of our financial situation."

"I want to do a first-rate job for you, my son." She stole a quick glance to see if Joseph had noticed her slip. *In all these years, I have never made that mistake before.* She waited, holding her breath for his reaction.

Joseph continued reading the file.

William's death announcement has made me careless. Should I tell him that William was his father? That I am his mother?

Joseph looked up. "What did you say?" He closed the file and walked toward the front of the desk. "I'm sorry. I was reading and probably not paying proper attention to what you had to say."

It's now or never, Hélène.

Joseph noticed her delay. "I promise to pay more attention if you will just repeat what you said."

"I want to do a first-rate job for you . . . ."

"Nothing less than I expect from the Mistress of Oakwood." He laid out the files on the desk. "I will be gone two or three seasons, just long enough to make sure that James is properly established on The Island."

"And Joseph?"

"Joseph will return with me to be Master of Oakwood in his turn."

"Of course, he being the eldest son."

"Yes, of course."

Endnotes

1. "During the night of Wednesday the Prisoner nearly effected his escape. He had filed off his irons, and was prizing open the bars of the window before he was discovered—when the guards were called and he was again secured without any resistance. Whether unfortunately for the prisoner or not, we cannot say, but at that time a petition was handed about on his behalf, which this attempt entirely silenced." *Royal Gazette of the Island of Saint John* (1792).

2. According to the write-up in the *Royal Gazette of the Island of Saint John* (1792), Joseph Farrow " . . . died with that composure which only a confidence in the mercy and goodness of his Creator could inspire." In his last words, Farrow declared to the world he was not guilty of the crime he was convicted of.

Chapter Fifteen
Last Word

Summer 1795
Rivière-du-Nord-Est

"You are not going to die, maman."

Reine LeBlanc Cameron smiled indulgently at her beautiful daughter. "Come sit by my side. I have things I would say to you."

"I will sit as long as you do not speak of old age and dying."

Reine patted the side of her bed. "I am old and I will die." She beckoned Rosalie Gallant to approach as she begged, "I need to speak with you before . . ."

" . . . before it's too late, I know." Rosalie gave her mother a lovely smile. "Tell me what is bothering you, ma chère maman."

Reine waited until Rosalie was seated on the edge of the bed. "I loved the man who was Robert Cameron." Reine had a random thought. "Do you know that in the beginning he was known as Carrot Top?"

"Why was that?"

"He had gorgeous red hair and freckles. Even the hated English knew him as Carrot Top—in battle he was easy to see—and they had a reward for his capture."

"I only remember him with grey hair."

"We lived a hard life—we both went grey early"—an expression of pain passed across the older woman's face—"and all our troubles will have no meaning unless our family knows what we went through to make a life for them here on The Island." Reine leaned forward and touched her daughter's hand. "Please listen carefully and tell your children . . ."

"I know most of the story, Mother."

"Be patient with me, Rosalie."

"Yes, Mother." Rosalie was going to say more but she could see that her mother was lost in her thoughts, miles away and a half century ago. She waited.

"He looked so . . . English! With his red hair and freckles he was . . . and he stood so straight . . . I loved him the moment I saw him but I had to wait until he was accepted by the community."

"He was accepted?"

"Well, no . . . I think not . . . but the priest gave us permission to marry and we were assigned a farm on new lands . . . but the English came. My dear, dear cousin, Abel Comeau, rescued me from the church . . ."

"I've forgotten, mother; why would you have to be rescued from a church?"

"So I could escape with Robert . . . and we came here, to Rivière-du-Nord-Est, and made a home . . . but then there was Beau Soliel . . . and we left Rivière-du-Nord-Est to fight the English. It was at Louisbourg that we had our first battle . . . but Louisbourg wasn't the first fight . . . we fought near Annapolis Royal . . . and . . ."—Reine passed her hand over her face as if to get rid of black flies—"I thought I was lost in the woods . . ."[1]

I wonder what woods she is talking about. However, this time, Rosalie held her tongue. She turned her head slightly, to look out the window, wondering where her boys were. She smiled, inwardly, because every time she thought about her babies, she included her husband, Jean-Pierre Gallant. *Jean-Pierre is such a child,* she thought. *It's not just because he is younger than I am . . . Oops! Mother is asking me a question.* "What did you say, Mother?"

"Did you know that I fought as a man at Louisbourg? I ran against the English guns and picked Robert up—he was bleeding so bad—and carried him back to our lines." Reine made the hand-passing motion over her face again. "I was so tired after that run." She closed her eyes. "I am tired, now." Reine opened both eyes with a snap. "You be sure to tell your children and their children about our lives." She closed her eyes. "It is important we remember what it was like during those days." She breathed softly, her head falling back on the pillow. A smile stole across her face. "I remember, Robert, when we could run for miles . . . and we did. Remember, Row-bear? We ran and ran and that tall officer—his name was Jerry—with the musket—he could have—but he didn't—and . . .."

Rosalie stepped out of the room.

"Rosalie!"

What does she want now? She took several steps toward the doorway but changed her mind. "Yes, Mother?"

"Like sheep we were led away. Not again. "

"Yes, Mother."

"Tell them to be warriors . . . like we were."

"Yes, Mother."

When there was no more, Rosalie peeked around the corner; her mother was asleep, breathing easily. Rosalie Gallant tiptoed out the front door, her hand shielding her eyes from the sun as she searched the fields for her two little boys and the one big boy.

Endnotes

1. Reine's life as a soldier is recounted in the second book of the *Abuse of Power* series, *The Colonials and the Acadians.*

Chapter Sixteen
Final Moments

April 1799
The Smallwood Farm
Lot 38, Prince Edward Island

"Who is that, Father?"

Young Joseph and his brother had been watching the visiting blacksmith as he shod the Smallwood horses when a figure passed through the trees at the bottom of their land near the creek. It wasn't the first time the brothers had witnessed the trespass but it was the first time it had happened when Smallwood Senior was present. The brothers looked to their father for a response. The younger brother was the first to realize that his father hadn't heard the question over the din the blacksmith was making, so he repeated it, a little louder.[1]

"Somebody just walked across the bottom of the lot, sir. Do you know who he is?"

Joseph patted the flank of the horse and walked a few paces around his boys to the doorway so that he might have a view of the retreating figure. "Cameron. His name is Cameron. I believe they call him Cuddy Cameron."[2]

"He crosses at the foot of our land. Did you ever give him permission?"

"That's not our land. That's his." Joseph Smallwood saw the strange look—perhaps of discomfiture—on his sons' faces. "You've had a run-in with him?"

"No," was Young Joseph's quick reply.

John avoided looking at his brother as he said, "Actually, we tore up a trap-line we found near the brook. It was probably his."

"Well, you'll get no complaints from him." Joseph turned away and devoted his attention to what the blacksmith was doing.

John looked relieved but continued to stand in the doorway, staring at the path where it disappeared into the woods between the two properties.

Young Joseph joined his father. "What kind of a man wouldn't complain if his trap-line were torn up?" He scratched his head. "I know I'd be as mad as hell."

"What kind of a man?" Joseph smiled at his eldest son. *So tall yet still so young at heart,* he thought. "He's the sort of man who will never speak to a Smallwood no matter what the provocation." He wagged a finger at Young Joseph. "I told you about the time Governor Patterson sold some of our land without our knowledge or permission?"

"Yes. Was Cameron one of the buyers?"

"His grandfather was."

"Then his grandfather should have known better than to buy our land."

Joseph looked through the trees as if he might be able to see the Cameron place. "His grandfather died in a mysterious fire back in '91." He sighed. "Cameron blames us."

"Seventeen ninety-one? That was before we arrived here. Surely he can't blame us."

Joseph shrugged his shoulders. "Cameron believes that our man Tierney was responsible for the fire, but Tierney couldn't have been involved since he was in Charlottetown all that week." He raised a bony finger to emphasize his point. "Mister Cameron holds a grudge and he'll hold an even stronger one if you and John ruined his traps."

John had sidled back into the barn in time to hear his father's comment. "I'm sorry, sir," he said.

Joseph lowered his finger. "Saying you're sorry won't help. Cameron will add it to his list of grievances." He shrugged his shoulders. "Can't be helped now, but I would wager that he still won't speak to any of us."

The blacksmith cleared his throat a couple of times before saying, "Beggin' yer pardon, sirs, but the mare's done." He took his cap off as Joseph approached. "Took me longer'n I thought . . .'n she's been a good girl . . .'n maybe one of the young gentlemen'll walk her to yer pond . . .'n let her sup while I do the roan."

John was eager to make amends—or to curry favour—so he was the first to speak. "I'll take her, Father."

Joseph swung his cane—once—twice—in little circles like a circus master directing a troupe. "Let's go for a walk. It might do my leg some good." He slapped his right thigh to get the circulation going in his leg. "The damn thing has been gimpy ever since my fall during the Atlantic crossing." He shook his head. "I am not looking forward to the trip home."

John was careful not to show any sign of his inner glee; he really didn't give a tinker's damn about Atlantic crossings since he wasn't returning to England with his father and brother. *I'm going to stay here on The Island. I'm going to be master of all I survey and, what shall I call it?* He pulled at his lower lip with his thumb and forefinger. *Can't call it Oakwood; Father wouldn't like that. Can't have two Oakwoods.* John was distracted from that line of thought as he watched his father toss the reins to the nearer son. Slowly John's face flushed with the jealousy he always felt when his father showed any kind of preference for the elder son.

"Lead her out, Little Joseph."

Now it was Young Joseph whose face turned crimson—with embarrassment—while John's beamed with pleasure at his brother's discomfort.

"Father, please do not call me Little Joseph."

The father didn't respond. Instead, he strode through the door out into the barnyard, expecting Young Joseph to follow—leading the horse—which he did.

John lagged behind, enjoying his thoughts. *Soon I shall not be the baby brother. I shall be master of . . . What shall I call it?* His thoughts were interrupted by his father's voice coming from down the hill.

"What happened to the pond?"

John ran outside. From the barnyard he couldn't see any pond. *Where did it go?*

It was Young Joseph, further down the hill, who saw the breach in the dam.

"Someone pulled down our dam. Look! There's a five-foot-wide hole; all the water is gone."

Both sons were surprised at their father's reaction.

"Well! I am surprised!" the senior Smallwood exclaimed. "In a way, Mister Cameron has spoken to us after all." Joseph Smallwood snorted and then chortled. "I hope you enjoyed pulling his traps because he's gotten back at us, nicely it seems. We won't have any water to fight fires or refresh our animals." He slapped the cane against his leg. "No, we won't have water until we get a good rain or two; probably not until the fall." He turned away. "Take the mare back to the barn." His limp was more pronounced as he began the trek back up the hill. After a few paces he stopped, waiting for his sons to come abreast before he resumed the climb. His breath getting shorter as he walked, the older man paused again and took a couple of deeper breaths. "I have no doubt but that the pond is the work of our dear Mister Cameron. I have no doubt of that." He pointed his finger at John, who visibly flinched but managed to meet his father's gaze with steady eyes. "Young Joseph and I will be gone by the end of the season and you will be acting on your own."

"Yes, Father." *I certainly will.*

"Take this piece of advice to heart. Do not strike back at Cameron."

Not likely, old man.

"You must understand that feuds can become deadly. They are born in real or imagined hurts, real or imagined," he repeated for emphasis, "and that man believes he has good cause for grievance." Something in John's face caused Joseph Smallwood to take the several small steps to where he could place his hand under his son's chin, lowering it so the father could look right into the son's eyes "And feuds are fuelled by acts of revenge."

John attempted to remove his chin but immediately thought better of it as his father improved his hold.

"I want you to listen to me, you little rapscallion!"

John swallowed, several times, before he could blurt, "Of course, Father!"

The chin released, the paternal finger was lowered to begin a tattoo on the young man's chest. "Let this all pass. You ruined his traps. He drained the pond. Leave it at that."

"But sir!"

"I have spoken on the matter." Joseph Smallwood wagged his finger under his son's nose. "You will do as you are told!"

"Yes, sir."

Joseph motioned for his other son to approach. He took his arm. "Help me up to the house, son." The father leaned on Young Joseph and the two resumed a slow ascent to the house.

John stood his ground, his hands on his hips and his eyes piercing the two backs. *I shall be master here.* When certain that he could not be heard, he growled, "I take shit from no man . . . not father . . . not brother . . . not . . . anyone." With long firm strides he marched to the house. He lifted the latch. *I certainly won't take any shit from a peasant named Cameron.*

The Next Farm Over

Cuddy pushed his way through the overgrowth at the edge of his first field. *Have to come over here and do some clean-out.* He looked ahead to the house. *Someone's here!* He slowed his pace. *I don't have friends. Who could it be?* He saw movement in the shadows at the side of the house. It was then that Cuddy regretted he didn't carry the old musket any more. He stopped and raised his hand to shade his eyes. *Damn! I don't like the looks of this!*

Whoever it was stepped out into the sunlight and waved.

Cuddy waved back but stayed where he was until he could see if the man was armed. He was. *Shit! Now what do I do?*

"Mister Cameron, sir, I am Hugh MacEachran."

Cuddy sighed. *I don't need this.* He put on a brave front and walked along to the house. "Pleased to meet you, Mister MacEachran." Cuddy walked the last few paces with his hand outstretched as if to shake the man's hand. *If I can get hold of one of 'em, he won't be quick to use the gun, one-handed.*

MacEachran took the proffered hand and shook it mightily.

Cuddy was somewhat startled when a young woman came to the door with a pot in her hand. "I'm making a stew, Mister Cameron. Where do you keep your salt?"

"Uh, I don't have salt." He scratched his head and mumbled, "Meant to get some but . . ."

"Spices?"

"Yes, Ma'am, in the can marked Peerless Spices . . . a friend used to bring them from a baker in Halifax who gave away small samples . . . they were free, you see, and I collected them because the can was pretty . . . and I don't use spices . . . not very much . . . and . . ." *Why am I talking this way?*

Hugh inclined his head and made a gesture of introduction toward the young woman. "This here is Rose Nelson. She come over last fall meant for my brother Andrew but he died and all my other brothers have wives." He turned to Rose and, with a broad smile, waved her back into the house with an admonition, "Get on with it, lass; we mean to have some stew today."

"Yes, Hugh."

Hugh took Cuddy by the arm and led him away from the front door. "She brought most of the fixin's with her in her pot. I'm surprised she forgot the salt. She's a dear thing, but she ought not to have left her mother. She's very young in her ways." Hugh's face turned crimson. "Not that there's a thing wrong with the girl . . . . And that's why I came this way today to speak to you."

"About her?"

"Is there somewhere we can go and have a mite of shade as we talk?"

"I have a bench down by the brook."

"That sounds just fine." Hugh took off his hat and wiped the sweatband as they walked along. "I find her openness most refreshing but the other women in our compound . . . . Oh yes, I should explain; I'm from over Scotchfort way. My father signed on with Donald Macdonald in 1772 and it cost him nigh onto thirty pounds for transportation—five boys and our mother—on the transport ship *Alexander.*

"What has that to do with a young woman in my house cooking a meal?"

"I believe you will understand if ye'll but let me finish."

Cuddy pursed his lips but inclined his head in acquiescence.

"So! Father spent at least thirty pounds of his wealth getting his family as far as Tracadie. It was good the *Alexander* brought us right into Tracadie so as to cut down on transportation expenses but it still cost a further five pounds to carry all of our supplies to Scotchfort . . ."

"Your supplies? Didn't your proprietor supply you?"

"We paid our own way and brought our own supplies." Hugh shook his head. "Father believed all the hokum. He believed that we were moving to a rich pastoral land where living was good and where the rent was only one shilling for each acre in paradise." He could see Cuddy shaking his head in wonderment so he continued. "We didn't know that most of the land was heavily wooded. We didn't know we had to pay five pounds for the local purchase of a cow." In a quiet, sorrowful voice Hugh added, "We didn't know that during the second winter we would be starving."

"My grandparents killed their horses."

"We killed our cow." Hugh made a quick swipe at some moisture on his cheek. "Some of the *Alexander's* passengers were getting supplies from the Scottish Catholic Church. They shared with us. We didn't starve." He looked away as he wiped at this cheek again. "Yes, they shared with us." Suddenly he laughed. "Almost made a good Catholic out of me."

They both sat there for a while, Hugh collecting his feelings and Cuddy trying to overlook the tears of a middle-aged man.

"We were out of money. The crops were poor; we had garden stuffs and of course potatoes, but the proprietor's agent was there with his hand out—wantin' his shillings." He

shrugged his shoulders. "We gave him everything we had."
Then Hugh leaned forward to get Cuddy's attention. "You
have to understand; my Pa was finished. When Pa realized that
he didn't have enough money to stay and not enough money
to leave, he gave up the ghost. So it was up to me, the eldest
son." With a sly smile, he said, "And I came up with a scheme.
I wrote back to some prominent families in the Highlands giving the same glowing report about Saint John's Island as the
proprietor had given us back in '71 and proposing that I
would marry one of their daughters if she were suitably dow-
ered. That's how I got my Mary. Robert, two years later,
married his Jean. By the time we got to Harry, the cat was out
of the bag. Unbeknownst to us, many Scottish tenants were
writing home telling the hard truth about life on this island
and the way we were being fleeced by the proprietors. It took
some little while before we found a girl on one of the outer
islands for old Harry."

"And Rose?"

"Rose Nelson was an English girl with no family but she
had an inheritance. We thought she would be happy with
Andrew but he died while she was on the way here." Hugh
turned to look toward the house. "She doesn't want to go
back."

Cuddy thought for a moment and then asked, "That's
four; you said there were five boys?"

Hugh swallowed twice before answering. "Willie isn't
interested."

"If your Willie isn't interested, why should I be?"

Again Hugh hesitated. "Our dear Willie has . . . mush for
brains." He appeared to regret his frankness so he explained,
"Willie is a good farmer. He's a hard worker."

"But?"

"But he doesn't catch on to things. When I say, it's spring,
then Willie does what he learned to do in the springtime."

Cuddy digested that fact and then returned to the original conversation. "You were saying that Rose has a sharp
tongue and the other women don't get along with her."

"No! I didn't say that!" Hugh scuffed his foot at a lump of clay at the foot of the bench. "Well, I suppose I would have to say that she does give her opinion quite freely. And I suppose I must admit that I find her . . . find her . . . well, too mature in the one sense and too innocent in another, if you know what I mean."

Cuddy sat on the bench and motioned to the other man that there was ample space for the two of them. "No, I don't quite know what you mean."

Hugh fanned himself with the brim of his hat. "On another woman you might presume to call it brashness the way she says what she thinks regardless if she is speaking to the senior wife of the compound." Hugh sighed. "And then there's the touching."

"Touching?"

"She is affectionate and loving to every living thing: animals, children . . ." He took a deep breath. "She never fails to give me a kiss on the forehead every morning and asks me if I had my proper sleep and how my digestion is." He smiled. "Oh, she is a lovely one, she is."

"And how come she is in my house, making a stew?"

"My wife suggested that she might be equally affectionate with you, since you don't have a woman or a family to help you tend the farm."

"You want me to . . .?"

"Yes. We would like you to . . . to try her out for a bit." Hugh saw the protest rising so he pressed on. "What I mean is, try her cooking. See if you like her disposition." Hugh could see that the protest had surfaced in the open mouth of his surprised listener so he hurried. "You would not have her stay with you. Let her sleep in the outbuilding, but please take her on a trial basis."

"Well! I can't believe that you would make such a proposal!"

"If you don't think it's appropriate for her to stay on the premises, you could have her come over every morning and return every evening . . . please. Even that little bit would help me with the problem I am having with the other women at the compound." Hugh touched Cuddy's arm, squeezing it to make his several points. "She is a good cook and has a sweet disposition. She is clean in mind and body and means no harm to any living thing." Hugh had a moment of inspiration. "She knows how to read and write and is good at her numbers." He stopped squeezing Cuddy's arm and raised his forefinger as he said, "And that's unusual for a woman." When Cuddy still hadn't said anything, Hugh made one last sally. "She's well read and can entertain you with her views on matters usually the domain of men folk."

Hugh placed his hands on his knees and pushed himself up. "If I know young Rose, she will have things all cleaned up by now." He saw the look in Cuddy's eyes and quickly added, "All bachelors' quarters need a little tidying, now and again." Inwardly cursing himself for the misstep, Hugh started again.

"Rose should be ready with a nice hot meal and a pleasant manner as she serves us." Hugh waited until Cuddy had stood up and had turned to face the cabin before he attempted to place his arm over the other man's shoulder in a comradely sort of way. "You can even ask her to join us—at the table—if you so have a mind."

Cuddy finally spoke. "You can take your arm off my shoulder Mister MacEachran. Asking me to take the woman is burden enough that I shouldn't have to carry any of your body parts up the hill."

August 1799
Charlotte Town

Joseph Smallwood stepped through the entry port of the transport ship. He paused on the ramp while he searched for his sons in the crowd that had come to give a send-off to the passengers of the *King's Ransom*. Instead, he caught the eye of Francis Tierney and waved him over to join him at the front of the pier.

Tierney gave a slight bow to his master. "Good morning, sir. Are you pleased with the thought of returning home?"

"Have you seen my boys?"

"Yes, sir. I saw them in Richardson's about twenty minutes ago."

"No, I am not looking forward to the trip." Joseph stepped closer to his agent and said, in a manner that made it obvious that he didn't want anyone else to hear, "John will be master at Seven Oaks."

"Ah, you have found a name for your farm."

"I want you to understand that John can be a trifle headstrong. I will count on your seasoned judgement to keep him from making any disastrous mistakes. But he is master . . . although you will be accountable to me. I will need reports, Mister Tierney, much in the manner you have been making for years." Joseph blinked his eyes a couple of times. "What was it you asked?"

"You have named the place Seven Oaks. Does the young master like the name?"

"Does who like . . .?"

"Does Master John like the new name?"

"We don't know her name yet. I want you to take John to Halifax and find him a suitable wife. Perhaps a widow stranded at the garrison by the death of her husband. A woman of some experience would be good for Young Joseph."

"I thought you were talking about Master John."

"Yes. I planned for the farm to be named Oak Grove but only a few of the transplanted trees survived. We had a problem with that Cameron fellow, you know, the one who owns the farm next to us." His voice suddenly very petulant, Joseph whined, "He stole our water and we couldn't look after the trees." Joseph picked at a spot on the sleeve of his coat. It was then that Francis Tierney realized that Joseph Smallwood's clothes were filthy. Joseph gave up picking at the stain and began flicking at it with his thumb and forefinger. "There may be more than seven oaks left but I liked the ring of"—he paused and savoured the words—"Seven Oaks. Much better than Five Oaks or Eight Oaks, don't you think?"

"Yes, Seven Oaks has a fine lilt." Francis cast a quick look for the Smallwood brothers. With an initial sense of relief he saw them approaching, but he became dismayed when he saw how flushed their faces were with drink. *Oh, this is going to be great! The father is losing his mind and, by the looks of it, the brats are inebriated.* "I was having a chat with your father, getting my final instructions . . ."

John took Tierney by the arm and turned him away, at the same time telling his brother, "Take Pa on the ship, Joseph. I will explain things to my agent."

Young Joseph growled something in reply but he did take his father's arm and lead him up the ramp.

"Father is indisposed, Mister Tierney. What did he have to say?"

"He said you were master of Seven Oaks and . . ."

"Do you have any problem with that? Because if you do, we should get it all straightened out before the old man leaves."

"You are master, sir."

"Good! I must go up now and make my farewells." He waved a hand in the general direction of the end of the pier. "Go along now and wait for me at Richardson's. See if you can get some Jamaican instead of that rotgut they make at Halifax." John turned around and gave his servant a broad smile. "Have them put it on my tab."

September 1799
Hillsborough River

Cuddy put over the tiller as he headed for the wharf at what was still known as the village of Rivière-du-Nord-Est. Two boys were sitting on the side of the wharf, feet dangling into the water. Cuddy reached forward and released the halyard, allowing the single sail to settle to the base of the mast. The little boat glided toward the side of the wharf where the boys were playing.

"Vous pouvez nous aider à accoster?" One of the boys looked up but the other one continued to hang over the side of the pier just about where Cuddy wanted to tie up. He repeated his question in English. "Push her off, will you?"

Both boys were instantly alert. "Sure thing, mister. Throw us a line." The way they moved, Cuddy could see that they knew their way around boats. The larger boy put his foot against the gunnel and guided the boat along the side of the pier while the other pulled back on the rope Cuddy had tossed—the sternfast—bringing the boat to a stop.

"Where's your bumpers?"

"Pardon me?"

"You don't want her to rub against the wharf. You should have bumpers."

"Oh, yes." Cuddy scrambled aft and retrieved a pair of fenders made of rope. He tossed them to the boys. "I'm not much of a sailor," Cuddy said by way of explanation.

"Give me your painter."

"Yes, of course." Cuddy searched around the bottom of the boat and then looked back to the boy for guidance.

"I got it!" The other boy had reached into the front of the boat and pulled out what Cuddy had thought should be called a front rope and not a painter. "It's not my boat. I just borrowed it to come visit my folks."

"Yeah, sure. How long you gonna be? My Pa will be back and want to tie his boat up"—he pointed—"right here."

"I suppose I had better move it then."

"Yeah, pull her ahead and you should be all right."

When the boys were satisfied that Cuddy's boat would not interfere with their father's boat, they went back to sit on the side of pier, their feet in the water.

Cuddy got a travel bag from under the thwart and stepped ashore. He started up the path leading to the top of the hill but changed his mind and came back to speak to the boys.

"Do you know where the Gallants live?"

The tall boy screwed up his face. "Sounds French. There's no French here any more."

The other boy laughed. "They were ordered off." It was a mean little laugh and Cuddy didn't like the sound of it.

"Would you please point out the way to where I might find someone . . ."

"You want a grownup? Sure. Take the path to the top of the hill and at the first house you'll find Ma and Grandma."

"Thanks."

Cuddy mounted the hill but the boys ran well ahead, shouting, "Someone's comin'." He was met in the farmyard by two women, the younger one holding a rake in both hands like a soldier holding a pike.

"I'm looking for the Gallant family. In fact, I'm looking for my Granma and my sister."

The rake relaxed a bit while the older woman asked, "Old lady? Spoke English?"

"Yes! That could be her. Please show me the way to her house."

"T'ain't there no more. Burned to the ground before they left. Didn't get no chance to say goodbye to the old dear. Name was Rayn?"

"Yes, that's her."

"She's still here."

The young woman leaned the rake against the side of the barn and pointed off to the side of the hill. "They planted her where she would have a nice view of the river."

"If'n one of the women was your sister, they stayed and faced up to the sheriff and his men until Rain died."

Cuddy leaned against the watering trough. He eased himself down to sit on the edge.

The young woman nodded her head. "Rain said she wouldn't be pushed off her land again—and she wasn't."

Warming to the story, they took turns telling the stranger what had happened to the Gallants. A proprietor's agent had arrived one day and had announced that unless the people at Rivière-du-Nord-Est paid their arrears in rent—arrears that amounted to many, many shillings more than they could pay—they were squatters and had better move along. The Gallants were the one Acadian family that stayed to the bitter end saying they wouldn't allow themselves to be chased off.

Reine Leblanc had stood up to the sheriff the first time and she faced them again when the sheriff and his men returned, holding an old musket on her knees as she sat in a chair at the front of her house.

"She war a sight to behold, sittin' there, fingerin' the trigger, the musket pointed in the general direction of the sheriff."

"Yeah, it war a stand-off."

"Oh, the sheriff was havin' his men spread out to take the old girl from the rear and I suppose they might have . . ."

" . . . but she got a surprised look on her face and grabbed the musket, pointin' at the sheriff . . ."

" . . . who tried to scramble out of the way . . ."

". . . fallin' all over hisself . . ."

" . . . but she didn't get to pull the trigger."

"Naw. She died right there."

Cuddy continued to sit on the trough. When tears began to fall, he made no attempt to stop them or hide them. He looked up at the women; "You're still here." He swept his eyes around the decrepit buildings and untidy farmyard. "If it was so much money, how did you manage to pay?"

"Now, don't get us wrong, Mister Gallant."

"My name is Cameron."

"Well, Mister Cameron, the agent told us—on the quiet—that there were no arrears for the right kind of tenants."

"And he said we were the right kind."

"Well, we kept our mouths shut."

"Looked to us like the landlord didn't want no Frenchies on his land," the older woman explained, "'cause when they was gone, he tol' us we had a year rent-free as well as no arrears to pay."

"And you didn't say anything to your neighbours?"

"You think we're stupid?"

Cuddy stood up. He brushed off the seat of his pants and walked toward the crest of the hill. "Over here, you say?"

The women followed him. "Yes. The sheriff gave them time to bury Rain before he moved them off."

"I think there's still a marker."

The older woman looked ahead. "Naw. It's gone. I sent the boys out lookin' for wood this spring. Sorry about that." She flashed a smile. "A marker don't mean much to the old girl, now does it."

Cuddy searched the ground for sign of a grave; he found several.

"Don't need no marker. I can show you where." She took several tentative steps. "I think she's right here."

"No, she's the one at the top. Remember the woman with the two boys? How she stopped the men from diggin' lower down?"

"Maybe so. Maybe so."

Cuddy forced his lips into a smile. "Would you please leave me? I would like to be alone here."

"'course." Both women moved away. The boys hesitated until Cuddy gave them a stern look. They ran off. Cuddy was alone, only the retreating voices of the women intruding on his grief.

"It war the woman with the two brats who sent her man off to set fire to the buildings."

"I believe so."

"They were tidy places . . ."

"Bigger'n ours and built some good."

"We coulda used them . . ."

"Do you think we woulda been charged rent for them?'

"They woulda belonged to the proprietor . . ."

"He don't give us nothin'."

"He gave us free rent . . ."

"Yeah, but that was . . ."

When he finally felt that he was alone, Cuddy pulled a small cloth package from his pocket. He unwrapped it and held the purple stone out to catch the sunlight. "The High Sheriff said it had belonged to Joe and that it rightfully belonged to me since I was his heir." He knelt and placed the stone where his grandmother's head might be. "There wasn't anything else left from the old days that you might have recognized." He sat back on his heels. He looked over his shoulders, making sure he was alone before he began to unburden himself to Granma as he dug a hole for the Nova Scotia amethyst.

"I think you knew, Granma, that, just like my Dad, I wasn't cut out to be a farmer." Recalling his trip down the Hillsborough River he hastened to add, "And I'm no sailor . . . so when I met Rose—her name is Rose Nelson—there were some other possibilities.

"Rose is teaching me to read and write and do my sums. We have some money: I have Donald McIntyre's money and what was left of Joe's. It's a tidy sum. Rose has an inheritance which comes to me if I marry her and . . . you know, Granma? I would marry her without the money because she is wonderful and she loves me." He paused as if gathering his thoughts, or maybe he was listening for a response.

"We won't lose the land. The MacEachrans believe that they will be able to buy the land next to ours from John Smallwood . . . Would you believe that? Willie MacEachran will do the chores and Hugh will keep an eye on things for me so the farm will be safe. No, Granma, no one will ever push us off our land." He cocked his ear to one side. "Believe me, sweetheart . . . they won't push us off our land, not ever."

Cuddy asked Mother Mary to be kind to his Granma.

Later, just as he pushed off to begin the trip back to the head of the Hillsborough River, he waved. Then he turned to the business of getting his sailboat to move against the current of the river.

"I think he saw us; he waved."

"He didn't see us."

"I think he did. We should wait until he gets out of sight."

"He won't come back. Do you remember where it was we said the old girl was buried?"

"Not this one. No, it's the next one over."

"Ah ha! I told you he was buryin' something!"

The young one—quicker or more agile—was down on her knees scrabbling at the place where the earth had been disturbed before her mother could move. "Look what I found!"

Endnotes

1. Gene Edward Smallwood of Brampton, Ontario, is one of the Smallwood family historians. He has evidence that Joseph Smallwood was a ship's captain who fled Virginia at the time of the American Revolution to avoid being forced to serve the rebel cause. Later, Joseph Smallwood was a grantee on Lot 56 and records show he lived on Lot 38; the Census of 1798 lists Joseph Smallwood as the head of a family of five females and four males living on Lot 38. For story purposes, I ignored the Lot 56 reference.

The Handsworth connection is another family story, evidence of which was presented to my father when a branch of the Smallwood family died out in England in the mid-twentieth century. My father was interviewed as a Smallwood with a possible claim to the Handsworth property. Unfortunately, someone in Virginia had a closer familial tie.

2. Just to inform the readers who might not have read earlier books of the *Abuse of Power* series, Reine and Robert Cameron are fictitious characters created to support a particular plot line. Cuddy Cameron and his father, Robbie, are also creations of mine. There is a close connection between the Camerons and the Smallwoods. The name "Cameron" has been carried on through several generations. It seemed logical to create a Cameron right from the beginning to help carry the storyline.

Chapter Seventeen
No Goodbyes

February 1800
Oakwood Manor
Handsworth

The winter's wind thrust against the windows with all its might, giving Hélène Smallwood the shivers. She pulled the lap rug higher, to her waist, and then shuffled her feet to better protect them from the penetrating cold. She glanced at the fire. Remembering that Digger had just stoked it, she thought, *can't get much more out of that. Perhaps I should take myself off to bed and have the upstairs maid put a hotpan or two under the covers to make it all cozy.*

There was a clatter in the main hall. Hélène was momentarily curious about the source of the noise but, with a slight shake of her head, she drifted along with her original thought.

In my earlier days, I could beat the cold by digging my fingernails into a set of flexing buttocks. She smiled. She remembered how skilled her fingers were in coaxing the boys along to a satisfactory—no, sometimes brilliant—climax. *If there wasn't enough heat in the hearth, I could always generate heat in the bedroom.* She glanced up at the family coat of arms. "Pro Aris et Focis," she read aloud, and then translated, "for home and hearth. *Yes, quite a few young men helped generate heat in the Smallwood hearth. Those were the days . . .*

There was another noise. Annoyed, she identified this one as coming from the door to the office. *Some clod is knocking on the door, trying to get my attention.*

"Go away! I told you I did not want to be disturbed again this afternoon. Go away!"

The door opened; it was Digger.

"He's back!"

Hélène didn't have to be told who "he" was. She sighed. "Damn!" She tensed her muscles, getting ready, and then every bone in her body complained as she pushed back the chair and rose. "Did we hear from the rector in time?"

"No. These days there's too much traffic on Church Street for the rector to keep track."

Hélène leaned against the edge of the desk as she gathered her strength. "Do we still tithe to that little man?" She answered her own question. "Yes, we do. We surely do." She pushed off from the desk. "I must remember to take care of that."

As she passed Digger, the servant reached out and touched Hélène Smallwood's arm. "Master Joseph won't get out of the carriage until . . . until you and the two boys are on the front steps to greet him."

"Tsk, tsk," was out of her mouth before she fully understood what Digger had said. "And the two boys?" She looked into Digger's eyes to see if he were jesting. "What does he mean, and the two boys?"

Young Joseph answered from down the hall. "His brains, my dear aunt, are addled. The only way we are going to get him out of the carriage is . . ."

Hélène motioned to Digger. "Alert the staff that the master has—"

"Excuse me, Aunt. I give the instructions around here now."

Digger continued toward the call station.

"You had better listen to me, old man, or your time here will be curtailed."

Digger stopped and looked to his mistress for guidance.

Before Hélène could speak, Joseph made it even plainer. "If you don't do as I say, I will have you thrown off the property."

Digger watched as his mistress turned away and marched—as well as her old bones would let her—to the staircase, where she ascended, one regal step at a time.

"We had better do as he says, Digger." She stopped and turned back to face the new Master of Oakwood. "The keys to the ledgers and the vault are in the seamstress's room behind the landscape with the gilt frame." Her eyes widened as the senior Joseph came through the main door. In a petulant, little-boy voice, the old man complained, "This is the first time the boys haven't been here to meet me. It's the very first time the boys haven't welcomed me home."

Household domestics had gathered at the servants' end of the hall. They observed the old man for a moment or two and then, one after another, looked to Young Joseph for direction.

Young Joseph was quick off the mark. "My father's clothes are dirty. When you get them off, throw them away. You!" Joseph pointed at one of the younger men. "What is your name?"

Before the servant could answer, the old man began crying. "I want to see my John, who is always nice to me. I want my other son to look after me."

Joseph ignored his father's blubbering and whining. "Well! What is your name?" Joseph made an erasing movement with his hand. "It doesn't matter what you are called. You are now John. Everyone will call you John and you will answer to John. Is that clear?"

"Yes, sir, it is."

Joseph pointed at his father. "Get him cleaned up. Keep him in his room . . . no! Not in *his* room! Take him to one of the lesser bedchambers on the main floor."

While the old man was being gathered up and led away, he pulled free for a moment. He searched the faces and then settled on Hélène, who was still standing on the staircase. Holding out both arms as if expecting an embrace, he bleated, "I'm home. I'm back."

Hélène fought back a tear. She smiled and whispered, "Welcome home, son."

It took eight months for the old Master of Oakwood to die.

After the ceremony at the family crypt, the rector was congratulated on his elegant eulogy for the deceased. He was also informed that the Smallwoods of Oakwood would no longer tithe to the church in town.

Hélène overheard the pronouncement and smiled; at least the new master had done one thing she agreed with. As to the rest: Cousin William was long gone, Oakwood was prospering without her input and, since she was not privy to any of the Lot 38 affairs, she could not be aware that serious problems were brewing between the Smallwood brothers. Nor would she have much cared; she had her flowers and Digger's companionship.

She looked for Digger's white hair in the cluster of servants. There he was, at the back. She didn't have to wait to catch his eye; his eyes always followed her every move. She beckoned to him. Excusing herself from the funeral party, she stepped away several paces and waited until Digger was by her side. Then the two of them, their silver and white heads together as they discussed the latest generation of their gorgeous roses, slowly walked down the path to the garden.

Joseph Smallwood paused at the front entrance to the house. He was waving the last of the guests through to the refreshments in the main hall when he caught sight of the pair. He beckoned to the nearest servant. "Tell my Aunt Hélène that the master requires her presence at the main house."

The servant hesitated. He was one of the older servants, who would never think of giving the mistress such an order.

"You're not deaf, man, are you?"

"No, sir. But—"

"You deliver my message, now! You tell her that the master demands her presence, immediately."

The servant bowed and backed away from his irate master. He knew where Mistress Hélène would be. He hurried.

It was about twenty minutes later that one of the guests mentioned that a gardener was stationed outside the windows overlooking the gardens. He wasn't peering in on the party but was obviously standing where he could attract attention.

Joseph knew who it was. He excused himself from his guests. *That goddamn woman! Sent her man to annoy me! They will both find out what it means to be annoyed.* He stepped outside and beckoned for Digger to approach. *This ought to be priceless,* he thought. *I'll let him speak first. I'll wait to see what tomfoolery she's up to.*

When the Master of Oakwood didn't speak, Digger said, "She heard her Master's voice and she is . . ."

"Well! Where is she?"

"She is seated on the bench in her rose garden."

"You said she got my message but still didn't come?"

"I'm truly sorry, sir."

Joseph could now see that the man was crying.

"She got your message, sir, but she heard her Master's voice and she is gone."

"Gone!" Joseph glanced at the garden area. He could see that his aunt was there, sitting on the bench. "I can see for myself that she is still in the garden."

"My mistress is dead, sir. She was called home to the house of God." Digger gave Joseph Smallwood a small bow as he backed away. Joseph watched as Digger walked down the driveway and out the main gate. Digger stood for a moment in the middle of Church Street, having a last look at the silver-haired lady sitting with her eyes closed, seemingly enjoying the scents from the beautiful flowers that surrounded her. Then he left.

Hélène Smallwood was placed in the family crypt next to her son. There was no eulogy.

A NEW CENTURY

Every New Year brings new hope. The arrival of the year 1800 brought increased expectations, probably because it was the beginning of a new century.

Islanders who were proprietors encouraged the local assembly to pass escheat laws (a legal process allowing the Crown to take back land titles). The argument was simple: a large number of absentee proprietors had not improved their lands as they had contracted to do, they had not paid their quitrents to the Crown, and the barren unimproved lands were interfering with the growth of the colony. In 1802, the local assembly petitioned the home government to force proprietors to do their duty or, failing that, that the delinquent proprietors' lands be escheated and granted to local settlers. The resident proprietors hoped the mere threat of the Crown resuming title to various lots would frighten some absentee proprietors to sell at depressed prices—sell at depressed prices to the Island politicians and landowners, of course. However, the escheat principle was not acceptable to proprietors who had fulfilled their obligations because having their tenants leave to take up free or cheap Crown lands and become proprietors on their own could not be permitted. The proposal became mired in political manoeuvring and was not implemented.

So, what was the situation?

When the magic wand of escheat had been first waved, some absentee landowners panicked and sold their holdings at bargain prices to the wealthy local proprietors just as the proponents of escheat (the local proprietors) had planned. As time passed and it became evident that there wasn't enough support for the escheat principle to become law,

273

the proprietors (both local and absentee) breathed a sigh of relief; change could lead to disruption and disruption was not good for business. Proprietors were willing to let escheat quietly pass into history.

However, the Island tenants had seen the magic wand and believed that escheat was the key to their economic freedom.

Tenants were obliged to work to pay rent to the proprietors, a fee that could be increased at any time. Come cold, heat, fire, or starvation, tenants were obliged to pay or face eviction without regard to any improvements to the property or any public works like roads and bridges that they might have found it necessary to build to support local commerce.

Perhaps they could complain to the government? The proprietors were the government.

Use their votes to effect change? Catholics were not permitted to run for office or vote. Catholics had no say in government until 1830, when the Test of Loyalty was repealed. Even then, there was no secret ballot; they would not dare to vote against the people who owned their land. To make matters worse for the Catholic Acadians, they could not speak the language of government and were generally illiterate.

Perhaps another escheat movement—or something like it—might improve the tenants' lot. So, at the beginning of the nineteenth century, the seeds of the Tenant League were planted in the rich soil of putrid politics and the compost of human misery.

⬛

Chapter Eighteen
Changes Are Upon Us

May 1817
The Smallwood Farm
Lot 38, Prince Edward Island

Francis Tierney closed the ledger. He was sitting at the side of the house, soaking up the sun's rays, trying to make up for the months of dismal winter weather by doing his bookwork outside. He lifted the chair—he didn't want to mar the wood by scraping it against the imported flagstones—and stood up so that he could see the bottom of the property, down by the brook. He waited; any moment now, whoever he had heard coming along the trail would be visible through the trees. *There! There he is!* As soon as he saw who it was, he returned to his chair. *An Acadian, he thought. Not many of them around these parts this last while.* Francis could see the stranger quite clearly now; *they wear such funny clothes.* He watched as the man followed the path and disappeared in the direction of the Cameron property. Flipping open the ledger, he tried to get back into his accounts, but he was distracted with errant thoughts about John Smallwood's quest for a wife.

Yes, the Master of Seven Oaks had asked his overseer to compile a list of all of the eligible females from as far away as Halifax. Through a systematic process of elimination, master and overseer had reduced the list to two young ladies of good repute and sterling upbringing—both residing in Charlottetown. The plan called for the master to arrange an invitation to one of the governor's fancy social occasions in the fall and then . . .

Francis Tierney could hear another traveller on the trail, this time going in the opposite direction. *Busy, busy day!* Again he waited to see who it was. He glanced at the ledger but made a conscious choice not to pick it up again, but rather to continue his reverie. Francis closed his eyes against the glare of the sun . . . *but then fate had intervened.* He smiled as he recalled the flurry of excitement as John Smallwood made a hurried business trip to Halifax, leaving no time for the final scrutiny of the unaware Island ladies.

He spoke softly to himself. "And, at a fancy dress ball, when John Smallwood saw Violet Owen, daughter of Captain Jack Owen of the Halifax garrison, all of John Smallwood's careful planning went out the window." Tierney shook his head. "His brains must have descended to his cock . . . all that work . . . gathering all that intelligence . . . and the planning! Dumb bastard! One look at Violet Owen and instant stupid!"

He could see who it was coming the other way; it was that same Acadian. "At least it could be the same man," he said to himself, "they all look the same to me in their dark suits and round hats." Tierney frowned as he watched the Acadian turn off the trail and start up the hill toward the Smallwood house. Tierney considered slipping back inside the house to get his jacket and hat but then thought, *he doesn't mean a thing to me. Probably just wants a drink of water . . . but the brook is right there for his use . . . wonder what he wants?* Tierney changed his mind and did re-enter the house to fetch his hat and coat.

Tierney waited for the knock on the door. He stood there, his coat buttoned and hat in hand, waiting. Finally, muttering something about curiosity and an unfortunate cat, he peeked through the window. There was no one on the front veranda! He opened the door. Allowing a moment for his eyes to adjust to the sunlight, Tierney placed his hat square on his head and then stepped forward to the top of the steps. He was startled when a pleasant voice said, "Bonjour, M'sieu. I tink you come back . . . da books . . . I wait . . . here."

"Yes, well, I suppose I would have come back there . . . but I didn't. Who are you? What do you want?"

"I look for . . . cousin, Robert Cameron. I speak to . . . the . . . farmer . . ."—he pointed to the next farm—"over dere but he not . . ."

"Yes, well, Mister MacEachran doesn't speak to many people."

"Quoin?"

Francis Tierney shook his head. *Language is always a problem with these people.* He made circular motions with his finger to his temple and then pointed at the Cameron farm. "He's slow in the head . . ." *Why bother. He doesn't understand.* "No. No Cameron here." He pointed at the other farm. "No Cameron there."

"Eh?"

Tierney shrugged his shoulders. He indicated the jug of well water on the table and motioned with his hands: "Would you like some cool water?"

The Acadian didn't respond to the offer but, instead, with an intense, pleading look on his face, explained in rapid French that he was the eldest son of Rosalie Cameron Gallant, who was sick and probably dying. She wanted to see her brother once more. If the kind gentleman saw Robert Cameron, would he tell Cameron that they were living as tenants near Seven Mile Bay.

"I don't understand, young man."

Rosalie . . . Rosalie Gallant. Me . . . moi . . . je m'appelle Pierre Gallant." He tapped his chest. "Pierre Gallant," he repeated.

This is impossible! Francis Tierney sat down in the only chair. He smiled up at the young Acadian as he opened his ledger. He gestured at the figures on the page. "I must work." He lowered his eyes and began muttering as he worked the figures. "The fancy wedding? £70 6/3. The fancy Boston honeymoon?" He tallied some figures. "That was budgeted at £175. And the tag-on visit to Maryland? Well, I won't know until they get back." He continued in that vein for some while. When he looked up again, the Acadian was gone.

"What ho, my love!" Cuddy Cameron posed dramatically in the doorway of the tailor shop.

Rose Cameron put down one of the men's jackets she was working on and ran to her husband, intent on giving him an embrace and a kiss.

Cuddy held her off with one hand while saying, "Don't crush the material, Missus Cameron! It's all brand new and never been hugged."

Rose stepped back to admire the scarlet coat with the green facings. Her voice full of admiration, she said, "Oh, my! You look so dashing! Doesn't he look handsome, girls?"

The Cameron twins, Mary and Flora, were quick to leave their sewing and gather around their father. Mary traced the line of the white cross-belts and felt the stiffness of the regimental gold lace. "It's so beautiful!"

Apparently Cuddy had not come home alone; Ewen Cameron stuck his head around the corner and then edged past the soldier in the doorway. "Is it real gold, Mother?"

"Gold wire, I do believe."

Cuddy reached into his cartouche-box and brought out some money. "This is real enough." He handed the money to his wife, who fingered the coins as she counted.

"That's my signing bonus—£2 6/8." Cuddy puffed up his chest and clicked his heels. He gave a slight bow as he introduced himself to the women of his family: "Private Robert Cameron of the Queen's County Regiment at your service, Mesdames."

"Just a minute, dearest." Rose opened the door to the living area at the back. "Robbie! Bring your brothers out to see who's here in the shop!"

Robbie Cameron, a red-headed fifteen-year-old with freckles, ushered two youngsters, equally befreckled, into the tailor shop. Robbie stopped, somewhat awe-struck, as soon as he saw his father in the splendid uniform. The two children, Thomas and Allan, ran forward. The mother managed to catch and hold Thomas, the middle son, as he ran by, but little Allan was far too agile to be stopped.

"Are your hands clean, Allan?" By this time it was far too late but she gave the caution anyway. "Don't touch your father with dirty hands!"

"What's this, Daddy?" Allan held the scabbard in both hands, his fingers seeking a way to separate it from his father's belt. "Can I play with it?" He pulled, hard.

Cuddy gathered the four-year-old into his arms and gave the boy a whisker rub in the hollow of his neck. When the boy's screams of displeasure at being denied the scabbard turned to giggles, Cuddy put the boy down by his mother.

Ewen, almost as tall as his father, leaned in close to examine the elegant epaulets. "What are these for, Father?"

"I don't know, son." Cuddy shrugged his shoulders. "Makes the outfit look good."

Rose kept a grip on Allan but she released Thomas as she said, "They are called epaulets. I sewed a new pair on for young Master DesBrisay just the other day."

Cuddy flipped one of his epaulets with his finger. "These are just tacked on. I'll need them properly sewn, too." He smiled as his wife retorted, "I plan to work only for the DesBrisays . . . _they_ pay well."

Cuddy took off his hat. "And there are enough DesBrisays to fill every officer position in the regiment," he said as he handed the hat to Thomas, who immediately ran his fingers over the bright green cockade.

"No, son! That's the wrong way!" Cuddy guided the boy's hands to move in the opposite direction. "Up," he said. "You can smooth the cockade up because it has to stand up, but never down." Cuddy took the twelve-year-old by the arm and pointed him toward the living quarters. "Put it on the shelf in the back hall for me, Thomas."

The family slowly moved to the back of the building, Thomas running ahead to put the hat on the shelf.

Cuddy hesitated at the doorway. "What if a customer comes; it's too early to close."

"The tinkle bell will let us know. We'll just bring the cash box with us." Hearing her mother, Flora reached back and scooped up a little leather-bound box.

Cuddy put his arms around the twins and gave them a squeeze. Once into the living quarters, he patted them gently and suggested they go into the kitchen to make some tea for the family. "Take Allan with you. Give him some sweets." Once Allan and the girls were gone, Cuddy announced, "I got a letter from Hugh MacEachran today." Cuddy handed the letter to his wife. "He says Willie is getting forgetful." More softly he added, "He suggests that it's time for us to go back to the farm."

Rose's reaction was quick. "We can't go back! Our lives are here." With a panicky look on her face she added, "And you have your bounty for joining the militia." She shook her head. "We can't just up and go back!"

"We can't allow anyone or anything to push us off our land. That land is our sacred trust passed down from . . ."

"I know. I know all about that but what can we do?"

"Someone has to go back."

They both looked at Ewen as Cuddy repeated, "Someone has to go."

Ewen's response was almost immediate. "I won't go!"

What followed was one of those intense silences where each person in the room knew they were on the verge of something terrible. Several times, Cuddy opened his mouth but closed it again, choosing not to be the first to speak.

Thomas came charging back into the room, bringing with him the sense of happiness that had pervaded the home just a few short minutes ago. "I put your hat up, Father."

Rose patted the bench beside her. "That's a good boy. Come sit with me." When the boy hesitated—sensing that something was terribly amiss—she held her arms out to him. "Come, Thomas."

The boy still lingered near his older brother. He looked

up. "What's wrong, Ewen?" His brother didn't answer. He looked toward his father. "Daddy?"

"Go sit by your mother, son. That's a good boy." Cuddy faced his eldest son. He began to speak, but Ewen interrupted him.

"You and Ma married Church of England; that makes me an Anglican."

"Well, yes, we married Church of England because he was the only priest we could find. What's that got to do with our problem?"

"You are a proprietor . . ."

"Not really."

"Yes, but all the big-wigs believe you have tenants on our land and, because they think you are one of them, they treat me as the son of an equal. I have a chance to make my way here, in Charlottetown. I can become part of the establishment!"

"You, the son of a mercantile?"

"You don't get it, Father. You're a proprietor."

Cuddy turned away and appeared to be staring out the window as he said, firmly, "Someone has to go back."

"I don't know anything about farming."

"Neither do I, but all it takes is someone to do the thinking for Willie. He knows what to do and when. Hugh says Willie is getting forgetful. All you have to do is be his memory."

"No. No sir, I will not go."

"I will go, Father."

Cuddy bent over and lifted Thomas into his arms. Giving him a hug, Cuddy set the boy on the bench so that he could stand eye to eye with his father.

His eyes gleaming with pride, Thomas proclaimed, "If all I have to do is remember things for Mister MacEachran, I can do that."

The second eldest son, Robbie, shook his head. He stood up and approached his father. "Thomas can't go; he has to stay in school. I can go, Father." Robbie was tall enough that he could almost look his father in the eye as he repeated, "I can go because I have all the schoolin' I need. You and Ma can't go. Ewen won't go. Thomas is in school. It's up to me."

Mother and Father exchanged looks.

"Tea is ready, everybody!" Mary poked her head through the door. "Come and get it."

Chapter Nineteen
Tears for Tierney

October 1825
Seven Oaks
Lot 38, Prince Edward Island

Violet Smallwood could hear the screams coming from down near the pond. She supposed they were fun screams but with three youngsters ranging in age from eleven to six running loose on a farm, a mother could never be sure. She continued to dandy little David on her knee while she looked for someone to go see what all the fuss was about. *Certainly life is more pleasant here at Seven Oaks than Halifax garrison life could ever be, but I would appreciate more servants. Where is that girl!* There was no help for it; she would have to put David down.

Mother kissed the little fellow and talked sweet-talk to him as she lowered the four-year-old to the sofa. David, of course, wasn't about to accept being discarded without a fight. He grabbed his mother's blond hair and held on while bellowing his most recently acquired war cry, "Not fair! Not fair," bringing the house-girl on the run to rescue her favourite child. The mother stepped back to watch the miracles being wrought by a little bit of shushing and a lot of nose-nuzzling in the boy's neck.

More screams, this time from behind the barn. Violet gathered up her skirts to allow enough freedom of movement for her to go quickly toward the noise. She glanced back at the maid; Violet could see the girl was whispering sweet nothings in the boy's ear. David was wearing a large smile of contentment.

"Lise! Do not speak French to my son!"

From down the hill, a male voice called out, "Don't worry, Ma'am; I have the rascal!"

Violet spun around to see Francis Tierney leading a dejected-looking William Frederick by the hand.

Feeling a little embarrassed at her exposure, Violet lowered her skirts and assumed a demure pose as she waited for them to approach. *Oh, my! Francis is limping again. He reminds me so much of my father; all stern and military on the outside but so thoughtful and caring towards me. I have no idea how old he is but he is such a dear, sweet old man. It's strange how the children obey his every suggestion. When he says he is going to skin them alive, they take him at his word. Imagine!* She felt some loose hair at the side of her face and she took the moment to tuck it back in. *I couldn't imagine our dear Francis Tierney doing anything nasty to anyone.*

"What was going on, Mister Tierney?"

"Mary Ann was playing nurse again."

"Oh, the devil! I will have her father chastise her."

"It's looked after, Ma'am. She won't be quick to pick on this little boy again."

"What was James doing?"

"He was holding the little one down. Eventually William Frederick bit James on the arm. Then he tried to take a chunk out of the girl, too. Picked up a hammer and chased the two of them into the barn. He had just cornered James when I came upon them."

"He hit me, Ma."

"Who? Was it James who hit you?"

"No, him." William Frederick pointed at the old man.

Tierney smiled at the mother. "He had a weapon and I didn't."

The little boy wiped his tear-smeared face with the back of his arm, his lower lip sticking out in a huge pout. "You hit me," he repeated looking up at the man.

"Did I hurt you?"

"Y-y-yes."

"Next time, do as I say."

Violet knelt so she was at almost the same level as the boy. "You must not bite your brother and sister and you must do what a grownup tells you."

"Yes, Mother."

"Now, go along to Lise and get cleaned up." She gave him a little spank to send him on his way. She groaned as she stood up clutching her distended belly.

Mister Tierney extended a hand but Violet declined any assistance.

"There was another little girl in the barn," he said. "She skedaddled the minute she saw me coming."

"Yes, I have seen her before. James tells me her name is Mary. I have made a pirate's pact with James not to mention her again; she's Mary Cameron." Violet Smallwood shrugged her shoulders. "If the children can get along, perhaps the adults will learn from them."

They strolled in silence. It was Violet who picked up the conversation again.

"I didn't know if I would have been able to run that far to see what was happening down at the barn. I'm glad you were there." She accepted Tierney's arm as they walked back up the slight incline, Violet putting pressure against the small of her back with her free hand to relieve some of her discomfort. "What about my other two?"

"You'd better call them up and look at the boy's bite."

"I will. What if they get into it again with William Frederick?"

"I told them if I caught them again I would . . ."

" . . . skin them alive," Violet interjected.

They both laughed.

This man is such a large part of our lives, she thought.

She sent the house-girl after James and Mary Ann.

It wasn't until after the evening meal that she found out she would soon have to get along without her Francis Tierney.

Same day
Cameron Farm
Lot 38, Prince Edward Island

"The Smallwood brats are at it again." Robbie Cameron tossed the reins to Willie MacEachran and then slid off the horse. He didn't expect much of an answer from the old man, but he watched for it because Willie surprised him sometimes. Robbie went on, making conversation. "I heard some commotion as I rode by. Sounded like a pig was stuck but I knew it was the kids again. Often wonder what they get into."

"Long as they don't come here."

Robbie smiled at Willie. "That's right, Willie; as long as they keep their distance." He recognized the look on Willie's face so he repeated himself to keep the old man in the conversation. "Long as they don't come here." He waited, but that was the end of that.

"I was out to the Old French Trail today. There's a new wooden bridge near Saint Peter's. It would be nice if they would build a road on the south shore of the Hillsborough River instead of using the Old French Trail on the north shore."

"Don't matter none."

"You're right. It don't matter none but maybe, someday, we could ride in a carriage all the way from Charlottetown to here."

Willie had turned away and was leading the horse to the barn. Robbie called after him, "Where is Mary?"

Robbie smiled to himself as he watched the man and horse enter the barn. If Willie heard him he had—he remembered how his father often said—"paid him no never mind." He went into the house looking to see what his sister Mary was up to. She was only here for the summer—to get away from the dirt and smell of the town—but she was proving to be a grand help. "Mary," he called. The twelve-year-old was nowhere to be seen. He poured himself a cup of water and went out to sit on the step to catch the last sunshine of the day. It was a beautiful late Indian Summer day. Out of the corner of his eye he saw Mary sneaking around the front of the house trying to enter the side door without being seen.

"Mary!"

She stopped running and, slipping her shawl back up over her shoulders, she walked slowly toward her brother. She made some adjustments to the garment to more completely cover herself and then said, "Hello, Robbie."

"Where have you been?"

"Playing down by the brook. It's beautiful there."

"You weren't at the Smallwoods', were you?"

"I wouldn't go there."

"Good. We don't have no truck nor trade with those people." It was then he noticed the blood. "Are you hurt, Mary?"

Quickly, Mary pulled the shawl closer to her body. "It's not mine."

"Then whose is it?"

Keeping the shawl tightly wrapped, Mary turned away. "I . . . I found a fox in a snare. I let him go. When he was struggling to escape, he leaked some blood on me."

"You're sure it didn't bite you? An animal in a trap doesn't know that you are trying to help it." Robbie thought for a moment and then asked the girl, just as she was opening the door to go into the house, "You know we don't have snares on our land?"

Mary knew what he was after so she gave it to him. "I was down by the brook and I might have strayed over the lot line."

"I didn't know the Smallwoods were setting snares."

"Maybe they didn't. Maybe someone else did. Anyhow, I let the fox go," she said as she entered the house, relieved to get away from her brother's questions.

By the time they sat down for supper, the sun had set but there was still a reddish glow to the sky. As they ate their meal, the blood-red colour spread further across the northern sky.

Seven Oaks
Lot 38, Prince Edward Island

John Smallwood poured a little brandy for his wife. He looked at the other man and asked, "Would you like a drink, Francis?"

"That would be nice. I would join the mistress in a brandy, please."

John served the brandies. On his way back to the rum decanter, he looked at the strange sky. "Looks like there's a fire somewhere. Either it's very, very close or it is very, very big." Francis was swirling his brandy. "It can't be close. With this wind, we would have live cinders and smoke coming this way." He sipped his brandy. "It must be a long way off."

"Yes, so true." John turned away from the window. "I mean to talk a bit of business, Francis." John bowed his head in the direction of his wife and asked, "If you don't mind, dear."

"No, of course not. Do you want me to leave?"

"Not at all. This has an effect on you as much as anyone."

Francis leaned forward. "Is it about your following my advice and selling off the land in fifty-acre lots?"

"Your advice has been sound. You convinced me that settlers on this island would eventually demand all the rights and privileges that Englishmen have at home. So, with that in mind, I had disposed of most of our excess lots before the proprietors started that escheat movement and the land prices fell." He paused and sipped his rum. "And now the rabble has formed the Tenant League." He smiled at the overseer. "It's just like you predicted; the peasants are in revolt. I am mightily pleased that I am in the enviable position of having lots of money and not lots of land." John reached over and squeezed Tierney's arm. "You are an excellent servant and advisor."

"Thank you." Francis Tierney waited while the master searched for something in the secretary desk. The "something" turned out to be a letter with an enclosure. The master separated the enclosure from the letter and handed it to the overseer. Francis could see by the coat of arms on the wax seal that the enclosure was from Oakwood. It was addressed to Francis Tierney. He opened it.

"I have been discharged for cause!" Tierney looked up to see a smug little smile on the master's face. "What does it mean?"

"It means, my dear Francis, that my brother believes me to be inept . . ."—here John paused for several heartbeats— "and you to be a thief."

The word "thief" did not register with the old man. "It says that I have been terminated and that I will not have claim to my severance." Stricken with the shock and suddenness of his change in condition, Tierney's voice quavered as he asked, "What have I done to deserve this?"

Concerned that the old man might have a heart attack, John hastened to explain that it had been years since Joseph had sent any funds to support Seven Oaks. "Not that we needed any—thanks to you—and I have not sent any of the profits from the land sales to my brother." Joseph sighed. "For that, he blames the overseer."

"I see." Some of the colour had returned to the overseer's face. "And my severance money?"

"I'm sure Joseph Smallwood will see the error of his ways and provide proper compensation . . ."

". . . as provided by my contract signed by your father."

"Of course."

Violet cleared her throat. Both men waited for her to speak. "After all these years, Mister Tierney only gets what is specified in a decades-old contract?"

John Smallwood quaffed his drink as he rose from his chair. "No, certainly not. I will match the amount specified in the contract." Seeing the questioning look in the old man's eyes, John moved to stifle any hope Tierney had of staying on at Seven Oaks _and_ collecting the severance from Joseph. "No, Francis, you cannot remain here at Seven Oaks. If you did remain, Joseph would believe that you are in league with me. I don't need that kind of trouble . . . and, indeed, my brother would make trouble."

The old man suddenly looked very old. He knocked back his brandy and stood. "Well, it's been an interesting evening."

Violet rose and hurried to Tierney's side. She didn't embrace him—although in her heart of hearts she wanted to—but she did give him her warmest wishes. "Where will you go, Francis?"

"Back to Maryland. I still have kin there." He took her hand and in an old-fashioned, courtly manner he kissed it.

Noting the flush on her face he asked, "Is the little passenger you're carrying giving you some distress?"

She smiled and took his hand in hers. "All the time, Francis, thank you." She released his hand when her husband cleared his throat and began to speak.

"In the morning, why don't we go out the Old French Trail as far as Saint Peter's? Someone will know what is causing that glow in the sky."

* * *

The next day, at Saint Peter's Harbour, they learned from ships' captains that the glow in the sky didn't come from anywhere on The Island. The source of the live cinders and billowing smoke was somewhere well to the northwest.

Wildfires were always a threat to the Islanders and John Smallwood didn't breathe easily until he found out the cause and the location. When he was escorting Francis Tierney to Charlottetown to catch the ship to Pictou, the town was abuzz with activities in support of a charity drive to load a ship with medicines and supplies for Newcastle on the Miramichi River in New Brunswick.[1]

Later, after he had said his adieus to his old overseer, John was having a couple of rums for the road when he was joined by an acquaintance. John allowed a few moments to pass following the usual exchange of pleasantries before he raised what he felt was the most important topic of the day.

"They are mostly French in New Brunswick, aren't they?"

The other proprietor preened his moustache and considered his reply, carefully. Finally coming to the conclusion that he could reveal his true feelings in the presence of another landowner he said, "Yes, I truly believe they are."

"I understand that hundreds are homeless and their animals and possessions destroyed?"

"Yes."

"Pity."

"Indeed."

It was John's turn to preen. "You are supporting the charity?"

"Oh yes, of course. We can't be seen to let the side down, you know."

Endnotes

1. The glow of the fire at Newcastle could be seen in the night sky at Charlottetown. Live cinders from the New Brunswick fire were reported on the northwest end of The Island.

Chapter Twenty
Catholic Emancipation

Spring 1830
House of Assembly
Charlottetown

"The Speaker recognizes the member for Queen's County, the Honourable Mister Ewen Cameron."

"Mister Speaker, I would like to speak on the resolution before the matter is put to a vote."[1]

"Proceed, Mister Cameron."

"In 1825, I was but a new member in the house when the Roman Catholics of our Island presented a petition asking for relief from the laws that prevented them from voting in elections or serving in this assembly. Unfortunately, discussion was postponed"—Ewen made an exaggerated shrug—"because of the lateness of the session."

"Early in the next session I suggested a resolution that would have extended the right of voting in elections to His Majesty's subjects of the Roman Catholic religion on our Island. You will, of course, recall that the resolution was defeated, the Speaker being called upon to cast the tie-breaking vote.

"Today, the mother parliament has suggested that we accept the principles of their Catholic Emancipation Act of 1829. I am always proud to be a member of this assembly but today, when I participate in the passage of this act, it will be one of those special moments that I will cherish for the rest of my life."

* * *

Later, at the tailor shop, Cuddy gathered the clan so Ewen could explain his participation in an historic event.

"Ewen was a part of a wonderful moment in our Island's history." Cuddy beckoned to his son. "Come up here where we can all see you, Ewen, and tell us about it."

Ewen walked to the front of the shop. He looked from

293

face to precious face of his family as he told the story of the
Test Act which required all civil and military officers to be
communicants of the Church of England, and to take oaths
of supremacy and allegiance. "That has been repealed," Ewen
said, proudly, "and the Catholic Emancipation Act now
allows all citizens of our Island to vote for members of the
assembly."

Everyone made congratulatory noises but it was Mary,
Ewen's favourite in the family, that he sought out for her special approval. He scanned the group. "Where is Mary?"

A very grumpy Flora complained, "It was my turn to
spend the summer at the farm but Mary—"

The mother interrupted, "Mary really wanted to go back
again this year. She said she had things she wanted to finish—
"

"She just made a bigger fuss than I did," whined Flora.
"Mary always gets her own way."

"That's not really true, sweetheart. She told me there was
one particular thing she wanted to do . . ."

"Did she tell you what it was?"

"No, Flora, she didn't. She said it was supposed to be a
surprise."

It was Cuddy's turn to interrupt. "She's there and we're
here. Let's not spoil Ewen's moment."

The family began to discuss Ewen's achievement but not
before Flora made one last sour comment. "She may be my
twin sister, but I hate her. I hate her very much because I know
what she plans to do."

August 1830
Seven Oaks

James Smallwood paced back and forth, his hands clasped
behind his back. "What did Father say?"

William Frederick was seated by the window, still dressed
in his dusty travelling clothes. "I found Father at the DesBrisays'
and I must say that he didn't have the time to properly con-

sider your dilemma. They were leaving to have dinner at Government House."

"For God's sake, William! What did he say?"

"Are you under any obligation with that family to marry the woman?"

"If you keep on like this, I will come over there and give you a punch!"

Mary Ann Smallwood made calming motions with her hands as she looked to her fiancé for help, but William Douglas was trying his very best to appear disinterested. Seeing little help could be expected from William Douglas, she continued on her own. "I believe that to be a very sensible question; what have the Camerons had to say about you compromising one of their little girls?"

"Oh, Christ, Mary Ann!" James ran his fingers through his hair in frustration. "She's not with child, if that's what you mean, and she's not a little girl. In fact, she's older than I am but if her family were aware of the number of times that . . ."

Mary Ann screwed up her face as she exclaimed, "You did compromise her!"

William Frederick leered at his sister. "I believe that's how the offended family would say it."

James stalked across the room and stood over his younger brother. "You'd better tell me what Father had to say." He lifted his fist as if to strike a blow.

William Frederick put his hand up to shield his face. "All right! I told you I didn't have much time with Father. He told me to tell you . . ."

"Get on with it!"

William blurted out the message. "You are a member of an honourable family; you should do the honourable thing."

James went back to the window, looking in the general direction of the Cameron place. "Oh sure! I'm supposed to get all dressed up, go over to the Camerons', ask for Mary's hand in marriage, and dodge musket balls as the Camerons come across the property line in a rage!"

Mary Ann said, very softly, "You won't have to worry about that."

"What?"

"The Camerons coming over here. I don't know what went on in the early history of this island, but you can be sure they won't come over here."

The room was silent for several minutes. James finally said, "Mary Ann, will you please come with me?"

"Yes, James. I will."

That afternoon

Although it wasn't far, it had been a hot walk. Mary Ann looked down at her shoes and then up at the Cameron house, where there didn't seem to be anyone in the windows. Satisfied that they would not be observed, she grabbed her brother's arm to stop him. She pointed down at her shoes. "Please knock the dust off them, James."

"You can't be serious!"

"James, I will not go with you up to that house if my shoes look like I have been working in the fields."

James took a handkerchief out of his pocket and bent down to clean Mary Ann's shoes. Neither of them saw the movement of the curtains in the front window.

Robbie beckoned to his sister. "Mary, there's a couple coming into our front yard. Do you know them?"

Mary studied the couple through the curtain.

"Well? Do you know who they are?" When his sister still didn't answer, Robbie said, "He's on his knees." Then he laughed. "It looks like he's kissing her foot!" He watched as the man straightened up and adjusted his clothing. The man offered his arm to the woman but she obviously declined, perhaps wanting to use both hands to keep her skirts out of the dust, Robbie thought. He looked more closely. No, she wasn't holding up the skirt because he could see she was making an adjustment to her waist . . . Robbie was surprised to see the hem of the skirt lower several inches. "What the hell?"

Mary spoke for the first time. "It's a dress elevator, Robbie. Mary Ann told me that the proper name is porte-jute. It turns her walking dress into a driving dress for afternoon visiting and—"

"Who is Mary Ann?"

"Oh."

"Well? Who is Mary Ann?" He pointed out the window. "Is that Mary Ann?"

"Yes."

"Who is the man?"

"James . . . James Smallwood."

"Coming here?"

"Yes."

"How do you know them? If I don't know any of them, how do you . . ." Suddenly Robbie had a sinking feeling. All those times that Mary disappeared on the farm somewhere. "Why are they coming here?"

Mary took her brother's hand in hers. "I know them because . . ."

"Have you been alone with that man?"

"Yes . . . and I love him." She turned away from her brother and looked out the window. The couple were almost at the front door. "James is coming here to meet you. He is coming here to talk about . . ."

There was a knock on the door. Speechless because of all he had suddenly learned, Robbie went to the door and opened it.

Strangely, it was the woman who made the introductions. "Hello. I am Mary Ann Smallwood. Unfortunately, we haven't met before. We have all lived here, side by side, but we have never had the opportunity to converse . . ."

"What do you want with us, Madam?"

"Well, we have a wonderful opportunity to overcome the strangeness between our families because . . ."

"Madam, I don't mean to be rude but . . ."

". . . because my brother, James, would like to speak to you about the young lady who was standing behind you . . ."

Robbie swivelled around to look to see if there was someone else in the house because this woman couldn't be speaking about his sister—not Mary—but Mary was not standing behind him nor was there anyone else. "You must be mistaken."

James finally stepped out from behind his sister's skirts. "May I please speak with Mary?" Suddenly he was overcome by a flood of words. "I look forward to every summer when Mary is here. I can't imagine my life without her and please, do not be alarmed. All the times we were together we didn't . . ." He was stopped by the anger that suffused the male Cameron's face.

"You were alone with my sister?"

"Yes, but we didn't . . . I mean . . . nothing much hap—"

"Good day to you, sir, madam."

"But, I mean to ask her to marry me."

"Get out!"

Mary had been waiting in the hall. When she heard James proclaim his intentions, she entered the front room from the hall carrying a small travel case with several coats over her arm. "Yes, James."

For a moment, it looked as though the brother was going to interfere with Mary's movement toward the door so James stepped forward and extended his arm. Robbie Cameron didn't move. Robbie watched his sister step outside the Cameron home.

Mary Ann took the coats and case while James and Mary turned to face the male Cameron unencumbered by luggage.

"Don't go with them, Mary."

"I love James. I must go with him, Robbie. I thought you knew about us, all these years, and would be on my side."

Robbie moved into the doorway. For a moment it looked as if he was going to offer his hand, but no, he put his hand on the door handle. "You can't go with them, Mary." With a catch in his voice he said, "Please don't go with them."

"I love him. I must go with him."

"You're a Cameron. He's a Smallwood."

"Please Robbie. Help me fix this."

Robbie slowly closed the door. He listened to the foot-steps as they retreated from the house. Robbie felt the tears on his cheeks but he ignored them. How was he going to explain all this to his father?

Endnotes

1. It is a matter of record that Ewen Cameron was a supporter of Catholic emancipation and spoke in the House on the subject.

Chapter Twenty-One
Succession

August 1831
Charlottetown

John Smallwood folded the letter once, twice, and put it in the pocket of his smoking jacket. He felt quite satisfied with the information it contained; Mister and Missus William Douglas had been well received by the English branch of the family at Oakwood. His brother Joseph had rolled out the red carpet for Mary Ann and her new husband. "That was nice," John said to himself. *You can always count on good breeding to have the right thing done at the right time to the right people,* he thought. *I should drop my brother a note expressing my appreciation . . . no, no, no. That would start the bickering all over again. It cost me the services of old Mister Tierney to put an end to the matter before. I mustn't do anything to start up that fuss again.*

He picked up the latest copy of the *Royal Gazette*. "I say, Violet, are the boys coming in or not?"

"I sent for them, dear. They shouldn't be long in coming." Violet entered the room as she asked, "Anything interesting in the *Gazette*?" She sat down.

"Just the usual . . . Oh! There are now two hundred coloured people from Ohio living at Wilberforce. The last time we read about them there were only eighty."

"I know you mentioned that before but, where is Wilberforce?"

"Upper Canada, my dear." He sat more upright in his chair. "Someone named Cameron is dead. I wonder if he's related to Mary!"

"Mercy of God! Poor darling Mary has already suffered such great losses. There can't be more!"

"I'll read it to you."

LAMENTABLE ACCIDENT—It is with the most poignant regret we have to announce the death of our much esteemed townsman and valued friend Ewen Cameron, Esq., which occurred yesterday under the following circumstances. It appears that about five in the afternoon, he passed the four gun battery at Fanning Bank after asking the gunner's wife where was the best place to bathe. Less than fifteen minutes after, a man came to the fort and gave the alarm that some person was drowned. Four medical gentlemen were called and every means that skill or ingenuity could prompt, in order to restore animation, was resorted to, in vain. The operation of bronchotomy, or opening of the windpipe, was performed, and the stomach pump introduced when the lungs were found completely surcharged with water. [1]

John skipped down the article. "Ah! Here is the clincher!" He traced the words with his finger as he read along. "Mr. Cameron's death will occasion a vacancy in the representation of Queen's County in the House of Assembly." John looked up. "I remember she said her brother was in the House."[2]

"She probably hasn't yet heard about the fire. Do you believe the letter would have caught up to them by now?"

"I doubt the postal services on the continent are as efficient as the Royal Mail."

"James promised to attend the consulate in Rome before leaving Italy."

"Come now, Violet; you know James and his promises."

"Perhaps having a wife will occasion changes in our errant son."

"Maybe. Maybe not." John Smallwood tossed the newspaper to one side. "It would probably be for the best if the letter doesn't find them. The news would spoil their honeymoon."[3]

"And when they return, Mary will learn—all at once—that she is alone in this world."

"Don't be melodramatic, my dear. She is not alone. True, her mother and father are gone . . ."

"And the rest of her family."

"No, you are mistaken there. I learned that there is a brother, Thomas, and a sister, Flora, who continue to live in Charlottetown, and the other . . ."

William Frederick came through the door. "Sorry I'm late." He kissed his mother on the forehead and nodded a "hello" to his father. "Who is it that still lives in town?"

"We were talking about Mary's family in Charlottetown."

"I do hope they are more civil than the one next door." William picked up the *Gazette* but, changing his mind, tossed it aside. "I met our dear neighbour, Robert Cameron, on the trail today and he didn't so much as . . ."

Violet, indicating the newspaper, interjected, "There's an article about . . ."

"Tut, tut, my dear. We didn't call the boys in to speak about the Camerons. We have more important fish to fry."

Without another glance at the paper, William sat down. "What is it, Father?"

"It is time to discuss succession."

William hardly breathed; he was aware that decisions would have to be made and papers drawn up so there would be no family bickering when his father passed on but he could hardly believe that the discussion would begin when he was the only son present. "Shouldn't we wait until sometime when my brothers are here?"

The mother looked as though she might have been ready to agree but the father waved aside the thought as he announced, "James—the eldest—will inherit Seven Oaks. He is on the Grand Tour and I will advise him of my decision when he returns."

William swallowed hard; *there isn't much left if my numb-skull brother inherits the land.* He tried not to let his sense of foreboding show, but his face betrayed him.

"That shouldn't come as a surprise, my son; the eldest always gets the land."

"Yes, of course, Father; James will inherit the land."

I won't be able to remain here. He looked out the window and pictured the only place for him if James owned all that beautiful green grass and red soil—over by the oak trees and six feet under. *Yes, I might as well be dead.* He glanced over at his mother. *Mother would miss me.* He looked back at his father who was meandering through a discourse that seemed to be touching on land values and money and then it was a history lesson again: the generations of Smallwoods who had followed the same rules so the land would remain intact. *Shit!* William continued on with his own thoughts.

I'd like to build my own ships and sail the world's seas. Now what's he saying?

"David has already indicated that he would like to own and run a sawmill. I do believe that is an admirable ambition but . . ."

David would make a fine businessman. If David knew about turning trees into lumber we could build a fleet of ships! The Smallwood brothers would rule the world while James could rot here with his piles of manure as much as we could care.

"I said, if you have any special interests I would like to hear them now."

"No, Father." William looked down at his feet as he added, "I should have expected that James would inherit everything."

"That's not what I said!"

Bridling, William Frederick shouted back, "Then what!"

His face turning red with his effort to maintain his composure, John replied, stiffly, "I was acting on information from your mother that you and David wanted to build ships. I ascertained . . ."

"I want to build ships; David wants to be a sawmill owner."

"If you will permit me to continue, I ascertained from Elisha Coffin . . ."

"The Coffins who have the boatyard at Saint Peter's Harbour?"

The father glared with exasperation at his middle son. "William Frederick, it is most difficult to converse with you."

"I'm sorry, Father." William put on his most winning smile—the one that usually melted his mother's heart, but it had no discernible effect on the male parent. "I am truly sorry, Father."

"You should be. The Coffin family will rent some living quarters at the harbour for you and David and allow you to learn shipbuilding . . ."

"And David would see how their sawmill is run! Wonderful!" William clapped his hands and then turned suddenly serious. "Why would the Coffins want to do that for us?"

"Money . . . I am going to pay them well and make the promise that no Smallwood would set up shop in Queen's County after they teach you everything they know."

"Done!" William grabbed his father's hand. "That's the best thing you could have done for us, Father." He shook his father's hand while planting a wet kiss on his mother's forehead. "Absolutely the best thing you could have done for us," he repeated.

Endnotes

1. The *Royal Gazette* article about the death of Ewen Cameron was kind in its praise of this fine Island citizen. For storyline purposes, I have Ewen dying at a younger age than he did in real life and so he wouldn't have had time to accomplish as much in the story as he did in real life.

2. It's time to "get real" about some of our Camerons. As you already know, Ewen Cameron was a real person. So was Thomas Cameron, who is recorded as being a tailor in Charlottetown during the same period as Mary and Flora Cameron, who were known as sisters, lived in Charlottetown. I don't know if these Camerons were related or not but I put them all in the same family and made the two girls twins.

3. In real life, records show that Mary Cameron was the first wife of James Smallwood.

Chapter Twenty-Two
Gone Fishin'

September 1837
Josie Anne *offshore*
Cascumpec, PEI

"I seen you wearing a fancy suit at Havre Saint Pierre an' the next t'ing I knows you been jiggin' along wit' us . . . who be you?"

William Frederick realized that the fisherman he was helping tie a mackerel barrel to the starboard bulwark of the *Josie Anne* was the one who hadn't spoken a word to him during the whole week they had been fishing off Cascumpec. William had asked John Baker, the ship's master, for the man's name, expecting to find himself in the company of a grumpy Cameron but, no, the captain said the man was John Shasong. William wanted to shake hands with his companion but the other man had squatted to heft the barrel and then push it closer to the tie-down. William bent to the task.

When they were walking to the starboard side to secure the next barrel, William took the opportunity to introduce himself. "I'm Willie. I'm here because I want to have my own boatyard some day."

"Why you want go jiggin' mackerel?"

"If I build boats, I want to be able to sail them. I sign on for any ship whose home port during the season is Saint Peter's." He stuck his hand out. "You're John Shasong and I'm Willie Smallwood and this isn't the first time I've been jigging mackerel." William took a firm grasp of the other man's hand. "But it's the first time I have sailed on anything as small as a pinky." The man's handshake and smile were firm and genuine; William took a liking to him.

"Moi, Jean Chiasson, I fish . . ."

"There's no time for scuttlebutt! Move your ass!"

Jean gave a curt nod in the direction of the voice and grabbed some lashings.

William, on the other hand, gave a friendly wave to the captain as he began to help his crewmate tie down the next barrel. They worked along silently, while William considered Jean's question: why was he, the son of a proprietor, out on the North Shore fishery working with a ten-man crew on a poky old fishing boat?

I won't be building any pinkies, he thought. *Josie Anne, old and cramped as she is, really suffers in rough seas. Being only 45 tons with a pointed stern, she has a tendency to bob and pitch. Her open deck gives little protection.* He took a moment to study the layout of the rigging for the jib, foresail, and mainsail. *Doesn't call for much of a crew. Most of the ten-man crew are here to handle the fish, not the boat.* He stood up to stretch his back muscles; *the helmsman wouldn't have much to hang on to.* He mentally shuddered when he pictured the sailor standing on the exposed deck, clutching a tiller instead of a wheel. *The boat would be heaving and the tiller would want to move with her. All the helmsman would have is the strength of his legs to hold her on course.* He stopped and examined the layout of the tiller to see if there was some sort of lashing points that a desperate sailor might use to hold the tiller steady. *No . . .*

Jean gave him a nudge. "He watches us," he whispered.

William nodded to show he understood. He looked around. There were no more barrels to secure. He pulled out his fish knife and joined the rest of the crew at the gutting table where the mackerel were split, gibbed, scraped, and washed. He didn't turn to look—he wanted to keep his eye on the blade of his knife—but he knew that, behind him, the mackerel were being salted and stowed. "Looks like there's forty barrels, Jean."

"Oui, we finish, we go home."

Again William nodded. His arms were sore from the hours of jigging, his back ached from moving the storage barrels, and his hands would soon be raw from gutting. Yes, he would be glad to head for home. He lifted his head—just a little—so he could catch the movement of the rat's tail hanging from the fore-stay. "There's a fair wind. The run for home won't take long."

Jean grunted.

By mid-afternoon, the wind had died. *Josie Anne* found herself alongside several other ships becalmed some three miles off-shore. They took to mackerel fishing.

In normal circumstances the ship would heave to and the crew would gather on the windward side to fish. Of course, on this day there was no windward side. The men were spreading themselves out on either side of the ship, but the captain soon corrected that.

"Let's not be lubber-like about this. Bait man midships like always. Port side for the jiggers. Hop to it, now."

Jean and William rolled an empty barrel to where they would be fishing and set it upright behind them. While the bait man spread ground bait on the water to attract the fish, William selected four lines. On each line was a single hook embedded in an oblong piece of lead called the jig. He forced a piece of tough pork rind onto each hook. Placing two of the lines to one side as replacements, he waited for the call to begin jigging.

Jean ran his fingers along each of his four lines. He grimaced as he found one of the lines damaged by its many encounters with tough mackerel teeth. He tossed it aside and chose another.

Seeing that, William checked his own lines but found no damage. For the first time that day he scanned the horizon. It was a beautiful day. The air was warm and still. Strangely, the setting sun seemed to fill the eastern sky with vivid golds and browns. The glassy surface of the water caught and held the colours and mixed them with the reds and blues of the western sky, making the dirty grey sails and black hulls of the other mackerel boats look terribly out of place. He sensed movement all along the deck. The fish were here!

Lines were over the side and the men began the little movements that would make the jigs look as if they were fish trying to escape mackerel jaws.

"Ten feet!" was the cry from the fishermen at the bow.

Jean was already hauling in his first catch. "More like eight feet, Willie." Jean snapped the first fish into the barrel, the fish's delicate jaw tearing apart and releasing the jig. He was pulling up the second line as he tossed the first jig back overboard.

William found he was breathing hard with the excitement of the catch. There was a rhythm to it all: the set of the jig in the fish's mouth, the quick ascent to prevent the fish from having any chance to spit out the hook but not so quickly as to tear the hook through the jaw before the fish was over the barrel, the snap to pull the hook free, and the rapid descent to where the fish were schooling, while the arm with the other jig was doing a similar dance all its very own. Someone rolled a second barrel behind them, then a third. It was getting dark.

"Wind's up!"

The sails that had hung slack all afternoon were now fluttering in a light breeze from the southeast.

Jean pointed at the southern skyline. At first William couldn't see what his friend was looking at. In the gathering dusk it was difficult to make out the hundreds of seabirds wheeling about the sky as they flew inland. When he did spot the fleeing birds, he didn't have time to consider the true meaning of their behaviour because the captain was giving orders.

"Back the jib! Set the mains'l! Helmsman, when she has way, steer east nor'-east! It's time to go home, boys!"

Before the crew could finish stowing the two dozen additional barrels of mackerel, the wind swung to the east. A heavy swell was rolling in from the Gulf and could be heard crashing onto the north shore not two miles to starboard. William cleared some of the spray from his eyes and stared off into the darkness, praying that he wouldn't be able to see the breakers, yet wishing that he could see them because they sounded much closer than they probably were. William gauged that the *Josie Anne* was sailing as close to the wind as she could. He shouted for Jean to hear. "She can't sail any higher. We are going to have to come about or run ashore."

Jean shook his head to indicate either that he hadn't heard in the rising wind, or he hadn't understood.

William leaned back into the wind as he walked to the stern, clutching the lifeline that had been strung along the deck. When he reached the three figures huddled around the binnacle, he saw that the compass was reading south of east. On this heading and with the wind now coming out of the northeast, they would not be able to make Saint Peter's Harbour. As he watched, the lighted faceplate of the compass box was blurred by some driving rain.

"Double reef the foresail!" The captain had decided that he couldn't continue to sail into the teeth of this gale. He would have to take up an easier heading or put the ship in the position of lying to.

Monstrous waves crashed across the deck, tearing loose several of the mackerel barrels which then slid across the deck until they struck the opposite bulwark. The barrels, heavy with salted fish, shattered, spreading debris everywhere. One of the sailors, who was reducing the size of the foresail by reefing it in, lost his footing in the mess and was only saved from going overboard by the safety line.

William worked his way forward to help with the foresail. It took a great deal of effort, but the amount of canvas was finally reduced. Before the crew could release the strain on the jib, it was torn away. Then the mainsail split and was torn to tatters. Suddenly, there was no choice; crippled enough that she could make no headway against the storm, *Josie Anne* hove to. Bow-first into the seas, she would try to hold her position using her double-reefed foresail and some skilful manipulation of the tiller until daylight revealed some harbour entrance or island where she could find shelter. Perhaps the storm would abate or the wind would veer enough to spare her from being driven onto the north shore, but only time would tell.

William and Jean were huddled in the lee of the bulwark where there was some shelter. Through eyes squinting against the rain and salt spray, William observed his friend; he could see that Jean's lips were moving. *He is probably praying to his saviour,* William thought. He considered making a prayer or two of his own but found he couldn't concentrate. Someone —or something—was trying to give him a message. He listened.

The rest of the mackerel barrels tore loose and hurtled over the side into the dark of the night, taking two sailors with them. For a moment William believed he could hear one of them crying to his mother for help. *When it's my turn, who will I ask for help?* He bowed his head to begin some sort of prayer but there was still that nagging feeling that he was missing something. He lifted his head and opened his mind to what was going on around him. He heard first the shouts of the crew as they fought to keep *Josie Anne*'s bow into the waves; he was concentrating on understanding their individual words when he became aware of a deeper, more commanding sound. Somewhere in the darkness astern, the breakers were calling to the *Josie Anne*, warning her of the fatal consequences of any mistakes. Then he became aware of the noise that the wind tearing through the ship's rigging was making; it did sound like *Josie Anne* was wailing and bemoaning the fate that awaited her on that hostile shore. William cocked his head. *What else was she telling him?* With his hands, he felt the planking of the wet deck beneath him. He could feel the shifting of the ship's timbers as she was first thrown one way and then wrenched back in a way that nothing built by man should be able to withstand. That was it! The ship was giving him a warning of . . . of what? William, with his shipbuilding mind, was hearing the sounds of a ship in mortal agony; *Josie Anne* was telling him that she was failing. She had reached out to the only man on board who could understand her. If Jean had opened his eyes, he would have seen that William's lips were moving, too; William was speaking to Josie Anne.

"Your timbers are shifting, letting the sea in, but you can handle that for a while." William took his weight off his backside so that he could disregard the sounds and tremblings of the hull. "If your foresail and mast were going to go, they would have gone before now." Squatting in the lee of the bulwark, eyes closed, he carefully listened to what else he could hear. "The foresail and the tiller are holding us into the seas . . ." He listened. There was a creaking sound. It was a sound he hadn't paid any attention to before because of all that was going on around him. "The tiller! If you lose the tiller we'll fall off and . . ."

William jumped up and made his way to the tiller. In the darkness of that terrible storm, he ran his fingers along the tiller until he found the source of the creaking. The long arm of the tiller was flexing at the top of the rudderpost. He leaned over Captain Baker and cupped his hands so he could shout into the captain's ear. Baker shook him off; he was far to busy working his ship to listen to a landsman.

William shouted, "I'll find something to support the tiller!" He searched along the deck and found some lashings and several staves from the mackerel barrels. He was on his way back to the tiller when it snapped off at the rudderhead. *Josie Anne*, now helpless, slewed and fell off into the next trough. The seas swept across her deck, each one forcing the hapless vessel deeper into the next trough.

The captain knelt to pray, as did the helmsman and two other crewmen. They recognized the end was near and they knew the proper way to meet their Maker was on their knees.

William grabbed the long arm of the tiller before it washed away. He tied a quick round-turn and two half-hitches on one end and slid the lashing to the centre of the pole. On his first attempt to tie it to the rudderhead, he was knocked over by a passing wave. The tillerpole was washed out of his hands but, fortunately, it became mired in the ranks of the praying men. Captain Baker's reflex action to prevent anything from being lost overboard caused him to grab the pole. He was the first to realize the possibilities . . . He helped jam the pole against the rudderhead using the barrel staves and the lashings. With effort—two men pushing on one side, two men pushing on the other—pressure was again brought against the rudder and the ship's bow slowly pointed back into the waves. For the moment, they were saved, but it was to be the beginning of an uneven battle.

Steering the ship's bow into the heavy seas coming out of the northwest left the hull of the ship exposed to the onslaught of the northeast winds. The bow would fall away from the proper heading and a heavy sea would sweep across the little boat, forcing her lower in the water. The four men would push and pull on the bar to steer the ship back into the waves, and the wind would again begin its attack on the exposed hull. Eventually the bow would be forced to one side or the other, allowing the monstrous seas to submerge the little craft. It was a titanic battle and there was no doubt in William's mind about the eventual outcome.

After several hours, the men were tiring and the jury-rigged tiller was suffering slippage. There was nothing else to do but take the pressure off the rudder. *Josie Anne* was brought around to run with the wind. They were now headed southwest.

The crew of the *Josie Anne* knew it would be a race. Would daylight come in time for the little ship to see the shoreline? Or would she come upon the unseen shore in the darkness, taking all aboard to their deaths?

After a while, the crew found that running with the wind was almost peaceful in comparison with the hours of lying to where, despite their best efforts, heavy seas continued to tumble across the open decks. The ship's timbers were still working and grinding but the rigging was singing a muted song and the enormous waves—instead of beating against the bow— were catching up with little *Josie Anne*, lifting her twenty feet and then letting her fall into the trough—each succeeding trough feeling deeper and wider than the previous wave—but it was all so . . . lady-like, so graceful. The crew began to believe they might survive.

At the crest of one of the waves, Captain Baker was the first to see the white line of breakers in the morning twilight. "Dear Jesus! Those breakers are mast-high! Oh my God! Help us."

William could see that the breakers stretched in an unbroken line—east and west—as far as he could see. As the light quickly improved, he was able to see further but the line was still unbroken. *We're going to die*, he thought. It was, indeed, time to pray. He joined the circle of kneeling crewmen around the binnacle. Someone began to recite The Lord's Prayer. Over the heads of the other men, William could see the spume from the breakers towering over them. *It won't be long now.* The prayer finished, William had a moment to ask forgiveness for his unchristian acts against his brother James. "I truly regret all the times that I . . ."

The ship was taken violently to starboard. Within seconds, the rudder tore loose from the makeshift tiller . . . which hastened William's confessions.

"Please look after little David. I shouldn't have a favourite brother but I just don't like James. It wasn't David's fault that I love him so." He opened his eyes a trifle to see the helmsman still standing, staring at the thrashing rudderpost. William stuck out his hand, which the helmsman quickly took as he too knelt to meet his Maker. William felt for the hand of the man next to him. When he made contact, he opened his eyes; it was Jean. In spite of it all, he smiled at his friend. In this his last look at the world, William could see they were being drenched in the spray and froth of the breakers. *At least we will be clean when we appear at the pearly gates.*

The ship was wrenched around, bucking and rolling in the choppy waters . . .

Choppy waters? William stood, dragging his two companions to their feet. They could see that the storm was behind them on the other side of two islands! They were saved!

"Get a hold of that rudderpost!" Captain Baker kicked one of the men still kneeling. "Move your ass, sailor. The good Lord has other plans for you, it seems."

"The rudder post is gone!"

"Get that sail down!"

"Aye sir!"

"Drop anchor."

"We don't got no anchor!"

"Stern anchor is still here, sir."

"Drop it right some quick, I say!"

Captain Robert Baker recognized where they were. *Malpeque Bay.* He studied the two islands. "That's probably

Hog Island over there and . . . that would be Fish Island. I didn't know there was enough water to pass between them."[1]

Jean Chiasson was standing nearest the captain and he had a simple answer. "God lift us over rocks."

"Maybe so."

William thought for a moment and then added, "There was enough water under *Josie Anne* because she rode a wave over the bar between those islands."

Jean had the last word. "Hand of God on tiller."

William Frederick took the several steps to the starboard bulwark. He stared back out at the Gulf where the huge waves were pounding against the little islands, totally obscuring them.

Jean Chiasson was saying a brief prayer of thanks for sending this man named Willie to be there when he was needed. Jean could see that William's lips were moving. He had never seen a man praying with his eyes open. Obviously, the man wasn't Catholic, he thought.

William wasn't praying; he was making some promises to himself. "I will never again go to sea on someone else's ship. I will build my own. I shall be captain of my own fate." He realized that Jean was staring at him, but he didn't feel the least bit self-conscious about someone witnessing his talking to himself.

"David will cut the timber; I will bring home our fortunes." He slapped the side of his leg and did a jig. "Yes!" he shouted as he raised his eyes to the heavens.

Endnotes

1. This miraculous escape is based on a portion of an historical article written by Edward MacDonald titled *The Yankee Gale* for the Fall/Winter edition (1995) of *The Island Magazine*.

Chapter Twenty-Three
A New Life

Spring 1847
Seven Oaks

James Smallwood didn't mind the hypocrisy. If polite Charlottetown society expected a memorial service at the end of the official period of mourning, who was he to deny them the charade? The black crepe, the posturing, the laments of the unfortunate death . . . it was nothing to James Smallwood. Members of his social group wanted it, they expected it, so he gave it to them, but that didn't make the time-consuming trip to Charlottetown any more palatable. Nevertheless, it was over now and he was back home. He slipped off his brown travel coat and passed it to his man. "Thank you, Jefferies."

Jefferies wrinkled his nose at the accumulated dust on the shoulders. "The weather has been remarkably dry for this time of the year." He took a whisk to the coat's shoulders and instantly regretted his lack of foresight; he would have to tidy up after dressing the master for dinner. To make matters worse, the cloud of dust made him sneeze just as the master asked him a question. "Beg pardon, sir?"

His voice showing his exasperation, James repeated his question. "Are there any cards?"

"No sir. There was one . . . gentleman . . . who came unannounced. I had him go around to the side door when he couldn't produce cards."

Now there was a trace of concern in James's voice. "Was that wise?"

Jefferies hesitated for the smallest moment before saying, "He was dressed like a . . . Acadian, sir."

"I understand, Jefferies." James snapped his fingers for Jefferies to return with his selection from the wardrobe.

Jefferies knew what was appropriate but with this master, he was never quite sure. "Late afternoon at home or would

317

you prefer to dress for dinner?"

"Let's not put on airs at Seven Oaks, Jefferies. I will sit for a while on the front veranda. The smoking jacket would do nicely, thank you."

Jefferies felt that things hadn't been the same since the mistress had died over a year ago from a growth in her female parts—all that bloating and distension—and the old master had succumbed to a choking spell within weeks. *At least the old man was neater about his departure.* "Very good, sir."

"I prefer my soft leather Italian shoes."

"Of course, sir."

James waited for Jefferies to help him into his jacket and shoes and then the master selected a pipe and descended the stairs to the front door. He felt in the pocket of his jacket for his pouch and matches and was on the verge of summoning Jefferies when he patted the other side and found that he was properly equipped. He stepped outside and selected the nearest chair. It was a lovely day. He expected an hour of repose and then he would be ready for the evening meal.

Through the pleasant haze of his pipe smoke, he saw movement at the bottom of the property. *Damn! Someone is coming up the walk to the house. What person with any sense of propriety would walk to an afternoon visit?* He found a pair of spectacles in his jacket's breast pocket and peered through them at the approaching figure. When he discerned who it was, he quietly complained, "Where do they all come from?" He pretended not to watch the fellow until he was standing at the foot of the veranda, cap in hand. *They always come cap in hand.*

The Acadian waited to be noticed.

At least this one knows his place. Looking over the rims of his spectacles James intoned, "Well, my dear fellow, what can I do for you?"

"May I please speak with Mister Smallwood?"

Impressed with the correctness of the Acadian's English, James was suddenly more convivial. "Please, come up out of the sun. Take a chair." As the Acadian passed by to take the second chair, James was able to see how threadbare the man's dark suit was. *Well, I'm in for the penny, at least.* "I am Mister Smallwood. Why have you sought me out?" Noting the dust on the man's clothing James added, "Did you come far?"

"I work for Mister Wright down near Seven Mile Bay. I came a few days ago and your gentleman told me when to return."

"You speak excellent English."

"That is my work for Mister Wright. I speak English and then I speak French for they to understand."

"You are an interpreter."

"No, I am Jean Chiasson and I seek Mister Willie Smallwood."

James blinked at the Acadian's misunderstanding but continued without making any reference to it. "William Frederick is one of my brothers. They no longer live here." James corrected himself almost immediately. "My brothers, William and David, have taken their share of a considerable estate and gone out into the world." James could see that this was beyond the Frenchman's grasp of English. "Willie is gone. Not here. No come back."

The visitor nodded his head to show he had understood and made a motion as if to rise. This time it was curiosity that prompted James to place a restraining hand on Chiasson's arm to invite him to stay. "Please, I would ask how you met my brother, Willie." He smiled at the use of the name Willie.

"We sailed on same ship out of Havre Saint Pierre."

"Saint Peter's Harbour," James corrected.

"Yes."

"Tell me what you wanted to tell Willie." James was thinking that this would make an interesting story next time he was at the club . . . as long as William's actions hadn't brought disrespect to the Smallwood name.

"When Mister Wright arrives from Boston . . ."

Absentee proprietor, James thought.

" . . . he go over the books with the overseer. They both sit before the tenants and collect rents. Each tenant has his

turn to pay rent or explain to Mister Wright what he will do
to get the money to pay his rent."

"Your Mister Wright has Acadian tenants?"

"He has Scottish but . . . yes . . . Acadians, also."

James had heard stories about the yearly rent judgements
made by some proprietors. As related at the men's club, those
stories had seemed unbelievable. Perhaps now was a good time
to get some first-hand information. "Tell me why you have
come here."

"This year not good for tenants. I was there when the
McBrides came—tenant and wife—and they said they had no
money but their crops were good. Would Mister Wright wait
until the crop was taken? Mister Wright told them to borrow
the money on the crop and pay him. He gave them to
Saturday. It was not my business; the McBrides speak
English."

"My business start with the next family. The Acadians said
they didn't have the rent. Mister Wright asked if they have
crops, oxen, or the like to pay down their debt. They had
not'ing. Tenant ask me to explain to Mister Wright . . . he had
paid rent every year for forty-six years. He gave me the receipts
to show to the proprietor but Mister Wright would not look
at them. Then the overseer warned the tenant that he would
put the law on him . . . and he did. The tenant is in the
Charlottetown jail. He asked me to find a certain relative who
spoke English and could read and write to speak on his
behalf."

"We're not related to any Acadians!"

Jean Chiasson was startled by the forcefulness of the
Smallwood denial. He considered the situation for a moment
and thought about withdrawing before he got into trouble
with this proprietor, but he had promised to do the best he
could for the Gallant family. "Oh, no sir. Tenant told me his
relative live near here. On my way to Havre . . . I mean Saint
Peter Harbour. I t'ink to ask Willie . . . Mister Smallwood . . .
the other Mister Smallwood . . . if he knew them."

"What is the name?"

"Tenant name is Gallant. Their relatives have name LeBlanc. LeBlanc live here since before proprietor agent come."

James Smallwood stood up. "I'm sorry that I can't help you with this. We have owned this land for many, many years. There are no LaBlanks here and there never were any Acadians here." When he saw the doubt in Chiasson's eyes, James repeated his position. "There are no LaBlanks near here. Believe me; I would have known it." He ushered the visitor to the edge of the veranda and was relieved when Jean Chiasson stepped down onto the walkway, but James wanted a little more detail for his men's club tale so he asked, "Why did Mister Wright put the tenant in jail?"

"Monsieur Gallant burned all his buildings rather than see the proprietor have them for a debt of less than three pounds."

"Shameful!"

"Oui, monsieur. Shameful!"

Chapter Twenty-Four
Tenant League

Resolution passed by the Tenant League in 1865
Whereas no government of this Colony has yet done anything calculated to relieve the tenantry from the leasehold system under which we are groaning and whereas the Tenant League seems to have the good of the Colony at heart, therefore be it resolved, first that something must be done to extirpate from our land the leasehold system, and secondly that the present league of tenants is the only scheme adopted likely to relieve us from proprietary tyranny, we will join the League and from henceforth pay no rent or arrears to rent until the present agitated land question be settled on just and equitable terms.[1]

17 April 1865
Southport
Prince Edward Island

High Sheriff John Morris, Esq., sat tall on his horse as he waved a copy of the Governor's Proclamation that called out the yeomanry of the county to proceed to Vernon River to capture the body of Samuel Fletcher of Alberry Plains. "You men are ordered to . . ."

Deputy Sheriff James Curtis urged his horse forward to join Sheriff Morris; he leaned across so that he could be heard above the din of two hundred men gathered to enforce the proclamation. "They can't hear you, John. I suggest you . . ."

A pistol shot brought instant quiet but it spooked the deputy sheriff's horse, which danced away. There was good-natured laughter as Deputy Sheriff Curtis attempted to regain control of the animal because most of the assembled force—legally described by the proclamation as a *posse commitatus*—was made up of proprietors and their friends and agents. They all knew Curtis for the good horseman that he was and it was amusing to see him lose control at least this once in his lifetime.

High Sheriff Morris cast a scathing look at James Smallwood, who was coolly recharging his weapon. "I want none of that, gentlemen. The indiscriminate discharge of firearms will not be tolerated." He stood in his stirrups as he ordered, "I will give the order when to fire and what to fire at. Is that clear?"

An unseen wiseacre shouted, "Oh, get on with it, John. Ol' James there was just tryin' to get everyone's attention for yuh."

"He sure enough got the attention of the deputy's horse," another voice cackled.

Morris couldn't see who was speaking from the back of the posse but he recognized it as good advice. As soon as the laughter had died away, he began giving his instructions.

"On Saint Patrick's Day, a mob of the Tenant Leaguers marched on the Colonial Building. It was probably their intent to disrupt the parliamentary session."

"And cause troubles for us when we next collect our rents," the same voice from the back shouted.

John Morris pressed on. "Deputy Sheriff Curtis recognized one of the league members as Samuel Fletcher who, by his continued refusal to pay rent to his proprietor, was wanted by the law. Our deputy sheriff attempted to arrest the culprit but was driven off."

John Morris had to wait until the catcalls and insults against Samuel Fletcher faded.

"Well, that won't happen again! We won't let that happen again, will we!"

The posse gave three rousing cheers for the sheriff.

"I will be in command of the cavalry. Our deputy sheriff will lead the infantry who are waiting for us on the high ground over in the orchard." Firming up his voice in a fairly good imitation of a drill sergeant, High Sheriff Morris ordered, "Take command of the infantry, Deputy Sheriff

Curtis." He waited until Curtis had moved off toward the orchard and then took a deep breath. He screwed up his eyes and tentatively commanded, "Form up in threes."

"Where, John? Where do you want us to form up in threes?" It was that same voice.

John Morris wished he could see who it was. Hurriedly he looked around, searching for something to "form up" on. "Form up on James." He sighed with relief when he saw Smallwood turn his horse and hold up his two arms—parallel and pointing back down the road the way they had come. "Facing me, gentlemen," Smallwood called out.

"In threes, gentlemen," Sheriff Morris ordered in a loud voice.

There was a great deal of backing and forthing—of splattering mud and horse droppings—of cursing and challenges—it was all still going on when Deputy Sheriff Curtis called from the orchard that his infantry was ready to march.

"Stay there until . . ." Sheriff Morris reconsidered and decided that his order wasn't military enough. He started again. "Hold fast! Hold fast there until . . . the cavalry moves to the front . . . er, until the cavalry moves to the fore!"

"Well, we're ready to go now, John," was the reply. The infantry began cheering and John could see figures leaving the orchard and slogging up the muddy road. *The proper place for the cavalry must be in front,* he thought. He spurred his horse and, raising his arm, made a dramatic gesture to advance, which the horse must have taken very seriously. John Morris raced down the road at the gallop, barely managing to hold onto his hat.

The mounted men followed—also at the gallop—splattering mud over the footmen at the side of the road.

The infantry was left to plod along in the badly muddied tracks of the cavalry.

After about an hour of marching, someone in the infantry ranks suggested they halt for a drink. Haversacks were opened, flasks were shared and, when the march continued, the infantry had assumed a far more casual military formation. The sun came out, seeming to have encouraged the birds to sing and, not to be outdone, the soldiers relied on their alcoholic stimulation to sing all of the verses of *The Bonnie Flag*. After the last faltering notes of that old song had died, a rest period, when it occurred, wasn't ordered; it just happened. The old-timers in this sort of military business warned the young volunteers not to loosen their boots; a good number of them did and were soon left behind by the main body as the march was resumed. Then Deputy Sheriff Curtis gave the order for a pee parade, when he saw how many men were breaking ranks, which caused a further delay. Once more on the march, it was evident that what had begun as a lark on a fresh spring morn had become a trek under a hot midday sun. The sheriff's men were visibly drooping. "Let's put on the feed bag, men," he ordered. The pause for dinner was to become the most serious threat to the completion of the military operation.

The men dropped their packs and hunkered down anywhere they could find a dry spot. Something to drink, some food, and a bit of rest improved the morale of the troops but, as Deputy Sheriff Curtis rode around the edges of the mass of sweating human beings that were his to command, he could see that his men were spreading out—seeking the shade of the trees—supping the water from the brook—climbing the hill in search of the faint breeze—hiking down the muddy road to the aid of the stragglers. The deputy sheriff's admonition to the men, "Don't wander off!," had no visible effect. His military organization was fading before his eyes.

Sheriff Morris was having problems of his own.

The cavalry had moved swiftly along the Georgetown Road and were within striking distance of the Fletcher home and Morris didn't know how he could stop the mad onrush of his excited troopers. It was one thing to lead a posse cross-country. It was something else entirely to lead them against a fortified position, but that's what confronted them. On the brow of the hill, a short distance from the Vernon River near Weatherbie's forge, there was a fort. The cavalry halted of its own accord when they came within sight of the cannon.

"Where the hell would that son-of-a-bitch Fletcher get cannons?" He turned his horse and led his troop out of range of the deadly-looking weapons.

He waved at James Smallwood to approach. "We need someone to go find the infantry, James."

"That's fine. I'll go."

"No, you stay. Send someone else."

"As you say, Sheriff." James selected two men he knew from the men's club and gave them their instructions. "Find the infantry and bring them up."

The younger of the two asked in a breathless voice. "Can't you send someone else? I'd like to stay here where the action is."

"I do believe that Sheriff Morris is going to assault that fort and would appreciate infantry support."

The elder man used his horse to shoulder his son's horse aside. "Do as you are told, son." He gave James a snappy salute. "We'll go find the sheriff's infantry."

James, half-embarrassed, returned the salute and rejoined Sheriff Morris. "They'll find the infantry for us."

"Take a couple of men and ride forward to get a better idea of what we're facing."

"Go up there?"

"Yes. With a couple of men. See what's there."

"Ride up to the cannons?"

"They won't waste powder and shot on a couple of riders."

Now it was James who had the problem. A number of his Charlottetown cronies were within earshot. If James refused to ride into danger, they would be the first to hear of it and James would never hear the end of it. James spurred his horse. "I'll go alone."

James Smallwood galloped toward the barricades. He could see the Tenant Leaguers behind the guns, bent over as if sighting along the long cannon barrels. *Gad! There are four cannons!* He reined in when he heard hoofbeats behind him. A proprietor—the one who had been riding alongside during the advance down the Georgetown Road—had come up to join him.

"You like living dangerously, eh?" James asked.

"Thought I would take a look. I wanted to see what we were up against before the fighting starts."

"That makes sense. What's your name?"

"Robert."

Several more proprietors joined him.

It was Robert who pointed out what should have been obvious from the beginning; none of the leaguers behind the cannons was moving.

James pulled out his pistol. "Let's go closer!"

A white flag popped up behind one of the cannon. A young lad stepped out and kept waving the flag. "We give up," he said in a piping soprano voice.

It was then the proprietors saw that the desperate Tenant Leaguers manning the cannon were hats stuck on poles to resemble men. Each cannon that seemed ready to rake the advancing government men with grapeshot was actually a stove pipe stuck through a board. James rode through the barricade; there was no one else there, just the boy. He waved the column of cavalry to advance.

Red-faced, High Sheriff Morris rode through the barricade with hardly a glance at James, the fortifications, the one-boy garrison, or the gun emplacements. He stopped long enough to question the solitary prisoner as to the location of the Fletcher home and then rode on in that direction with one hundred of his men. On their approach to the Fletcher farm, they could see the culprit was waiting for them, sitting in a comfortable chair at the front gate. With loud huzzahs, the men surrounded the farm. Morris, with a personal guard of a dozen riders, dismounted at the gate and took possession of the body of Samuel Fletcher.

Standing on a farm cart at Burke's Mill, Deputy Sheriff Curtis looked out over the mass of men who were loosely spread across the road and into the field. His men were tired—expended—and they had nothing to show for it but sore feet, dirty clothes, and empty haversacks. There were rumblings of revolt and complaints against certain colonial officers who didn't know whether their assholes were punched, reamed, or bored.

Curtis raised his arms to quell their disquiet. "We don't have much further to go. I want you to think of what we have at stake here. The leaguers are not paying their rent and that is more than just a threat to our society, that is a . . ."

"Look! Here comes the cavalry!"

A smile crossed the deputy sheriff's face as he saw the riders approach; they were all as muddy as his men were. His smile widened when he saw that the cavalry had a prisoner. "They musta got him!" he shouted. He squinted as he tried to make out the features of the man seated in front of one of the riders.

"They got somebody!" one of the foot soldiers bellowed.

"I'd knowed him anywhere!" another confirmed. "That's Sam Fletcher, all right. That's his coat and hat!"

"Three cheers for our gallant comrades! Hip, hip, hooray!"

There wasn't a second cheer. The cavalry hadn't captured the body of Samuel Fletcher. High Sheriff John Morris, Esq., had arrested a straw dummy dressed in Fletcher's clothes.

In disbelief, someone shouted, "Sucked in!" which was followed by a moment of nervous laughter. The crowd turned sullen and watched as the rider who was carrying Fletcher's "body" dismounted and cast the dummy into Millview Creek.

The two sheriffs rode off in the direction of Charlottetown without a word.

If there was an order for disbandment, nobody heard it.

"Is that bloody all?"

"Just ride off?"

There was some hesitation and then, by threes and fives, the posse began to fade away.

James wandered over to the side of the stream and watched Fletcher's "body" sail serenely down to the sea. Several of the proprietors joined him. They sat there in silence watching the figure vanish into Island folklore.

The man known to James as Robert spoke first. "Why did the sheriff pick up the damn thing and bring it with him?"

After a moment, James made a guess at the answer. "Maybe the sheriff knew that Fletcher and his boys would be watching and laughing at him."

"Yeah, I suppose. At least, this way, Fletcher lost his favourite jacket and hat."

James turned to face Robert. "Thanks for being there with me. They looked like real guns." He stuck out his hand, saying by way of introduction, "My name is James Smallwood. We worked well together . . ." James might have said more, but Robert jerked his horse's head around and rode off.[2]

"What the hell!" He watched the stiff-backed rider until he was out of sight. "What the hell," James repeated. "Anybody know him?"

"Robert Cameron. He's a proprietor from up near Saint Peter's Harbour. I thought you knew him by the way you two hung together today, especially when he joined you at the barricade."

"Well, you won't see anything like that again," James said. Then, to himself, "I can't imagine another circumstance where a Cameron would let a Smallwood get that close. Nope! Not ever again in a hundred years."

* * *

Endnotes

1. I found the Tenant League Resolution quoted in an article written by Peter McGuigan for *The Island Magazine*'s Fall/Winter edition (1992) titled "Tenants and Troopers."

2. The confrontations between the Tenant Leaguers and Island officials are the stuff that folklore is made of. There are several articles on the period and I have not strayed from the facts as reported. I have no evidence that Camerons or Smallwoods were present at one or any of the conflicts.

THE PASSAGE OF TIME
BROUGHT CHANGES TO THE
PROPRIETOR/TENANT SITUATION

The Samuel Fletcher Affair was the first of a series of confrontations between representatives of the proprietors (government officials) and members of the Tenant League during the summer and into the fall of 1865.

There was the Archibald MacDonald Barn Affair, where, in late May, 1865, Archibald MacDonald had his barns burned on Lot 36 when he successfully served writs against some Leaguers.

The barn-burning was followed in July by the James Proctor and Charles Dickieson Affair where fighting occurred and blood was drawn. Deputy Sheriff Curtis carried writs against the goods of James Proctor and against the body of Charles Dickieson. Dickieson was eventually hauled off to the Charlottetown jail. During the ensuing riot, twenty-five special constables armed with clubs and pistols barely stopped the irate mob of Leaguers from releasing the prisoner.

After the riot at Charlottetown (and there were other disorders), the Executive Council requested British regulars from Halifax to restore order. Eventually, the regulars were sent out into the countryside to support the constables in the serving of writs. The Tenant League's resistance collapsed and, by January 1866, the tenant ringleaders, Peter Gallant, Charles Dickieson, and Joseph Doucette, were found guilty of common assault and imprisoned. However, There was so much popular support for the League that the government of the day was probably brought down because of its handling of the proprietor/tenant problem. Then the proprietors began selling off their excess lands and, soon, the large-scale dispersal of estates began in earnest.

Shortly after The Island joined Canada's Confederation in 1873, $800,000 was made available to buy out the last of the proprietors. Following the passage of compulsory land purchase legislation, the proprietor/tenant land system finally disappeared.

THE CAMERON/SMALLWOOD SITUATION CHANGED VERY LITTLE WITH **THE PASSAGE OF TIME**

Mary Cameron had been the last of her clan to publicly cross the Cameron/Smallwood property line. Her marriage to James was attended solely by Smallwood friends and relatives. Her death during childbirth gave rise to the first occasion where both clans were present at any sort of function at the same time—albeit on separate sides of the grave—where some polite words of commiseration were exchanged. It held promise that perhaps the rift between the two families might heal; perhaps the list of grievances between the families would be allowed to fade along with the now-forgotten proprietor/tenant quarrel. There was scant possibility of that happening when Mary Cameron's twin sister, Flora, crossed the line and became the second Mrs. John Smallwood.[1]

John Smallwood and Flora (Cameron) Smallwood enjoyed a nice-sized family: Susan, Mary Ellen, Charles, and Young James. Young James married Charlotte Holman. James Smallwood and Charlotte (Holman) Smallwood had at least one son, John Holman Smallwood.

Cuddy and Rose (Nelson) Cameron had given issue to Ewen, Robbie, Thomas, Allan, Mary, Flora, and David. Robbie married Eleanor Watts. Robbie and Eleanor (Watts) Cameron had a number of children: Mary, Peter, Joan, and Robert Watts Cameron.

During the years up to the end of the century, a Smallwood and a Cameron met once to determine that a common fence would better separate the properties than two parallel and opposing fences. They found it necessary to leave the details up to lawyers.

Near the turn of the century, John Holman Smallwood and Robert Watts Cameron found themselves serving as privates in the same Charlottetown militia unit (but in different sections). They served—without incident—until Robert Cameron departed with the Royal Canadian Dragoons for South Africa.

THE PASSAGE OF TIME
HAD WROUGHT SERIOUS CHANGES IN SOUTH AFRICA

At the middle of the century, the British had challenged the Boers of South Africa (white people of European origins) when they established two Boer colonies in South Africa: Cape Colony and Natal. Resenting British interference in their lives, a number of Boers abandoned the British territories and made the "Great Trek" north and east into central Africa. After defeating the African tribes, the Boers created two republics: Orange Free State and Transvaal. With the discovery of gold and diamonds in Transvaal, British businessmen sought control of the mines and British politicians planned to acquire sovereignty over the new-found riches. All it needed was a little war to clear things up.

The war started in 1899 and the Boers were surprisingly effective in the defence of their new homeland. When the British Empire called upon her sons to defend imperial interests in South Africa, troops from British colonies responded to the call. By the time of this story, the war had finally turned in the British favour and Canadians were marching on the capital city of Transvaal, Pretoria.

Endnotes

1. It is a matter of record that Flora Cameron became the second wife of John Smallwood.

Chapter Twenty-Five
Robert Watts Cameron

Marching to Pretoria
21 April 1900
Near Boschmann's Kop
Orange Free State, Africa

The civilian got down from the cart and motioned to his companion with the camera to set up his tripod off to one side. "I want that big hill in the background," he said. Then he walked on to accost the soldiers who were watering their horses. *They should make excellent subjects for my piece,* he thought as he approached the horsemen. *Those cowboy hats are novel but the horses aren't much to look at—all skin and bones.* As he got closer he could see the khaki riding pants and tunics were torn and threadbare. *They are sorely in need of refitting . . . or resupplying . . . or whatever it is the army does when its soldiers' equipment is wearing out.* He examined the face of the nearest horseman. *He looks tired.*

"Hello, there!" He didn't wait for a response. "I'm John Timmins of the *Guardian*, Timmy for short. I'm here to get some stories about our Canadian boys in battle. I'll trade yuh a couple of snorts for a bit of talk." He held out a pewter flask, the top dangling from the end of a short chain.

Three of the troopers made no move to take the reporter up on his offer, but the one with the reddish hair and flashing eyes handed the reins of his horse to one of the others and then held out his hand for the flask. "I wouldn't mind a libation . . ."—he grinned—"or two."

Timmins waited until the trooper stopped for a breath. "What's your name, how old are you, and where are you from?" Timmy turned the pages of his notebook until he found some space. He licked the end of his pencil, prepared to take notes.

"Robert Cameron, twenty-two, from Charlottetown.

"When did you enlist?"[1]

"I enlisted after my Pa said I could. I come from a military family. There was a Robert Cameron at Louisbourg and another at Quebec. Then my granddad was a volunteer in the Queen's County Regiment; he looked right some smart in his uniform. And me? I was a member of the Charlottetown Engineer Company. Soldierin' is in our blood and when the Brits needed good horsemen to catch the Boers . . ."—Cameron turned to include his friends—"they got us, eh boys?"

The three other troopers introduced themselves to the reporter: Joseph Brown, Ernest Cox, and Andy Boudreau. Andy had to spell his last name a couple of times for the reporter to get it right.[2]

"So, you must have landed at Capetown in April."

"Yeah, we went off to Stellenbosch to get some more horses for the ones that died on the ship."

"The 'we' being?"

All four men responded with pride, "Troop number 4, B Squadron of the Royal Canadian Dragoons."

Mister Timmins flipped back a page. "Yes. I have a list of your movements up until yesterday." He ran his finger down the page as he read, "You were on a train as far as . . ."

"Cattle car."

" . . . as far as De Aar and then trekked to Norval's Point, where you entered the Orange Free State . . ."

"They blew up the regular bridge," Joey Brown interjected. "We crossed the river on a pontoon bridge, which frightened ol' Clemçon."

Sensing a story, Timmins was quick to pounce on the mention of a fifth trooper who was no longer present. "Clemson? What happened to . . ."

In a disgusted tone of voice, Boudreau explained that Clemçon was a horse. "He brought his own horse from The Island."

Timmins regarded this common-looking trooper in a different light. Only men of influence were able to bring their own horses to a theatre of war. "And then, Trooper Brown, what happened?"

"Clemçon balked and I had to blindfold him and lead him across."

"Er, yes." Timmins resorted to his notes. "After Springfontein there was Bloemfontein, where you encountered over a thousand Boers entrenched on a large kopje, giving them a commanding view of the whole valley." He looked up from his notes. "Were you involved in the fighting?"

"No. We were on the wings . . . both days. It took the Brits and some of our boys two days to force them Boers to withdraw." Ernie Cox had spoken for the first time. "Then we went down to see what was goin' on in the house flyin' the white flag."

"There was a farmer in that house who said he was neutral."

"Some neutral!"

"Yeah, we took him out of there and set fire to the place . . ."

"Blam! It was an ammunition storage dump."

"Blew all to hell!"

"Clemçon got concussion!"

Boudreau gave Brown a punch on the arm. "You and your goddamn horse! You get to hold the horses while we go forward to make the attack!" Boudreau looked embarrassed to open up in front of a stranger but he finished it off anyway. "We had a shooting competition to see who holds the horses while the other three goes forward . . . .. He wanted to be with his precious horse so he made himself the worst shot."

"Oh shit, guys!" Cameron didn't like the look on the reporter's face. "Joey is the best horse handler, so shut up!" He pointed at the note pad. "Make some more notes. We returned to Bloemfontein, confiscatin' Boer livestock, burnin' and lootin' . . . I say, burning Boer farms on the way."

Ernie Cox waved his hands as if brushing cobwebs. "That's it, boys. Thank the man for the drink, Rob. Let's mount up!"

Timmins raised both arms to stop the horsemen. "Wait! I don't have your picture yet." It looked as though they might dismount but Boudreau reined his horse around.

"That's the recall." He spurred his horse and off he went.

"Where are you going?"

"We're going to Pretoria. Gonna chase those Dutchmen right up this valley until we take their capital city." Joey Brown gave the reporter a casual salute. "And the war will be over." He gently turned Clemçon's head. "You can take our picture in Pretoria."

"No, I meant, where are you going now?"

"Up the valley. The Boers retreat and then they dig in behind the next hill and river. The dragoons ride ahead and find them. The infantry and artillery come up and the Boers retreat." He spurred his horse. "See you in Pretoria."

23 April 1900

"I bet they're dug in on that hill."

B Squadron, Royal Canadian Dragoons, was drawn up in close-order troop formation just out of range of any enemy guns that might be hidden on top of Boschmann's Kop. They watched as a message was delivered to their headquarters group. Shortly after, approximately eighty men—the two troops led by Lieutenant Young and Lieutenant Van Straubenzee— began their advance.

The two remaining troops watched as the battle developed. They knew that it was the dragoons' job to ride forward and draw the enemy's fire, so they watched as their comrades moved from column into extended order and cautiously continued their approach to the hill.

Ernie Cox repeated himself, saying it louder to be heard over the thundering hooves of the advancing dragoons. "I bet they're dug in on that hill."

"Maybe not. Our boys are well within range of their Mausers now."

"Yeah. Should have seen some action by now . . . if the bastards are there."

Still the dragoons rode on.

Joey Brown looked up from watching the military splendour of two troops of mounted rifles trotting in extended order across the waving sea of brown grass. He raised a hand

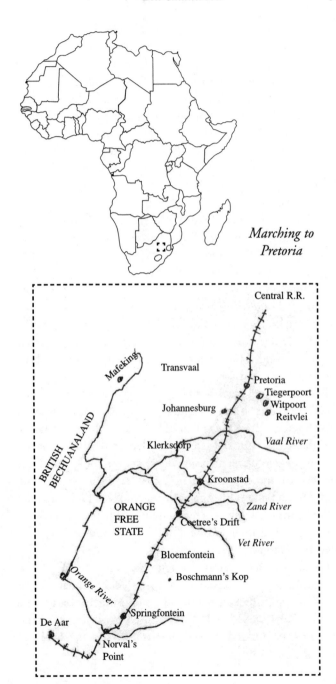

Marching to Pretoria

to shield his eyes from the harsh sun as he measured the height of the sun against each horizon. He didn't have time to say that he thought it was noon before the hills on either side of Boschman's Kop erupted in rifle fire. Two Canadian horsemen went down in that first fusillade. Then the biggest hill, Boschman's Kop, was shrouded in smoke from the British artillery as it added to the rain of lead. In the crossfire, two more riders fell. Another Canadian slouched in the saddle but managed to continue at the gallop to a ridge at the base of Boschman's Kop, where there was shelter behind big flat stones several feet high.

Cameron shouted, "We're ordered up!" He also said, "This is what we came for!" but his voice was lost in the crack of the British artillery and the staccato of the machine guns firing on the newly discovered Boer positions.

Troops 3 and 4, followed closely by the Canadian Mounted Rifles, trotted onto the plain in column of route. At the gallop, they changed to line of squadron and charged into the battle. Once at the ridge, Private Brown gathered the reins of the other three horses and led them back the way they had come, and the dismounted riflemen sought shelter behind the rocks.

Before taking up his firing position, Andy Boudreau glanced back at their horse handler, who was scampering back across the plain chased by a hail of bullets. He lifted his heavy Lee Enfield rifle and sighted on the top of the hill. "Maybe this is the best job after all." Of course no one could hear him, so he didn't mind admitting it. He estimated the range to the top of the hill and set his sight. All ready for his first battle, he searched for an enemy. There wasn't much to see. The Boers were dug in and their Mausers didn't give much smoke. He waited for a target.

Looking at his nearest comrade he shouted, "What are you waiting for, Cameron?" Andy smiled to himself. The group's self-proclaimed warrior had been lusting for battle ever since . . . He watched as Cameron lifted his head above the rock and then flipped back as if pushed by some invisible force.

Andy and Ernie, careful not to raise any part of their bodies above the shelter of the rocks, crawled to Cameron's side. With the noise all around them, they thought he was crying but . . .

"Sons of bitches almost got me! Lookit the hole in my tunic." That he was laughing was more evident now that they were huddled closer together to examine the tiny hole in the uniform.

"Tore my bandolier right off." He raised himself to a crouch to retrieve his equipment but his comrades pulled him down.

"Leave it until we're finished." They picked up their rifles and joined the battle.

The Canadians fought from the shelter of the ridge for two hours.

The British brought up reinforcements and extended the firing line.

The Boers, fearing encirclement, withdrew along the valley toward Pretoria.

It was becoming routine. The Boers would select a defensive position, taking good advantage of the terrain to hide their men. The Canadian horsemen would then press forward, forcing the Boers to reveal themselves as they subjected the horsemen to intense gunfire. The British artillery and infantry would come into play and the Boers would execute an orderly withdrawal to the next defensive position.

5 May 1900

Lieutenant Borden signalled for his men to gather 'round. "We have our orders. The Boers are probably in those bushes on the other side of the river. Other troops will continue up this side of the river to seize the crossing at the little village of Pretoius. As part of the same operation, B Squadron will force a crossing here . . ."[3]

"What's this place called, Lieutenant?"

It's always Cameron who asks the questions, Boudreau thought. *He's a real suck-up.*

"This is the Vet River. The crossing we are going to force is Coetzee's Drift." Lieutenant Borden paused and then continued. "As I said, B Squadron will force a crossing here; the Mounted Rifles will act as support. Hopefully, we will find the Boers somewhere in the middle between Pretoius and here. Maybe, this time, we can force them to stand and fight."

The men of Borden's troop cheered. At almost the same moment, they could hear the cheers of Lieutenant Turner's troop.

"Lieutenant Turner's boys seem just as ripe for a good fight as you are. Good thing, too! They will be on point with us during the initial probe." Borden gave his men a wide smile. "See to your gear. Assembly in fifteen minutes."

Cameron was talkative as he saddled his horse. "This will be the real thing. We'll gallop to the edge of the river, send some scouts across, the Boers will retreat and . . ."

"Goddammit, Cameron!" Annoyed, Joey Brown pulled so hard on Clemçon's cinch strap that the beast sighed and farted at the same time. Joey's concern for his horse made him forget what he was going to say, but Ernie was quick to pick up on the observation.

"Let someone else ask the questions. Don't be such a prick! Do more fightin' and less shootin' from the lip."

"I didn't . . ."

Now it was Boudreau's turn. "That's right. That time you lost your bandolier, you didn't fire a shot." He looked Cameron right in the eye. "You got down behind those rocks and played with the hole in your tunic." Boudreau saw the flash of anger in Cameron's eyes so he continued. "Don't bother to get mad at me. Show some balls when we go into action, instead."

"Mount up!"

"Form column."

"For-ward!"

Colonel Lessard led his squadron toward the river. He

gave the order to dismount when they were in sight of the water. Leaving the horses with their handlers, the rest of B Squadron advanced in extended order. Within five hundred yards of the bank, the dragoons lay down. Scouts cautiously crept forward but were soon peppered with bullets from the opposite shore.

"They better get out of there!" Cameron shouted. He must have raised his head and attracted the attention of some Boer sharpshooters because several bullets struck near him.

Boudreau cursed the day he had ever met anyone called Robert Cameron as the Boers, having lost sight of the Canadian scouts scuttling back to the main body, poured a dozen rounds into the area where they had last seen a Canadian. Andy Boudreau continued to curse even after the recall was sounded and they had crawled out of range of the Boers' deadly Mausers.

"Calling for volunteers!"

The men of Troop number 4 recognized the voice of their Lieutenant Borden.

Boudreau pushed Cameron's shoulder. "Here's your chance, soldier boy." Boudreau raise his arm. "Here, sir! Private Boudreau."

"Thanks, guys, but I have enough. Thank you."

B Squadron advanced in skirmish order along a dry ravine as far as the low bushes lining the river. Turner's volunteers pushed through the bushes and entered the water, holding the rifles over their heads. The water was soon up to their chins but all of the troopers reached the other side. Meanwhile, Borden's volunteers crossed the river further downstream. Both Canadian groups came under heavy fire from Boers hiding in a stone kraal. The Canadians, severely outnumbered, were forced to withdraw.

Borden and Turner called for fresh volunteers. Cameron, Boudreau, Cox, and others followed the lieutenants even further downstream. Borden signalled his men to take cover. "We'll wait until the squadron gives us supporting fire on the kraal. The colonel means to keep the buggers busy until we get across."

Heavy rifle fire erupted upstream.

"Let's go, boys."

The men stepped into the water, holding their rifles over their heads. Halfway across, with the water only knee-deep and getting shallower again, Borden ordered the nearest trooper, "Run like hell back to the colonel, Cameron. Tell him there's a ford here. It's narrow, but it's only knee-deep. Tell him we will give supporting fire as he brings the squadron across."

When B Squadron had gained the Boer side of the Vet River, the entire brigade soon followed and the Boers withdrew.

That night, at the campfire, there was talk of medals.

As Cameron was removing several eggs from the pocket of his tunic he said, "Turner is getting one."

Boudreau held out his hand. "Gimme the eggs. Turner don't need one. Let the officers get their own."

Cox was quick to comment. "Yeah, they get good rations and better billets."

"And medals. They get the medals."

Cameron watched as Boudreau placed the eggs on the ground and got out his mess tins. "I didn't mean Turner got one of our eggs! I meant Turner is gettin' a medal."

"What about _our_ boy?"

"Borden will get mentioned in despatches."

"What does that mean?"

"The Queen gets to read his name in a letter."

"That's better than a medal."

Boudreau cracked an egg on the side of the tin. "Not as good as an egg." He looked up. "What did you get from the mess tent?"

"Hardtack and some biscuits. No water."

"Bloody Brit supply system will end up killing us all."

"Did ya get some water from the river?"

"I didn't go. The boys say the river is runnin' blood."

Boudreau had cracked the last of the eggs. "Anyone got some pepper in their kit?" When he saw Cox nod in the affirmative, he went on. "Need some water. Someone get some water from the river."

"What about the blood?"

Brown ferreted a piece of biscuit out of his tunic. "Won't matter much . . ."—he held up the biscuit—"when you consider we eat this stuff." He sang a popular tune but changed the words slightly. "Have you ever seen a biscuit walking? Well, I did."

The men guffawed.

Brown stood. "I'll get the water. They say we'll be taken out of the line for a rest. We're gonna spend a few days at Kroonstad."

"Maybe the Brits will give us better supplies at Kroonstad."

"Yeah. Maybe they'll have some sugar and coffee this time."

"I betcha the officers get coffee."

Boudreau gave the eggs a turn. "We need that water, Joey."

As Joey Brown was leaving with a canvas water bucket in his hands he said, "If there's sugar and coffee and we don't get some, we'll send Cameron out."

The men grinned. In the traditions of practical soldiering, Cameron was the best scrounger in the squadron. Even Boudreau admitted that when they were taken out of the line, Cameron would "find" all kinds of things that would improve their existence. They were looking forward to Kroonstad.

Their time at Kroonstad was a disaster.

The first days of rest were truly appreciated. Of course, every day had its routine of patrol and outpost duty but there was plenty of time for the dragoons to wash their gear, forage for their horses, and rest. The boys would cover off Cameron's duties to allow him to disappear into the countryside for hours at a time because he always returned with trophies such as honey, butter, chickens, and containers of lamp oil for the fires. Even Boudreau stopped complaining about Cameron's soldiering abilities. Boudreau was so quiet that the boys didn't realize he was ill until he put himself on sick parade.

Dysentery was the camp doctor's diagnosis—probably caused by the drinking water or the camp's poor drainage, he said.

On the day B Squadron rode off to Pretoria, seventy-eight troopers were on the sick list and had to be left behind. Four consecutive spaces on the sick list read: Boudreau, Brown, Cameron, and Cox.

4 June 1900

Andy Boudreau was the first back up on his feet, attributing his early recovery to the fact that he was of strong Acadian stock. Ernie had recovered enough to argue that there weren't any Island Acadians named Boudreau, which Andy vehemently denied. When Cameron, raising his head slightly from the pillow, claimed to have Acadian ancestry, even Brown joined in on the laughter. "Imagine! A Cameron being Acadian!" he said.

Boudreau put an end to the argument by saying, "You said a Cameron served at Louisbourg. What regiment?"

"Well, I don't know."

The boys were quiet for a while until an excited orderly stuck his head in the tent.

"B Squadron rescued the Mounted Rifles at the Klip River." When the four patients didn't respond enthusiastically enough, the orderly came into the tent. "The Mounted Rifles were cut off for two days. Our boys went in and covered their retreat, but the way is now open to Pretoria."

"The war will be over."

"We can go home."

The dragoons and the Mounted Rifles were on the dusty Rustenburg/Pretoria road, the dragoons still acting as rear guard, when the British took formal possession of Pretoria, 5th June 1900.

Their horses spent, the Canadian horsemen were not able to enter the city until the next day.

But the war didn't end with the capture of Pretoria.

16 July 1900
Witpoort

Lieutenant Borden handed his reins to Boudreau. "Wait here. I must report to the colonel before we rejoin the troop."

Borden entered the bell tent that was being used as a headquarters for B Squadron and saluted. "Lieutenant Borden reporting, sir, with four troopers now fit for duty."

"Good to see you, my boy." Colonel Lessard took a closer look at one of his most effective lieutenants. "Are you sure you are well enough to resume duties?"

"Yes, sir. Doc signed me out." Borden changed the subject, quickly. "I understand the Boers attacked the ridge along Kafferspruit Pass."

Lieutenant Colonel Lessard waved the young lieutenant over to join him at the planning table. "This morning they struck on a line from Tiegerpoort, Hekpoort, and here at Witpoort." He jabbed his finger at the chart. "They drove in our pickets and B Squadron was forced to withdraw. That left the defence of Witpoort Pass to three companies of the Royal Irish Fusiliers on either side of the pass. The New Zealand Mounted Rifles, who were in support of the Irish, were overrun and surrendered."

"Leaving the Irish on their own?"

"I have sent A Squadron to the New Zealand position in support, but I must put more men into the Irish position."

"You mean to add more men to the Irish position? Wouldn't it be better if we could extend the firing line?"

Both officers studied the map.

Lessard stated the obvious. "There is another ridge line but it has a steep cliff."

"But the cliff is out of sight for the Boers." Now, somewhat excitedly, Borden drew a finger along the top of the ridge. "If we could get to the top, it would be a short run across the flat to the edge of the ridge facing the Boers."

"You would be in full view during that run."

"Yes, but just a few of our squadron rifles on the edge of

that ridge would force the Boers to withdraw."

"And if they were forced to withdraw from Witpoort . . ."

"They would have to retreat."

Lessard clapped Borden on the back. "The Irish will laud your name forever if you can pull it off."

"I won't be pulling it off, sir. My men will do it."

Boudreau was griping. "We left our horses five miles back and we been walking for hours and—"

Joey, usually the quiet one, interrupted. "We've been marching for less than half an hour."

"Seems longer."

"I don't like being this far away from Clemçon."

"You and that damn horse." The going was rough underfoot but Boudreau took a moment to look up. For the first time he saw the cliff. "That's too big to go around."

"We're goin' to climb over it."

"How do you know that?"

"Heard Borden talking to that new lieutenant . . . Burch is his name. Tol' Burch we were climbing up to the top and catch the Boers by surprise."

Boudreau stumbled but Joey caught him before he fell. "I tell you what will be the big surprise," Boudreau said with a smile of thanks to his comrade. "The big surprise will be if I can lift this damn old rifle after I climb to the top."

The men stopped at the base of the cliff and lengthened their rifle straps so they could sling them over their shoulders.

Cameron jumped up to a ledge that ran along the base of the cliff. He extended his hand. "Grab hold, you old horse lover." He boosted Joey up. Joey then continued climbing hand over hand up the rubble.

"You next, old man."

Boudreau grimaced at Cameron, who was the youngest of the quartet by several months, but he put a good face on the situation. "Thank you, my son."

Ernie jumped up to the ledge without assistance.

Cameron was about to follow his comrades up the slope

when the voice below asked, "Would you give me a hand up, Cameron?"

He doesn't look good. He should still be on the sick list. Cameron gave his lieutenant a boost and then let the officer go ahead. Every now and then during that long climb to the top, Cameron would give an assist from below, or Ernie would haul from the top. They were all breathing hard when they took shelter behind the small ridge of rocks at the summit.

"What's it look like, Cameron?" Lieutenant Borden was sitting with his back to the rocks, breathing hard. "How far is it to any shelter on the flat?"

Cameron stuck his head over the rocks. Rock splinters and dust sprayed in his face as a Boer sharpshooter sought him out. Cameron ducked back down, wiping his forehead as an expression of relief. "Whew! That was close." He looked at his bloody hand. Tugging at Joey's arm, he asked, "Am I hurt bad?"

"Naw. Just a scratch. Probably from a rock chip."

Borden's voice was tired but still carried its old authority. "Cameron! How far is it across that flat to some shelter?"

"I didn't have time to see, Lieutenant."

Lieutenant Borden pushed himself upright and peeked over the rock. His head snapped back and he threw his arms wide as if he were meaning to fly. Joey caught the body before it fell over the cliff. "My Christ! We lost our officer!"

The new lieutenant, Lieutenant Burch, probably heard the note of panic in Joey's voice. He drew his pistol and shouted in a commanding manner, "Let's go, boys!"[4]

Boudreau, Brown, Cameron, and Cox ran forward with the officer. Lieutenant Burch was hit almost immediately but he continued running. He must have been wounded a second time because he fell, hard, about halfway across the flat. Private Joseph Brown died a few paces further on. Cameron stopped to help his comrade but Boudreau, a slower runner, caught him up and dragged him to the shelter of the rocks on the rim of the ridge. More dragoons were joining them. Boudreau unslung his weapon and began to harass the Boers with accurate rifle fire.

"Dammit, Cameron! Unsling your gun. Shoot some of the bastards!"

"I can't, Andy."

Angry, Boudreau reached over and jerked Cameron's hand away from his chest. It was then he saw the tiny hole in the tunic, just above the breast pocket. "Oh, shit! Robbie, you've been hit!"

"I know, Andy. I know."

Andy pulled Cameron's rifle sling away from the wound. "Them Mausers make small holes, Robbie. You'll be all right."

"Yeah, Andy." He took a short breath and gasped, "See you in hell, Andy."

* * *

Near a farm at Rietvlei, the Royal Irish Fusiliers were the honour guard for the Canadian dead. Flags were at half mast. As the sun set, torches were lit as the men of the Royal Canadian Dragoons honoured their own. A private of Troop #4, B Squadron, Royal Canadian Dragoons, was selected to place flowers on the graves. Private Ernest Cox's cheeks glistened in the soft light of the torches but, otherwise, he properly performed his duty to the dead. The senior officers spoke of the British victory bought with the lives of these soldiers of the empire. The Colonel of the Irish Fusiliers expressed his deep gratitude to the Dragoons for so fearlessly coming to the succour of the beleaguered Irish detachment at a most crucial moment and saving their lives. Taps was sounded and there was a moment of silence. The soldiers marched away. The torches burned the night through and, in the morning, the war continued.

15 November 1900

Corporal Ernest Cox sat on the edge of the hospital bed. He patted the lump under the bedsheet that he presumed was the patient's foot. "You didn't miss much. We've been the fist inside the British Empire iron glove. The Brits have been using the dragoons to force the Boers to their knees." He patted the foot again. "No, you didn't want to be there."

Robbie Cameron's voice was husky as he asked, "The Boers started it, didn't they? They didn't fight fair."

"After takin' Pretoria, we annexed Transvaal and the Orange Free State. The Boers had no cities, no farms; they were forced to live off the land. The Brits saw this and began a scorched-earth policy. We started fighting dirty and they fought worse." Ernie shifted his weight carefully on the bed. "How are you, Robbie?"

"Like Andy said, the Mauser makes a small hole. I got caught high in the chest and the bullet went straight through." He pretended to pound his chest like a gorilla. I'll be as fit as a fiddle. They tell me I can go home with the rest of you next month." Suddenly very serious, Robbie asked, "What happened to Clemson with Joey gone?"

"We went back to the horse picket and we saw that Clemson was lying down. He tried to get up when we approached but . . ."

"He saw Joey wasn't there." When Ernie didn't respond, Robbie continued with the thought. "Horses are smart that way."

"I sat down and held his head; I talked to him just as if I was Joey. He didn't see the revolver." Ernie sighed. "Andy is a sure shot."

"How's Andy?"

"Fine. He has dysentery again. He'll survive."

Real concern clouded Robbie's face. "Tell him not to eat off the tin plates."

Bert shrugged. "Why not? I've been at the hospital. The plates looked clean."

"The orderlies are Brit soldiers. If it shines, it's clean."

"That's right. I could see my face in . . ."

"You don't understand. In the Brit army, it's spit and polish—if it needs cleanin', it gets spit and polish."

The colour drained out of Joey's face. "Andy had left some duff on his plate; I ate it."[5]

"Sorry to bring it up. Tell Andy about it, will you?"

They sat there for a while. Robbie asked about letters from home, the weather, when would they get their pay . . . When he asked about the scorched-earth policy, Ernie went into detail.

"We were on a farm-burning detail at the beginning of November."

"How does it work?"

"We surround the farm or the village. Under cover of the artillery, we order the people out. We tell them to take what food and clothing they want and then we go in."

"We still do some looting?"

For a moment, Ernie was back reliving the experience. "What we want, we eat or take. What we don't want, we destroy." He leaned forward. "You know, it's not hard to burn a house. Take some bedding and hang it over a table and throw a brand under it. Whuff! It's gone!" He was pensive for a moment. "There was this one house . . ." He stopped.

"Well, tell me."

"The woman didn't come out. I helped lift her up but she was stiff as board and it was some hard to move her around." He flexed his hands as if he were still feeling the softness of the woman's body. "She suddenly put her feet down and we let her go. She ran to her piano and asked, "You vill not burn my haouse?"

"I said, Lady, you have to get out of here."

"Burn my haouse?"

"I nodded my head and said that we were going to burn her house."

"Take my piano out, please," she pleaded.

"We took her piano out and moved it far enough away from the house. She didn't go back in for anything else." He shook his head at the memory. "The house was burning. We were pushing the women and children up the trail—they have to go into a concentration camp, you know—and we heard this beautiful music. One of the infantry officers was sitting at the piano, his hat on the lid, playing a waltz or somethin' like that. When he was finished, he ordered some of his men to smash the keyboard with the butts of their rifles. Then they pushed it over." He sighed. "The woman didn't look back."

"I have no sympathy for the Boers. They should have stopped fighting when we captured Pretoria."

"Another time, we were up near Lillefontein on an expedition to destroy the homes of farmers suspected of blowing up our trains and bridges. The Boers were waiting for us. They retreated until we were facing carefully prepared positions on the rocky ridge leading into Lillefontein, about four hours south of here. We made the attack but . . ." Joey stopped to think about what he was going to say.

"But what, Joe?"

"We were going to withdraw—you know—leapfrog with the infantry providing support for the artillery while we kept the Boers busy."

"No machine guns?"

"Oh yes. We had machine guns with us."

"Then, I know the drill. What happened?"

"The Boers kept on pushing. Some of our dragoons were overrun and taken prisoner. They fought until they ran out of ammunition and they were taken. The Brit infantry broke and ran . . ."

"No!"

"We were in a pickle. The horses hauling the artillery began to tire, the Boers were upon them . . . it looked like we were about to lose everything, but Lieutenant Turner had a plan. He took a dozen of his men and hid in the grass between the Boers and the guns. When the attack came, the Boers didn't see Turner's men in the grass and rode right into the ambush."

"Having you tell a story is like pulling hen's teeth! What happened?"

"Two of the Boer commanders were killed. The fight went out of them and we saved our guns." Joey leaned back, almost crushing Robbie's foot. Robbie yelped and moved his foot but

Joey didn't seem to notice. "It was a great day to be a Canadian Dragoon."

Full of awe and respect, Robbie said, "It was a great day to be a Canadian."

"Yes, indeed, it was."[6]

The Royal Canadian Dragoons returned to Canada in December 1900. Robert Cameron and Ernest Cox—proud as punch to have served their empire—were welcomed back as heroes.[7]

Endnotes

1. The National Archives has the records of the enlistment for Robert Watts Cameron for military service in South Africa. Robert Cameron, 22 years old, 5 ft. 9 3/4 in. tall, with brown eyes and dark hair, enlisted March 9, 1900. His birthplace is shown as Charlottetown Royalty, next of kin is "father," he is unmarried and a present member of the Canadian Militia (Charlottetown Engineering Company) at the time of enlistment. The period of service was expected to be one year but Cameron signed the usual document that stated: "I swear that I will well and truly serve our Sovereign Lady the Queen in the Canadian Volunteers for Active service, until lawfully discharged . . . ."

2. The Boer's defensive tactics were causing large losses to the forces of the British Empire. The British Press, long used to virtually bloodless victories over African tribes, were shocked. They dubbed the British defeats in late December of 1899 as Black Week. Black Week spurred recruitment throughout the Empire. Fifteen young men from Charlottetown responded to the call to arms. I used the family names of Cox, Boudreau, and Brown—as representative of the population of The Island at the time—to serve with Cameron.

3. I invented nothing about the Boer war. I followed the campaign records as closely as I could while maintaining the novel's flow.

4. The war diary of the Royal Canadian Dragoons has both Lieutenant Borden and Lieutenant Burch dying as they peeked over the edge of the rocks. I needed someone to lead the Canadians on and let Burch live a few minutes longer.

5. The words "duff" and "tuck" were army talk for military issue food.

6. There is a wonderful book about the Boer War that was produced by the Canadian War Museum: *Painting The Map Red: Canada and the South African War 1899–1902* by Carman Miller. It contains the type of detail I needed for this section of *The Islanders*.

7. Records show that Robert Cameron was discharged from the Royal Canadian Dragoons on 25 December 1900.

Chapter Twenty-Six
Robert Watts Cameron
Charles Gallant
Joseph Holman Smallwood

23 March 1902
Klerksdorp
Transvaal

"I don't get it. We're gonna herd the Boers, men women and children, eastward to a barbed-wire fence?"

Private Robert Cameron removed his hat as he sat down on the campaign stool. "Never mind that."[1]

If there was one thing that could be said about Charles Gallant, he was persistent. "No, I want to know what we are doing. Are we treating women and children like cattle?"[2]

"We'll be making an arc ninety miles wide and sweep across Boer territory, but I don't want to talk about that."

Gallant tried once more. "You were here before with the dragoons. Is that the way the war was fought? Against children?"

"Patterson isn't coming back. He's dead."

Gallant's face registered his shock. "He had the shits! How can he be dead?"

"He's dead and we are getting a replacement."

"First Willie and now Don." He looked up as he realized what Cameron had said. "We gettin' just the one replacement?"

"He'll join us before assembly."

"Do you know who it is?"

"Nope! Get your gear ready. Remember, half rations and 180 rounds of ammunition. Put the rest of your stuff in the tent on either of the empty cots."

While Gallant put his greatcoat, feed bag, and blankets in the tent, a trooper dressed in the uniform of the 2nd Canadian Mounted Rifles walked toward Robbie, leading a horse.

By way of welcome, Robbie said, "Put your extra gear in the tent. Take the cot that is free." It was hard to see in the evening twilight but Robbie felt a long-forgotten sense of antagonism as he checked the replacement's face. *I know him from the Charlottetown Engineers. He is . . .*

Gallant came out of the tent just in time to help their new comrade put his extra gear away. "My name is Charles Gallant . . ." he began.

Robert Cameron grunted. "He's a Smallwood."[3]

Surprised, the newcomer responded, "Yes, John Smallwood from . . ."

"Seven Oaks. After today, you'd better take yourself off to another group. I don't want you here." Robbie swung his saddle up onto the horse. "I'm senior and . . ."

"What the hell! Who the hell do you think you are?"

Cameron pointed to his campaign ribbon identifying him as soldier who had been awarded the Queen's Medal for service in Transvaal, Orange Free State and Cape Colony. "I'm senior to you and that's all that matters." He didn't bother to look up. He tugged on the saddle blanket and then began working with the straps. "You'd better get ready. Assembly is at dusk. We have to ride to Witpoort about forty-five miles from here. Then we spread out to extend our lines and drive the Boers and their livestock east to the Brit blockhouse at Schoonspruit. The men will be taken prisoner there. The women and children will be shipped to a camp." Cameron didn't expect any comment from the newcomer and he got none.

The bugler gave first call for assembly.

The members of the 2nd Canadian Mounted Rifles readied their mounts. Cameron peered through the gathering darkness at the faces of his two men. "This is our outfit's first operation," he said. "Let's make it a good one." When the bugle sounded again, they mounted and joined their troop leader.

At assembly the troops were told that there would be no noise, smoking or lights once the 2nd Canadian Mounted Rifles moved out of Klerksdorp. Success of the mission depended on mobility and surprise. Through the night, the

2nd would move west at a fast trot. Since the ground would be rough in places, the major expected there would be some injured horses or riders. They were to be left behind. The major was emphatic about it. "Make no effort to help injured horses or pick up fallen riders. At first light, we must be ready to begin the sweep. All of the units will begin at the same time."[4]

They rode through the night. When the 2nd arrived at the rendezvous, Charles Gallant was missing. Neither Cameron nor Smallwood had seen him fall behind.

"Do you think he will be all right?" John Smallwood was adjusting his harness by feel in the darkness. He couldn't see Cameron's face and had no idea what sort of reception he would get but he had to ask anyway. He asked again. "You've done this before with the dragoons; will Gallant be all right?"

"We never did this sort of thing. This is a new tactic."

"Do you think he'll be all right?"

"Out here, what happens, happens."

In the hour or so until daylight, Smallwood didn't ask any more questions.

When it was daylight, the British forces could see Boer wagons and cattle about a mile from the British lines. The men of the 2nd watched as Lieutenant Callaghan's scouts were sent out to investigate. The scouts found a Boer advance party approaching and laid a trap for them. When the three-man party was within rifle range, Callaghan called upon them to surrender and, when they showed no signs of surrendering, fired on them. Riding forward to make sure the three men were dead, the scouts sighted an even larger enemy force. Callaghan was not able to call up reinforcements because the British line was moving off in the opposite direction. With a sour taste in his mouth, he and his scouts rejoined the British sweep.

The sweep had gone for about seven miles when the colonel called a halt. There were no Boers. Systematic searches of every gully, building, and bush yielded very little. The Boers had escaped.

On the way back to Klerksdorp, Cameron and Smallwood rode side by side in silence. Cameron was the first to see Gallant. "At least he's alive," he said.

Charles Gallant was squatting behind an ant nest, embarrassed that a thousand troopers were witness to his shame. The Boers had found him and stripped him of his weapons, horse, clothing, boots, and pride.

The men of the 2nd had nothing to cover him with. Normally there would be blankets or greatcoats but, on this expedition, there was nothing.

John gave him a boost up behind and they rode along in silence until they saw the solitary figure in the distance.

"That's my horse," Charles shouted.

The Boer had been leading the horse. When he saw the approaching troops, he sprang into the saddle and spurred the animal harshly but to no avail. He shrugged his shoulders and slid off the horse.

"He looks just like a Canadian!" someone said.

"Sure he does. He's wearing my uniform." Charles called across to Cameron, the old campaigner. "Why would he want my uniform? Does he want to spy on us? Pass himself off as a Canadian?"

"Naw. He needed some clothes. His were worn out."

Two scouts had dismounted and disarmed the Boer. They said something to him that he didn't seem to understand, but Cameron knew what was going on.

"He's wearing one of our uniforms so he gets shot."

Charles couldn't believe what he was hearing. "What! Right here? Right now?"

"No, probably tomorrow; we don't have a spade to dig the grave." Cameron gave his two comrades an ironic smile. "Remember? We are travelling light so we don't have anything like that." Cameron looked down at the young man who looked so Canadian. "He'll be shot tomorrow." He rode on.

The scouts yanked the Canadian uniform off the Boer and handed it up to Charles. They gave Charles back his rifle. Then Charles and John rode on. Charles looked back. Two scouts were taking the equipment off the horse.

Cameron said over his shoulder, "They'll shoot the horse."

One of the outriders from the headquarters group rode back past them holding a shovel on the pommel of his saddle. Cameron added, "Now they'll probably shoot him, too." There were two shots.

31 March 1902
Boschbult Farm
Klein Harts River

"We've just made another mistake."

Gallant and Smallwood knew that the first mistake had happened that morning. Callaghan's scouts had run across some Boer gun tracks leading away from the British column. They had followed them into an ambush: two Canadians dead, nine wounded, and fifteen horses lost. Only the arrival of the main column had prevented greater losses.

Cameron gazed out over the little valley as he explained the present situation to the rookie troopers. "We are in a little hollow with our backs against the river." He patted the stone of the farmhouse. "The only strong point is here where we've been assigned. If there are any Boers out there, they'll have cover in those trees until they hit the edge of the farm clearing"—he sucked his teeth—"and we haven't set the camp up properly." He shrugged his shoulders. "Maybe the colonel will get around to it when the last of the supply wagons gets here."

As the last of the wagons entered the camp, the Boers attacked.

"Someone's catching it on our right flank." Smallwood stood up on tiptoe trying to see what was going on.

"That trooper, there!" a loud voice commanded, "get down! Get down, I say."

Red-faced, Smallwood scrunched down as far as he could get behind the wall.

"Did you see anything? Gallant asked.

"Is he gone yet?"

Gallant knew who the "he" was. "Yeah, he's giving someone else shit. You can get up now."

In an undertone John said, more or less to himself, "That
sergeant is a bully."

"Stickin' your head up can get your face blown off; seen it
happen a couple of times." Cameron tapped Smallwood's
shoulder. "That shootin' is on our left flank—not our right—
remember in case you have to know sometime. It's like your
left hand and right hand. But when you talk about the enemy,
it's their left hand and right hand as they face you." He smiled
for the first time since Smallwood had joined them. "Not to
confuse you little puppies, I do believe that the Boer right
flank is attacking our rearguard."

"Will they attack us here?"

"You can count on it."

Boer activity suddenly increased. Men from other regi-
ments sought shelter within the walls of the farmyard and the
farmhouse. The shout went up when the infantry broke and
ran, leaving the rearguard's flanks exposed to the Boer horsemen. Lieutenant Carruthers dismounted his men and formed a
crescent to meet the onslaught. Led by their sergeant, ten horsemen from another troop also dismounted and joined the
rearguard in their fight. These Canadians knew it would be a
desperate battle and they knew what would be the probable outcome, but they joined the half-circle of men crouched in the
grass ready to receive the Boer horsemen, who would ride forward firing from the saddle and then retreat as the next wave of
horsemen took their place. One by one, the men of the rearguard were wounded, and wounded again and again until they
died or began to run out of ammunition. As each trooper emp-
tied his rifle and then his bandolier, he would remove the rifle
bolt and throw it into the long grass so the weapon would
be of no use to the Boers. Eventually, the rearguard was overrun.

The defenders of the farmyard were not yet aware of the fate
of the rearguard, but the numbers of Boers attacking their
position suddenly increased. The Boers were now attacking

from three sides under the umbrella of an artillery barrage provided by cannons captured from the British earlier in the campaign. It was devilishly hot work in the farmyard.

Cameron reached over to stop Gallant from firing. "Slow down, Charles. You'll melt your barrel."

"That's the third time that fellow with the long beard has come up to shoot at me and I haven't been able to bring him down. He rides up and stops and shoots and his bullet comes right through here . . ."—he made a whooshing motion past his left ear—"and here . . ."—he did the same thing with his other ear. "The bugger's gonna get me!"

Cameron rested his weapon on the top of the wall. "Show me which one."

They didn't have long to wait. A large fellow riding a buff-coloured horse presented himself at the firing line and raised his weapon . . ..

Cameron raised his and the Boer dropped his rifle and hauled his horse around.

"Shoot him now, Charles."

Cameron watched carefully while Gallant took his shot. The bullet hit the ground in front of the Boer, who rapidly withdrew from the fight.

"You're firing over fixed sights! Adjust your sight to two hundred yards."

"How do I do that?"

"Shit! I suppose no one showed you." Cameron adjusted the sight and handed it back to Gallant. He moved off to look at Smallwood's rifle. He adjusted the range on that weapon. No wonder the Boers seemed invincible! The rookies of the 2nd had not been given any instructions on how to use a rifle. As Cameron worked with the rifles, he came to realize that the gunfire had lessened, but he knew it had stopped when the foghorn voice of the sergeant got his attention.

"Now laddies, the thoughtful Boers have given us some time to do some trench work which you little buggers should have done this morning." He pointed a finger at Cameron. "You, Cameron, will take your section—"

"I don't have a section, Sergeant."

"I beg your pardon, Cameron! You interrupted *me*! That would be the last time we have that sort of thing, wouldn't it Cameron?"

"Yes Sergeant, it would."

"You now have a section, Cameron, because Corporal Tanner is wounded and has gone to the hospital. Now, be a good lad. Take your section and lay some trip lines, Cameron, so we don't have any nasties sneaking up on us during the night."

Cameron led the section out past the point the Boers used as a firing line. To be effective, the trip lines had to be further out into the scrub trees. He smiled as he watched Smallwood walk three or four paces and then turn and look back longingly at the comparative safety of the farmyard. He could almost hear Smallwood's sigh of relief when Cameron said it was far enough and they could get to work. Before Cameron's section had finished laying the trip lines, it rained. The section soldiered on with its work. When they had finished, they returned to the farmhouse where they hoped to find shelter.

"No room at the inn," complained Smallwood when they were ordered outside to spend the night in the freshly dug trenches.

Gallant was more plain-spoken. "This is the shits!"

Cameron thought he would have the last word when he intoned, "None of us wants the shits. Get the shits and you go to the hospital. Go to the hospital and . . ."

"We'd be out of this rain," Smallwood said quietly.

The men around him laughed.[5]

7 May 1902
Klerksdorp
Transvaal

"Let's hope this is the last sweep. Charles Gallant leaned forward and patted his horse's neck. "Easy girl, it won't be long now." He smiled up at Cameron. "She knows when it's time to go."

"How far do we go this time?" John Smallwood sounded tired. "This is my third horse and this one's a pig so I hope it isn't too far." He patted the horse's shoulder. "No offence, old boy, but . . ."

The horse farted. The three men laughed.

"We go from here to Vryburg." Robert Cameron shook his head. "Don't know how far it is." He regarded the sky. "Here comes the sun. We'll be leaving soon."

John, still with a tired voice, said, "They're dying by the thousands in the concentration camps . . . by the thousands. The kids die first. Then the old . . ."[6]

"It's not our fault. It's the water and the drainage. Just like some of our camps. Donnie Patterson went that way. Remember? Oh, I forgot, John. You didn't know Donnie. Well, he was at the hospital and they couldn't do anything for him." Charles saw that Robbie was going to speak up so he raised a hand to stop him. "And these people are a lot weaker than we are. We burned their homes and crops, killed their animals . . ."

Robbie interrupted and, speaking sarcastically, he said, ". . . herded them like animals . . ." He sighed. "I've heard all that stuff from you before . . . but we herded them so they couldn't support their soldier boyfriends. Those boyfriends killed friends of mine."

"The Boers started it all . . ." John was going to say something else but Robbie butted in again.

"The Boers should have quit when we beat their armies and occupied Pretoria. They should have quit then and none of this would have happened."

John was intent on making his point. "They started it all but we shouldn't have come in here to tell them what to do in their own country." He looked from one comrade to the other. "Imagine if the British came to Charlottetown and told us that we have to be nicer to . . ." he almost said the Acadians but remembered in time that the Home Parliament had done just that, so instead of Acadians, he said, " the Micmac."

"The Brits wouldn't do that."

"Why not, Charles?"

"We're part of the British Empire. That's why we're here."

"You think you're British? You're Acadian, aren't you?"

"No, I'm not British, and yes, I am Acadian."

"You love the British Empire?"[7]

"We have rights and the British Empire protects them." He anticipated Robbie's next argument so he rushed along. "If the Empire looks weak, someone like the Yankees might think they can come along and push the Brits out. The Americans don't go around granting rights to people like Acadians."

"I'm here because I couldn't find a job back on The Island," Robbie snorted, and made a dry, rasping sort of sound that might have passed for a laugh. "I was a hero for about three months but, after that, the medal didn't work any more. I faced a choice: I could go back to the farm or go work for somebody." Again he made that almost-like-a-laugh sound. "If I was going to work for somebody, I wanted to do it here. The money's better here."

The bugle sounded assembly.

"About time," Robbie said and led the group into action.

For the first time on one of these sweeps, the troopers could see the true extent of the expedition. Ten thousand mounted men of the British Empire spaced no more than thirty feet apart stretched from the Vaal River to Mafeking—driving every living thing before it—destroying everything as they moved along—leaving nothing usable. Behind them were batteries of artillery and rank upon rank of infantry. The Boers were the problem; the problem would be removed—and destroyed, if they made it necessary.

On the third day of the sweep, as the line approached the Transvaal/Bechuanaland border, groups of Boer horsemen could be seen searching for a weak link in the string of blockhouses and barbed wire that marked the border. The next day would tell the tale when the net was closed. There could be little choice: any Boers who were not able to flee the net would fight or surrender.

The British forces camped close to the wire that last night of the sweep. The next day almost four hundred prisoners were taken prisoner along with most of the Boer livestock, weapons, and supplies. Surely now the war was over.

31 May 1902
Klerksdorp
Transvaal

"They expect the war to be over today."

"That's what they said yesterday."

Charles and John looked at each other for a moment before Charles said, "Let's go out in the country."

"Think we should?"

"Since the fighting stopped, nobody cares what we do. We can go armed."

"There's no one out there to give us any sort of trouble."

"Should we ask Robbie to come along?"

John thought about it for a minute. "Naw. He's been a real stick-in-the-mud since we came back from the border. He'll spoil the day."

Like schoolboys playing hooky, they saddled their horses and rode down to the mess tent. There was no mess staff so they helped themselves to some food and took off at a fast trot, giggling as they went.

"We can be shot for stealing the King's stores."

"Deserting our post . . ."

"Having a good time."

"In the presence of the enemy."

They both put on very stern faces. "Can't have a good time, no, that's not allowed in the 2nd Canadian Mounted Rifles."

"Soon to be the Canadian Dismounted Rifles."

They rode along in silence, each taking the measure of how they would feel when all of this was over.

As they passed a couple of burned-out houses, John suggested they stop and have a look. "We might find something."

"Like what."

"I was told that when the Boer women could see the Brits approaching, they would bury their wealth so the Brits wouldn't get it."

"Then when we were gone, they would dig it up?"

"Yes, until we started doing the sweeps. When we were doing the sweeps, we pushed them along and they couldn't possibly go back to dig it up."

They tethered their horses and approached a house that had been blown up.

"No sense looking in the house."

"The easiest place to bury something in a hurry would be in the garden."

They attached the bayonets to the rifles and spent the rest of the afternoon happily prodding the earth at a number of farms. When the shadows grew longer, they returned to the camp to find that the war was over and the announcement had been made that the members of the 2nd were going home. Tomorrow, they were told, the paymaster would be at the mess tent.

"Tomorrow we get paid!"

Charles gave his friend a wicked smile. "Tonight we get drunk!"

Robbie showed up as they were finishing the third beer. He sat down with them and joined in the revelry but refused to drink. "I have to keep a clear head. I am taking my discharge at Klerksdorp. There will be plenty of work in South Africa once things settle down. We killed enough of them so there shouldn't be much competition for the jobs."

John, ever the wag, said, "We didn't know that when we were out fightin' the Boers, we were fixin' up things for our friend Robbie Cameron."

That brought a smile to Robbie's face. "I'll say my good-byes now." He offered his hand to John. They shook hands.

John Smallwood held on to his comrade's hand. "When we first met, you said you didn't want me around."

Robbie tried to release his hand but John held on so Robbie said, jokingly, "I was just talkin' through my hat. Didn't mean a thing."

"I don't agree. Our families have had troubles for years." John grasped Robbie's hand even harder. "We are comrades, Robbie. We have shared more than most brothers get to share. Can't we go back to The Island and take that with us?"

"We are comrades, John. We have shared a lot, but we can't take that back home. On The Island we have too much history." Robbie gently pulled his hand away. "What we have here would be lost on The Island, John. Let's just leave it at that."

Robbie held his hand out to Charles. "I know where John hails from. I didn't ask you . . ."

Charles ignored the hand and gave Robbie a big hug. "Us Gallants live in Charlottetown now but, once upon a time, we came from a village called Rivière-du-Nord-Est. Do you know where that is?"

Neither John Smallwood nor Robert Cameron knew the village of Rivière-du-Nord-Est.

Robbie stepped back from the two men. He took one last look at them as if to remember them forever, and then walked away.

Endnotes

1. April 18, 1902. R.W. Cameron, 23 years of age, height 5 ft. 10 in, enlisted in the 4th Canadian Mounted Rifles, B Squadron. Records show that he had previous service with the Royal Canadian Dragoons and possessed the Queen's Medal with bars for his service in Transvaal, Orange Free State, and Cape Colony. He was still unmarried. Additionally, he had a scar.

2. April 17, 1902. Charles Gallant, 22 years of age, height 5 ft. 6$^{1}/_{2}$ in., enlisted in the 4th Canadian Mounted Rifles, B Squadron. He had no previous military service.

3. April 17, 1902. John Holman Smallwood, 21 years of age, height 5 ft. 6$^{1}/_{2}$ in., enlisted in the 4th Canadian Mounted Rifles, B Squadron. He was a member of the Canadian Militia (Charlottetown Engineers Company).

4. The war ended 31 May 1902. The 4th Canadian Mounted Rifles arrived in time to be shipped home again. I moved our three warriors to the

2nd Canadian Mounted Rifles to give us a better story. The campaign to depopulate the Boer countryside began just about the time that the 2nd Mounted Rifles arrived in South Africa.

5. There were more sweeps in real life than I have used in the story. Otherwise, I have tried to follow the actual campaigns as best I could. I didn't invent anything; if it was raining in real life, it rained in the story.

6. Most of the Boer women and children were in the concentration camps and they were dying. If the campaign had continued a little longer, there would have been an end to them as a people.

7. Governor Cornwallis came to Nova Scotia in 1749 fresh from the brutal subjugation of Scotland. In the first books of this series we learned that men like Cornwallis employed a large number of Scots to help set the scene for the depopulation of Nova Scotia (expulsion of the Acadians). In this book, we learn that during the depopulation of the Boer states, there were Irish, Acadians, and Scots serving as the iron fist of the British Empire against the Boer population. History is interesting, isn't it?

Final Notes

Robert Watts Cameron took his discharge in Durban, South Africa, 2 July 1902.

John and Charles returned to The Island with the rest of their regiment. They applied to the Department of Militia for their veterans' benefits in a timely manner.

Robert Watts Cameron waited until 2 February 1948 before he made application to the Department of Veterans Affairs. My guess is it took him that long to find his way back to The Island.

But then, Islanders always come back, God willing.

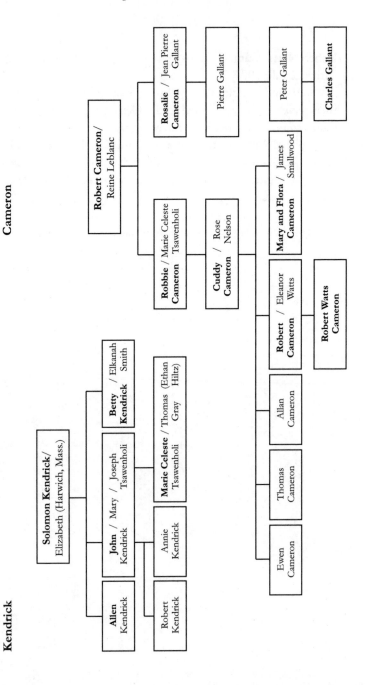

Smallwood

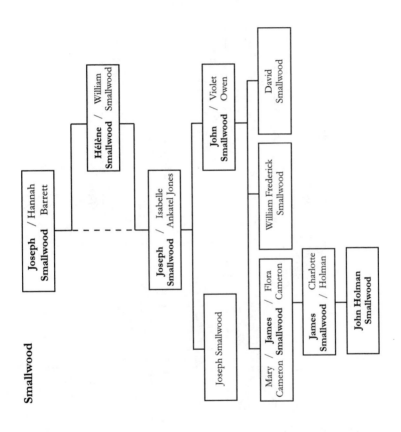

Gray

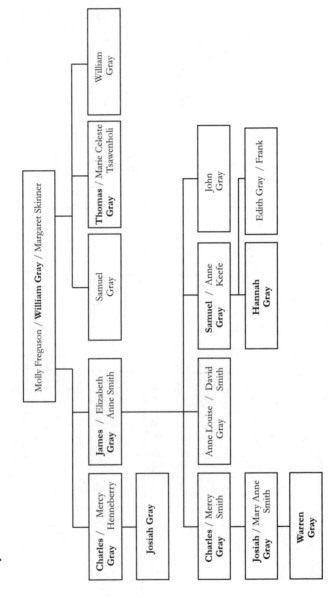

Smith

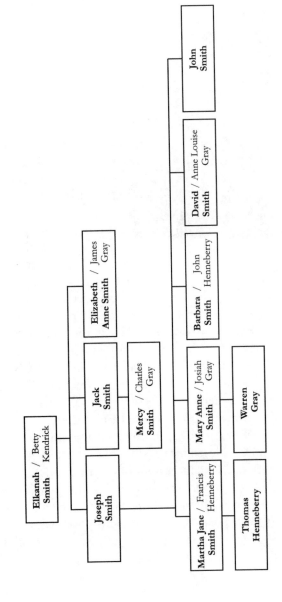

ABOUT THE AUTHOR

It is every boy's dream to be just like his Dad. Bill Smallwood's father was the best cookie and candy salesman in Nova Scotia. Perhaps that might have been good enough if Bill had been born somewhere else, but Bill was born in Halifax and his Dad raised him on stories about the world's largest natural harbour.

Excited by life's prospects, and encouraged by his father, Bill graduated from the Royal Military College with a degree in history and an officer's commission in the Royal Canadian Airforce, going on to navigate transport aircraft in the Korean War and jet fighters along the East German border during the Berlin Crisis. With the Cold War drawing to a close, Bill joined the Public Service at HMC Dockyard, Halifax. Before his retirement from the Canadian Public Service in 1986, he was Director of Civilian Training and Development for the Department of National Defence and, after retirement, became the right hand man for his wife in her highly successful real estate career.

When it was grandchildren time, Bill recounted the old stories. He came to realize that each story had a thread that entwined with the threads of other stories. Giving them a little tug here and a pull there, a picture emerged as to what it must have been like in the early days of Nova Scotia. *Expulsion and Survival* is the fifth of a series of novels about six families who came to Nova Scotia. If Bill's Dad were alive today, he would be proud of his son's storytelling.